With my thank
Miles Bennett, ba
and to
my wife, **Debbie**, for her
continued love and support,
and for her enthusiasm for this story.

At Cheltenham Racecourse in November 2024,
a named character in this book was bought at a
charity auction, with the proceeds going to Racing
Welfare and the Countryside Alliance.
Hence, **Sophie Burnett** appears in these pages
as herself, but her character is used fictitiously.

DARK HORSE

A *New York Times*, *Sunday Times* and international bestseller, acclaimed author, Felix Francis, was born in Oxford, England, son of the famous mystery author, Dick Francis and his wife, Mary. Felix graduated from London University with a Bachelor of Science degree. His initial career led him into physics, where he was a successful teacher of A Level Physics for 17 years, becoming head of the science department at Bloxham School. Felix next went into business, spending 13 years as a company director and deputy chairman of World Challenge Expeditions Ltd. But he could not deny that his family's gift of writing had been passed along to him, so, in 2005, he started his third career – as an author. His many other accomplishments include being an expert outdoorsman, marksman and pilot. He lives in rural Northamptonshire with his wife, Debbie, and their dogs, who are the ones really in charge!

DARK HORSE

FELIX FRANCIS

ZAFFRE

First published in the UK in 2025 by
ZAFFRE
An imprint of Bonnier Books UK
5th Floor, HYLO, 105 Bunhill Row,
London, EC1Y 8LZ

A CIP catalogue record for this book is
available from the British Library.

Hardback ISBN: 978-1-78512-587-4
Trade paperback ISBN: 978-1-78512-588-1

Also available as an ebook

1 3 5 7 9 10 8 6 4 2

Typeset by IDSUK (Data Connection) Ltd
Printed and bound in Great Britain by Clays Ltd, Elcograf S.p.A.

The authorised representative in the EEA is Bonnier Books
UK (Ireland) Limited.
Registered office address: Floor 3, Block 3, Miesian Plaza,
Dublin 2, D02 Y754, Ireland
compliance@bonnierbooks.ie
www.bonnierbooks.co.uk

PART 1

IMOGEN DUFFY

Chapter 1

'**D**ON'T YOU BLOODY TOUCH ME!'
I instinctively pulled my arm away from his grasp.

'Ah, come on, Imo,' he said, in a somewhat pained County Carlow lilt. 'I'm only wishing you good luck.'

'I don't need your good luck,' I replied, perhaps rather too sharply. 'Go away.'

'But you're my girlfriend,' he whined.

'Not any longer, I'm not,' I said. 'I told you last week it was over.'

'But I love you.'

I stood and looked at him – the man with whom I had been in a relationship for almost four years, and not once before had he told me that he loved me.

I remained staring at him for some time, maybe a full minute or two.

'I'm sorry, Liam,' I said finally. 'I don't love you.'

'You did once,' he said unhappily.

Did I?

Maybe I *had* loved him once, in an adolescent sort of way – an eighteen-year-old girl falling in love with a man five years older than her. But, if so, it had been a long time ago now.

I knew I hadn't loved him for at least the past year. But I'd felt trapped in an abusive entanglement that I hadn't known how to end. That was until the previous week when I had finally plucked up the courage to pack my suitcase and leave the house we had shared, going home instead to my parents.

'Maybe I loved you once,' I said. 'But I don't any more.'

I could tell that he was hurt, and he was also angry.

But Liam had always been angry.

'Duffy, you're late,' shouted a racecourse official. 'Get outside now!'

I turned away from Liam and faced the official. He gestured for me to go out of the open door. Everyone there turned to look at me.

'Sorry,' I mumbled, and brushed quickly past the official, and out through the doorway into the watery March sunshine.

I almost tripped down the three steps to the crowded parade ring and searched frantically amongst the throng for Paddy Murphy, the trainer of City Flyer, the horse I was about to ride in the Queen Mother Champion Chase.

He saw me and waved me over to join him and the horse's owner – a large man in a grey tweed overcoat and a black cap.

'Where have you been?' Mr Murphy hissed at me as I approached, clearly not amused by my tardiness. 'The other jockeys have been out for ages.'

'Sorry,' I said again.

I could see doubt in his face, as if he was wondering whether it had been a good idea to offer me this ride after his first-choice jockey had been concussed from a bad racing fall the previous afternoon.

The Queen Mother Champion Chase was the feature event on the second day of the annual four-day Cheltenham Festival, the most prestigious steeplechase race meeting of the whole year, and it was my first ride in any race of such importance.

I was desperate not to make a fool of myself, but I had already done that by being late out of the weighing room.

'Are you ready?' Mr Murphy asked with apparent concern.

'Yes, sir. I am.' I smiled at him and pulled myself up to my full five foot five inches.

'She's nothing more than a slip of a girl,' the owner said rather disdainfully, especially considering I was listening. 'Everyone's been telling me it's madness for you to put a young girl in such an important race. Is she up to it?'

'Well, she'll have to be,' Mr Murphy replied to him bluntly. 'I've made the decision, and it's too late to change it now. She'll be fine. She's ridden for me before and done really well. She's much stronger than she looks.'

'Humph!' said the owner, clearly not much placated. 'I'll still blame you if she falls off. Or gets blown off by the wind.'

'I'll be fine, sir,' I said to him, but I could see that he didn't believe it.

The bell rang for the jockeys to get mounted.

'Let's go, Imogen,' Mr Murphy said, heading off towards where City Flyer was still walking round the ring.

'Now remember everything I told you as we walked the course this morning,' he said over his shoulder. 'This race is only two miles. They'll all set off fast, so don't get caught napping at the start. Flyer will likely run too free if you let him, so tuck him in behind the leaders, and save some energy for the finish.'

'Yes, sir,' I said, hurrying along behind.

City Flyer was one of the fancied runners, having won the Dublin Chase at Leopardstown last time out in February, and I began to feel the huge responsibility that I'd been given.

What if I made a complete hash of it?

There was no other place like Cheltenham to make an impression, either good or bad, in front of the fifty thousand spectators in the grandstands, and almost a million more watching live on television. Every single British or Irish jump trainer, my potential future employers, would be scrutinising every move.

I suddenly began to wish that Paddy Murphy hadn't offered me the ride.

As he'd told the owner, I'd ridden for him before, but that had mostly been at the local Irish courses at Thurles and Clonmel in County Tipperary, when the average attendance was only a few thousand at best, and where a riding mistake could easily be forgiven, and quickly forgotten.

The Cheltenham Festival was on a different scale altogether, and especially in one of major championship races. Make a balls-up of it here and now, and everyone would know about it all right, and they'd remember it too.

My whole future career as a jump jockey might rely on the upcoming four minutes of racing. I started to become very nervous.

We reached the horse, and Paddy Murphy gave me a leg-up onto its back.

'Just be yourself,' he whispered into my ear. 'You'll do fine. If I didn't believe you could win, you wouldn't be here.'

I knew that was why he had offered me the ride. But he'd also taken a huge risk with his own reputation. Inexperienced jockeys like me didn't usually get to ride in major championship races, let alone on one of the favourites. So now was the time to grasp the opportunity, to show the horse's owner, and the other doubters, that I was good enough.

'Thank you,' I said, collecting the reins with shaking hands. 'I'll do my best.' And I hoped that my best would do.

The nine runners made one more complete circuit of the parade ring, sorting themselves into racecard order, ready to go out onto the racecourse.

As I passed by the owner, he pursed his lips and shook his head, and I wondered how Paddy Murphy had convinced him to allow me to ride his horse. Perhaps he hadn't. Maybe the trainer had simply declared me as the rider without telling the owner, just as soon as his original jockey had failed the concussion tests. It made me all the more determined not to let him down.

Liam was standing on the weighing-room terrace, and he watched as City Flyer walked past him. He was wearing a navy puffa jacket over white britches and black riding boots. He half raised a forlorn hand in my direction.

I hadn't expected *I love you*.

In recent months, he hadn't exactly behaved as if he loved me, continually belittling my ability as a jockey, or as anything else for that matter, including as his lover.

I now couldn't get *I love you* out of my head.

City Flyer and I made our way out onto the track, and after the brief parade in front of the grandstands, we were finally released to canter down to the start. Only then did my nerves begin to subside.

I suddenly felt at home, where I was at my happiest, astride a fast-moving muscular Thoroughbred, staring forward through the gap between its ears.

The two-mile start at Cheltenham is down the far end of the home straight, half a mile away from the winning post, and well out of earshot of the enormous crowd.

'It's just like Clonmel on a wet October Wednesday,' I told myself quietly. 'Keep calm. Keep calm.'

The nine horses circled as their girths were checked and tightened, and the official starter took a roll call to ensure everyone was present and ready. There was a distinct lack of the usual banter between the jockeys that I had become accustomed to at the start of other races, and I wondered if the rest of them were as nervous as I was.

How could Liam have said *I love you*?

I shook my head.

Don't even think of that now.

Concentrate. Concentrate!

Don't get caught napping at the start.

I kept my eyes firmly on the starter as he walked across to his rostrum.

Unlike flat races, which begin from a single line of starting stalls, jump races get under way when the starter lowers his flag and simultaneously releases an elastic tape that has been stretched across the course.

The starter climbed onto his rostrum and raised his small orange and yellow flag.

We were now *under starter's orders*.

'Come forward,' he shouted. 'Slowly, now!'

The nine runners stopped circling and began moving in a group, at no more than a walking jig-jog, towards the two-mile start line. I kept City Flyer in the centre of the pack, just behind two other horses. As instructed, I didn't want to allow him to start too freely, but equally I didn't want to be caught flat-footed and give the others an undue advantage.

We were still some fifteen yards behind the actual start line when the starter shouted 'Come on, then,' dropped his flag and released the tape.

We were off.

Two miles is the shortest length of a steeplechase, so this race was akin to a jumping sprint, and as Paddy Murphy had said, the field started fast. But I was ready for them, tucking in behind the leading pair as we all popped safely over the first of the thirteen obstacles.

The field remained closely bunched as we negotiated the four jumps in the long straight, and the crowd gave us a huge cheer as we passed them and turned away for the remaining full circuit.

City Flyer was travelling well beneath me as we jumped the cross fence and set off along the back stretch. Here the pace picked up even further and a few at the rear were beginning to struggle, but my horse was still bowling along comfortably in third place without any apparent problems.

Next came a plain fence, and then the water jump.

One of the two in front of me was beginning to tire, so I pulled City Flyer slightly wider to give him a clearer view. He immediately took that as an invitation to move forward.

We had now travelled well over half distance and my horse was hardly puffing at all. City Flyer jumped the next fence up-sides with the long-time leader. We were now at the top of the hill and soon swung sharply left-handed, back down the slope towards home.

Just three fences to go.

I had a quick look through my legs to try and spot any approaching danger, but those behind were now spread out some distance to the rear. I glanced across at the other horse, trying to gauge how well it was going.

Rather too well, I thought.

As we sped down the hill, I had a decision to make. Did I just allow City Flyer to freewheel, giving him a bit of a breather, or did I kick on hard and try and establish a lead that would last all the way to the winning post?

I glanced across again, this time at the jockey, one of the top ones in the sport.

I saw him drop his hands fractionally, loosening the reins. I knew what that meant. *He* was giving his mount a breather.

And that made up my mind for me.

I kicked City Flyer and slapped him down his shoulder with my whip. He understood the message and surged forward, quickly opening up a lead of four or five lengths before my rival had a chance to recover.

The third last was once a notorious fence where, over the years, many hopes had come to grief as fast horses overjumped and pitched forward onto their noses, before crashing to the turf at this most difficult of downhill obstacles. However, in recent years the ground on the landing side of the fence had been levelled to try and reduce the danger to both horse and jockey.

But it remains a considerable test, especially for a tiring horse.

So, did I steady City Flyer – the safer option – or did I push on hard, chancing the likelihood of a bone-breaking fall?

Fortune always favours the brave.

I kicked him again and he met the fence perfectly.

True to his name, the horse flew over the fence and continued galloping forward unchecked. I glanced back. We were still almost three lengths in front but had not shaken off the challenge.

I hugged the inside running rail round the final turn into the finishing straight, taking the shortest possible route. There were just two fences left, but there was also the punishing steep incline from the last to the finish line. Had I kept enough in reserve for City Flyer to climb it?

But never mind the horse, I was already completely knackered.

I dragged in several lungfuls of oxygen, blowing out the excess carbon dioxide from my body, but the muscles in my arms and legs still felt like jelly.

'Come on,' I shouted to myself. 'Don't lose this race because of your own failings.'

Perhaps City Flyer's owner had been right when he had described me as nothing more than a slip of a girl. And that thought alone gave me a renewed determination and increased energy.

As we approached the second-last fence, I didn't need to look behind to see where the other horse was – I could hear it coming up on my inside. I stared at the ground, trying to measure the stride, to meet the obstacle perfectly, but I realised that we were wrong. He was either too close to it, or too far away, and I wasn't quite certain which.

Did I ask City Flyer to put in a short stride to get us right?

That would have involved taking a pull – slowing him down – something I couldn't afford to happen if I wanted to retain any chance of winning.

So, no. No pull.

Instead, I kicked hard and asked him for a big leap.

'Come on, Flyer, fly!' I shouted loudly into his ear.

He responded and soared over the birch, gaining distance in the air.

Now just one fence to jump.

But I could tell that my horse was tiring. His stride was shortening, and he was slightly swinging his head from side to side.

'Come on, boy, you can do it.'

He steadied himself and jumped the last, brushing tiredly through the top and pitching forward on landing. I grabbed the reins and lifted his head up, preventing him going fully down.

Only the infamous Cheltenham finishing hill remained.

City Flyer began to wander off a true line, drifting over to the right, towards where we had entered onto the track from the parade ring, as if to imply that he reckoned that *enough was enough*, and it was time to go home.

I pulled my whip through from my left hand to my right, and gave him a reminder to stay straight, but he was definitely slowing despite my best efforts. Out of the corner of my eye I could see the head of the other horse getting ever closer, and much too rapidly for my liking.

And there was still fifty yards to go.

But horses are naturally herd animals. They love to run, and some love to run in front. The very presence of the other horse alongside seemed to stir that instinct in City Flyer, and he picked up, regained his stride, and stuck out his head, refusing to be beaten.

We won the race by half a length.

As we crossed the finish line, I was totally spent with no energy left even to celebrate. Instead, as the horse slowed to a walk, I lay down on his neck and hugged him with both my arms. Meanwhile, the tears streamed down my face from both emotion and exhaustion.

It is the custom at Cheltenham for the winner to remain out on the course, circling for a couple of minutes while the other runners return to the unsaddling areas. During that time, the winning jockey is interviewed for the television viewers.

I managed to regain some sort of composure, wiping away the tears on the sleeve of my silks, just before a microphone was held up to my face on a stick.

'Congratulations, Imogen,' shouted up the interviewer. 'What a great ride. At what stage did you believe you would win?'

I laughed. 'Only when we crossed the finish line in front.'

'And what was the decisive moment in the race?'

'The stand-off leap at the second last. Magic.' I affectionately slapped City Flyer's neck. 'What a fabulous horse.'

And now it was time to make the historic *Walk of Champions* along in front of the grandstands. I stood up on my stirrups and saluted the packed crowd as they cheered us.

It was, without doubt, the best moment of my entire life.

At Cheltenham, the space reserved to unsaddle the winner is at the far end of the parade ring, so City Flyer needed to be led right round the stands and back up the chute from which we had appeared, seemingly half a lifetime ago. And all the while people were shouting their congratulations and appreciation.

'I love you, Imogen Duffy,' someone yelled loudly to my right in a Carlow accent.

My heart missed a beat, and I glanced across, but it wasn't Liam. It was another man, standing next to the rail wearing a bright green leprechaun hat, complete with black strap, gold buckle and an attached false ginger beard. He was holding a half-drunk pint glass of Guinness, which was clearly not his first of the day. I waved at him.

'You just won me a fortune off the bookies,' he shouted. 'Good on you, girl.'

'Don't spend it all on drink,' I shouted back at him, laughing.

And I remained laughing all the way onward.

Arriving into the unsaddling enclosure as the victor of a championship race at the Cheltenham Festival is one of the great examples of sporting theatre, comparable to the presentation of the FA Cup at Wembley, or the winner of the King's Prize for shooting being carried shoulder-high in a sedan chair around Bisley camp.

City Flyer was led down the centre of the parade ring into the jaws of the Roman-style amphitheatre that is built around one end, with all its steps crammed full of cheering racegoers.

Added to that was a mass of press photographers, plus the uplifting strains of 'Heart of Courage' by Two Steps from Hell blaring out loudly through the public address system. A suitable choice, as my mount had shown both heart and courage, especially at the second-last fence.

I held my arms up high in triumph as we arrived at the space reserved for the winner to a renewed cheer from the crowd, especially from the Irish contingent.

The horse's owner was already standing there, beaming from ear to ear.

'Well done, Duffy,' he said, as I dismounted. 'I never had any doubts you could do it.'

I looked at him and wondered what other lies he might add.

I removed my saddle and the weight cloth from the back of the steaming horse. So tired was I that I almost dropped them straight down onto the ground.

'Don't forget to weigh in,' Paddy said, putting his hand on my shoulder while smiling broadly. 'It would be a shame to ruin such a great ride by not weighing in. Well done, Imogen.' He patted my back with real pleasure, both for him and for me. 'Well done, indeed.'

I posed for a few more photos with the horse before I staggered up the three steps to the weighing room to stand on the electronic scale.

I looked nervously at the red digital readout on the wall.

'City Flyer. Eleven stone, ten,' said the Clerk of the Scales, typing a note on his keyboard. 'Perfect. Weighed in.'

All the nine horses in the race had carried eleven stone and ten pounds, which was one hundred and sixty-four pounds, whereas my body alone weighed only a hundred and twenty. So, there was an extra forty-four pounds to add.

I had used the heaviest saddle I could borrow, plus ultra-thick riding boots, but I'd still needed thirty pounds of lead plates placed in the weight cloth to bring it up to the required total. No wonder everything was so damn heavy.

The Clerk of the Scales looked up from his computer. 'Well ridden, Imogen,' he said, smiling.

'Thank you, sir,' I said, stepping off the scale.

I handed my saddle, weight cloth and skullcap to my waiting jockeys' valet, and then turned to go back outside for the trophy presentations, but I found myself face to face with Liam.

'Congratulations,' he said, with a forced smile that didn't make it up to his eyes – not even close. 'That was great.' It was as if he was saying it through gritted teeth.

He put his arms out and came towards me, as if to give me a hug.

I stepped back, away from him.

'This doesn't change anything,' I said quietly but firmly. 'It's still over between us.'

In fact, this win *had* changed things. It made me even more determined to spread my wings, to move on.

Liam dropped his arms, and his paltry smile rapidly disappeared altogether, to be replaced by a scowl.

'You'll regret it,' he said with real menace. 'I'll make sure of that.'

Chapter 2

I DIDN'T HAVE MUCH TIME TO celebrate my victory in the Champion Chase, as I had to catch a train at eight o'clock that evening to start the long journey home.

I had originally only intended being at Cheltenham on the Tuesday when I was due to ride in the three-mile Ultima Handicap Steeplechase, the third race on the first day of the Festival.

A top Irish trainer from County Meath had four horses confirmed for the race, and he had called to offer me the ride on one of them, having watched me come a close second in a Grade 2 steeplechase at Navan the previous week.

I'd never ridden at Cheltenham before, so I had eagerly accepted, subject to my principal employer's approval, but I had not fully appreciated the logistics required to get there, and also to find somewhere to sleep.

Of the quarter of a million race fans expected to pass through the racecourse turnstiles over the four days of the Festival, about a third would have made the trip across the Irish Sea, either by plane or by boat, most of them having booked their passage many months in advance.

And all the hotels within fifty miles of the racecourse would have been fully reserved for at least a year, with the same guests returning time after time to the same establishments, mostly to the same rooms.

I had known that Liam was going to Cheltenham. He had three rides booked and had had his air ticket and accommodation sorted and paid for by the horses' owners. He had been boasting about it for weeks and had used the fact to further denigrate my own riding skills.

Hence, he'd been absolutely furious when I'd announced that I also now had a ride at the Festival, and it had been his overtly negative reaction to my exciting news that had been the final straw. The following morning, while Liam was still riding on the gallops, I had nervously packed my stuff and walked out, taking a taxi home to my parents.

Predictably, Liam was incandescently furious when he came home from work to find I'd gone.

When I refused to answer his calls, he left message after message on my voicemail – half of them loving and pleading for me to return, the other half threatening what would happen to me if I didn't.

I had spent most of that day in tears, but my overriding emotion was one of relief – combined with a huge measure of embarrassment for not having left him sooner.

*　*　*

Securing a seat on any flight out of Ireland to England the day before the Cheltenham Festival had proved to be impossible. Instead, I had booked myself as a foot passenger on the overnight ferry from Dublin to Holyhead. After disembarking,

I made the long, tortuous rail journey from Anglesey to Cheltenham – changing trains at Crewe, Stafford and Birmingham – arriving around midday on Monday after fourteen hours on the move.

Before I'd left home, I had called the County Meath trainer to ask if he could help find me accommodation for Monday night. He had laughed down the line. 'You've got to be joking, Imogen. My kids want to come over for the Gold Cup on Friday, so I've tried to find something for them. In the end, I had to tell them there's no chance of finding a room anywhere nearby.'

But, even so, he had rung me back about ten minutes later, as I was seriously contemplating calling him to say I couldn't ride his horse after all.

'I've found you a sofa bed,' he'd said. 'If that's OK? It's in a rented house with some other Irish jocks.'

'Which ones?' I'd asked warily.

The last thing I wanted to do was to find out I would be sharing a house again with Liam, even if there were other people there.

The trainer mentioned three names that I recognised, but not one of them was Liam Carson.

'Fine,' I'd said. 'I only need it for one night as I'm returning home on Tuesday evening after my race.'

In the end, of course, I'd been on the sofa for two nights because on Tuesday afternoon I'd been offered the ride on City Flyer, even though I'd hardly slept at all during the second night due to nerves.

So here I was now, on Wednesday evening, on a train to North Wales to catch the overnight ferry to Dublin, and then on to Thurles via the Irish Rail intercity service.

I had considered staying on for another day at Cheltenham, partly to wallow in my own success, and in the hope I might be offered another ride on the Thursday. But I was provisionally booked to ride one of my employer's five-year-olds in a two-mile maiden hurdle at Cork races on Saturday, and I'd already outstayed my welcome on the sofa in the rented house.

I'd been tempted to buy an airline ticket from Birmingham to Dublin, using some of the twenty-two thousand pounds I'd received for riding the winner of the Champion Chase. It was more than I'd earned before in a whole year. But I'd already paid for a return ticket on the ferry, and it seemed like a waste of good money not to use it.

I did, however, indulge myself a little by upgrading my ferry ticket from an upright seat to a cabin with a single bed, so I could get a few hours of proper sleep. I needed it.

On the last leg of the journey, the hour-and-a-quarter intercity train trip from Dublin to Thurles, I sat watching the rolling Irish countryside rushing by, thinking about my future.

I was now twenty-two years old, and I was in my fourth year as a professional steeplechase jockey, having started straight from secondary school. And my parents were both horse mad, so I'd been riding ponies since before I could remember.

Even though I regarded myself to be Irish to the core, I'd actually been born in England during the time my Irish father and Irish mother were both settled and working there. As such, I automatically acquired both British and Irish citizenship, but I chose to have only an Irish passport.

My father was a doctor; having graduated from Trinity College Medical School, he completed two years at St James's

Hospital in Dublin, before leaving his native Ireland to further his training in the Emergency Department of St Thomas' Hospital in Central London, across the River Thames from the Houses of Parliament.

He'd catch the train every day from Woking Station, near our home, to Waterloo, while my mother, who was a qualified midwife, worked at the nearby Chertsey Maternity Hospital, where two years later, I would arrive into the world.

I know they would have loved to have given me a baby brother or sister, but it never happened, something that greatly saddened my mother, especially as she delivered so many babies for other women.

When I was ten years old, my parents returned to Ireland, taking everything they owned with them, including me and my much-loved pony.

Over the years, my dad had steadily climbed the medical-career ladder from Senior Houseman to Registrar, to Senior Registrar, and finally to Consultant in Emergency Medicine. Now he had accepted the role of Senior Consultant and Head of the Emergency Department at the Tipperary University Hospital, and my mum took a midwifery job in the Maternity Department of the same establishment.

As soon as we had settled into our new home, I enrolled myself into the local branch of the Irish Pony Club, and when I was fifteen, I had been one of only ten club members nation-wide selected to participate in the week-long Jockey Skills Training Course at the Racing Academy in Kildare Town, near the Curragh Racecourse.

That was when I had become determined to become a jump jockey.

For the next three years, I spent every spare minute at the stables of Cormac Fitzgerald, a local licensed racehorse trainer, eventually graduating to ride his horses on the gallops and over the schooling fences. In addition, he arranged for me to get a Qualified Rider's permit from the Irish racing authority, which allowed me to ride as an amateur in races for a local point-to-point stable during the summer holidays.

I absolutely loved it, and I had some limited success, enough for them to provide me with regular point-to-point rides on weekends throughout my final year at school, winning two and coming second on four other occasions. I'd even won a race 'under rules' at nearby Thurles Racecourse when I was still only seventeen.

Considering the amount of time I spent riding horses rather than doing my homework, I did surprisingly well in my final school exams, and my Leaving Cert grade was easily good enough for me to have gone on to university. But, in spite of my parents' pleading, I was determined to leave academia behind me and pursue my ambition to be a jockey.

My schooldays were done, and Mr Fitzgerald offered me a job at his stable as a 'conditional', that is an apprentice professional jump jockey.

I was in heaven.

His stable was small, with only twenty horses, so the opportunities were limited. But I made the most of them, having a winner on only my fourth ride, in a two-mile hurdle race at Clonmel races.

By the end of my first season, I had ridden two further winners, but by the close of my second, I had a total of eighteen, and finished fifth that year in the Irish Conditional Jockeys Championship.

People were beginning to notice me, and I was occasionally being asked by other local trainers to ride their horses. Then, the previous July, I'd received an offer of a new job, one at a much bigger stable, as third stable jockey and work rider.

I'd been loath to leave Mr Fitzgerald, as he had given me my big break, but he had insisted that I should take the job, to further my career, though it had meant a major change to my circumstances.

The new stable was in County Carlow, an hour's drive from my parents' house, so I could hardly continue to live at home and be available to ride each morning at seven, or even earlier in the height of the summer.

'Come and live with me,' Liam had said. 'My place is only down the road from your new job. Walking distance.'

I had met Liam at a charity ball in aid of the Irish Horse Welfare Trust. I'd only just started work, while he was already an established jump jockey, and he had bowled me over with his exciting stories of daredevil riding over fences.

Despite the physical separation between our respective homes, we had by then been 'going steady' for more than eighteen months. Although the relationship had developed into a sexual one, with me staying over with him occasionally, was I ready to move in with him permanently?

But it seemed like the perfect arrangement, especially after I had spent a fruitless evening on the internet searching for an affordable place of my own. Hence, I had packed my suitcase, and my father had reluctantly driven me the fifty miles to Liam's small house in Leighlinbridge, County Carlow, to start a new chapter in my life.

Initially, everything had been great, and I had eagerly settled into my new surroundings, and into my new job.

Instead of sixteen horses, I now had over seventy available and, in spite of being only number three in the stable's jockey-pecking order, the number of rides I was given, and the winners, increased steadily, such that by mid-December I was lying second in the conditional jockeys' table.

But despite my professional success, it was in the run-up to the Christmas period that cracks first began to appear in my seemingly domestic bliss at Liam's house.

I had two rides booked at Thurles races on the Saturday before Christmas and then a couple more at Limerick on Boxing Day, when the other stable jockeys would both be riding at the major meeting at Leopardstown, near Dublin. With no race meetings scheduled during the four days before Christmas, I decided that I would go and spend the time between Thurles and Limerick races with my parents, including Christmas Day itself.

Liam didn't like it. Not one bit.

He accused me of being disloyal and placing my family ahead of him. I pointed out that I had hardly seen my mum and dad for months and that he was being unreasonable.

'Don't you accuse me of being unreasonable,' he had shouted at me. 'You're the one who's being unreasonable by leaving me alone at Christmas.'

But I knew he would be seeing his own family. He'd already said so.

Over the following few days, he wouldn't stop going on about it, not until I reluctantly agreed to spend Christmas Day with him, albeit with his other family members also present.

'Thank you, my darling,' he had said, giving me a hug and a kiss. 'You know it's the right decision.'

But, quite apart from not seeing my parents at all over the Christmas break – something that dismayed them hugely – it made my Boxing Day arrangements far more complicated.

Even though Liam had taught me to drive, and I had passed my test, I still had no car of my own, and Liam would never let me drive his to go anywhere without him.

If I'd been staying at home, my father or mother would have driven me the hour to Limerick races. But as I'd been in Leighlinbridge with Liam, the journey had been twice as long, and I'd had to go in the horsebox with the horses. With racing during the winter months starting soon after midday, the box left the stables well before six o'clock in the morning, almost three hours before the sun was up, so I didn't exactly have the relaxing Christmas evening in front of the television with my feet up that I had hoped for.

Having had his own way in that first instance, Liam obviously grew in confidence, and over the following few months, he became more and more controlling of my life.

I could see that now, but at the time, it had all seemed to creep up on me unawares. Throughout, he largely remained very affectionate, and would even buy me flowers and other small presents but, nevertheless, he was exerting increasing control over everything I did, and with whom.

Often, I would simply agree to his demands – I wouldn't go out for a coffee with some of the other stable staff after work, or to have lunch with my mother – because it made for a quiet life. And it usually wasn't a great issue. I was always so tired from work that I didn't want to go out much anyway.

He, meanwhile, did exactly what *he* wanted, often coming home very late at night, worse for drink and smelling of cigarettes, before apologising profusely and promising to never do it again – but of course he did, often.

If I objected to anything he said, he would fly into a rage and maintain that he was only saying it for my own good, to protect me, although to protect me from what, he never revealed. During these rages, he never actually hit me, but he did threaten to do so on several occasions.

One of his favourite tactics was making me feel guilty that I didn't appreciate him enough for all the help he was giving me by allowing me to live in his house, in spite of him also insisting that I paid him rent, plus half the household bills.

But he could also be very charming, especially to other people, and he would bestow endless thanks and praise on anyone who did what he asked, though he was equally quick to berate and criticise them when they didn't.

It was as if he craved to be the centre of everyone's attention, especially mine.

He didn't like it if I wore high heels or sexy clothes when we went out together, in case other people looked at me rather than at him, and he began telling me what I must wear – mostly baggy, shapeless tops rather than the tight-fitting ones I liked.

He also had an inflated idea of his own importance, and of his ability as a jockey. He kept telling everyone that he would be champion jockey, and that he would win both the Punchestown and Cheltenham Gold Cups but, so far, none of those things had happened, and they didn't look much like happening anytime soon. In truth, he was a middle-ranking jockey with middling ability – just about able to eke out a decent living from riding, but unlikely to ever break into the elite.

Looking back, I realised that he had always been jealous of my own victories in races, and his less than lukewarm reaction to my big win at Cheltenham showed that he clearly still was. My reiterating to him that our relationship was over had simply poured petrol on his already burning fire.

You'll regret it, he'd said. *I'll make sure of that.*

It had been the degree of menace in his voice as he'd said it that had shocked me most.

And I *was* really worried about what he might do. Not least because my employer, the trainer at the big stables in Leighlinbridge, was Michael Carson – and he was Liam's father.

Chapter 3

I ARRIVED AT THURLES RAILWAY STATION at a quarter past eight in the morning, after another lengthy overnight journey.

I had expected to have to get a bus to my parents' house, but my father was standing waiting on the platform to welcome me.

'You're our heroine,' he said, giving me a huge bear hug. 'Everyone at the hospital watched the race on the television. It's given the place a huge boost.'

'Why aren't you there now?' I asked, knowing that he was meant to be on early shifts all week.

He laughed. 'Being the department boss has certain advantages. I told the others I was going to meet you off the train and that I'd be in later. No one objected. Quite the reverse. Even the hospital manager as good as told me to come here. But he also said that he wants you to go in and see all the staff. You're quite the local celebrity now.'

I didn't feel it. I was totally worn out.

'Not today,' I said, yawning. 'I'm too tired. All I want to do is go home and go to sleep.'

Dad laughed again. Then he carried my holdall out of the old nineteenth-century grey station building to his car and tossed my bag into the boot. I climbed in beside him.

'Tell me about it,' Dad said, starting the engine. 'Were you nervous?'

'Nervous? You're joking! When I was given a leg-up onto the horse I could hardly hold the reins because my hands were shaking so much.'

'They said on the television that City Flyer wouldn't have won without you on his back. They simply couldn't believe your jump at the second last.'

'Neither could I.' I laughed. 'I didn't really think about it. I just kicked the horse hard, and he did the rest.'

'They likened your riding to that of Rachael Blackmore.'

Rachael Blackmore had been born and raised in the small Tipperary town of Killenaule, only a few miles away. She'd won just about everything in jump racing that was worth winning, including being the only female jockey so far to win either the English Grand National or the Cheltenham Gold Cup, and she'd won both of them, not to mention five Champion Hurdles – two English and three Irish. Like me, she'd also won the Queen Mother Champion Chase.

To be compared by the television racing pundits to Rachael Blackmore was praise indeed.

I laid my head against the headrest and closed my eyes, but I was smiling both on the inside and the outside.

It was six miles south from Thurles Station to my mum and dad's house in the appropriately named village of Horse and Jockey, and I was fast asleep before we'd even gone halfway.

'Wake up, Imogen,' my father said, shaking my knee. 'We're home.'

I slowly opened my eyes as he turned the car through the gate, but then they were suddenly wide open with delight.

Strung across the first-floor windows of the house was a line of white sheets with the words CONGRATULATIONS IMOGEN, CHELTENHAM CHAMPION CHASE WINNER painted on them in big bold black letters, and outside the front door were about thirty people all waving wildly, my mother amongst them.

Dad stopped the car, and I climbed out to be embraced by my mother while everyone else clapped and cheered.

'Well done, darling,' my mother said into my ear. 'We are so proud of you. The whole village has turned out to welcome you home.'

She had tears of joy in her eyes, and I was speechless.

People came up to shake my hand or slap me on the back. One man I'd never seen before even gave me a hug and a big kiss on the cheek.

'Wonderful,' he said. 'Wonderful.' There were tears in his eyes too.

'Thank you,' I finally managed to croak.

In spite of it still being well before nine o'clock in the morning, trays of champagne appeared, and everyone toasted my victory, then we all crammed into my parents' front room to watch a recording of the race, with me sitting squeezed on the sofa in the middle of them.

Even though I'd been shown the last few furlongs before, during a press conference held after the race, it was the first time I had watched the whole thing in its entirety, and it was just as I remembered.

There were gasps as they watched City Flyer jump the second-last fence, and then cheers all the way to the finish line.

Many more drinks were then consumed, and my mother appeared with trays of bacon rolls to try to soak up some of the alcohol.

'How have you done all this?' I asked her. 'What time did you start?'

'Well before five,' my mother replied, smiling. 'But I could hardly sleep anyway, what with the excitement.'

The party would go on all morning, and probably well into the afternoon. Like at all good Irish parties, no one appeared keen to go home.

Shortly after the ten o'clock Thursday deadline for declarations for Saturday's racing at Cork, I slipped out into the garden to look at the Horse Racing Ireland website on my phone – to see if the horse, which I had been provisionally booked to ride in the maiden hurdle, would be running.

I scanned down the card of runners and the horse was there all right, but the trainer hadn't declared me as its jockey.

I stared at my phone in disbelief.

Instead of Imogen Duffy being listed as the rider, it was Liam Carson.

* * *

My first thought was that there must have been an error in the rider declaration because Liam had told me that he intended staying on in England for a couple of days after Cheltenham, to visit a cousin who was working as an assistant trainer at a stable in Yorkshire.

If I phoned Michael Carson, the error might be corrected before the midday deadline for changes. He would still be at Cheltenham, but he would have his mobile with him. I dialled his number.

'It's not an error,' he said coldly. 'Liam will ride for me at Cork on Saturday.'

'But he told me he was staying on in England for a few days.'

'He's not doing that any more. He's flying home tonight.'

'Oh,' I said. 'Is that why you've taken me off the ride?'

There was a pause from the other end of the line.

'You must know the reason why,' he said eventually.

'No. I don't.'

'Liam tells me that you've been having sex with other men behind his back. Three of them, he told me, other jockeys. He's so upset. How could you do such a thing to him after all he's done for you?' He was angry now. 'He also told me that he's breaking off your engagement.'

'Engagement?' I said, incredulously. 'We were never engaged.'

'So you admit you were sleeping around?'

'No,' I spluttered. 'I don't. Absolutely not. I never did. I stayed in a house in Cheltenham with three other jockeys on Monday and Tuesday nights, but I slept on the sofa, not in any of their beds. Nothing happened.'

'That's not what they say. They were bragging about it last night – about how they each took turns with you.'

I could hardly breathe, let alone speak.

'Who told you that?' I asked, almost in a whisper.

'Liam. He was having dinner with them, that's until he left because he was so distressed by what he heard.'

'But it's not true.'

'Are you calling my son a liar?' he asked furiously.

'Well, someone is definitely lying,' I whispered.

And I knew who it would be.

But Michael Carson wasn't finished yet – not by a long chalk.

'I have also decided to terminate your employment contract with my stable,' he said. 'You won't ever ride for me again, either at home or in races.'

I was stunned.

'I'll sue you for unfair dismissal,' I said, finally finding my voice, and my own anger.

'I think you'll find that Irish law states that, within a year of taking you on, I have the right to terminate your contract at any time, and without having to provide a reason. So, you can't sue me.'

It was as if he had already done his homework – or maybe Liam had done it for him.

He hung up and I was left there in the garden, holding my phone and wondering how I felt. At least it seemed that Liam had finally accepted that our relationship was over, even if it had been me who had finished it rather than him.

But I was worried about what he would now be saying to everyone else.

If he'd told his father such a huge bunch of lies, he would clearly have no qualms about repeating the same nonsense to anyone who would listen, and there would be plenty of those who'd believe it. And nothing moved so fast in racing circles as a juicy bit of sexual tittle-tattle, whether it was true or not.

How could someone tell me that *he loved me* one minute, and then set out to destroy me the next? But the truth, of course, was that Liam never did love me. He'd only ever loved himself, and having me hanging on his arm for everyone to see had simply added to his self-adoration. Only when I'd told him that I wouldn't be there any longer had his true feelings shown through.

I felt wretched at the thought of him still peddling those dreadful lies at Cheltenham to everyone in racing, to both the Irish and the English.

Any future I had as a jockey would probably already be destroyed, despite my big win yesterday. No trainer's wife would allow their husband to employ a female jockey with a tarty reputation, one who might end up putting their own marriage at risk.

My glorious day of celebration had suddenly come crashing down around my ears. What should have been a time of happiness and joy was now anything but.

My father came out of the house onto the patio.

'Ah, there you are, Imogen,' he said. 'I've been looking all over for you.'

I turned towards him, tears now welling up in my eyes.

'What's wrong?' he asked, quickly striding over and putting his arms round my shoulders, while I buried my face into his pullover.

What could I say?

He and my mother had gone to such an effort to put on this celebration for me. And they were so happy and proud. I couldn't ruin it for them.

'Nothing's wrong, Dad,' I said, pulling away and smiling at him. 'I'm just tired. That's all. It's a great party.'

He gave me a tissue to dry my eyes, and then I held his arm as we walked together into the house.

Everyone in there was so delighted for me, while at the same time, a huge mass of dread sat heavily in the pit of my own stomach.

* * *

Most of the guests drifted off home around lunchtime, but a hardcore few remained into the afternoon to watch the racing from Cheltenham on my parents' television.

I sat amongst them in the sitting room, but I wasn't really paying much attention.

What did I do now?

Conditional jockeys in Ireland are officially known as 'claiming professionals'.

To make up for their inexperience as riders, they receive a weight allowance, or a claim, compared to more seasoned jockeys, meaning that, in certain races, the horses they are riding carry less weight on their backs.

In Ireland, jockeys can claim a seven-pound allowance if they have ridden fewer than twenty-five winners, five pounds from twenty-five to forty-nine, and three pounds from then until they have ridden sixty winners, after which they are said to have 'ridden out their claim', and they then become full professionals. A similar system applies in Great Britain although the numbers of winners for each weight stage are slightly different, being twenty, forty and seventy-five.

Since taking out my jockey's licence, I had ridden a total of fifty-two winners, so I was still able to claim a three-pound allowance for many races – although not in the Champion Chase, as that is what's known as a Pattern Race, where the claiming of weight allowances is not permitted.

In Great Britain, the 'condition' for someone having a conditional jockey's licence is that he or she is directly employed by a racehorse trainer, and hence losing their job would also mean losing their licence.

However, in Ireland, claiming professionals are considered freelance and self-employed for race riding, even if they are employed by a trainer. Hence, I still had my jockey's licence and was therefore able to have rides in races, but how would I get any?

Almost all my rides in races, including those for other trainers, had been booked through my employer – now my ex-employer – and after what he'd said, it was most unlikely he would pass on any future requests.

Perhaps I should employ a jockey's agent to act for me.

But would I get any rides anyway, given what Liam was saying about me?

You'll regret it. I'll make sure of that.

Well, I didn't regret it, in spite of what he was doing to me.

I was so glad it was finally over between us.

I suddenly felt free, and I was damned if I was going to allow Liam to ruin my life, either personally or professionally.

But little did I realise what was coming.

Chapter 4

FIRST THING FRIDAY MORNING, I called Cormac Fitzgerald, the local trainer who had given me my initial break.

'Hello, Imogen,' he said warmly. 'Well done at Cheltenham. You were brilliant. I always knew you had it in you to win big.'

'It was all down to you,' I said.

He laughed. 'Nonsense. I knew you were destined for greatness ever since that first day you walked into my stable yard as a young schoolgirl.'

'So will you take me back?' I asked quickly.

'Back where?'

'Will you give me my old job back?'

'Don't be silly,' he said, laughing again. 'Why on earth would you want to come back here, to such a small stable, when the world is now your oyster?'

'Because I need a job,' I said. 'And some rides.'

There was a slight pause from the other end.

'What's happened?' he asked, now very serious. 'What did Michael Carson do to you?'

'He fired me.'

'Did he actually fire you or did you quit?'

'He fired me,' I repeated.

'Why?'

Now it was my turn to pause.

'Because I broke off the relationship I was in with his son.'

'Don't be ridiculous,' Cormac said. 'That's not a good enough reason for firing anybody.'

'You try telling him that,' I said. 'He also accused me of sleeping around behind his son's back.'

'And were you?'

'No. Absolutely not.' Although I wasn't sure that it was any of his business. 'I just broke off the relationship.'

'Then sue him for unfair dismissal.'

'I can't. He claims he could end my employment any time he likes because I haven't been with him for more than a year. He made it quite clear that, under Irish law, I'd have no grounds to sue.'

'When did he tell you all this?'

I could tell that he was getting quite angry on my behalf.

'He called yesterday afternoon. He's cancelled my contract. He also said that I'd never ride for him again, either at home or in races.'

'So that was after your big win at Cheltenham?'

'Yes.'

'Then Carson's more of an idiot than I realised. He had one of the country's best jockeys at his beck and call, and now he's fired her. It's total madness.'

It made me feel a bit better hearing him say that.

'So will you take me back?' I asked.

He hesitated.

'I'm so sorry, Imogen, but I can't,' he said slowly. 'I'd absolutely love to, but I took on someone else when you left, and I can't afford another salary on top of that. The government keeps putting up the bloody PRSI, and I'm totally squeezed.'

PRSI stood for Pay Related Social Insurance – similar to National Insurance in the United Kingdom, or payroll tax in the United States – used to fund welfare payments and retirement pensions.

'But I'll do my best to get you some rides, either on mine or on others'.'

'Thanks,' I said, rather forlornly.

'But don't you worry,' Cormac said. 'After that win of yours at Cheltenham, you'll have trainers queuing up to have you on their horses.'

'I'm not so sure. My ex made it quite clear that I'd regret leaving him, and now he's spreading awful lies about me. He told his father I had sex with three other male jockeys at Cheltenham, all of them in one night. It's absolutely not true, but that's why his father sacked me.'

'It sounds to me that you're much better off without either of them.'

'I am,' I agreed. 'But I'm terrified that people will believe what they hear, and I'll never get a job ever again, not in racing anyway.'

'What rubbish,' Cormac said. 'The only thing that people will remember is that jump of yours at the second last in the Champion Chase. Everything else will soon be forgotten.'

'Not if my ex goes on telling the same lies about me.'

'Can you prove they are lies?'

'I don't know. I think so. I'll have to speak to the other jockeys. They surely can't have said it, because it didn't happen.'

'If you're that worried, stop him telling them.'

'How?' I asked.

'Take legal action against him. Get a court injunction to stop him repeating lies about you.'

'How the hell do I do that?' I asked.

'First of all, you need to find yourself a lawyer.'

'I can't afford to pay a lawyer.'

'Can you afford not to?'

* * *

Cormac Fitzgerald called me back at eleven with the name of a lawyer.

'His name is Jim Wilson. He's one of my owners from Limerick. Specialises in libel and slander cases. I called him and he's agreed to give you an initial phone consultation for free.' Cormac gave me Jim's number. 'I have to tell you, though, he wasn't particularly hopeful. But give him a call anyway. He's expecting you.'

I called Jim Wilson straight away but, as Cormac had implied, he wasn't very enthusiastic about my chances.

'Since 2009, both libel and slander have been dealt with in the same way by the Irish courts, and are jointly known simply as defamation,' he said. 'Spoken defamation, or slander, is particularly difficult to prove unless it's recorded, like on a radio or TV programme. You have to get statements from people who heard it, getting them to remember exactly what was said, and it's notoriously difficult to find witnesses who will help you in slander cases, especially if they initially believed the things said about you were true.

'And suing people in the High Court is not cheap. Indeed, it can be eye-wateringly expensive. Even if you win, you are unlikely to recover all your costs, and if you lose . . . Well, don't even go there as you would also have to pay the costs of the other side.'

'But what my ex is saying is a lie,' I said. 'So how could I lose?'

'Very easily,' Jim said. 'There is a much-used defence for defamation known as Honest Opinion. If your ex states that what he originally said was *honestly done* – that is he thought it was true when he said it – then you might well lose.'

'But that's ridiculous,' I said, exasperated. 'He knew damn well it wasn't true when he said it.'

'You might believe that, and I might believe it too, but are you certain a judge or a jury will? And are you willing to take that risk? I advise all my clients to think very carefully before going to court. You never know what will happen. Some of them still do, mind, but it's a huge ordeal for them, even if they win.

'And some people mistakenly think that by suing, everyone else will then believe them, even if they are actually in the wrong. It's a very expensive error. Do you remember the case of those two footballers' wives in England? One accused the other of leaking her private information to the press. The second one sued the first for defamation, in spite of the fact that what the first had said was substantially true. Hence, the second one lost the case, and it cost her millions in legal fees.'

'So, what can I do?' I asked gloomily.

'If you instruct me, I could write a cease-and-desist letter to your ex, demanding that he stop telling lies about you. It's a formal legal document, and if he ignores it and goes on repeating the lies, then you would have a much stronger case if you ever do go to court. And it would also show him that you are serious.'

'How much would that cost?' I asked.

'A few hundred euros.'

'Is that what you would advise?'

'Maybe,' Jim said. 'Or maybe I'd ignore it. Making a fuss is likely to make the lies heard by more people, not less. I know it's unpleasant, but what harm can they really do?'

'I lost my job because of them.'

'Then sue your employer. Much safer, and cheaper.'

'He told me I can't because he'd employed me for less than a year.'

'Oh,' he said. 'Well, in that case, my best advice is to do nothing. Find another job, and another boyfriend, and move on.'

'But it's so unfair.'

'John F Kennedy once said that *life is unfair, but we still strive*. Hence, my advice to you, Imogen Duffy, is to put this behind you and strive hard.'

* * *

On Friday afternoon, in stark contrast to Thursday, I sat alone in my parents' sitting room watching the racing from Cheltenham while my mum and dad were both at work, saving people's lives and bringing babies into the world.

And that thought alone put my own situation into perspective.

Find another job, Jim Wilson had said, *and strive hard*.

Striving hard was not a problem – I'd been doing that for years – but how did I find another stable job? And did I actually need one?

Even before winning the Champion Chase, I had about reached the point where my earnings from races – riding fees plus my share of prize money – meant that my stable salary had become less crucial to my survival. And now my slice of the Cheltenham purse gave me time to decide where I wanted to go.

Maybe things weren't so bad after all.

But I had to find a way to maintain the number of my race rides, or even to increase them, so I reached for my phone and searched for 'jockey's agent' on the internet.

* * *

The Aintree Grand National is called *The World's Greatest Steeplechase*, and has the largest purse for any jump race, in excess of a million British pounds, but winning the Cheltenham Gold Cup is the more prestigious triumph for any horse or jockey.

This is because the Grand National is a handicap race, which means that the better the horse, the more weight it has to carry on its back, so theoretically, every horse in the race has an equal chance at winning. Hence, the 'best' horse doesn't necessarily win. Whereas, in the Gold Cup, as in the Queen Mother Champion Chase, all the horses carry the same weight, so it is a true test.

The only exceptions to this are that young, five-year-old horses get a four-pound allowance, and mares get seven, although no five-year-olds, and only one mare have run in the race during the past ten years, and the last mare to win it was Dawn Run in 1986.

Whereas the Champion Chase on Wednesday had been a sprint, run over the minimum distance of two miles, the Gold Cup on Friday was for stayers, negotiating twenty-two fences, over three and a quarter miles. It is described as the *Blue Riband* of British steeplechasing, and the winner is lauded as being the very best of the best.

I watched on the television as the twelve hopefuls for this year's race circled behind the start, having their girths checked. It made me think back to how I had been feeling in that same position just two days previously on City Flyer. I wondered if the jockeys were as nervous now as I had been then.

And then they were off, galloping past the grandstands with two complete circuits of the course ahead of them.

As well as it being an individual event, the race was, as always, viewed as a duel between the very best British- and Irish-trained horses, this year with six of the twelve runners coming from each country. This international rivalry is always intense and there is even a trophy, the Prestbury Cup, awarded annually to the trainers and jockeys of the country with the most winners at the Festival.

I was, of course, cheering on the Irish, even though the short-priced favourite in the betting was trained in England – a twice previous winner, hoping to retain his crown for a third consecutive year.

And it was this favourite, Multistorey, a renowned front-runner, that led the field down the back of the course for the first time, skipping over the water jump some two lengths to the good. But it was at the next fence that he came to grief, hitting the top of the birch, screwing sideways in mid-air, and going down to the turf in a heap, sending his yellow-clad jockey hard into the ground.

There was a huge groan from the crowd as they realised that their beloved champion was out of the race, but relief too when

Multistorey was seen to get up quickly and gallop away unscathed. The same, however, could not be said of his rider, who remained motionless on the grass.

I was never pleased to see any horse fall, but I felt that, in this instance, it gave the Irish runners a better chance of victory.

However, my concerns for the jockey were multiplied when, on the second circuit, the remaining runners had to bypass that fence completely, because he was still being treated by the medical team.

Racing falls, and the associated injuries, are an occupational hazard for any jump jockey. I'd had my fair share of spills, but so far, I'd been lucky to sustain nothing more serious than cuts and bruises, plus a dislocated thumb, which had been very painful at the time but had not kept me out of the saddle for long.

My interest in the race waned as I waited to hear news from the television commentator concerning the injured jockey.

One of the Irish raiders won the race, its owner's euphoric reaction in stark contrast to my own feelings as the TV images showed an ambulance moving along the course very slowly, a sure sign that there was serious trouble within.

There is a special camaraderie uniting all jockeys when it comes to injuries, irrespective of nationality, and that's especially true amongst jump jockeys. We are as competitive as hell when we ride against one another, but there is also a brotherhood, or sisterhood, between us away from the track, bound together by an appreciation that every time we go out to race we are putting our bodies, and our lives, on the line.

The TV director cut between the joyous images from the unsaddling enclosure and those of the ambulance making its slow way, not to the racecourse medical centre, but out onto the main road, turning left towards Cheltenham Hospital, now with its blue lights flashing.

Maybe the jockey was only concussed. Perhaps he was being taken to hospital as a precaution. Or maybe not.

No jump jockey likes to dwell on thoughts of serious injuries.

Despite overwhelming evidence to the contrary, everyone believes they will get round every time they ride, and racing falls are simply for others to worry about. But all of us have to learn how to fall at jockey school – there is even a mechanical fall simulator to assist with the training.

There are far fewer falls today than there were forty, fifty or sixty years ago when the fences were both higher, stiffer and with much larger spreads. Especially at the open ditches, which used to have a wide, deep ditch dug out in front of the fence, but now mostly they only have the take-off board placed further from the obstacle than at a regular 'plain' fence.

And horses now tend to be better schooled in the art of jumping, with every trainer having their own practice hurdles and fences built at home on the gallops.

Nevertheless, statistics show that, on average, a jump jockey will hit the ground at thirty miles per hour, about once in eighteen to twenty rides. Compare that to one fall in every ten to twelve rides in the 1960s. However, for a top jockey today, that will still mean having at least one racing fall every single week. Even if they don't break anything, they live permanently with bruises.

And hitting the ground at speed is not the only problem.

The jockey in the ambulance had been leading the field when his horse fell, so once down on the ground, the other runners had to gallop right over him. Horses are usually pretty good at avoiding someone lying on the ground, but there's not much they can do if they are already airborne themselves.

I knew from experience that half a ton of Thoroughbred landing on your thigh was bloody painful – and I'd sported a horseshoe-shaped bruise on my leg for months.

The last two races from Cheltenham were less eventful, and so the Festival ended for another year, the Prestbury Cup safely in the hands of the Irish for the next twelve months.

At the close of their transmission, the TV company played a montage of the best moments of the week and there I was, shown jumping the second-last fence in the Champion Chase astride City Flyer.

It made me smile.

Not even Liam could take that away from me.

The front doorbell rang.

I stood up from the sofa and went to answer it.

Liam was standing there, carrying a large bunch of flowers.

'Hi, Imo,' he said, smiling and holding the flowers out towards me.

I didn't take them.

'What do you want?' I asked.

'I want you to come home.'

'I am already home.'

'I meant to come home to my house with me,' he said.

'And why on earth would I do that after what you've been saying about me?'

'It was only a little joke. I didn't mean it.'

'Your father didn't think it was funny,' I said. 'He fired me.'

There was no shock or surprise in Liam's face. He already knew.

'So go away, and take your bloody flowers with you. I never want to see you again.'

I stepped back into the house and began to close the door.

Liam stuck his foot into the gap, stopping the door from shutting completely.

'Come on, Imogen,' he said. 'Give me another chance.'

'Is that another of your little jokes?' I replied through the gap, still leaning hard on the door trying to push it shut. 'You really must be crazy if you believe I would go anywhere with you, let alone back to your house. Get it into your head that I've left you. Now get your bloody foot out of my door.'

'I can't move it,' he said. 'Release the pressure.'

I eased it, but he didn't remove his foot.

Instead, he came crashing through the doorway like a charging rhinoceros, sending me sprawling backwards onto the hall floor.

'Get out,' I shouted, but he ignored me.

He advanced along the hallway.

'I'll never let you leave me,' he shouted. 'I'd rather kill you first.'

Then he started kicking me, first my legs and then my body. Next, he tried to stamp on me, aiming for my head.

I curled up into a tight ball, putting my jockey fall-training to good use, but still I was certain I was going to die.

Chapter 5

'LIAM CARSON! LEAVE MY DAUGHTER alone and get the hell out of my house!'

My father was standing in the open front doorway.

Liam suddenly stopped trying to crush my skull, as if the sudden presence of a third person had somehow brought him to his senses. He stood above me for a couple of seconds before turning and running out of the house, disappearing off down the road.

Dad came forward quickly and crouched down beside me.

'Darling, are you all right? I'll call an ambulance.'

He started to dial on his mobile phone.

'I'm fine, Dad,' I said, sitting up. 'No ambulance. I've had far worse bruises from falls in races. But I'm really glad you arrived home when you did. I feared he was going to kill me.'

I was shaking.

'I'm going to call the Gardaí,' Dad said.

The Gardaí were the Irish police – their official name being An Garda Síochána, meaning *The Guardians of the Peace* in the Irish Gaelic language.

'Liam Carson needs to be locked up,' Dad said, making the call.

I couldn't disagree.

'They're on their way,' he said to me, hanging up, a look of concern on his face. 'What the hell was Carson doing here anyway?'

'He wanted me to go back to live with him. I told him there was no chance of that, and he should get lost. And that made him angry.' I paused. 'But there's much more to it than that, Dad.'

As we waited for the police to arrive, I told my father everything that had been going on, including losing my job due to the lies Liam had told his father about me, and how he had threatened to kill me if I left him.

'I never liked that young man,' Dad said, becoming increasingly angry on my behalf.

After ten minutes or so, the Gardaí arrived in the shape of two uniformed officers in a blue and yellow patrol car, and the four of us sat around the kitchen table, while I gave them a statement of exactly what had happened. They both made notes.

'So, this is a domestic violence incident,' one of the guards said when I was finished, his tone implying that he believed that made it less important.

'No, it's not,' I objected. 'The relationship between Liam Carson and myself finished more than a week ago. This was a forced invasion of *my* home – not his – and a sustained assault on my person. He also made threats against my life.'

'Do you have any injuries?' the other guard asked.

'Some bruising to my legs and to my upper body.'

And also to my state of mind, I thought.

'We will arrange for you to be seen by a doctor,' he said.

'My father is a doctor. I do not wish to see anyone else.'

'We will require a proper assessment of your injuries. And it must be produced by a Garda medical examiner, not by a family member of the victim.'

I suppose I could see the sense of that.

'You will need to come with us now to the Garda station in Thurles for a full examination. In case it's ever needed in court.'

'Will you be arresting Liam Carson?' I asked.

'That will be a decision for our inspector. We will be making a report to him.'

I didn't think that sounded too encouraging.

*   *   *

I spent about three hours with the Gardaí in Thurles, first being poked and prodded by the medical examiner, and then being questioned by the inspector.

'There's not much wrong with you,' said the doctor, when he was finally finished. 'Some of those bruises on your upper arm are not new.'

'I had a fall,' I said. 'About a week ago.'

'A fall? At your age?'

'A racing fall,' I explained. 'I'm a jockey. The horse I was riding fell. That bruise is from being kicked by one of the other horses in the race.'

'Oh,' he said in surprise. 'I don't deal much with jockeys.'

'How about my left ear?' I asked.

'What about it?'

'It was stamped on. Liam Carson was aiming for my head, but I moved. He caught my ear.'

He inspected the appendage.

'Only a very minor abrasion,' said the doctor. 'Nothing to worry about.'

'I'm not worried about it,' I said. 'But it is an injury caused by the assault and it should be recorded, in the same way as the bruises on my legs.'

I could tell that he was reluctant to add to his workload. And the inspector seemed equally disinterested when he interviewed me.

'This interview is being recorded,' he said, pushing a button on the black box on the table. The box emitted a long beep, then fell silent.

'Do I need a solicitor?' I asked.

'Not unless you particularly want one. This is a witness interview only. You are not being interviewed under caution. The recording is so we can produce an accurate statement for you to sign later. It prevents disagreements over what was said, or not said.'

He paused, looking at me.

'Fine,' I said, waving a hand. 'Go ahead.'

The inspector glanced down at the papers in front of him.

'Now, Miss Duffy, tell me what happened to you this afternoon?'

I went through the whole thing again, from the moment Liam rang the doorbell to when he ran out of the house. At the time, the confrontation between us had seemed to go on forever, but in fact, it had been only a minute or two.

'It was hardly a serious incident, now, was it?' said the inspector. 'Are you sure your memory is accurate?'

'Absolutely,' I said. 'It was a ferocious assault.'

'But the medical examiner says that the injuries you have are merely superficial.'

52

'It would have been much more serious if my father hadn't arrived home when he did. In fact, I'd probably be dead.'

I could tell from his demeanour that the inspector didn't agree with me.

'Look,' I said. 'I was in fear of my life. He threatened to kill me, and I believe Liam Carson may very well do that unless you lock him up.'

The inspector looked at me in a manner that suggested he reckoned that either I was lying, or I was as nutty as a fruitcake. But at this point, another man came into the interview room and whispered into the inspector's ear.

The inspector stood up and moved towards the door.

'Please wait here, Miss Duffy. I will be back shortly.'

I sat and waited for more than five minutes.

'Sorry about that,' the inspector said, returning to the interview room and sitting down. 'There has been a development. Mr Liam Carson has voluntarily attended the Garda station at Kilkenny.'

'Was he arrested?'

'No. Not at this time.'

'Why not?' I demanded.

'He was told to report to the station in the morning, once my investigation is complete.'

I stared at him. 'So that means he is free to attack me again tonight.'

'He was told not to contact you.'

I almost laughed. 'And you think he will take any notice of that?'

'Miss Duffy, we can't arrest someone without an investigation first. We have to weigh up the available evidence.'

'Is my word not enough for you?' I was almost shouting at him. 'Ask my father. He was there too. He saw what happened.'

'Dr Patrick Duffy has already given us a statement.'

'What more do you need? If my skull had been fractured and my brains spilt all over my parents' hallway floor, then you might be taking more interest. And it was a damn close call that they weren't.'

I was becoming quite agitated.

'So, if you won't lock *him* in a cell for the night, then you'd better lock *me* in one. That way he can't get at me, because, next time, he might bring a proper weapon with him, rather than just his shoes.'

* * *

In the end, I didn't spend the night in a cell, but only because the Gardaí wouldn't allow it.

Instead, my father came to Thurles to collect me at nine o'clock.

'They didn't even arrest Liam when they had the chance,' I said in the car.

I told him about Liam surrendering himself to the police at Kilkenny and then being allowed to leave again.

'Unbelievable,' Dad said.

'And all because I wasn't sufficiently injured. It was as if the inspector would have preferred it if I'd had something much more serious.'

'Thank God you didn't.'

'It was only because you came home early. So, thank you, rather than thank God.'

When we arrived home, I refused to get out of the car until Dad had checked that Liam wasn't waiting for me in the shadows.

He wasn't. But I still believed he would come after me again – if not tonight, then sometime. He was nothing if not obsessive.

But it is no secret that almost all jump jockeys are obsessives.

AP (Sir Anthony) McCoy, a fellow Irishman of mine from the north, had been an obsessive all the way through his riding career – obsessive about winning. He had starved himself and driven himself beyond any reasonable measure to win more than four thousand jump races and secure a record twenty consecutive British Champion Jump Jockey titles right up until he retired in April 2015.

Like me, AP had ridden his first ever winner at Thurles Racecourse when aged only seventeen, but his had been a flat race while mine had been over hurdles. His obsession to win had always been an inspiration for me, as it was for all jockeys.

He'd also been the UK Sports Personality of the Year in 2010 and the Irish Sports Person of the Year in 2013, before being knighted by Queen Elizabeth II in 2016.

So, obsession has its proper place, as long as it is directed in the right manner. But I felt that Liam Carson's chief obsession was not with his riding career, but with me.

I'll never let you leave me. I'd rather kill you first.

Having checked that the coast was clear, I rushed into the house, and then my father locked and bolted the front door.

But did I feel safe?

Not a bit. I was shaking all over.

How could I live the rest of my life like this?

And unless Liam was locked up soon, the rest of my life could prove to be extremely short.

* * *

At eleven o'clock on Saturday morning, having heard nothing, I finally rang the Gardaí at Thurles and asked to speak to the inspector, but predictably, he didn't work at weekends.

However, I did speak to another officer who knew about my case.

'Liam Carson attended the Garda station in Kilkenny this morning at eight a.m. as instructed,' he said. 'He was interviewed and will be summonsed to appear before a district judge to answer the charge.'

'What charge?' I asked.

'Using threatening behaviour in a private place.'

'Is that all?' I asked incredulously. 'Why not attempted murder?'

'You will have to take that up with the Office of Public Prosecutions. They decided there was insufficient evidence for a more serious charge.'

'What sort of evidence did they need? Blood on the floor?'

'That might have helped,' said the officer. 'Or a broken bone.'

I sat there holding my phone in disbelief.

But at least Liam had been charged with something.

'When will he appear in court?' I asked.

There was a short pause, and I could hear papers being rustled.

'April tenth, at Thurles District Court.'

'But that's nearly a month away,' I said. 'Will he be in prison until then?'

'Oh, no, Miss Duffy,' replied the officer, with a small laugh. 'He is not in prison. He wasn't arrested. Mr Carson is free to go about his business. He only has to appear at Thurles District Court on the specified date to answer the charge before the district judge, that's like a magistrate. You will receive a summons to attend as a witness. It will be in the post to you in the next couple of days.'

I wasn't really listening to the last bit.

Mr Carson is free to go about his business, the officer had said.

Free to murder me, more like.

*   *   *

During the afternoon, I watched the racing from Cork on the television and, as if to rub salt in my wounds, Liam won the two-mile maiden hurdle on the five-year-old that I should have been riding.

It made me feel like throwing up.

How could they have let him go again? And for a month!

How could I keep safe from him for a month? And what sentence would Liam then get anyway?

I looked up the Irish sentencing code on the internet.

The maximum term of imprisonment for using threatening behaviour was just three months. And, because he had no prior convictions, the likely sentence would be a fine or a community order – no prison time at all.

What good would that do?

Perhaps I should emigrate to Australia.

They had racing over there. But it was almost all flat racing. Jump racing has all but disappeared, and did I really want to be so far away from my parents?

And would it make me any safer?

According to the Australian visa page on the internet, anyone with an Irish passport was welcome to visit Australia any time they liked. It also said that having been fined for something was not a sufficient reason to refuse a tourist visa. But having been jailed for attempted murder would be.

How could I get the charge against him upgraded to match what actually happened in my parents' hallway?

I decided to call the Garda inspector first thing on Monday morning.

That's provided I survived until then.

Chapter 6

IT SEEMED STRANGE TO NO longer have a job.

Even though I'd been employed by Michael Carson mostly as a work rider and a jockey, I had also been expected to help care for the horses in other ways, often stepping in to act as a stable lass if anyone was away on holiday or off sick. Hence, I had done more than my fair share of mucking out and grooming.

I'd always been at the stables very early, even on Sundays, so it was a peculiar feeling on this particular Sunday morning to be still lying in bed well past eight o'clock.

But at least the night had been uneventful, and I was still alive, not that I'd slept particularly well. Every slight creak of the cooling house, or the bark from a dog or a fox, had me instantly awake and on edge, listening intensely for sounds of an intruder, despite me placing a chair under the door handle of my bedroom.

I'd moved the chair by the time my mother brought me in a cup of tea at half past eight.

'Here you are, dear,' she said, putting it down on the bedside table. 'How are you feeling?'

I almost burst into tears.

'I'm so sorry,' I said.

'Why?' she asked. 'You have nothing to be sorry for.'

'I'm sorry for all this worry. I feel so ashamed.'

Mum sat down on the edge of my bed.

'You don't need to feel ashamed,' she said. 'It's not your fault.'

'But I chose to go and live with that man in the first place. And I'm ashamed of myself for not having left him sooner, and I'm embarrassed too for all the hurt I must have caused you and Dad.'

Mum leaned over and gave me a hug.

'What's past is past,' she said. 'It's now time to look to the future.'

She was right. I had to move on. To simply lie in bed, become a recluse, and feel sorry for myself was nothing more than an acceptance that I shouldn't have left him. And I should have, ages ago.

As Mum had said, I had to look to the future and trust that I'd be around to enjoy it.

'OK,' I said with a sudden firmness of purpose. 'I'll get up, get dressed, then we can start making plans.' But any plans we might have made were made irrelevant by a telephone call I received at nine o'clock precisely.

I had just stepped out of the shower and was wrapped only in a towel that was rather too small, even for my slight frame.

'Is that Imogen Duffy?' said an English male voice on my phone.

'It is,' I said.

'Thank God,' he said. 'I've been trying to find your number since yesterday.'

'It's not a secret,' I said.

'Tell Michael Carson that. He refused point-blank to give it to me, and Paddy Murphy didn't have it.'

'So how *did* you get my number?' I asked.

'In desperation I called Cormac Fitzgerald because I discovered from the *Racing Post* results data that you had also ridden for him, but years ago. He gave me your number straight away.'

'So how can I help you?' I asked.

'Will you come to England to ride for me?'

Would I? Damned right I would. I'd go anywhere to get away from Liam.

'I don't even know who you are,' I said.

'Oh, yes, sorry. I'm Freddie Swinton.'

Now my ears really pricked up.

'*The* Freddie Swinton?' I asked.

'The one and only,' he said with a laugh. 'Except for my son, Freddie Junior.'

Freddie Swinton, in his mid-forties but already a six-times champion jump trainer in Great Britain. One of the true heavyweights of steeplechasing.

'You may have seen the Gold Cup on Friday,' he said. 'My horse, Multistorey, had a bad fall at the open ditch.'

'I watched it on the television.'

'Well, the horse is fine but the same can't be said for poor Jimmy Tucker who rode him. Broke his shoulder badly. Needs an operation, so he'll be out for several months, maybe more. That's why I'm calling you.'

My heart was beating fast.

'I watched your ride on City Flyer in the Champion Chase,' he said. 'Impressive. Very impressive.'

'Thank you.'

'And I've now been back and looked at all your other rides, those that are on the *Racing Post* website, and I liked what I saw. I think you have great potential.'

'Thank you,' I said again.

'And you're still a claimer?'

'Three pounds,' I said. 'But, of course, I didn't get that in the Champion Chase.'

'No, you wouldn't. But does Paddy Murphy employ you?'

'No. He asked me to ride City Flyer because his usual jockey got concussed in the Arkle Chase on Tuesday.'

'Are you employed by anyone?'

'No,' I replied. 'Totally not.'

'Great,' he said. 'That makes things much simpler.' He paused. 'Imogen Duffy, will you come and ride for me, as my second-string jockey to Adrian Shaw?'

Adrian Shaw was the current British champion jockey.

What an opportunity!

'I would need to be employed by you,' I said. 'I'm still a conditional.'

'No problem. Shall we say initially for six months? Then see how we're doing. Either of us could end the arrangement at that time if we want to.'

'Sounds good to me,' I said. 'But where would I live?'

'I have two small cottages adjoining my yard. One of them is currently empty. You could have that. And I'll organise a car for you to use. I assume you can drive?'

'Yes,' I said.

He must really want me, I thought.

'When would you want me to start?' I asked with excitement. I could hardly believe what I was hearing.

'How soon can you come?'

'Anytime,' I said.

'Good. I'll get my staff to make the arrangements. Where are you now?'

'At my parents' home near Thurles, County Tipperary.'

'I know Thurles,' he said. 'Nice little racecourse. OK. I'll sort it. Imogen, welcome aboard the Swinton ship.' He sounded almost as excited as me. 'I'm quite sure you'll do great.'

He hung up and I stood there holding my phone, needing to pinch myself to check I wasn't dreaming.

Second jockey for Freddie Swinton!

About ten minutes later, my phone rang again. Another English number.

'Hello,' I said.

'Hi, Imogen, this is Stacey. I'm one of Freddie's secretaries. I've booked you onto the Aer Lingus flight from Dublin to Heathrow this evening at six thirty. A car will pick you up from your parents' home at half past two. What's the address? And I also need your email address to send you the boarding pass.'

I gave both to her, somewhat in a daze at how fast things were moving, especially as it was a Sunday.

'Freddie runs a seven-day-a-week operation here,' Stacey said, when I remarked on it. 'There are four secretaries, and someone is always on call, twenty-four hours a day, every single day of the year, even on Christmas Day. You can't simply switch off the horses, now, can you?'

Stacey told me some of the things I should bring.

'I've added extra baggage to your flight booking,' she said. 'Make sure you also bring your paperwork: passport, driving licence, and your jockey's licence and medical book.'

'My jockey's licence and medical book are both now digital.'

'Then I will get those from the British or Irish racing authority data systems. Do you have your own saddle?'

'I do,' I said. 'But it's with my valet. I was meant to be riding at Cork yesterday and he took it with him to be there.'

I gave her the name of the valet.

'Don't worry. You can borrow one until I arrange for yours to be sent over from Ireland. Right, that's all. Do you have any questions?'

Yes, I thought, *hundreds of them*.

'How will I get from Heathrow?' I asked. 'And where exactly are Mr Swinton's stables?'

'Freddie,' Stacey said. 'Everyone calls him Freddie. Even the stable staff. That's what he prefers. It may sound relaxed but, I assure you, there's nothing relaxing about working here. It's high pressure all the time.'

What was I letting myself in for?

'A driver will be waiting for you. He'll have a board with your name on it when you exit arrivals. The stables are outside the village of Lambourn, near Hungerford, in West Berkshire, about seventy miles west of London. The whole area is called the Valley of the Racehorse. There are lots of racing yards nearby.'

'I've heard of it,' I said. Everyone in jump racing had heard of Lambourn.

'Good. Right, anything else?'

'Do I need to bring any bedding and how do I get into the cottage?'

Stacey laughed. 'I'll make sure that the bed is made up, the place is warm and there's some basic food, and a pint of milk in the fridge for coffee. The driver who meets you will have your key. His name is Spencer. He's our horsebox driver.'

'Great. Thank you.'

'I'll see you tomorrow,' Stacey said. 'Be at the yard by seven a.m.'

* * *

My Aer Lingus flight from Dublin to Heathrow was delayed by more than an hour, due to the late arrival of the incoming aircraft, but I didn't care. I was floating on air, with or without the aeroplane.

Everything had been such a rush, so much so that I hadn't even had time to worry about Liam.

Mum and Dad had been wonderful, despite their real concerns about their twenty-two-year-old daughter going to live in England on her own.

'I'll be fine,' I said to them. 'Probably safer than staying here at the moment. And it's a golden ticket for any jockey. I couldn't say no.'

They helped me pack my stuff, lending me one of their large suitcases to take in addition to my own, in order to get in all my riding clothes, body protector, and my racing boots. And I carried my racing skullcap in a separate holdall as hand luggage.

Dad helped load everything into the smart black chauffeur-driven Mercedes that arrived on the dot of half past two to collect me.

I stood beside the car giving them both hugs. It had been only three days since I'd arrived home on this spot with a hero's welcome, and here I was leaving again. My mother was in tears once more, although these weren't tears of joy at my arrival, but tears of sadness at my departure.

The Mercedes whisked me the hundred and sixty kilometres to Dublin Airport, north of the city centre, arriving in good time for me to check in without any fuss. To my delight, I found that my business-class booking allowed me fast track through security, as well as access to the airline lounge. Hence, I was able to sit in comfort throughout the delay, enjoying a complimentary glass of champagne.

I felt that I deserved it, and I made a silent toast to my new adventure.

And what an adventure it turned out to be – but it was not the one I was expecting.

Chapter 7

STACEY HAD WARNED ME THAT there was nothing relaxing about working for Freddie Swinton – and she'd been absolutely right.

Spencer didn't deliver me to the empty cottage until almost midnight on that Sunday night, but I was standing in the Swinton yard just before seven o'clock the following morning, appropriately dressed to ride out, including wearing my body protector and skullcap.

The rest of the stable staff were there well ahead of me, scurrying around carrying muck sacks, buckets of water, or other equipment. Indeed, the whole place was a hive of activity, and I felt a touch foolish standing there doing nothing.

'You must be Imogen,' said a small man with a weather-beaten face, coming over to greet me. 'I'm Wes Duncan. Head lad. Nice to meet you.' We shook hands. 'Freddie has you down to ride Grapejuice for first lot. She's in box sixteen.' He pointed to my right. 'We pull out at seven thirty sharp.'

I walked down to box sixteen, wondering where I would find the necessary tack, but I needn't have worried. Grapejuice was already being saddled by someone else, a young man similarly dressed to me, except that his blue padded jacket had FREDDIE SWINTON RACING in yellow on the left breast.

'Hello,' I said. 'I'm Imogen.'

'And I'm Tom,' said the young man, smiling. 'Juicy is almost ready for you.'

'Do you normally ride her?' I asked.

'Often,' he said. 'But not always. I'm riding another one today.'

'Then please show me the ropes. It's my first day here.'

'I know,' Tom said. 'Freddie told us all yesterday at evening stables that you were coming. He seemed very pleased, excited even.'

That was good to know.

Tom finished tacking up Grapejuice, then he went away, presumably to get his own mount ready.

I looked at my watch – 7.20. I didn't want to be late.

As I was waiting, Freddie Swinton came into the box. He too was wearing a FREDDIE SWINTON RACING branded blue jacket.

'Hello, Imogen,' he said with a friendly smile. 'How lovely to have you join the team.'

'Thank you,' I said. 'And thank you for all the arrangements in getting me here yesterday.'

'No problem. Have you settled in?'

'Not really,' I said. 'I only arrived at midnight. My flight from Dublin was delayed.'

'I'm sorry to hear that,' he replied, but his tone gave the strong impression that he wasn't really interested in other people's problems. As long as I was here now was all that mattered to him, along with the welfare of the horses, of course.

'Grapejuice, here, is a six-year-old star.' He gave the horse an affectionate slap on its neck. 'She was second in the mares' hurdle last week at Cheltenham, beaten again by the bloody

Irish.' He grinned at me. 'She will probably go next in the Aintree Hurdle at the Grand National meeting, two weeks on Thursday. She's had a few days' rest to recover from Cheltenham, and we'll soon start the process to get her back to absolute peak fitness for Aintree. Today, you'll just be giving her a couple of gentle canters up the all-weather track.'

'Right,' I said. 'And I'm Irish.'

'Not any more, you're not,' Freddie said with a laugh. 'It's where the stable is situated that counts, not where you were born.'

'I was born in England,' I said. 'In Surrey. But I'm still Irish.'

He looked across at me. 'I'd heard you were feisty. I like that.'

'Don't believe everything you hear.'

Especially, I thought, *if it comes out of Liam Carson's mouth.*

'Pull out!' came a shout from outside.

I led Grapejuice out of her box, and Freddie gave me a leg-up onto her back.

'Feisty,' he said again, then he laughed and walked away.

'Imogen, follow me,' Tom called over from his position on another horse to my left.

So, I did, out of the rear of the stable yard into a sort of collecting circle where Grapejuice was one of a string of twenty-two horses that walked round and round, waiting.

Freddie came over and stood in the centre, giving each rider in turn his instructions.

'Imogen,' he called out towards me. 'Twice up the all-weather, just gentle canters. Just sit still on her. Let her do all the work.'

'Yes, Guv'nor,' I called back.

I couldn't quite bring myself to call him Freddie, and Guv'nor was what I'd always called Michael Carson, at least within his hearing.

When all the instructions had been given, the string left the collecting circle and walked out towards the gallops, climbing the hill above the yard. It was my first view of the beautiful rolling Berkshire Downs, although I wondered why they weren't called the Berkshire Ups, because there was certainly nothing *down* about them.

Nowadays, training racehorses is a science as well as an art.

In the past, the prevailing opinion had been that, to get a horse ready to race, you ran it fast over longer and longer distances, maybe two or even three times a week, interspersed with days of 'road work', that is long-distance walking and trotting on a hard surface, which was believed to strengthen the bones and tendons.

But 'interval training' is now seen as the magic key to success, while road work was limited due to its tendency to adversely affect the joints, increasing the likelihood of arthritis.

Interval training involves several short periods of high-intensity exercise interspersed with periods of rest. It is how human athletes have trained for donkey's years, and throughout the last quarter of the twentieth century, Martin Pipe started applying the same principle to the training of racehorses.

It was revolutionary and was instrumental in Pipe becoming British Champion Jump Trainer on a record fifteen separate occasions, thirteen of them consecutively.

But it wasn't the only thing that he did differently. He started blood-testing his horses on a daily basis, building an on-site laboratory at his stables to get faster results, and he kept his horses skinny, so you could see their ribcages.

'You don't see any fat human athletes in the Olympic Games,' Martin would say. 'And you can turn a really good horse into a very slow horse if you run him when he's twenty kilograms overweight – that's equivalent to giving the other runners a forty-five-length start. A racehorse is an athlete, and it has to be properly fit. It's only common sense.'

Hence using interval training, keeping horses very lean, weighing them daily and regularly testing their blood, have become normal practice for almost all racehorse trainers, and Freddie Swinton was one of the best in the business.

The string walked to the bottom of Freddie's all-weather gallop, a half-mile-long strip of Polytrack, designed such that the horses run quite steeply uphill during the last two furlongs, enhancing the aerobic effect of their exercise.

The first time up, all of us cantered gently in line astern, warming up for the more vigorous work to come.

Having taken his Land Rover to get ahead of us, Freddie stood at the top of the hill, watching every horse in turn through his binoculars, as they cantered up towards him. I was probably under particular scrutiny as the new girl, and I felt quite self-conscious as I passed him, but Freddie made no comment, and I didn't fall off or otherwise make a fool of myself.

I pulled up at the top of the hill and walked the horse back down again, giving her heart time to return to a resting rhythm.

Second time up, I sat quite still on Grapejuice as I'd been instructed, allowing her to canter easily beneath me. In spite of it only being gentle, it was exhilarating to be on such a good horse in such magnificent surroundings, with the wind blowing through my hair beneath my skullcap.

'Perfect, Imogen,' Freddie called across. 'Well done. That's enough for her for today. Dismount now and walk her back to the yard. Wes will arrange for someone to deal with her. Then go over to the office. Second lot pulls out at ten past nine. You'll be on Multistorey.'

Multistorey! Two-times winner of the Cheltenham Gold Cup.

'He needs to regain his confidence,' Freddie said. 'My plan is for him to run in the Grade 1 three-mile chase on the first day at Aintree, but I need to know he's recovered from his fall, so you'll be taking him gently over the schooling fences.'

To say I was excited at the prospect would have been an understatement.

*　*　*

'Hi, Imogen,' said a friendly voice as I walked into the stable office. 'I'm Stacey. We spoke yesterday. On the phone.'

'Of course. Hello, Stacey. It's very good to meet you, and thank you for making all the arrangements to get me over here.'

I reckoned that Stacey was in her mid-forties, petite, with dark brown hair pulled back into a ponytail. Like everyone else, she was wearing FREDDIE SWINTON RACING branded clothing, in her case a polo shirt.

'We need you to sign some papers,' she said. 'The conditional jockey training agreement and your contract of employment.' She held them out to me. 'Would you like to sign them now, or would you rather get some advice first from a solicitor?'

'Do I need advice?' I asked.

'The training agreement is the standard form for all conditional jockeys. The employment contract is also standard for all of Freddie's employees. Read them through first, then decide.'

I sat down on a chair and went through them. The conditional jockey agreement was far more formal than I'd had before with Cormac Fitzgerald or Michael Carson, setting out the obligations and duties of both the trainer and the jockey. But it was also quite straightforward in easy-to-understand language.

The same was mostly true of the employment agreement, which was for an initial term of six months, with an option to extend beyond, and with a minimum notice period of two months by either side. There was some legal jargon concerning the dispute, disciplinary and grievance procedures that I skimmed through quickly. The only thing I was really interested in was how much I was to be paid, and I was pleasantly surprised at what was being offered, especially when I realised the amount shown was in British pounds, not euros.

Perhaps I should have asked about that before jumping on the aeroplane.

'How about any race riding fees?' I asked.

'You keep all of those, except for a small percentage paid to the racing authority to cover industry training.'

'And jockey's share of prize money?'

'You get to keep that too,' Stacey said.

I wondered if there was a catch.

'How much do I have to pay in rent for the cottage?' I asked. 'And for the use of a car?'

'Hasn't Freddie already discussed that with you?' Stacey asked.

'We didn't discuss anything to do with money.'

She laughed. 'Typical Freddie. As far as I'm aware the cottage and the car are available for your use free of charge for the first six months. You only have to pay the household bills, insurance, council tax, and your petrol.'

'That's very generous,' I said, quite surprised.

'Freddie is very generous, but he expects total commitment and absolute loyalty in return. He'll be very nice to you, just as long as you give everything you've got for him. But he will also come down heavily on you if he believes you're slacking.'

I reread the dispute, disciplinary and grievance procedures in the employment contract, this time with greater scrutiny. Did I need a solicitor? But would I really give up this chance even if the solicitor advised me not to sign?

I signed the papers and handed them back to Stacey.

'Great. Thank you. I'll also sign them as the witness and get the training agreement form emailed off right now to the authority. And I'll get Freddie to apply for your conditional jockey's licence. You will get an email form to complete, after which the licence will be issued. It should only take a few days, but it might depend on whether they accept your Irish medical or require a new one, and also if they require you to undergo a skills assessment or any training. But you rode twice at Cheltenham last week and won the Champion Chase, so I can't think there'll be any problems with that.'

She then reached down behind her desk and handed me a large carrier bag.

'Branded clothing,' she said. 'Freddie expects everyone to wear it whenever they're at work, either here or on a racecourse. It's part of the deal with our sponsors.'

I lifted out the clothing – two blue padded riding jackets, three green polo shirts, and one green fleece gilet – all with FREDDIE SWINTON RACING embroidered in yellow on the front, and *BETFRED* in large white capital letters across the back.

'Are they the right size?' Stacey asked. 'I had to guess.'

I removed my own padded riding jacket and replaced it with one of the branded ones.

'Perfect,' I said.

'Good. Anything else?'

'I'll need a new SIM card in my phone. My current one is Irish. And I'd like a new phone number.'

'No problem,' Stacey said. 'I'll sort it.'

'Do you sort everything?' I asked, smiling at her.

'Pretty much. Either me or one of the others.' She waved a hand at the other two people in the room – one man and one woman, both sitting at desks with computers. 'Peter is our wizard at race entries and declarations.' Peter waved a hand at me and then turned back to his screen. 'And Clare's speciality is ensuring we have enough feed, hay, bedding, tack and other equipment – anything for the horses. While Julie, who's on her day off today, deals mainly with vets, farriers and transport, plus stable visits, race-day tickets, and entertaining for the owners. My primary role is our staff – contracts, payroll, and everything else they throw at me – plus sending out bills to our owners and syndic-ates. But each of us can do it all if necessary.'

'Impressive,' I said.

She smiled at me. 'We're a good team. We've been here together for the last eight years, and the system seems to work. If you need anything, just ask one of us.'

'Thanks,' I said. 'I will.'

I thought about asking them for special security measures to protect me from an aggressive ex-boyfriend, but I decided against it. It would take too much explaining.

And surely I'd be safe here, with hundreds of miles, plus the Irish Sea, between us.

If only.

Chapter 8

RIDING MULTISTOREY AT SECOND LOT was everything I could have hoped for.

Even being close to such a fabulous horse was exhilarating, but his fall in the Gold Cup had clearly affected his confidence. He was a little wary as I took him over the line of three schooling fences for the first time, cautiously approaching the first obstacle and popping over it at little more than a canter. But his self-assurance grew, and on the third trip, he was at his best, stretching out fully in the air and landing with aplomb.

'Great,' Freddie said when I pulled up. 'He'll have a full gallop tomorrow and then I'll decide, but on that evidence, he should be fine.'

I walked the great horse back to the yard, and I don't know who was more pleased – Freddie, me, or the horse, who seemed delighted to be safely back home in his stable without any further mishaps.

*　*　*

Over the next couple of weeks, I settled into the daily routine at the Swinton stables, if 'settled in' was the right term for a life that was so hectic that my feet hardly touched the ground.

I thought I'd been tired every evening when I worked for Michael Carson, but I was in a completely different league of tiredness here.

But, somehow, it was all worth it.

The alarm on my phone sounded each morning at five thirty, and I was at the stables well before seven. I rode out every day except Sundays, usually two lots, but sometimes three, unless I was going to the races.

On the days I wasn't racing, I would exercise myself in the afternoons, working on getting as fit as the horses, by running on the Downs above the stable yard. I quickly discovered a route that involved running up and across the gallops, through the village of Upper Lambourn, and then back along the roads to Lambourn village proper – a distance of about three miles.

I would time myself from my cottage to the front door of the small supermarket in the village, aiming to be quicker each time. Then I would buy myself something to cook for supper from the shop before walking back home.

Even though I'd lived with Liam for about eight months, he had enjoyed preparing our meals, so I had done almost nothing on the cooking front.

Hence, feeding myself was full of trial and error and involved some hilarious mistakes – such as failing to remove the plastic bag of giblets from inside a chicken before roasting it, and exploding a carton of soup inside the microwave as I tried to defrost it too quickly.

In spite of such catastrophes, I didn't starve, although once or twice I had to resort to getting a pizza from the local village takeaway.

*   *   *

My first day at the races in my new job was on the first Wednesday after my arrival, when Freddie drove me to Huntingdon Racecourse to assist him saddling two horses he had running, both ridden by Adrian Shaw.

During the journey, he told me that he'd heard from the racing authority that my conditional jockey's licence had been approved with immediate effect, and therefore my first ride in a race for him would be on Friday at Newbury.

'I have two runners in the two-mile handicap hurdle. I've declared Adrian to ride one, and you to ride the other. I hope that's OK?'

He looked across at me.

'Absolutely,' I said. 'Can't wait. Which horse?'

'Point Man. You'll ride him out tomorrow morning to get acquainted.'

I was both hugely excited and extremely apprehensive.

What if I made a complete hash of it?

'You'll do fine,' Freddie said, as if he was reading my mind. 'And I have another ride for you on Saturday, also at Newbury. Maybe two of them. I'll decide whether to run the second one before the declarations close at ten tomorrow morning. Some overnight rain would help.'

I'd never in my life prayed so hard for rain.

'Then you'll be riding two for me at Exeter on Sunday, one at Taunton on Tuesday, two at Hereford next Wednesday, and one at Warwick on Thursday. Then it'll be either Stratford or Uttoxeter the following Saturday, depending on where Adrian wants to ride. And maybe one at Fontwell on Friday too, that's if it rains before then.'

Perhaps I should pray instead for dry weather, to give me a rest.

I stared at him.

'Is it like this every single week?'

'Oh, no,' he said with a laugh. 'Sometimes it gets busy. You wait until the summer when there are evening meetings as well, and my first lot pulls out at six o'clock to use the daylight and avoid the heat.'

The thought of having to ride races in the evenings, travel home, and then be up ready for work at six the next morning filled me with trepidation. The past two nights, I'd been so tired that I was fast asleep well before nine o'clock.

'Seriously, though,' Freddie said. 'I have a hundred and sixty-two horses in my stables at the moment. During the height of the jump season, that's from October to April, it's not unusual for twenty or more of those horses to run in any given week, often with runners at more than one meeting on the same day. Even Adrian, for all his undoubted magic, can't be in two places at the same time, so quite a lot of them will be ridden by you.

'It gets quieter between May and September but there are still jump meetings on most days, although there is a brief break at the end of July into August when the ground is usually too hard for jumping. That's when we all go on holiday.'

He laughed once more.

I looked over at him again. I liked Freddie. He was fun.

* * *

Point Man and I finished a close fourth in the two-mile handicap hurdle at Newbury on Friday, one length and two places behind the mount of Adrian Shaw. Freddie seemed to be satisfied, although I know he had really hoped that one of us would win.

'Maybe two miles is a bit short for him,' Freddie said to me in the car on the way home. 'I think we should try him over two and a half next time out, perhaps at next month's meeting at Cheltenham. What do you think?'

I was flattered to be consulted. Michael Carson had never once asked for my opinion about how a horse of his had run.

'He did find the early pace today rather quick,' I said. 'But he stayed on well towards the finish, so I think the extra distance might suit him.'

'Right, then,' Freddie said. 'That's the plan. And you will ride him at Cheltenham at their April meeting.'

Perhaps for the first time, I felt like a proper jockey, being offered a ride on a horse because of my skill and input, rather than simply as a favour to me.

And it was a major turning point.

I suddenly felt that I was now in control of my life, rather than continually running as hard as I possibly could just to keep up. My confidence was hugely boosted, and it had even more of a lift the following day, again at Newbury, when I won the first race, the John Haine Memorial Novices' Hurdle on Silver Bliss, another Swinton-trained horse.

'Well done, Imogen,' Freddie said in the unsaddling enclosure. 'Now, don't forget to weigh in.'

*   *   *

By the following Saturday evening, I had notched up fifteen rides since my arrival – all of them for Freddie Swinton – and two of them had been winners.

But I was totally exhausted.

The racing regulations state that every conditional jockey must fully acquaint themselves with any racecourse at which they are riding, including walking the course on the first occasion they ride there.

All the courses were new to me, so I'd spent many hours trudging around, digging my heel in to test the turf and feeling the stiffness of fences, all the while making sure I was aware of the numerous undulations that could catch out even the best of riders.

And, most importantly, I would check where the winning posts were. I did not want to be one of those jockeys who mistakenly dropped their hands too soon, only to then get caught on the line, something that was done all too often.

But it meant getting to the racecourses very early to complete a circuit on foot before racing started, and some of them were many hours away from Lambourn.

I did have a car to use but I was nervous of driving when I wasn't sure where I was going, and there was so much more traffic in England than I was used to in rural Ireland.

So Freddie would drive me in his car – that's if he was going to the same racecourse. But he sometimes attended a different meeting or didn't go racing at all. On those occasions, I was left in the care of his assistant or one of the stable's two travelling head lads. Then, I would mostly sit up front in the horsebox, next to Spencer, which made for an even earlier start, plus a much later finish to the day.

But I was living my dream, and I could cope with the tiredness.

I was suddenly a known face in the weighing room, accepted as a regular, and I'd heard no tittle-tattle about me having had sex at the Cheltenham Festival with three Irish jockeys.

But I did worry that some people might be saying it behind my back.

* * *

My second Sunday in Lambourn was my first full day off in two weeks.

I had a luxurious long lie-in until almost nine thirty, then I thoroughly cleaned the cottage and washed some clothes, using the machine in the corner of the kitchen.

When all was spick and span, and my clothes were neatly drying on the airer in the sitting room, I decided to indulge myself and bake a chocolate cake.

I meticulously followed the online recipe to the letter, but unfortunately, I failed to appreciate that I had to butter the insides of the baking tin before pouring in the mixture and cooking it. Hence, it stuck tight – totally immovable. Also, the oven must have been at a lower temperature than it indicated on the dial, because the centre was still rather gooey.

In the end, I ate the cake with a spoon, straight out of the tin, while lying on the sofa, still in my pyjamas, watching the afternoon's racing from Ascot on the television.

Such decadence!

Indeed, it was so out of character for me that it made me feel really guilty – so much so that, at five o'clock, I went upstairs, got dressed into some jogging pants and a top, and went out for a run.

I did my usual circuit up the gallops to Upper Lambourn, and then down to the village supermarket, where I popped in to buy myself some fresh fruit for supper.

As soon as I went back in through the front door of the cottage, I felt sure that someone had been in there. There was a slight alien smell of stale tobacco, which had not been there when I went out.

My heart started racing.

'Who are you?' I shouted loudly, my voice reverberating off the walls.

I went through into the kitchen, placed the fruit on the table, and pulled a large carving knife from the wooden block on the worktop next to the sink.

'I have a knife,' I shouted. 'Now get out of my house.'

There was no sound – no call, and no movement.

Why had I left the cottage front door unlocked?

But I always did when I went out for a run. I was away for no more than half an hour, and it wasn't as if I had anything worth stealing, while I had nightmares about losing my door key up on the gallops, and being locked out.

Now I had a different kind of nightmare.

'Come on,' I shouted again. 'Show yourself. Get out of my house.'

Nothing.

Gingerly, I went silently out of the kitchen and into the sitting room.

No one. I checked beyond the airer, and behind the door – still no one.

'I'm coming upstairs,' I shouted. 'And I still have my knife.'

I started to slowly climb the stairs, holding the knife out in front of me.

Was I doing the right thing?

Would it be more prudent to simply get out of the cottage alto-gether, and then call the police?

But what if I were wrong?

Had I only imagined the smell? Or maybe a smoker had brushed against me in the supermarket, and I hadn't been able to smell anything on my clothes until I was back inside my cottage?

I sniffed at the sleeves of my top, but I couldn't smell anything.

There were two bedrooms plus a bathroom upstairs. I went into each in turn, searching anywhere where someone could hide – under the beds, behind the shower curtain, and in the solitary wardrobe.

I found nothing.

There was nobody here.

As I went back down the stairs, I began to feel a bit foolish, but there it was again, close to the front door – stale tobacco.

I locked the door and did another full circuit of the cottage, both up and down, even checking in the tiny cupboard under the stairs, where there was hardly enough room for a small dog, let alone a human being.

And there was no smoking dog to be found – no souls at all.

Still feeling slightly uneasy, I returned the carving knife to its slot in the wooden block.

I checked that the front and back doors were both locked and bolted, then switched on all the lights and closed the curtains. Next, I turned on the television, as if I needed it for some company.

Had I been wrong?

Now I went right round the place for a third time, this time not looking for an intruder, but searching to see if anything was missing.

My most valuable possession, by far, was my mobile phone, but that had been with me all the time, held in a special holster attached to my upper arm during my run, so I could also listen to music through my earpods.

Next in line would be my racing skullcap, but that was still in its bag, hanging on the hook in the hall, as usual. My racing saddle had now arrived from Ireland, but that was currently being stored in the stable office.

I had no jewellery to speak of – and no expensive watches. In fact, the only watch I owned was a very moderately priced Timex, which my parents had given me for a twelfth birthday present, and that was still in my box of trinkets on the bedside table. Ever since I'd acquired my first mobile phone at age fifteen, I had used the readout on the screen to tell me the time.

What else would an intruder want to steal?

I opened the fridge and the freezer, but the meagre contents didn't seem to have been diminished since I'd last looked, and there were no bottles of alcohol to pilfer, because I hadn't had any to start with.

I came to the conclusion that I must have been mistaken, not least because I could no longer detect any lingering tobacco smell near the front door.

I ate my fruit supper while half-watching a television programme about lions in the Serengeti, then it was time for me to go up to bed.

I had an early start.

I was due to ride two at Newton Abbot in south Devon, about a hundred and fifty miles away, and the stable's horsebox would be leaving Lambourn at six o'clock – and I'd be going with it because Freddie would be at Chepstow races with Adrian Shaw.

Just before I went upstairs, I checked to see if my washing had dried, and that was when I discovered that something *was* missing.

When I had hung everything on the airer, I remembered quite clearly that there had been four, but now there were only three.

I searched under the other clothes, on the floor, and behind the curtains, even bending right down and peering under the sofa, but without finding the missing item.

Now I was certain.

Someone had indeed come into my house – and they had stolen a pair of my black lace panties.

Chapter 9

I HAD A DISTURBED NIGHT, NOT due to any external influences, but because my mind was racing.

I hadn't known what to do.

I could hardly dial 999 and report the theft of a pair of panties.

I felt that the police would laugh at me and suggest that I must have left them behind in Cheltenham when I'd had sex with the three Irish jockeys.

So, what did I do?

Had someone been watching my house and seen me go out for a run? Or had they just struck lucky? Were they watching it even now?

I was in a cold sweat thinking about it.

And perhaps the biggest question of them all kept resurfacing in my brain – had it been Liam who had entered my home?

I'd checked, and then double-checked, that the front and back doors were both locked and bolted, and that all the windows were firmly latched shut. Then I'd gone up to bed, leaving all the lights switched on downstairs. But sleep hadn't come easily, and every slight noise had left my nerves jangling.

I must have slept during some of the night, but it hardly felt like it, and by the time the alarm on my phone had sounded at five o'clock, I was a complete nervous wreck.

I dragged myself out from under the duvet and dressed in my going-to-the-races outfit – smart chinos rather than my faded denim jeans, and a coordinating bomber jacket over my branded polo shirt.

I decided to leave the curtains closed and, because I wouldn't be back here until it was nearly dark, I also left the ceiling light on in the sitting room.

The clocks had gone forward early on Sunday morning, which meant it was still pitch black outside as I prepared to leave the cottage, collecting together my racing clothes, boots and skullcap into a holdall by the front door.

I was loath to abandon the relative sanctuary of my locked-up home, but I knew I had to.

I took some deep breaths and unbolted the door.

My hands were shaking as I turned the key in the lock.

Come on, I told myself. *If you can fearlessly ride horses over fences at thirty miles per hour, you must be brave enough to walk a hundred yards down the road to the stable yard.*

I opened the door and peered out.

The sun wouldn't be up for another forty-five minutes but there was already a sliver of light in the eastern sky, and it was enough for me to see that there was no one waiting there. I quickly locked the door again, slung my kit over my shoulder, and sprinted along the road.

* * *

'You look like you've seen a ghost,' Spencer said, as I climbed up into the horsebox cab alongside him, having first collected my saddle from the stable office.

'Just tired,' I said. 'I had a bad night.'

But it felt good to be in his company, and that of Jason, the travelling head lad who joined us up front, with me sitting between them. There was also another member of the stable staff coming, and he was sitting on the bench seat behind the driver as we pulled out of the yard at five past six, the two horses securely loaded in the stalls behind us.

I suddenly relaxed, feeling safe, and I was fast asleep before we had even joined the westbound M4 motorway towards Bristol.

I woke up as we stopped briefly at Taunton Deane Services on the M5, with still about an hour to go to Newton Abbot.

'Better?' Spencer asked me, as he pulled the horsebox into the lorry-parking area.

'Mmm, a bit.'

'You should have got your head down properly,' he said. 'You could've lain down flat in the back, next to the horses.'

'I'm fine,' I said. But the truth was that my neck was quite sore from sleeping for two hours sitting up.

'Right, fifteen-minute fag and loo break,' Spencer said, switching off the engine.

'I'll stay here with the horses first,' Jason said. 'Can someone get me a coffee? Milk. One sugar.'

'I'll do it,' I said.

I climbed down from the cab and walked over to the main building, but I wasn't at ease. I spent the whole time looking around me, wondering if someone was watching me.

Stop it, I told myself. *Be sensible. Who could be watching you here?*

However, it didn't prevent me continually glancing from side to side, scrutinising everyone, looking for any face that I recognised.

I went to the ladies, then over to the coffee shop to buy two coffees, one for Jason and the other for me, and I also bought myself a hot bacon roll, filled with lashings of tomato ketchup.

A great blessing for me was that I was naturally short and slim, and I didn't have to worry about what I ate, at least not how it might affect my riding weight. But that wasn't true for almost all other jockeys.

Flat-race jockeys have the worst of it, because flat-riding weights are so much lower than those over the jumps.

Lester Piggott was five foot seven inches tall, and he starved himself for forty years to ride at thirty pounds or more below the ideal healthy body weight for someone of that height.

And the great Fred Archer was even taller than Lester, at five foot ten. Archer was champion flat jockey on thirteen consecutive occasions – riding 2,748 winners from only 8,084 starts – but he had to starve himself so much that it disturbed the balance of his mind. Having gone without any food for three whole days to make the weight for a ride in the Cambridgeshire Handicap, he shot and killed himself, aged just twenty-nine.

But jump jockeys are not immune from weight problems. Far from it. And one former jump champion recently claimed that he had retired from riding much earlier than people had expected, simply because he was fed up with always being hungry and having to survive on a diet of laxatives and diuretics.

I quickly ate my bacon roll and went back out to the horsebox to give Jason his coffee. The two of us then stood outside next to the vehicle, waiting for the others to return. Jason lit a cigarette.

'Imogen, could you stay with the horses for a few minutes?' he asked. 'While I go for a pee.'

'No problem,' I said, but as he walked away, I suddenly felt hugely vulnerable, standing there on my own, so I climbed up into the horsebox cab and locked the doors.

Hence, I was more than a little relieved when I finally saw Spencer walking towards me.

How could I be in such a state?

* * *

I spent some of the remaining journey on my mobile phone.

The *Racing Post* website has a very useful search tool, where anyone can look up any British or Irish registered horse, or any licenced owner, trainer or jockey to find out their current form, and their stats going back many years.

With sweaty hands, I typed 'Liam Carson' into the search bar.

It immediately responded, showing me that he had a flat and jump jockey's licence and that his minimum riding weight in the last twelve months was ten stone, two pounds. It also showed that in the current jump season, he'd had three hundred and twenty-six rides, almost all of them in Ireland, and twenty-eight winners. But I was looking for something else.

There had been only one meeting in Ireland yesterday, at Fairyhouse, about twenty-five kilometres northwest of Dublin city centre, and I wanted to know if Liam had been riding there. If he had, he couldn't have also been in Lambourn when I was out for my run.

I clicked on the 'Form' tab, which showed all his rides during the previous fourteen days. There were nine of them, but the most recent had been at Cork the previous Wednesday. So, Liam hadn't had a ride for five days, and that worried me. I wondered if he was injured.

Next, I clicked on the 'Booked Rides' tab, to show any horses that Liam had been declared to ride during the next two days.

I stared at the screen, and I could feel the panic rising in my throat.

Liam was scheduled to ride in the first race at Newton Abbot today, the novice hurdle – the very same race in which I would be riding.

I felt sick.

How could he be riding at Newton Abbot today?

Sure, Irish jump jockeys often come over to ride in England, and vice versa, but usually only for the really big races, or for the main steeplechase festivals like those at Cheltenham, Aintree or Punchestown.

What was Liam doing riding at Newton Abbot on a Monday, and in a race worth less than five thousand pounds? Surely, no one would pay to bring a horse over from Ireland for a purse that small.

But the horse wasn't trained in Ireland. Instead, the website told me it was trained by someone called Sophie Burnett, in a place called Eastbury in Berkshire.

I clicked on Sophie Burnett. She was a jump trainer with thirty-six horses in her yard, and she'd had eighteen winners from a hundred and thirteen runners in the current season, a perfectly respectable win rate.

Next, I looked up Eastbury on Google Maps and was mortified to discover it was a small village very close to Lambourn – only two miles down the road from my cottage.

What was Liam doing riding for a trainer from there?

Had he picked up a spare ride, or was he now also based in England? And on my doorstep?

I stared ahead at the road, dreading the afternoon.

I was now convinced that it was him who had been into my cottage. Did I confront him about it? Or did I ignore him completely? But that might be difficult as we were riding against each other. All I was sure about was that I didn't want to be left alone with him.

Well, that was the plan.

*　*　*

We arrived at Newton Abbot Racecourse just before ten o'clock, almost four hours since we left Lambourn, and more than three and a half hours before the first race, ample time for the horses to recover from the journey before they ran.

Jason and the other stable-staff member settled the two horses into the racecourse stables, but only after an official at the entrance had scanned the microchips in their necks to establish that they were indeed the horses that Jason claimed them to be.

After all was satisfactorily completed, the four of us went along to the stable lads' canteen for another breakfast.

Jason turned to me.

'You can go to the Owners' and Trainers' Lounge as Freddie's representative if you want to, or even to the jockeys' café in the weighing room,' he said. 'Are you sure you want to come with us and slum it in the lads' canteen?'

'I'm quite certain,' I said, laughing and taking his arm. 'Those other places won't be open yet, and I'd much rather be slumming it with you lot anyway.'

Safety in numbers, I thought.

* * *

Liam was waiting for me when I finally went to the weighing room, about an hour before the first race. He was standing inside the door, and he had clearly been looking out for me.

'Hello, Imo,' he said, all smiles. 'Fancy meeting you here.'

'Leave me alone,' I said, trying to get past him and into the safety of the lady-jockeys' changing room. But he stepped across, blocking my path.

'Come on, Imo,' he said. 'Give me a chance.'

'You had your chance, and you blew it,' I said. 'Now get out of my way.'

'Give me another chance,' he said, not moving.

'You must think I'm stupid or something. Don't you remember what you did to me at my parents' house?'

'That was nothing. I didn't mean it.'

I stared at him. It had not been nothing to me, and if I remembered correctly, which I did, he had meant every kick and stamp. If my father hadn't arrived home when he did, Liam would have killed me. I was sure of it.

'What are you doing here?' I asked. 'Why are you not at home in Ireland?'

'England is my home now,' he said, smiling. 'I've moved over here to ride. More opportunities. I now work as stable jockey for a trainer in Eastbury, and I'm living in a flat over the yard.'

It was the news I'd been dreading. I'd come to England to get away from him, only to find out now that Liam had followed me.

What did I do?

I could hardly pack up and go home to Ireland after only two weeks in my new job. Anyway, my contract of employment stated that the minimum notice period I could give was two months.

'Can we meet later, after racing?' he asked.

'No.'

'Perhaps have a meal together?'

'No.'

'I could give you a lift home. I brought my car over.'

'I don't need a lift home,' I said.

'My car is much more comfortable than a horsebox.'

How did he know I'd come here in a horsebox?

'Look,' I said forcefully. 'I don't want to meet you later, I don't want to eat a meal with you, and I don't want a lift home. In fact, I don't want to see you ever again. Stop spying on me, and don't ever come to my home again. Do you understand?'

'What do you mean, again?'

'You were there yesterday.'

'No, I wasn't. I don't even know where you live.'

I didn't believe him.

I tried to get past him again, but he refused to budge.

'If you don't move out of my way,' I said calmly but quite clearly, 'I'll make a complaint that you are bullying and harassing me in the workplace.'

The racecourse official by the door looked over towards me and raised a questioning eyebrow.

Everyone in racing was aware of a recent high-profile case that had resulted in a male jockey being banned from riding for up to eighteen months for bullying and harassing behaviour towards a female rider.

There was a brief but clear flash of anger in Liam's face at my threat, and he glanced across at the official, who was still taking a keen interest in our standoff.

Finally, and reluctantly, Liam did move to one side, and I dived past him into the relative safety of the female changing room, breathing hard.

Will no one rid me of this turbulent priest?

Chapter 10

THERE WERE TEN RUNNERS IN the novice hurdle.

My mount, Sweet Sheila, was a five-year-old mare that had graduated to hurdling after running six times on the flat aged three and four. This was only her second outing over jumps, having broken her maiden at the very first time of asking at Warwick in February, when she'd won easily by eight lengths.

Consequently, she was a very short-priced favourite for this race.

Jason told me earlier that she was only running here, in this modest contest, because her owner lived close by, and he was desperate to see her run – and win – at his local course, so he could impress his friends.

I weighed out, handed my saddle to Jason, then went back into the lady-jockey changing room to wait for the call to the parade ring. As I was the only female declared to ride at Newton Abbot on this day, I had the place to myself, or at least I should have done.

I was sitting on the bench, waiting to go out, when the door opened, and Liam brazenly walked straight in.

'Get out,' I shouted at him. 'Men are not allowed in here.'

'Come on, Imo,' he said. 'Be reasonable. You're my girl.'

I stood up.

'I am certainly not your girl. Now get out, or I'll scream.'

He didn't get out. Instead, he took a step towards me.

I picked up my riding whip and held it above my head in a threatening manner. But a race whip is not much of a weapon. Whereas once it might have raised a welt or two on a horse, or even on a human face, these days the whips have so much cushioning on the ends that the horses can hardly feel them. I'd have much rather had the carving knife from the wooden block in my kitchen.

'I'll scream,' I said again.

He took another step towards me.

'Help!' I shouted. 'Help!'

'Shut up!' he barked angrily, but he hesitated slightly.

'Then get out of here.'

I swished the whip rapidly through the air towards him, but he grabbed it as it passed in front of his face, and he tugged it sharply out of my grasp, dropping it to the floor.

He smiled maliciously and advanced another step forward.

I did scream, but so frightened was I that the sound seemed to stick in my throat, making it out of my mouth at hardly more than a whimper.

The changing-room door opened a crack.

'Jockeys out,' an official called through the gap.

The call seemed to unnerve Liam, and he half turned away from me. I took the opportunity to lean down, pick up my whip, and push past him out of the door.

'Are you all right?' Jason asked when I joined him in the parade ring with the horse's owner. 'You look rather flushed.'

'I'm fine,' I said.

But was I?

What had just happened? It seemed incongruous that one moment Liam was asking me to go out for dinner with him, and the very next he was intent on injuring me.

'Imogen?' Jason said, bringing me back to reality.

'Yes.'

'Mr Walton asked you a question.'

'Sorry. What was it?'

'I asked if you had ridden Sweet Sheila at home on the gallops?' the owner asked again, his tone and facial expression clearly indicating rising irritation.

I smiled at him. 'Of course, sir,' I said. 'Several times. She's a fine horse. Moves really well. She should have a great future ahead.'

The irritation faded from Mr Walton's face, replaced by a look of pride. He smiled back at me. 'Good. Thank you. She's named after my daughter.'

To be honest, I couldn't remember whether I had ridden Sweet Sheila before or not – probably not – but I did know how to keep the owner sweet, eh, Sheila?

The bell sounded, indicating it was time for the jockeys to get mounted.

Jason gave me a leg-up onto Sweet Sheila's back and I took her out onto the course, all the while checking where Liam was on his horse. I preferred to keep him in view in front, rather than have him creep up on me from behind.

Newton Abbot is a flat squarish course with sharp bends on the corners. It is situated near the centre of the town, on the banks of the River Teign, close to where the river becomes a tidal estuary. Consequently, there is always plenty of water available to use on the course, so the going is never too hard, even through the hot summer months when most of the fixtures are held.

Today, however, the going was officially 'good', 'good to soft' in places.

The two-mile-one-furlong start is at the beginning of the back straight so that the runners have to negotiate almost two complete circuits of the course, and eight flights of hurdles.

While the ten runners circled, having their girths checked, Liam kept staring straight at me and smiling. I found it most unnerving, and it didn't help my preparations for the race.

Indeed, when the starter climbed his rostrum and raised his flag, I still had my lightweight plastic goggles up on my skullcap, above the peak of my cap.

'Hold on, sir,' I shouted across at him. 'Not yet. Not yet.'

I reached up to bring the goggles down into position, while there were some murmurings from the other jockeys, Liam included, about 'bloody women drivers'.

And, of course, they didn't wait for me.

They moved forward towards the tape at a jig-jog, with me a little bit behind, due to the goggles fiasco. I did my best to catch up without letting my horse break into a canter and was almost on the tail of the others when the starter dropped his flag.

We were off.

There are two flights in the back straight and all ten runners popped over the first one safely, with the characteristic clack-clack-clack as they brushed the tops of the hurdles with their front hooves.

The second comes up quite quickly and we all jumped that safely too. Then there was the long sweeping bend around the far end of the course, furthest from the grandstands, before the next two flights of hurdles in the home straight.

As we swept around the turn, Sweet Sheila was in fifth place, on the inside, while Liam had somehow managed to get his horse alongside mine, fractionally in front, and on the outer. Now, he began to squeeze me up against the running rail.

'Give me room,' I shouted at him, but he didn't. If anything he leaned in harder, forcing his horse against mine.

'Give me some bloody room,' I shouted again, looking at him. But all Liam did was look back at me, smile, and squeeze again.

I could feel my left boot rubbing hard along the white plastic rail, and I was worried that there might be a loose joint, one with something carelessly left sticking out, which could pull me off the horse – or worse, wrench my foot clean off my leg.

I had no option but to take a pull, to slow Sweet Sheila down a bit, and allow Liam to go completely ahead of me, but it wasn't ideal, and I knew it would look dreadful from the grandstands, from where everyone would have the perfect side-on view.

If I subsequently lost this race, they would all blame me.

Sweet Sheila was obviously confused by being asked to slow down, and she slipped right to the rear of the field before I managed to get her going again at full speed. Hence, we were still in ninth place as we passed the winning post for the first time, some seven or eight lengths behind the leader. There was even the sound of boos coming from the stands, with some punters clearly thinking that their money was already lost.

But my horse was still travelling well beneath me, and I slowly eroded the deficit such that we were again up into fifth place by the time we approached the final hurdle in the back straight, the third last.

Liam, however, was still making a nuisance of himself.

He had positioned himself so that he was again alongside me, on my right. Thankfully, on the straights there is no running rail between the hurdle and steeplechase courses, so there was nothing for him to squeeze me against, but that didn't stop him pressing me to my left.

I suddenly realised he was trying to force me out of the hurdle or put me through the six-foot-high wing.

It was far too late in the race to take another pull, to move back. With only another half mile to run, there would be no time to recover.

Liam forced his horse further over, pushing me wider still.

At the last moment, I kicked Sweet Sheila hard, and she shot forward. I pulled her sharply to the right and just made it inside the wing, clattering across the hurdle.

There was a loud shout from behind me, followed by a crash, but I didn't care about what was going on back there – I was only intent on the action in front.

My poor horse was now more confused than ever, with first a 'go slower' message and then a 'go faster' one from her rider. But Sweet Sheila really was a class above the other runners. She was in third place approaching the second-last hurdle, a close second at the last, and won easily by two lengths easing up.

Those who had booed her before were now cheering, and I was hugely relieved.

'Well done,' Jason said, as I dismounted in the unsaddling enclosure. 'Bit of a strange race, though. Why did you suddenly drop back to last like that?'

'She stumbled,' I said. 'I took a pull to steady her.'

Jason didn't look convinced, but he nodded. I don't know why I didn't tell him the truth. Perhaps I didn't want an inquest.

'And what on earth happened at the third last?'

'I've no idea,' I said. 'It was all behind me.'

The owner, meanwhile, was absolutely delighted with the win, but as we were all posing for a victory photograph with the horse, there sounded the familiar triple-tone signal through the public address system, which indicated that the stewards had ordered an enquiry.

I weighed in, and as there would be no presentations until after the enquiry was concluded, I returned to the female changing room.

There was a television high up on the wall and I sat down on the bench and watched the replay of the race.

My pull on the bottom bend looked dreadful, far worse than I remembered, with Sweet Sheila appearing to come almost to a complete standstill before resuming. But it was the action down the back straight towards the third last that I was most interested in. The angle of the TV shot wasn't great, but it was quite clear that my horse was drifting left, even though it wasn't obvious that it was due to Liam pushing me out.

My surge forward and sharp rightward movement to get myself inside the wing of the hurdle was also not particularly well shown, as the camera position at that point had been in front of the hurdle looking backwards. But even from that angle it was possible to see Liam and his horse crashing through the wing behind me.

Serves him right, I thought, with a laugh.

I watched the television until the replay concluded.

After a couple of minutes or so, there was a knock on the door. I went over and opened it.

'You're wanted in the stewards' room, miss,' said the official standing there.

The stewards' room was next door to the female changing room. I knocked on the door and opened it.

There were three men sitting at a table, with a fourth at a desk behind them with what looked like a computer screen in front of him. Liam was standing to one side, his white britches muddied and grass-stained.

'Ah, Miss Duffy, thank you. Please come on in,' said the chairman, the man in the centre. 'There are two incidents in the race we are concerned about. The first was on the initial circuit.' He turned to the man with the screen. 'Please play the first videos.'

The large-screen TV on the wall came to life with four simultaneous videos of the horses moving round the curve at the end of the course, each one taken by a camera at a different location. One was the view I had seen on the broadcast race replay, while the others were from the three other racecourse patrol cameras. All the videos clearly showed Sweet Sheila almost coming to a halt and dropping to the very rear of the field, before getting going again.

'Miss Duffy, can you explain what happened to your horse at that moment?' asked the chairman of the panel.

'Yes, sir,' I said. 'I was being squeezed badly, with my left leg forced hard against the plastic running rail. I took a pull to relieve the pressure, but my horse reacted more than I had anticipated.'

'Did you not ask the other jockeys for more room?'

'I did, sir, twice, but none was forthcoming.' I glanced briefly across at Liam, who was looking down at the floor. 'In fact, if anything the pressure increased further, and I was worried my foot might get caught in a joint in the rail. I felt I had no option but to slow my horse to extricate myself from the position, but I didn't expect her to slow as much as she did.'

'But you must agree that your actions decreased your horse's chances of winning. The rules state quite clearly that a rider must ensure that, at all times, they give their mounts the best chance of gaining the highest possible placing.'

'But, with respect, sir, my horse did go on to win the race. I couldn't have gained a higher place than that.'

'As may be,' said the steward, seemingly disregarding that crucial fact. 'Nevertheless, your actions at that time would not have helped.'

'Sir,' I insisted. 'I was getting myself out of danger, and it didn't decrease our chances of winning. Quite the reverse – as was proved to be the case.'

However, I could see from his expression that my pleas were falling on deaf ears.

'Let us now move on to the second incident,' he said. 'Play those videos.'

The images on the screen switched to the last flight of hurdles in the back straight on the second circuit. We all watched in silence as the events unfolded, culminating in Liam and his horse going through the wing and falling.

Like the running rails, all fence wings are now made of plastic and are designed to come apart if struck, and the images showed both Liam and the horse safely climb to their respective feet.

The videos stopped.

'Now, Miss Duffy,' said the chairman, 'Mr Carson, here, claims that your riding was dangerous, and you put him and his horse through the wing of the hurdle. What do you have to say?'

I stared across at Liam.

Dangerous riding was a most serious charge, and implied that actions were deliberate, reckless, and knowingly far below the standards expected of a competent and careful rider. If the stewards agreed on the balance of probabilities that I was guilty of dangerous riding, then Sweet Sheila would automatically be disqualified from her win, I would forfeit my riding fee, and a lengthy suspension from racing would undoubtedly follow.

I turned back to the stewards.

'Sirs,' I said slowly. 'Mr Carson was trying to force me out or put *me* through the wing. If it were not for my avoiding action, that would have been the case. The patrol camera from behind shows quite clearly that he was forcing me wide. I believe it was done on purpose.'

The chairman turned towards Liam. 'What do you say to that, Mr Carson?'

'It's total nonsense,' he said. 'Why would I purposefully try to force another jockey out, or put them through a wing? My riding was firm but fair. It is quite clear from the video that Duffy's late swerve to the right unsettled my horse and left him with no alternative but to go left through the wing. I maintain that the manoeuvre constituted dangerous riding, and I put it down to Duffy's inexperience, as a claimer.'

I was steaming with anger, but I kept my composure, at least outwardly.

'Sirs,' I said calmly. 'Please show one of those videos again, the one taken by the patrol camera positioned behind the horses on the back straight.'

The man at the rear tapped his control and the relevant image filled the whole of the large TV. Without the distraction of the simultaneous recordings from the other cameras, it clearly showed Sweet Sheila being forced to the left as we approached the hurdle.

'So why were you not keeping a straight course?' asked the chairman.

I thought he was asking Liam, but when he looked up, he made it clear that the question was directed towards me.

'Because, as you can see, sir, Mr Carson is pushing me wide,' I said.

The recording moved on and showed me forging ahead of Liam and making the sharp change of direction to the right, followed by the dramatic sight of Liam and his horse crashing through the wing of the hurdle behind me.

'My move to get inside the wing was towards the right,' I said. 'Mr Carson was on my right-hand side, so surely if my movement had affected his horse in any way, one might expect him also to have gone to the right, not to the left as actually happened.'

I took a deep breath and dived in further. 'I am convinced that Mr Carson was deliberately attempting to either push me out of the race or to put me through the wing. When I surged forward relative to him, such that I was suddenly no longer there to lean against, his horse moved rapidly to the left, as it had repeatedly been asked to do by its rider, and hence it collided with the wing.

'Furthermore, it had been Mr Carson who squeezed me against the rail in the first incident, and I believe that was also done deliberately. If anyone is guilty of dangerous riding in this race it is Mr Carson, not me, and on two separate occasions.'

I stopped talking and there was a silence in the room, broken only by Liam saying 'Bollocks' almost under his breath, but we all heard it.

The chairman cleared his throat. 'Mr Carson, Miss Duffy, please wait outside while we deliberate and make our decision.'

The two of us left the room and stood waiting outside.

'Bastard,' I said.

'Have me back then,' Liam replied.

'No bloody chance.'

'You'll regret it.'

Chapter 11

'MISS DUFFY, WE FIND THAT you caused interference due to careless riding,' the chairman of
the enquiry said. 'Suspended for three days.
Placings remain unaltered.'

Liam and I were back in the stewards' room, standing in
front of the table.

'What about Mr Carson?' I asked.

'We take no action against Mr Carson.'

I stared at the three stewards, but I knew that arguing with
them was not advisable. Racecourse stewards never change their
minds, and it could get you into far worse trouble. At least
they hadn't upheld Liam's claim that my riding was dangerous,
although they hadn't upheld mine against him either, for the
same offence. And Sweet Sheila had not been disqualified, so
we would keep the prize money, and I'd be paid my riding fee.

'You may both go now,' said the chairman.

I went out first. Liam followed.

'Imogen,' he called from behind me. 'I'm sorry you were
suspended.'

I didn't turn round because I did not believe him, and I also
didn't want to give him the satisfaction of having me see him

smirking. He had done his utmost to ensure that I was suspended, lying through his teeth, as he always did.

Jason was waiting for me outside the stewards' room. I took his arm and, despite it being against the rules, I steered him directly into the lady-jockeys' changing room, firmly closing the door behind us.

'What happened?' he asked.

'I've been given a three-day suspension for careless riding.'

'What!' Jason said. 'But you won the race fair and square.'

'They said I caused interference at the third-last hurdle, but I didn't. I think the bloody stewards must be blind.'

Jason was angry on my behalf, but he was mostly angry with himself.

'I'm so sorry,' he said. 'I should have been there with you. Conditional jockeys are entitled to have somebody accompany them at a stewards' enquiry – the stewards should know that. But I was too busy looking after the horse and getting it to the vet.'

'Don't worry,' I said. 'I'm going to appeal anyway, so that might actually help.'

Anyone has the right to appeal a racecourse stewards' decision by submitting a written report to the racing authority within seven days, or within forty-eight hours if it involves a jockey's suspension, as in this case. But the report has to be accompanied by a hefty deposit, which is forfeited if the disciplinary panel subsequently determines that there were no reasonable grounds for the appeal.

'You need to talk to Freddie first,' Jason said, pulling out his mobile phone and dialling the number.

Freddie was not pleased, and that was putting it mildly, and his ire seemed to be shared equally between Jason and the stewards.

'Jason, you should have been with Imogen.' Freddie said it so loudly that I could hear it clearly, even though Jason's phone was not on speaker. 'I told you to look after her.'

'I'm sorry,' Jason replied stoically. 'But the horse had cut into itself, so I was arranging for the vet to check it over.'

'Cut into itself' is when a horse overreaches while galloping or jumping, such that its rear hoof makes contact with the front leg, resulting in cuts or bruising.

That seemed to placate Freddie a little, as his volume decreased.

Jason held his phone out to me. 'He wants to talk to you.'

To prevent the passing on of 'insider information' for betting purposes, jockeys are only supposed to speak on a mobile phone during racing in the 'phone zone', a small area set aside close to the desk of the Clerk of the Scales. The penalty for using a phone anywhere else can be as much as a two-thousand-pound fine plus a year's suspension from riding.

But did I care? No one could see, and there would be no tell-tale record on my own phone bill.

I reached out and took Jason's phone. 'I'm sorry,' I said.

'Don't be,' Freddie said. 'I watched the race from here at Chepstow, and you won it well. But what happened round the first bend, when you almost stopped?'

'I was being squeezed hard against the inside running rail by another jockey. Even though I shouted at him, he wouldn't give me any room. My boot was rubbing hard up against the rail, so I took a slight pull to get away, but the horse slowed down more than I expected.'

'Who squeezed you?'

I hesitated, but only for a split second. 'Liam Carson,' I said.

'Michael Carson's son?'

'Yes.'

There was a pause from the other end.

'Weren't you and he an item?'

'Yes,' I said again. 'For almost four years. I broke it off about three weeks ago.'

'Amicably?'

'No. My choice, not his.'

'So, he was exacting revenge?'

'Yes.'

'Did you tell the stewards that?'

'No. Of course not. But it wasn't that incident that caused my suspension. It was the one at the third last.'

I explained to him about Liam Carson again trying to push me out, but how he had been the one who ended up going through the wing due to his own misjudgement and foolishness.

'I couldn't see that on the TV,' Freddie said.

'It wasn't really visible from in front,' I said, 'but it was clear as daylight from the patrol camera behind.'

'So why did the stewards suspend you?'

'God knows. Liam claimed that my riding was dangerous, and I put him through the wing. I replied that he was the dangerous one, but the stewards clearly believed him more than they believed me, because he didn't even get a caution. I want to appeal their decision, but Jason said I needed to talk to you first.'

'Tell Jason to get copies of the race videos – from every angle. Get the stewards to email me the links. And also a copy of their deliberations and report. We will look at it and discuss our options tomorrow – we have until Wednesday to lodge an appeal. I want you to concentrate now on the handicap chase.'

The handicap chase was the fourth race of the afternoon, and I would still be riding in it as planned – jockey suspensions didn't come into force for a minimum of fourteen days.

* * *

In comparison to the first race, the fourth was very uneventful.

My horse didn't win due to him being outpaced around the final turn, and then he completely ran out of puff between the last two fences. Hence, we finished a distant third, but Liam hadn't been riding in the race, so there was no disruption, and no stewards' enquiry.

'Don't forget to weigh in,' Jason said to me in the unsaddling enclosure. 'We'll leave for home just as soon as this boy is washed down and recovered.'

He patted the horse affectionately on the neck.

I carried my saddle into the weighing room and stood on the scales.

I sighed. Another loser.

Since my arrival at Freddie Swinton's stable, my personal strike rate, up until today, had been thirteen per cent, that was I had won thirteen per cent of the races in which I had ridden – which I reckoned was pretty good – more than twice the rate I'd achieved when riding for Michael Carson. True, I had been riding some of the best horses in the country, but I was still number two behind Adrian Shaw, and he had first pick.

However, that meant that eighty-seven per cent of the horses I had ridden had lost. Even Adrian rode a loser almost four times as often as he rode a winner, and he was the champion. Hence, horseracing is full of disappointments, and all jockeys, even the very best, have to get used to them.

Compare that to Usain Bolt, the greatest sprinter the world has ever seen. In the twenty-two individual Olympic and World Championship sprint finals in which he raced, he was never out of the medals, and nineteen of them were gold.

Not much disappointment there, then.

I went into the female changing room and had a shower – if the horse could have a washdown after the race, then so could I, but thank goodness, mine would be warmer. Then I changed back into my day clothes and packed up the bag containing my riding kit.

I realised with dismay that I'd have to go into the male changing room to find my valet, to give him my saddle. I was due to ride the following afternoon at Ludlow, and he would be taking the saddle there overnight in one of his large wicker baskets.

As I went in, I kept my eyes firmly down, staring at the floor, mostly because I didn't want to see Liam, but also because I did not particularly want to be confronted by any naked men, flaunting their wedding tackle.

I walked through to where I knew my valet would be, each valet having his own section within the room.

'Hello, Imogen,' he said, as I handed my saddle to him. 'My, what an exciting life you lead. You're quite a girl.'

'And what is that meant to mean?' I asked warily, perhaps not really wanting to hear the answer.

'We've been hearing about it throughout the afternoon,' he replied. 'Liam Carson has been regaling us all with stories of your sexy foursome at Cheltenham during the Festival.'

Regaling us all. Oh God!

I had always been afflicted with involuntary blushing when I was embarrassed, ever since I was a child. And I blushed now. I could feel the warmth in my face, and my valet saw it.

'It's not true,' I croaked, but I could tell that he believed it was.

I wanted the floor to open up and swallow me.

I rushed back to the female changing room in tears – tears of anger, embarrassment and frustration.

How could I stop this happening to me?

* * *

The journey home seemed never-ending, not least because of a car on fire north of Taunton, which resulted in a forty-five-minute holdup on the motorway.

I sat alone on the bench seat behind Spencer, as I couldn't bear to be in very close proximity to anyone.

I'd waited in the changing room for more than an hour before Jason came to fetch me, saying that the two horses were now loaded into the horsebox, and they were ready to leave. I had grabbed my stuff and rushed out, staring straight ahead, not saying a word to anyone.

Freddie called me as we were leaving the M4 motorway at Swindon.

'I've watched all the videos of the Newton Abbot novice hurdle,' he said. 'And I agree that the stewards were very harsh on you, but is it really worth an appeal? Probably not. You did make a sudden movement, and it's only a three-day suspension.'

'But I had to make that movement to get inside the wing, otherwise I'd have been pushed out completely,' I said with exasperation. 'It's so unfair.'

But I remembered what President Kennedy had said about life being unfair and to carry on striving rather than whinging about it.

'Every jockey gets into trouble with the racing authority at some time or another,' Freddie said. 'Even the best. I know for sure that Rachael Blackmore had more than twenty suspensions during her illustrious career, and I bet she didn't think that any one of them was fair.'

That made me feel slightly better. But it was the fact that I had been punished for careless riding while Liam had got off scot-free that really put my nose out of joint.

'I'm worried about it happening again,' I said. 'Liam Carson seems to be obsessed with me. He forced his way into the female changing room at Newton Abbot before the race. First, he asked me to take him back. Then he threatened me when I said I wouldn't.'

'Did you report him to the stewards for that, or to the police?' Freddie asked.

I thought back to when my father had called the Irish police after Liam had attacked me at home, and how little notice they had taken because I hadn't been sufficiently injured. They had almost made me feel like I was the one at fault.

'It wouldn't do any good,' I said. 'And it might make things worse. But I would still like to appeal against my suspension, if only to let Liam Carson realise that he can't push me around whenever he likes.'

'We'll discuss it again in the morning. Let's sleep on it.'
'OK,' I said.

That was assuming I'd be able to sleep in the first place.

Chapter 12

I T WAS NEARLY NINE O'CLOCK and fully dark by the time we arrived back in Lambourn from Newton Abbot, so I asked Spencer to drop me outside my cottage on the way to the yard.

'Could you wait a moment while I unlock the front door?' I asked as I climbed down from the horsebox cab with my bag.

'You all right?' he asked through the open driver's window, concern clearly showing on his face.

'Yes, fine,' I said. 'I'd just feel safer if you waited.'

And my hands were shaking as I undid the lock.

I opened the door and put the light on in the hall, then I turned, waved and smiled at Spencer, who drove off. Next, I closed the door and locked it, pushing across the bolt for good measure.

We had stopped at the motorway services south of Bristol for some supper, but I went through to the kitchen and put the kettle on for a cup of tea. It had been a very long day, and I was ready for my bed.

I took my tea through to the sitting room and stopped dead in the doorway.

The curtains were open.

I was quite sure I had left them closed when I had departed that morning. The ceiling light was also off, when I clearly remembered leaving it on.

My heart was pumping hard.

Was someone here? And was that someone Liam Carson?

I went into the kitchen and again drew the large carving knife from the wooden block on the worktop.

'Liam,' I shouted loudly. 'I have a knife. Get out of my house.'

There was no response.

I'd already been everywhere downstairs, so now I went up, the knife held at the ready.

I put on all the lights and searched everywhere, as I had done the previous day, but there was no sign of an intruder, Liam or otherwise.

I went back down to the kitchen to replace the carving knife in the wooden block, and my heart rate began to return to normal.

I wondered about calling the police, but I had nothing to show that anyone had been here, other than a pair of opened curtains and a switched-off light. I was simply too tired to wait several hours for them to come, and then to ask me hundreds of meaningless questions. And, all the time, they would probably be doubting my memory or my sanity – probably both.

But I was quite certain that someone had been in my house again, and I didn't like it.

* * *

The rest of the night was uneventful, not that I slept soundly despite again wedging a chair under the door handle of my bedroom.

When my alarm went off at six o'clock on Tuesday morning, it felt like I'd only been asleep for about five minutes. Nevertheless, I dragged myself out of bed and got dressed. I was due to ride out both first and second lot, before leaving with Freddie for Ludlow races.

As I went downstairs, I could see a white envelope lying on the mat, beneath the letterbox.

Bit early for the postman, I thought.

I picked it up, but there was no address on the front, and no stamp. It had been delivered by hand.

I opened it.

There was a single folded sheet of paper inside with one word written on it in black ink.

Sorry.

So much for Liam claiming that he didn't know where I lived. But he never had been truthful about anything, and I didn't believe for a second that he was sorry about what had happened at Newton Abbot. Or maybe he was only sorry that I hadn't received a much longer suspension for dangerous riding.

I angrily ripped the paper and the envelope into tiny pieces and threw them in the waste bin.

Sorry, my arse!

How dare he?

My anger carried me all the way to the stable yard and only subsided when I was mounted and walking out to the collecting circle on a horse called My Wife's Mink. It was his name that made me smile, and I could only imagine the awkward conversations that must have taken place between the owner and his wife over whether he would buy her a mink coat or a racehorse.

'Right, Imogen,' Freddie shouted across from his position at the centre of the circle. 'Twice up at a fast canter as a pipe-opener. He's entered on Sunday at Stratford. You'll be riding him if he runs. It depends on us getting some rain.'

I inwardly sighed. Another racing Sunday – so no day of rest for me this week.

There had been no horseracing on any Sunday in Great Britain until 26th July 1992, due to a long battle against it by various protest groups including the influential Lord's Day Observance Society.

More than twenty-two thousand spectators turned up at Doncaster Racecourse on that first Sunday, but due to the law at the time, it was still illegal to charge entry for horse racing on a Sunday. Hence, they all had to pay a fee to listen to the band of the Irish Guards, and then had the racing thrown in for free afterwards.

Now, more than thirty years later, there is racing on every Sunday of the year, and on almost every Sunday in Ireland as well.

I took My Wife's Mink to the bottom of the all-weather track and gave him a gentle giddy-up, plus a light kick in the ribs. He instantly understood the message, and I had trouble restraining him from breaking into a full-blown gallop.

'Whoa,' I said to him, pulling hard on the reins. 'Save that for Sunday.'

The horse finally settled into a fast canter, and I took him up the hill towards where Freddie was now standing.

'And again,' he bellowed at me as I rode past.

I walked the horse down the hill and then we repeated the canter, Freddie watching every step intently through his binoculars.

'OK,' he shouted as we passed. 'Take him back to the yard.'

I slowed the horse to a walk, dismounted, and then led him down the hill as he cooled off after his exertions.

It had been a misty, cold start to the day, but the early April sunshine was now breaking through the gloom, and by the time I reached the yard, I could feel its warmth on my face.

Somehow, whatever demons are lurking in the recesses of the mind, sunshine makes things brighter in so many ways. Hence there was a happy spring to my step as I returned My Wife's Mink to his stable, removed the tack and gave him a rub-down. Next I buckled up his blanket, fetched him some water, and placed a small amount of hay in the corner.

'Good boy,' I said, patting his neck as he reached down to eat.

There is something very calming about being around these imposing and majestic creatures, and it's no surprise to me that equine-assisted psychotherapy is gaining in popularity.

Horses have been used for therapeutic purposes since before the time of the Greek physician Hippocrates of Kos, the 'Father of Medicine' and the supposed author of the doctors' Hippocratic Oath. He wrote about the healing effects of horses in about 400 BC. Indeed, ancient Greeks admired and loved the horse so much that they often incorporated 'hippo' (Greek for horse) into their children's names – hence possibly Hippocrates himself.

I gave My Wife's Mink another last affectionate pat on his neck and then went across to the stable office, bolting the stable door as I left.

'Hi, Imogen,' Stacey said as I walked in. 'How's it all going?'

'Fine, thanks,' I replied almost automatically. 'But who has a key to my cottage, other than me?'

'We have one here,' Stacey said, pointing at a cupboard on the wall. 'Why? Have you locked yourself out?'

'No. Nothing like that. I'd just like to know who else has one.'

'Freddie has,' Stacey said. 'Though goodness knows where it'll be.' She laughed. 'He's not the tidiest of men – not since Susie left.'

'Susie?' I asked.

'Freddie's wife – or rather his former wife. She left about four years ago. I think she got fed up with always being second fiddle to the horses. She and Freddie finally divorced last year, but they're still good friends. She even stays over here occasionally.'

Stacey raised her eyebrows, and this time we both laughed.

'Anyone else?' I asked.

Stacey tipped her head to the side as if thinking. 'I don't think so. I know we got Dean's back. He was one of our travelling head lads. He was the tenant before you. Left in February. And it's his key you now have.'

'And that's everyone who has a key?' I pressed.

She thought again. 'Yes. Except for Louisa, of course.'

'Louisa?'

'The cleaner.'

'I don't know anything about a cleaner,' I said.

'I've arranged for Louisa to come in and clean for you, once a fortnight – every other Monday. She has a key. She should have been in yesterday, while you were at Newton Abbot.'

I stared at her. If I'd known there had been a cleaner coming on Monday, I clearly wouldn't have spent several hours cleaning everything myself the day before.

'But she didn't come the first Monday I was here.'

'No. I had her go in the day before that week, so it was all nice and clean for your arrival.' Stacey smiled at me.

'Do you have her phone number?' I asked.

'I have somewhere.' She picked up her phone and scrolled through her contacts. 'Here we are.'

Stacey held up her phone and showed me the screen.

Louisa Jacobs. Cleaner. Together with her number.

I took my own phone out and called it. She answered on the second ring.

'Louisa,' I said. 'I'm Imogen Duffy. I work for Freddie Swinton. You went in to clean my cottage yesterday.'

'Yes, that's right,' she replied. 'But it didn't really need much cleaning. It was already spotless.' She sounded a bit sheepish, as if she'd accepted payment for doing nothing.

'Tell me,' I said. 'Did you open the curtains in the sitting room?'

'Yes, I did,' she said. 'And I turned off the lights. I assumed you must have left early, when it was still dark.'

I breathed a sigh of relief.

'Was that all right?' Louisa asked, now sounding worried.

'Perfectly all right,' I assured her. 'I look forward to meeting you next time you come.'

I hung up.

'It would have been nice to have been told she was coming,' I said to Stacey sharply. 'I was afraid I'd had an intruder.'

'I'm so sorry,' she said. 'I thought you knew.'

'Is there anyone else I should know about? Any maintenance men?'

'We do have a maintenance man. He's called Simon Potter, but he doesn't own a key to your cottage. He collects the one here in the cupboard if he needs it.'

'Please don't give the key to anyone without telling me first,' I said. 'And could you ask Simon Potter if he could fit a security chain to the front door, so I can open it a fraction to see who's there, before having to open it fully.'

I was getting quite agitated.

'Imogen,' Stacey said with concern. 'Are you all right?'

'Yes,' I said, breathing deeply to control myself. 'I'm fine. I'm only a bit concerned about my safety. It's the first time I've ever lived on my own, and Louisa having been in there when I didn't know she was coming has spooked me somewhat.'

I decided not to mention anything regarding Liam having been in the cottage on Sunday afternoon, about him stealing my panties, or him putting an envelope through the letterbox last night.

It would all sound too dramatic and far-fetched.

* * *

'Tell me all about Liam Carson.'

Freddie and I were in the car on our way to Ludlow races.

'There's not much to tell really,' I said. 'We were in a relationship for almost four years, since I was eighteen, but he gradually tried to take total control of my life, so I left him. But he won't accept that. He told me he'd rather kill me than let me leave him.'

'Did you report him to the police?' Freddie asked.

'Yes, in Ireland, but they didn't really care. Liam had attacked me, but they still let him go. It seems I wasn't injured badly enough.'

Freddie glanced over at me. 'Are you serious?'

'Absolutely. They didn't charge him with assault because there wasn't enough evidence – no blood or broken bones, just some bruising.'

'That's outrageous.'

'It certainly is,' I agreed. 'I called the police inspector to complain, but he told me there was nothing more he could do. The decision had already been taken.'

'Was he charged with anything?'

'Using threatening behaviour. It's a joke. But he has to appear in court a week on Thursday.'

'Where?'

'Thurles. I've been called to be there as a witness. But it's a complete waste of time. Even if he's found guilty, he'll only get a fine, and there's no guarantee of even that. I don't think I'll bother going.'

'In that case he'll definitely get off. Can't you go and ask the judge to impose a restraining order to stop him coming near you?'

'And how is that going to work if we're both declared to ride in the same race? Like yesterday at Newton Abbot. What I'd really like is for him to have remained in Ireland.'

'Why didn't he?' Freddie asked.

'Why do you think? He followed me. And if I leave here to go home, he'll go back there too.' I paused. 'And you don't even know the half of it.'

Freddie glanced across at me again.

'So, tell me.'

I hesitated – out of embarrassment. But I shouldn't be embarrassed – I had done nothing wrong.

'Liam Carson went into my cottage on Sunday afternoon while I was out for a run. He stole something.'

'What?'

I hesitated again.

'What did he steal?' Freddie pressed.

'A pair of my black lace panties.'

I blushed – feeling the all-too-familiar unwelcome warmth in my face – so I turned my head away, staring out of the passenger-side window, so Freddie wouldn't see.

'And you're sure it was him who took them?'

'Who else would it be? He must have been outside, watching, and seen me go out. I left the front door unlocked because I was worried about dropping the key up on the gallops. And I was only gone for half an hour.'

'But you didn't actually see him?'

'No. But I know it was him. I smelt him. There was a lingering stale tobacco smell, like I remembered before, after he'd been smoking.'

'Could it have been another smoker?' Freddie asked.

'I know it was him,' I said determinedly.

'Then you should report him to the police.'

'They won't do anything.'

'They might if I report it. I own the cottage.'

'Liam told me at Newton Abbot that he didn't know where I lived. But I know that was a lie because he put an envelope through my letterbox last night.'

'What was in the envelope?' Freddie asked.

'A note saying he was sorry. But I don't believe that either. He would only be sorry that I didn't get suspended for longer.'

'Where is the note now?'

'In my waste bin.'

'We'll get it out later. Then I can take it with me to the police.'

You'll be lucky, I thought. I remembered venting my anger towards Liam by tearing his note into little pieces.

Freddie drove on in silence for a while, as he navigated around the outskirts of Gloucester and then north towards Ludlow Racecourse.

I had two rides that afternoon, one in the first race, a two-mile novice hurdle, and the other in the fourth, a three-mile handicap steeplechase. Both were designated as Great British Bonus (GBB) races, which meant that the winner of each would be eligible to earn a sizable bonus for both their owner and their breeder, provided they were fillies or mares, hundred per cent British-bred, and registered with the scheme, as both my mounts were.

I had already checked the declared runners for the seven races, and in particular the declared jockeys, and I was relieved to see that Liam Carson was not amongst them, but that didn't guarantee that he wouldn't be at the meeting. There were always jockeys on the lookout for spare rides, hopeful that one of the expected riders might fall ill or become injured during an earlier race.

I wondered if he would be there simply because he knew I would be. If so, how could I avoid him? I hoped there was a lock on the female changing room door.

'So, are you looking forward to this coming weekend?' Freddie said, snapping me out of my daydreaming.

'Why? What's happening?' I asked.

Freddie looked across at me.

'It's Aintree. The Grand National meeting.'

'But will I be going?' I asked. With Adrian Shaw going to Aintree, I'd been quite expecting to be sent to one of the other meetings on each of the three days.

'Of course you'll be coming,' Freddie said. 'You'll come up with me early on Thursday morning. I rent a house in Knowsley.

It's about five miles away from the course. I've had the same place for years.'

'And will I be riding?' I asked.

'You certainly will, but not in the National itself. I have only one runner in that, and Adrian will be riding it. But I have fourteen runners in total going up for the three days and you'll be on a share of them – three or four at least. I've asked Peter to declare you to ride on Thursday in the Red Rum two-mile handicap chase – I have two runners in that. And you'll also definitely be riding in the three-mile chase and in the conditional jockeys' hurdle on Friday.'

Wow! I thought.

I'd often watched the three-day Grand National meeting on the television at home in Ireland, but I'd never been to Aintree, not even as a spectator. But now I was going to be there as a jockey!

Chapter 13

NEITHER OF THE TWO MARES I rode at Ludlow collected a Great British Bonus for their owners.

One was second in the novice hurdle, while the other fell at the third fence in the three-mile handicap steeple-chase.

It wasn't a particularly bad fall – the horse simply pitched forward on landing and crumpled down to the turf – but I went over its head and, to add injury to insult, it kicked me on the left knee while it was standing up.

I lay on the ground vigorously rubbing my sore knee, worried that it might prevent me from riding at Aintree. I was quickly joined by one of the racecourse doctors, who came running over to me with his bright red medical bag.

'You OK?' he asked.

'Perfectly fine,' I said with a forced smile.

'Where does it hurt?' he said, clearly not believing me.

'My knee,' I said, still rubbing it. 'The horse kicked me.'

He stretched out my left leg and felt around the joint.

'Does that hurt?' he asked, pressing in on all sides.

'A bit,' I said. 'But not too bad.'

He lifted my knee up, bending it through ninety degrees.

'How about now?'

'Not too bad,' I repeated.

'I don't think anything is broken but you might need an X-ray to be sure. Anything else hurt?'

'No,' I said.

'Neck OK? And your back? No pain.'

'None,' I assured him.

'Blurred vision?'

'No.'

'OK. Shall we get you up? The others will be round again soon.'

I could see the fence attendant looking over towards me with a concerned expression on his face. If I wasn't able to get clear well before the remaining field came round on their second circuit, he would have to initiate the 'bypass' procedure, whereby the horses would be directed around the outside of the fence instead of over it.

The doctor helped me up, and even though my knee was sore, I could still walk on it. And the fence attendant appeared much happier when I finally limped off the racing surface, ducking under the white rail when the other runners were still three fences away.

There was a car designated to collect fallen jockeys, and I was grateful for the lift back to the jockeys' medical room situated inside the weighing-room building, where I was examined again, this time by the senior racecourse medical officer.

First, she asked me some questions – the concussion test that all fallen jockeys must take, apparently injured or not – designed to test both long- and short-term memory.

'Which racecourse are we at?' she asked me.

'Ludlow,' I answered instantly.

'Trainer of your horse that fell?'

'Freddie Swinton.'

'Type and length of the race?'

'Three-mile handicap chase.'

'Name of the current champion jockey?'

'Adrian Shaw.'

'OK,' she said. 'That'll do.'

Satisfied that I wasn't concussed, she next examined my knee, deciding that sending me to hospital for an X-ray was unnecessary, at least for now.

'I don't think any bones are broken or tendons ruptured,' she said, 'otherwise you wouldn't be able to walk on it. It's only soft tissue bruising, but if your leg swells up badly overnight, I suggest you go straight to your nearest hospital emergency department. I am going to stand you down for the rest of the day, so you'll have a red entry on your medical record. You will need to pass the doctor before you can race again.'

Being stood down for the rest of the day was not a problem because I had no more rides booked today anyway, and *passing the doctor* was slang for being assessed by the senior medic at the next course where I was due to ride, and being declared fit to resume.

The doctor gave me a couple of tablets to swallow for the pain, and then I limped along the corridor to the female changing room.

Freddie was waiting for me outside the door.

'You all right?' he asked.

'I have a sore knee,' I said. 'I got kicked. How's the horse?'

'Thankfully sound, but I expect she's also a bit sore. I gave your saddle to your valet.'

'Thanks.'

'Ready to go in twenty minutes?' he asked.

'No problem.'

* * *

Freddie drove most of the two and a quarter hours home in silence, as if he was thinking. I closed my eyes and dozed, but the ache in my knee prevented me from falling asleep completely.

Only when we were on the last stretch into Lambourn did Freddie speak.

'So, would you like me to report Liam Carson to the police?' he said. 'For stalking you?'

Was it stalking?

I certainly felt intimidated by his actions.

'Yes,' I said. 'And also for theft.'

'I'll come in with you and get the note he put through your door.'

'I tore it up,' I said.

'Then I will get the pieces.'

He pulled up in front of my cottage. He turned and faced me.

'If you don't feel safe here on your own, you could always come back to my place.'

It sounded to me like a chat-up line.

'I'll be fine,' I said, and I climbed out of the car.

My knee was stiff from being immobile for so long, and it hurt as I repeatedly bent and straightened it to get it moving. I limped to the front door of the cottage as Freddie lifted my stuff out of the car boot.

I unlocked the door and pushed it open.

There was another white envelope lying on the doormat. I picked it up and stepped into the hallway. I opened the envelope.

Again, there was a folded single sheet of paper inside.

Sorry, it said again. But this time there were more words written underneath, all in the same black ink: *Hope you're all right after your fall.*

As before, there was no signature, but I knew it was from Liam – who else would it be from?

I found his *love me/hate me* flip-flop behaviour very strange – one minute he cared for me, the next he tried to do me harm. But I didn't believe the former. It was nothing but a ruse to get me back, to allow him to control me further.

'What's that?' Freddie asked, walking through the door behind me.

'Another note. It must be from Liam.'

'Try to touch it only on the edges. You can get fingerprints from paper. They might prove it's from him. Unwanted mail is a clear indicator of stalking behaviour.'

I carefully placed the paper back in the envelope and laid it down on the hall table.

'Where do you want this?' Freddie asked, holding up my kit bag.

'In the kitchen. I need to wash some of it.'

He started to sidle past me, as I pressed myself up against the wall. The hall was quite narrow, and we found ourselves face to face and very close. He looked down at me, and I looked up at him.

I suddenly had goosebumps all up my arms. But I also felt awkward, convinced he was about to lean down towards me, perhaps even to try to kiss me. I turned my head and moved quickly away in the direction of the front door.

Like him as much I did, I did not want to get involved romantically with Freddie. For a start, he was more than twice my age, and he was also my boss – so it would make my life far too complicated.

He, too, seemed to realise that a frisson moment had occurred between us. He mumbled 'Sorry', and went on through to the kitchen, while I hung my skullcap on its hook in the hall.

Freddie came back into the hall, keeping his eyes firmly on the floor, as if embarrassed.

'I'll be off,' he said, picking up the white envelope from the table by its edges. 'I'll take this to Newbury Police Station in the morning.'

'Won't I need to come with you?' I asked.

'I'll call them first, and I'll let you know. Take the day off from riding tomorrow, to give that knee a chance to recover. I want you fit for Aintree. We will be leaving here at seven o'clock sharp on Thursday morning.'

'OK,' I said, worried that my knee wouldn't be better by then.

Freddie finally looked up at me and smiled. 'But call me tonight if you need anything.'

'OK,' I said again. 'I will.'

But I knew I wouldn't call him, not even if the whole place was burning down.

He went quickly out of the front door, and I closed it firmly behind him, locking it securely. Then I turned round and leaned back heavily as he drove away.

What the hell had just happened?

Had I been sending out the wrong signals?

I didn't believe so, but I had been trying very hard to please him with my riding.

Had he misinterpreted my actions?

Indeed, had the whole thing been my fault?

Or had it been his?

* * *

The soreness in my knee kept me awake for much of the night, despite taking more painkillers, but my leg wasn't noticeably swollen in the morning, which was a good sign, and I found walking on it easier when I went downstairs to make myself a cup of coffee.

Maybe I'd be fit to ride at Aintree after all.

Freddie called me at quarter past ten, after second lot, while I was back upstairs, lying on my bed, drinking my coffee.

'The police say you need to come in with me,' he said. 'Because it has to be you making the complaint in person, not me on your behalf. I'll pick you up in ten minutes.'

He was there in eight, but I was ready, having quickly changed out of pyjamas into jeans and a sweater.

I locked the cottage and then climbed into the passenger seat of Freddie's car alongside him.

'Lovely day,' Freddie said. 'This sunshine should help dry the ground at Aintree.'

'Is that good or bad?'

'Good for me, I think. My horses tend to like going firmer rather than softer. How's the knee?'

'Still a bit sore. But improving,' I replied.

Pleasantries over, he drove on in silence for a while, into the centre of Lambourn and then out again on Newbury Road, while I wondered what I would tell the police.

'Oh my God!' I suddenly blurted out loudly, breaking the silence.

'What is it?' Freddie said, clearly alarmed at my outburst.

'Eastbury,' I said, breathlessly. 'We've just passed a sign saying this village is Eastbury.'

'So?'

'Liam Carson lives here. He's stable jockey for Sophie Burnett.'

I slid down in the seat so the top of my head was barely above the bottom of the window, in case Liam was about and would see me.

Freddie glanced across.

'He really does spook you, doesn't he?'

'Bloody right, he does. And I'm afraid of him. With good reason. He has threatened to kill me. He also tried to put me through the wing at Newton Abbot, so I wouldn't put it past him carrying out his threat.'

'Then it's a good job we are on our way to see the police.'

'Don't hold your breath,' I said. 'They probably won't do anything.'

Freddie drove out of Eastbury; I sat up, and we went on, again in silence.

Only as we were coming into Newbury did Freddie talk again.

'I'm sorry about last night,' he said quietly, looking forward through the windscreen, rather than at me.

'Don't worry about it,' I replied, also staring straight ahead.

'But I do worry about it. That's not who I am. I'm not sure what came over me. I am so sorry.'

'It's OK, Freddie. Apology accepted. Nothing more needs to be said.'

He nodded, as if relieved. 'It won't happen again.'

'No,' I agreed.

It certainly wouldn't.

* * *

PC Tate, the young policeman who met us, was surprisingly understanding, caring even.

Freddie and I were sitting at a table in an interview room, with the uniformed police constable sitting opposite us.

'So let me get this straight,' said the officer. 'This man Liam Carson attacked you, Miss Duffy, in your parents' home in Ireland, last month, soon after you broke off your relationship with him.'

'Yes,' I said. 'My father intervened, and we reported him to the Irish police, but they didn't charge him with assault, only with using threatening behaviour.'

'Did they say why?'

'They said that I wasn't sufficiently injured.'

The officer made some notes in his notebook, and then he looked up at me. 'Tell me about your relationship.'

'We lived together for almost a year, but as time went on, he tried to take more and more control of my life – what I did, what I wore, and who I could see. He was forever telling me that he was better than me, that I was nothing without him, and everything I had was because of him. In fact, he undermined my confidence in any way he could, and he tried to separate me from my parents and friends by saying that I didn't need them any more, not now that I had him. And if I ever disagreed with him, he would shout at me and claim that I was being unreasonable or even that I was insane.'

PC Tate nodded. 'Typical behaviour of a gaslighter.'

'A gaslighter?' I asked.

'Someone who psychologically manipulates a partner through controlling behaviour, making them believe something that is untrue.'

'And now he's stalking me,' I said. 'I left my home in Ireland and came to England to get away from him, but he's followed me here. He told me that he'd never let me leave him, that he'd rather kill me first.'

'When did he make that threat?'

'When he attacked me.'

'In Ireland?'

I nodded.

'Did anyone else hear him make it?'

I thought back. He had made the threat before my father had arrived home. I shook my head. 'But I'm frightened,' I pleaded.

'Understandably,' the officer said sympathetically. 'Has Mr Carson been in touch with you since your arrival here in England?'

'Yes, he has,' I said. 'We're both jockeys and, much to my dismay, I found myself riding against him at Newton Abbot on Monday. He forced his way into the female jockeys' changing room and confronted me. He said he wanted to have me back as his girlfriend, but he reacted violently, shouting at me when I told him there was no chance of that. Then in the race, he tried to put me through the wing.'

'Through the wing?' the officer asked.

'Every fence has large panels on either side, to guide the horses in,' I said. 'They are the wings. They were once constructed of solid timber but, for safety, they are now made of white plastic tubing, which separates if a horse hits it. But it's still dangerous. Liam forced me wide with his horse, and he was definitely trying to do me harm.'

'But he didn't actually put you through the wing?'

'No. I managed to escape.'

I decided not to tell the policeman that it had been Liam who had ended up going through the wing, and it was me who had subsequently been suspended for careless riding.

'So has Mr Carson struck you at all, or caused you any injury, since you've been over here in England?'

'Well, no, but it's not from his lack of trying.'

The officer stroked his chin, as if thinking.

'So, you are not making a complaint of assault?'

'No,' I said. 'Only of harassment and stalking. And theft.'

'Theft?'

'Yes. Liam Carson entered my home last Sunday, when I was out, and stole something.'

'Did he break in?'

'No. I'd left the front door unlocked while I went for a run.'

The officer looked at me and raised an eyebrow, as if in reprimand for being so lax with security, but almost no one locked their doors at all in rural Ireland. It was what I was used to.

'I was only gone for a short while,' I said.

'What did he take?'

'A pair of black panties.'

I was trying very hard not to blush but without much success.

'And you're certain it was him?'

'Absolutely,' I said.

'Did you actually see him in your house?'

'No, I didn't. But who else would it be?'

'Miss Duffy,' PC Tate said seriously. 'We would need solid evidence that Mr Carson was the perpetrator before we could take any action.'

'Then search his flat for my panties.'

'Even if we could search his home – which we can't – could you prove that they were yours and not someone else's? Would your DNA be on them?'

I felt myself blushing again.

'They were clean,' I said. 'He took them from the airer in my front room, where they were drying.'

'Then even finding them would only be circumstantial evidence. That's not strong enough. Patently not strong enough to issue a search warrant.'

'He's also put two unwanted notes through my front door.'

'What sort of notes?'

Freddie cleared his throat. 'I have one of them here.' He placed the white envelope down on the table, now safely enclosed within a clear plastic bag.

'What does it say?' the officer asked.

'It says he's sorry, and hopes I am all right after a racing fall.'

'And has he signed it?'

'No.'

I could tell that was another problem.

'But can't you lift fingerprints from paper?' Freddie said.

'We could try. But have either of you touched it?'

'I have,' I said. 'I opened it.'

'Then I'll arrange to have your prints taken so they can be eliminated.' He closed his notebook. 'But I have to say, Miss Duffy, there's not much substance here for us to go on.'

'Isn't the fact that he threatened to kill me enough?' I asked in despair.

'It would be if we had corroboration from a third-party witness that Mr Carson had said it, but as it stands, it would be just your word against his. Not enough for us to charge, let alone for a jury to convict. We need more.'

'Like my lifeless corpse?' I asked sarcastically.

Chapter 14

FREDDIE AND I WALKED OUT of the police station to his parked car.

'I told you it would be a waste of time,' I said as we climbed in.

'But that policeman promised to speak to him, so he'll know that you've made an official complaint.'

That's what I was worried about. I didn't know how Liam would react, but I feared it would be badly.

The policeman had kept the envelope with its note, and a technician had taken my fingerprints for elimination purposes. I'd expected to have black ink put all over my fingers, but he took the prints with a handheld digital device – I simply had to place each finger, and then my thumbs, on a piece of glass which was then automatically scanned from beneath. Clean and easy.

'How long will you keep them for?' I asked the technician.

'Only as long as necessary for this particular job. They won't be uploaded to the national fingerprint database – not unless you get arrested.'

He laughed.

Freddie drove us back to Lambourn and this time I did not slink down in my seat as we went through Eastbury, rather I sat up proud and straight. Somehow, in spite of their apparent indifference, going to the police had emboldened me.

Bugger Liam, I thought. *I'm not going to hide from him any more.*

'Continue to rest that knee,' Freddie said as he dropped me at my cottage at midday. 'I need you to be passed fit to ride at Aintree tomorrow. I'll pick you up here at seven.'

'What do I need to take? Should I take anything smart?'

'Not unless you intend going out clubbing in Liverpool.'

It sounded like an attractive option, but not one I'd take if I was riding the following day.

'Who else is staying in the house in Knowsley?'

It was a question that I'd been itching to ask, ever since the events of the previous evening in my hallway. I was worried it would be only Freddie and me.

'Adrian will be there, plus his wife Mandy, and my ex, Susie, is coming up on Friday night. She's coming to the National with me on Saturday, and she's also bringing Freddie Junior. It's quite a houseful. Should be fun.'

I was relieved, and also looking forward to meeting Freddie's ex-wife and son, to say nothing of spending some quality time with Adrian Shaw. We'd met a few times, when he'd been on visits to the stables, but we had often been riding at different racecourses on any given day.

'We traditionally have a pre-Grand-National dinner together at the house on Friday evening,' Freddie said. 'I've booked someone to come in and cook, so you might want to bring something reasonable to wear for that.'

'OK, I will,' I said. 'See you in the morning.'

I went into the cottage and my phone rang.

'Hello, Imogen,' said a female voice, when I answered. 'Stacey here. Is it all right for Simon Potter to go round to your cottage and fit your security chain?'

'Oh, yes, please,' I replied. 'That would be great.'

'Good. He'll be there in about twenty minutes.'

I went upstairs to start my packing for the Aintree trip, but I had hardly begun when the doorbell rang.

That was a quick twenty minutes, I thought.

I went down the stairs as quickly as my knee would allow.

'Coming, Simon,' I shouted.

I opened the door. But, of course, it wasn't Simon Potter standing outside. It was Liam, holding another bunch of flowers – red roses this time.

'Go away,' I said.

I tried to shut the door again, but as before, he put his foot in the way, preventing it from closing fully.

'I only came to see how you are,' he said. 'After your fall at Ludlow. I watched it on the television.'

'Go away,' I said again. 'Move your foot or I'll call the police.'

Still leaning hard on the door, I felt for the phone in my pocket, but it wasn't there – I had put it down on the bed while I was choosing what to pack.

Needless to say, Liam didn't move his foot.

'I'm calling the police,' I shouted through the gap.

How could I have let this happen again? As it had been before at my parents' house. But I was determined not to let him in this time.

'Come on, Imo,' he pleaded. 'Open the door. I'm being nice.'

'Police, please.' I said it loudly so Liam would hear. I then waited a second or two. 'Help me,' I shouted in a panicky voice.

'A man is trying to force his way into my house. Yes, he's here right now. Help me.' I paused again. 'How long?' Another pause. 'Please hurry. Yes, I'll stay on the line.'

Surely Liam wouldn't know that my phone was lying unused and untouched upstairs on my bed.

'I've brought you some roses,' he said calmly through the gap.

'I don't want your bloody roses. Now go away, before the police arrive.'

'But the police aren't coming, are they, Imogen?' he said, confidently. 'Because you never called them, did you? Because you never said your address.'

Damn it.

He gave another hard push on the door.

What did I do now?

I was quite certain that Liam would attack me if he got into the cottage. I was also sure he would complete the task he had planned to carry out when my father had interrupted him last time – to kill me for leaving him.

I leaned against the door with all my weight – all one hundred and twenty pounds of it – but for how long could I keep him out? He was stronger and heavier than me, and he had correctly worked out that the police were not coming.

'Help!' I screamed. 'Somebody please help me!' But the sound of my voice simply reverberated off the inside of the hall walls.

No one outside would have heard a word.

Liam pushed again at the door, and this time, he managed to open it another couple of inches. I decided that trying to hold it shut against him was a fruitless task – he would eventually make it through.

So much for me being emboldened and not hiding away from him. Right now, I'd have gladly been hiding somewhere else – anywhere else but here.

'How dare you complain about me to the police,' Liam shouted angrily. 'I'll give you something to bloody complain about.'

He pushed hard against the door once again, and it opened another couple of inches. His hand even appeared on the inside.

'Fuck off!' I shouted at him, but it was like King Canute shouting at the incoming tide – hopeless and futile.

I suddenly let go of the front door and ran to the kitchen, quickly grabbing the carving knife from the wooden block by the sink.

'Leave me alone,' I shouted.

'Never,' Liam said, advancing along the hallway, the bouquet of red roses having been long discarded somewhere outside. 'You'll be mine, or you'll be nobody's.'

'Liam,' I screamed at him. 'Stop and think about what you are doing! You will be ruining your own life, as well as mine.'

But he was obsessed and seemingly well beyond any sensible reasoning. Or maybe he believed that spending the next twenty years of his life in prison was worth it, to have killed me.

How could I get through to him?

He came into the kitchen. I was leaning against the sink unit, facing him, with the long carving knife held out in front of me, its blade glinting brightly in the afternoon sunshine coming through the window. He wavered when he saw it but only for a split second.

'I'll use it,' I assured him. 'Now get out of my house.'

He took a step towards me, and I slashed the knife through the air in front of him.

'I mean it,' I said. 'Come any closer and I'll stab you.'

'You wouldn't dare.'

'I certainly would dare. And can you take the chance?'

He wavered again, but he didn't retreat.

We stood there, silently facing each other like cowboys in an old-style gunfight, waiting for the other to draw, to make the first move.

The silence was broken by the doorbell – one long ring.

'Miss Duffy,' called a male voice through the open front door. 'It's Simon, the maintenance man, I've come to fit your security chain.'

I could have kissed him.

'Come on in, Simon,' I called.

Liam looked at me. 'Next time,' he said menacingly, 'I'll bring my own bloody carving knife.'

He turned, and calmly walked away, pushing past Simon in the hallway, and out through the front door.

I slid down to the kitchen floor and burst into tears. I sat with my head down, hugging my knees, sobbing uncontrollably.

Simon came through into the kitchen.

'You all right, miss?' he asked with obvious concern.

I couldn't reply. I just went on sobbing.

'Stacey, I think you'd better come round here straight away.' I looked up. Simon was talking into his phone. 'Yes. Imogen's cottage. And hurry. She's holding a knife.'

I let the carving knife slip from my fingers, and it clattered down onto the stone floor. Simon advanced and dragged it away from me with his shoe.

'That's better,' he said.

* * *

It wasn't only Stacey who arrived, but Freddie too.

By the time they appeared in my kitchen, Simon had helped me move from the floor to a chair, and my uncontrollable sobbing stage had passed.

Freddie crouched down beside me.

'What happened?' he asked.

'He was here,' I said.

'Who? Liam Carson?'

I nodded. 'He forced his way in.'

'But what about the knife?' Freddie asked. 'Did Carson bring that with him?'

'No,' I said. 'It's mine. From there.' I pointed at the wooden knife block by the sink. 'I grabbed it for self-defence. But I'm sure he would have attacked me if Simon hadn't arrived.'

Freddie looked up at Simon, who was still standing by the kitchen door.

'What are you doing here anyway?' Freddie asked him.

'Miss Duffy asked if a security chain could be fitted to her front door. I came round to fix it.'

'Do you need an ambulance?' Stacey asked me, also crouching down to my level.

I shook my head. 'I'm not hurt.'

Not physically anyway, although my emotional wellbeing had taken a huge battering.

'Right,' Freddie said decisively. 'No arguing, you are not staying here tonight. You will sleep in the spare room of my house. We will go there now, and then we will call the police. What do you need?'

'My riding kit and some clothes for Aintree,' I said. 'I had only just started packing when Liam came.'

'Stacey,' Freddie said, 'go upstairs with Imogen and help her pack. I'll go and get the car. Simon, you stay here.'

'Shall I still fix the security chain?' Simon asked.

'Yes,' Freddie said. 'Do that, although it's a bit late now, at least for today.'

'Come on, Imogen,' Stacey said to me kindly. 'Let's go and see what we can find.'

I stood up, treading on the carving knife. I leaned down, picked it up carefully by the blade, and returned it to its designated slot in the wooden block. You never knew when I might need it again, and I couldn't continue to rely on someone turning up to save me in the nick of time, like the US Cavalry in all those western flicks of the 1950s that my father so loved to watch when I was a child.

Stacey and I went upstairs and packed my stuff – one relatively smart outfit for Friday night, but mostly jeans, jumpers and sneakers. Gone were the days when jockeys turned up at race meetings wearing smart suits, ties and shiny black shoes to impress the owners and trainers of the horses they rode.

I collected my wash bag, shampoo and dressing gown from the bathroom, and added them to the pile, along with my hairbrush.

'Make-up?' Stacey asked.

I wasn't really a make-up sort of girl. Being covered in kicked-back mud or hitting the deck at thirty miles per hour somehow didn't sit very well with eye shadow, mascara and face powder. Sometimes I'd apply the occasional bit of lippy, but mostly only then to prevent my lips from cracking in the cold dry early morning air up on the gallops.

Maybe it was time to experiment.

'Top drawer,' I said, pointing at the pine chest of drawers. I had brought with me the all-in-one make-up kit that my mother had given me for Christmas more than a year ago. The see-through bag still had the label attached, plus the little plastic tag that held the zip closed before use.

Stacey put it in my suitcase.

Finally, I collected a couple of racing undershirts, two pairs of leggings, my remaining black lace panties, a new pack of tights, and some clean socks.

'Coat?' Stacey asked.

'I'll take the Freddie Swinton branded one. It's on the hook in the hall downstairs with my skullcap. The rest of my riding kit is in a bag in the kitchen. I was going to wash some of it this afternoon.'

'I'm sure Freddie has a washing machine in his house. Do it there.'

I took my suitcase downstairs.

'How's that?' Simon asked, proudly showing me the security chain he had finished fitting. 'It'll stop a charging elephant.'

It wasn't elephants that I was worried about. I'd be happy just as long as it stopped a charging Liam Carson.

'Thank you, Simon,' I said. 'And thank you for arriving when you did to save me. Did you see Mr Carson?'

'Is that the man that pushed past me?'

'Yes.'

'I didn't really see his face, but I did like his shoes.'

'His shoes?'

'Yes. Nike Air Jordans – red and white. I think they were real ones too. I've been saving up for ages to buy a real pair, rather than these cheap fakes I found at Hungerford market.'

He pointed down at his own rather scruffy red and white sports shoes.

I wasn't at all sure that the police would consider positive identification of his shoes as conclusive evidence that Liam had been there wearing them.

Chapter 15

WHEN WE ARRIVED AT FREDDIE'S house, he called Newbury Police Station and was put through to PC Tate, the same police officer who had interviewed us earlier.

Freddie put the phone on speaker.

'Did Mr Carson use force to enter the building?' the constable asked.

'Yes,' I replied. 'I opened the door because I believed it was someone else arriving. But it was Mr Carson, and he wouldn't let me close the door again. Then he pushed his way in.'

'So, he didn't actually break in, as such?'

'It felt like it,' I said.

'But did he damage the fabric of the building?'

'No.'

'And you say that he then attacked you?'

'Yes.'

'Do you have any injuries?'

'Not physical injuries. I managed to hold him at bay with a carving knife.'

I suddenly wondered if it had been a good idea to tell the policeman about the knife. Police have a strong aversion to anyone holding a knife, either villain or victim.

'You mean you threatened him?' the policeman asked slowly.

'I told him to get out of my house and leave me alone.'

'But you still threatened him with a knife?'

'I told him that, if he came any closer to me, I wouldn't hesitate to use the knife to defend myself.'

'I cannot recommend the use of a knife as a weapon under any circumstances,' said the officer.

'So would you rather he had killed me?'

He didn't reply.

'What are you going to do about it?' Freddie asked. 'Miss Duffy is in fear of her life because of this man. He has to be stopped.'

'I will ensure that he is interviewed today and warned as to his future conduct.'

'That won't make any bloody difference,' I said angrily. 'Liam is obsessed, and he needs to be locked up. Otherwise, I'm a dead woman. He told me he'd bring his own knife next time. If that isn't a threat to kill me, what is?'

'Did anyone else hear him make that remark?'

I thought back. 'No. We were alone in the kitchen.'

'Did anyone else see Mr Carson while he was in your property?'

'Simon Potter saw him. It was only his timely arrival that saved my life.'

'Simon Potter is my stable maintenance man,' Freddie interjected.

'Could he positively identify Mr Carson as the person in Miss Duffy's cottage?' the policeman asked.

Only by his shoes, I thought.

'Don't you believe me?' I asked with irritation.

'Of course I do,' he replied. 'But the prosecution service always prefers two or more witnesses. It makes for a much stronger case.'

I could tell we were getting nowhere, and so could Freddie.

'But someone will definitely talk to Mr Carson today?' he asked.

'I will do it myself,' replied the officer. 'You told me earlier that he lives in a flat above some racing stables in Eastbury. Is that correct?'

'Yes,' Freddie said. 'But there are two trainers in Eastbury village. You want Boxtree Stables. The trainer there is called Sophie Burnett. I know her. We're both members of the Lambourn Trainers Association.'

'Right. Thank you. In the meantime, could you speak to your maintenance man to find out if he saw or heard anything that might be relevant.'

'Yes,' Freddie said. 'I'll do that.'

He disconnected the call.

'Why can't the police simply arrest Liam?' I asked. 'You would think they would rather prevent a murder than have to solve one.'

'Like in *Minority Report*,' Freddie said.

'What?'

'*Minority Report*. It's a science fiction film starring Tom Cruise. Would-be future murderers are arrested before they can commit their crimes. They are then detained in an everlasting coma-like state.'

'Sounds like a great plan to me,' I said with a laugh. 'I wish someone would put Liam into an everlasting coma-like state.'

'Look, Imogen,' Freddie said. 'I have to go back to the stable office. I have stuff to do before I go away for the next three days. Will you be all right here on your own, or would you rather I asked someone to come and sit with you?'

We were in what he called his snug, a large room attached to his kitchen, containing literally hundreds of racing trophies and photographs, together with two very large flat-screen television sets fixed one above the other on the wall opposite a leather sofa and two matching armchairs.

When I asked him about the two TV sets, and how he could possibly watch both of them at once, he simply said that one was permanently tuned to Racing TV, and the other to the Sky Racing channel, so he could watch every race from every British and Irish racecourse, without missing any of the action. He simply switched the sound from one to the other as required.

'I'll be fine here on my own,' I said. 'But can you please lock the door?'

He smiled at me. 'OK. I won't be very long. You can put the racing on if you want. And help yourself to anything in the kitchen. There's tea, coffee and some mugs in the cupboard above the kettle, and milk in the fridge.'

'Thanks. Can I use your washing machine?'

'Help yourself. It's in the utility room.'

He went out of the back door, locking it, leaving me alone in his house.

I didn't put the racing on the TVs, not immediately anyway. Instead, I put my dirty racing kit in his washer, and then spent some time looking round the snug, at the huge treasure trove devoted to the ongoing success of Freddie Swinton, racehorse trainer.

Trainers' trophies were always much smaller than those presented to the owners, which was just as well or else Freddie would have needed an extension to house them all.

On one side of the room was a table straining under a mass of silver and gold salvers, all standing upright on small stands, and an array of different-sized glass bowls and platters, each of them engraved with the name of a race in which one of Freddie's horses had triumphed.

Against the opposite wall was a floor-to-ceiling bookcase holding a vast collection of silver-plated racing horseshoes, each mounted on a stand with a small plaque detailing the Grade 1 race or Premier Handicap won, together with the name of the Swinton horse that had been wearing the shoe while winning it.

In pride of place on an antique writing desk in one corner were three Cheltenham Gold Cup Winning Trainer goblets, another for the Champion Hurdle, plus two Leading British Jump Trainer trophies.

And every square inch of free wall space was filled with framed pictures of horses winning races or of trophies being presented to smiling connections, Freddie always included.

I was impressed – very impressed.

I knew Freddie was one of the sport's all-time leading race-horse trainers but perhaps I didn't realise quite how successful he had been. Here was the proof. I was only glad that I wasn't the person who had to dust them all.

* * *

Freddie didn't return home until almost six o'clock, when I was still in the snug, having watched the racing from Sedgefield on one of the TVs.

'I'm sorry I was so long,' he said. 'Everything OK?'

'Fine,' I said. 'I've been having a good look at your collection.' I swept my hand round in a circle. 'It's very extensive.'

'But incomplete,' Freddie said.

'Incomplete?'

'Yes, there's one thing missing.'

'What's that?' I asked.

'The Grand National. But it's not from a lack of trying. I've had twenty-five runners in the last eighteen Grand Nationals, and the closest I've come to winning was to be second. There's no silverware for coming second in horse racing.' He sighed. 'But at least my record is not as bad as that of the great Nicky Henderson. He's been trying to win the National for over forty years without any success. Maybe this will finally be my year, or his.'

I suddenly realised how important the next few days were to Freddie – and I didn't want to be a distraction from his primary objective.

'Right,' he said, snapping himself out of his melancholy. 'What shall we have for supper? I'm starving.'

I was too, not having had any lunch.

'What have you got?' I asked.

'Well, I'm not much of a cook – that was Susie's department – but I am a real wizard at heating up ready meals in the microwave. What do you fancy? Cottage pie? Fish pie? Chicken tikka masala? Thai green curry? Chinese? I have a freezer full of all sorts.'

I laughed.

'The fish pie sounds great.'

So that was what we had, sitting opposite one another at Freddie's kitchen table.

'Would you like a glass of wine?' he asked. 'I'm having one.'

I was suddenly wary again – dinner for two, glasses of wine ... where might it lead?

'Best not,' I said. 'I don't want to give the Aintree Racecourse medics any reason for not passing me fit tomorrow morning.'

'As you like,' Freddie said. 'But I'm sure one glass of wine won't affect that.'

'Still no, thank you.'

He poured himself a glass of red, and it did look rather good, but I resisted. Maybe tomorrow night at the house in Knowsley, when there were more people around.

At half past seven, when we had finished eating, Freddie's phone rang. It was PC Tate, from Newbury Police Station. Freddie put him on speaker.

'I'm sorry it's so late in the day,' he said. 'But I thought I should update you on my enquiries. I interviewed Liam Carson this afternoon at his home. Suffice to say that his account of this morning's incident differs considerably from your own, Miss Duffy. He says that he came round to check that you were all right after your racing fall, and he brought you some flowers to cheer you up. He claims that you welcomed him into your home before confronting him with a knife, threatening him for no apparent reason. So he left.'

'That's a lie,' I said.

'Furthermore, he denies having entered your property last Sunday or having stolen your underwear. He told me that he is very upset that you have accused him of harassment when he only has your best interests at heart.'

'More lies.'

'What happens now?' Freddie asked.

'I have warned Mr Carson regarding his future behaviour, but I must also tell you that threatening a person with a knife is a serious offence under the Offensive Weapons Act, 2019.

Do you realise, Miss Duffy, that you can be sent to prison for up to four years for threatening someone with a knife? However, after a discussion with my senior officer, we have decided not to initiate legal proceedings against you on this occasion, but I must officially warn you as well about your own future conduct. Do I make myself clear?'

He made me feel like I was the villain here. Perhaps I was.

'Yes,' I said.

'Good,' he said. 'This incident will go on file, but I will not be making any further enquiries or taking any further action at this time.'

He disconnected.

'Well, that didn't go very well, did it?' Freddie said.

No, it hadn't. But, on the bright side, I had dodged being sent to prison.

'Can I have that glass of wine now?' I asked. 'I think I need it.'

He poured me one, and I took a sizable swig.

'What do I do now?' I asked.

'Well, for one thing, I'd keep well away from Liam Carson,' Freddie said.

'Don't worry, I intend to. I've already checked tomorrow's declarations. Thankfully, he's due to ride at Plumpton. And he's also not declared to ride anything at Aintree on Friday, but I suppose he might still be there. If he is, I'll have to hide from him in the female changing room, not that that has stopped him in the past.'

'Only declared jockeys are allowed anywhere near the changing rooms at Aintree,' Freddie said. 'They're very strict on it. I know because even Adrian was refused entry last year. He was injured and not riding.'

I'd been declared to ride two of Freddie's runners on Friday, one in the Grade 1 three-mile novice chase, and the other in the Class 2 conditional jockeys' handicap hurdle, but both were dependent on my injured knee being successfully passed by the doctor, as was my ride in the Red Rum two-mile handicap chase on Thursday afternoon.

I finished my wine.

'More?' Freddie asked, holding up the bottle.

'No, thanks. I think I'll have an early night, if that's all right.'

'Sure. Your room is at the top of the stairs on the right. I've already put your suitcase in there.'

'Thank you.'

'Breakfast at six. We must be on our way by seven.'

'Aye, aye, sir,' I said, making a mock salute.

Maybe that glass of wine had gone to my head more than I realised.

But I had a much better night, sleeping soundly in Freddie's spare room with no pain from my knee. Freddie had been the perfect gentleman all evening, and I wondered what I'd been worried about. However, that hadn't prevented me from again placing a chair under the door handle – just to be sure that neither he nor Liam Carson could get into my room while I was away in the land of Nod.

* * *

Lambourn to Liverpool is nearly two hundred miles, and even at Freddie's breakneck pace on the motorway, it took him almost three and a half hours to drive there on Thursday morning, skirting round Birmingham during the rush hour.

'We'll go to the house in Knowsley first and drop off some stuff,' he said. 'It's not far out of our way.'

'OK.'

The stuff we dropped off were two suitcases – his and mine – a box of mixed red and white wines, plus a case of the finest Bollinger champagne.

'You never know,' Freddie said, grinning, when he saw me looking at it. 'It's always worth being prepared.'

'Whose house is it?' I asked, looking up at the modest detached property only a stone's throw from Knowsley Hall, seat of the Earls of Derby for more than three hundred years.

'Some people called Ferguson. Local family. They rent out their home just for Grand National week. I have to pay for the whole seven days, mind – Sunday to Sunday – same every year, and they use my money to take their kids away on holiday. I think they've gone skiing in Austria this time. Last year it was Disneyland Paris.'

'Nice.'

'Yes, but it's also nice for us. Renting the house is cheaper than booking multiple rooms in one of the local hotels, what with their Grand National inflated prices, and it's infinitely more private. We can let our hair down during the evenings, after the stress of the races, without anyone spying on us and reporting what we do to the damn newspapers.'

Aintree Racecourse was only ten minutes down the road from Knowsley – at least it would have been only ten minutes if it hadn't been for the race-day traffic. Even at ten thirty in the morning, some three hours before the first race, the Ormskirk Road was bumper to bumper past the racecourse, mostly because the Merseyside Police had decided for some reason to close one of the two lanes and severely restrict the traffic flow in the other.

Hence it took many more frustrating minutes for us to cover the last few hundred yards to the trainers' car park, but we were in before eleven o'clock.

'Go and see the medics,' Freddie said. 'If they pass you fit, we'll go and walk the course.'

'And if they don't?' I asked.

'Then I'll be deep in the brown stuff,' he said. 'I'd have to find another jockey for the Red Rum chase this afternoon, and on top of that, if you're still not fit to ride tomorrow, I'll get fined by the stewards for declaring a jockey who was on the red list at declaration, and who is still on it at the off. So don't mess it up.'

I hadn't properly realised the risk he had taken. Declarations for today, Thursday, had been made on Tuesday morning, before my fall at Ludlow, but those for tomorrow had been made after it. He must have been confident that I would be fit. Now was my chance to prove him right.

I climbed the steps to the weighing room, took a deep breath, and went in.

* * *

'Any pain?' the senior racecourse doctor asked, as I lay on the treatment table in the medical room.

'None,' I said, although my left knee complained a bit when he fully flexed it so that my foot touched my bottom.

'Push against my hand.' I did so. 'Any pain now?'

'No.'

'Stand up,' he said.

162

I did as he asked.

'Now stand only on your left leg.'

I did that too.

'Close your eyes.'

I closed them.

He counted seconds – one, two, three, four, five – and I didn't fall over.

'OK,' he said. 'You're fine. Fit to ride. I'll remove the red entry on your medical record.'

'Thank you.'

I replaced my shoes and went out. Freddie was waiting for me, a worried expression on his face.

'All good?' he asked.

'Yup, I'm fit to ride,' I replied.

The worried look only partially disappeared.

'That's lucky,' he said, 'because Adrian Shaw isn't. He's just called me. Seems he woke up feeling unwell. He hoped he'd be better after taking paracetamol, but he isn't. He now thinks it's the flu, and both he and Mandy have taken to their beds with high temperatures.' He smiled at me. 'I hope you've had a hearty breakfast because you're now riding four this afternoon, including Multistorey in the big three-mile chase. If Adrian doesn't recover overnight, you'll ride five tomorrow, and if he's still not fit by Saturday, you'll be on another three then, including on my runner in the Grand National. Is that OK?'

OK?

I'd say so.

But I didn't know whether to be hugely excited or bloody terrified.

Chapter 16

MY FIRST RIDE WAS NOW in the very first race of the meeting, a Grade 1 two-and-a-half-mile novice chase.

Adrian Shaw had been declared to ride an animal called Carbon Dioxide, the ante-post short-priced favourite in the seven-horse contest. Carbon Dioxide, or C-O-2 as he was known at home, had easily won the Golden Miller Novices' Chase at the Cheltenham Festival on his last outing, and he was strongly fancied to repeat the victory today against many of the same opponents.

I only hoped that, as Adrian's late replacement, I wouldn't let all the punters down. It made me quite nervous.

As I walked down the steps from the weighing room to the parade ring, I heard one racegoer loudly complaining to his friend that *'Swinton should have substituted a proper jockey, not a bloody girl, and a claimer to boot. My bet now has no chance of winning. I think I'll lay it to cover my losses.'*

The comment gave me added determination.

If Freddie believed I was good enough to substitute for Adrian, then I was. All my pre-race nerves disappeared in that single moment. If C-O-2 didn't win this race, it wouldn't be from any lack of application on my part.

And win it he did, jumping brilliantly over all sixteen fences. He took the lead coming towards the second last, and went further ahead after it, triumphing by three lengths without me even having to raise my whip.

As at Cheltenham after the Champion Chase, ITV Racing were on hand out on the course with a cameraman and an interviewer holding a microphone on a stick, which he held up to my mouth.

'Well done, Imogen,' he said. 'Another Grade 1 success for you. You're making a habit of picking up winning rides from other indisposed jockeys.'

'Yes,' I said, ignoring the slight jibe. 'And it's all very exciting. This horse jumped like a stag all the way round. He gave me a great ride.' I gave him a pat on his neck. 'But I do feel sorry for Adrian Shaw. It should have been him here talking with you right now.' I looked straight into the lens of the camera. 'Get well soon, Adrian.'

But not too soon, I thought. *Not before Saturday.*

Interview over, C-O-2 was led through the passageway between the grandstands and into the unsaddling space reserved for the winner. The large crowd cheered enthusiastically, and I wondered if the disgruntled punter I'd heard before the race now regretted laying the horse to '*cover his losses*'.

What a horse! What a feeling!

'Well done,' Freddie said as I dismounted. 'Great ride.'

All I'd done was sit there and let the horse do all the work beneath me. Anyone could have won on him. And I hadn't fallen off.

'Don't forget to weigh in,' Freddie said.

* * *

Next up for me was Multistorey in the three-mile chase, the third race of the day, another Grade 1 event, this one with a total purse of a quarter of a million pounds, of which £140,000 would go to the winning connections – almost £13,000 of it to the jockey.

It was in a different league to the paltry £540 I had won for steering Sweet Sheila to victory at Newton Abbot the previous Monday. But the riding fee was the same for both, as it was for any race, win or lose.

After his fall in his last race, Multistorey was not the betting favourite this time, that distinction going to the Irish raider that had actually won the Gold Cup.

How circumstances had changed. I remember being quite pleased that Multistorey had fallen at Cheltenham as it had given the Irish a better chance of victory. Now, I was desperate to turn the tables. As Freddie had said, perhaps I wasn't Irish any more, at least not in racing terms.

There were ten runners in total for this race, half of which had also lined up at Cheltenham twenty days ago for the Gold Cup. Much had changed for me in the last twenty days. Would the outcome of this contest also be changed?

I skipped down the steps to the parade ring wearing Multistorey's bright yellow silks, joining Freddie and the owner on the grass.

'He's a natural front-runner,' Freddie said firmly, 'so give him his head and let him go on at the start, but try and save something for later. If you try and hold him back initially, he'll waste all his energy fighting you rather than using it to run. Once he's established himself in front, he should settle down, so don't worry.'

I nodded.

'And remember what I told you when we walked the course. The three-mile-one-furlong start is at the beginning of the home straight and you have to race over two complete circuits of the Mildmay course. It's a very tight track, with sharp bends, so keep as close to the inside rail as you can. And watch out for the cross fence at the far end. It comes up very quickly after the bend and can catch a horse out.'

I nodded again.

'And he hasn't got a strong sprint, so try and run the finish out of the others before you get to the last two fences.'

I nodded once more.

The bell for mounting was rung, and Freddie and I went towards the horse.

'Tell me,' I said on the way over, 'why wasn't Adrian Shaw riding him when he fell in the Gold Cup?'

'Because Jimmy Tucker won on him when the horse first ran as a young novice, and the owner has insisted on being loyal to him ever since. Jimmy always rode him – and he won two Gold Cups on him. And now it's your turn.'

He gave me a leg-up onto Multistorey's back.

'Good luck,' Freddie said, as the horse and I moved away.

'Thanks.'

My turn indeed.

*   *   *

The starter dropped his flag, and we were off.

As expected, Multistorey went immediately to the front, and he had established quite a big lead almost before we even made it to the first of the nineteen fences. But, as Freddie said he would, he soon settled and, by the time we passed the grand-stands for the first time, he was in the lead by only four lengths, travelling easily.

As with schooling at home when I'd first ridden him, he was a little wary over the first few obstacles, jumping somewhat higher than was needed, but he grew in confidence down the back straight and began extending in the air over the fences, jumping like a true champion while better maintaining his momentum on landing.

As we raced past the stands for a second time, I glanced across at the big-screen TV set up for the crowd. It showed me that we were still several lengths to the good and Multistorey was bounding along with no apparent problems. I hugged the rail round the sharp bend, taking the shortest route, and we increased our lead down the back with four perfect leaps, before flying over the cross fence.

'Come on, boy,' I shouted as we turned into the final straight, giving him a sharp tap down the shoulder with my whip. 'Now's the time.'

He responded immediately and even though he got rather close to the last open ditch, we were not headed all the way to the finish line.

Having safely passed the winning post in front, I stood up in the stirrups and saluted the crowd.

Two rides. Two winners. Both at Grade 1.

I was beginning to rather like this racecourse.

After another short on-track television interview, Multistorey and I were led through again into the space reserved for the winner. Both the owner and Freddie were grinning from ear to ear.

'Bloody marvellous,' Freddie said as I dismounted. He rubbed my back. 'I always knew you were a good thing.'

I removed my saddle.

'Now, don't forget to weigh in,' Freddie said. 'Then go and quickly change and weigh out for the next. It's only thirty-five minutes between races. Jason will collect your saddle. Then put these silks back on top of the others and come out for the trophy presentation, so you're wearing the right colours in the photos.'

The next race was another Grade 1, the Aintree Hurdle, and I was riding Grapejuice, the very first horse I had ridden on my first morning at the Swinton stables.

I carried my saddle up the steps to the weighing room and stood on the weighing platform.

'Eleven stone, ten pounds,' said the Clerk of the Scales, tapping it into his computer. 'Multistorey. Weighed in.'

'Thank you, sir,' I said.

I dashed into the female changing room, switched Multistorey's yellow silks for the red and blue ones of Grapejuice, removed seven pounds of lead sheets from the weight cloth, and went back to the scales.

'Eleven stone, three pounds,' the clerk said this time, checking the digital readout. Then he consulted his computer screen, ensuring I was wearing the correct colours, had been given the right number cloth, and was at the correct weight. 'Grapejuice. Number nine. Eleven stone, three pounds. Weighed out.'

'Thank you, sir,' I said again.

Jason was waiting close by.

'Bloody brilliant,' he said, beaming. 'All the lads at home had their weekly pay packet riding on Multistorey.'

I was glad I didn't know that before the race.

'And you didn't let them down.' He took my saddle. 'I'll go and put this on Grapejuice.'

'Thanks.'

I quickly returned to the changing room, put the yellow silks back on top of the red and blue ones, rushed out again and down the steps, making it just in time for the presentations.

Phew!

The owner of Multistorey was presented with a large silver bowl by the managing director of the race sponsors. Freddie received a smaller silver bowl and there was a small silver goblet for me – all of them gratefully received, with lots of pictures taken by the massed ranks of media photographers.

The trophies were then taken away for engraving, while I rushed up to the changing room, removed the yellow silks, collected my racing helmet – with the correctly coloured cap – before going down again to the parade ring.

The Aintree Hurdle has been a feature of the Grand National meeting for half a century and is one of the main feature races. It attracts the very best hurdlers from both Britain and Ireland, many having stepped up from the shorter trip of the Champion Hurdle, with others have stepped down from the longer Coral Cup.

Grapejuice had run second in the mares' hurdle at Cheltenham, over the same two-and-a-half-mile distance of today's contest, but this was a sterner test against the boys, despite her receiving a seven-pound allowance because she was a girl. Needless to say, I couldn't claim my own three-pound allowance in this class of race.

'All set?' Freddie asked when I joined him and the owner.

'All set,' I agreed.

'Grapejuice is a very different horse to Multistorey. She doesn't like to be in front. Whatever you try to do, she will tend to start slowing down, waiting for the others to catch her up – and it's not the best attribute for a racehorse.' He laughed. 'Hence, you need to keep her covered up until the last possible moment before asking for her final effort. It's a long way from the final turn up the home straight to the finish line, much longer than it looks, and there's also quite a long run-in from the last flight of hurdles to the winning post. But provided she's not in front for too long, you'll be all right. Understand?'

'Yes,' I said.

'Same Mildmay course as before,' Freddie said. 'But over hurdles this time, of course, not fences. The start is at the beginning of the back straight, so you do almost two complete circuits. Three flights of hurdles down the back and three more in the home straight on each circuit, so twelve in total.'

'Got it,' I said.

The mounting bell rang, and we walked over to the horse. Tom, the stable lad from Freddie's yard, was leading her round.

'Hello, Tom,' I said, smiling at him.

'Hello, Miss Imogen,' he replied. 'Juicy here is raring to go.'

Freddie gave me a leg-up.

'Give her every chance,' he said, looking up at me. 'She can win this.'

Could I really win three Grade 1s in a row?

There was only one way to find out.

* * *

171

I gave Grapejuice every chance.

We raced mostly in third or fourth place around the whole of the first circuit and down the back straight for the second time, only a few lengths behind the leading pair.

As we turned into the home straight for the last time, I sat very still, biding my time, not wanting to ask for an effort too soon.

Over the third-last flight of hurdles, and the race was now on in earnest around me, but still I sat quietly, content to bound along steadily behind the leaders.

As Freddie had said, it was a very long way from the final turn to the finish line, much farther than it looked, and some of the others had clearly gone for home too early. The horse immediately in front of me started to waver coming towards the second last, so I pulled my mount slightly to the right, in case it went down in front of us. We safely jumped the obstacle, and only now did I ask Grapejuice for an effort.

She glided up almost alongside the remaining leader as we approached the last flight, and I steadied her.

Not too soon. Not too soon.

We were still in second place as we landed and now I asked her for everything, kicking hard and giving her a couple of sharp reminders with my whip.

She drifted up alongside the leader, and then went ahead with just fifty yards to go.

I pushed and pushed and pushed, as hard as I possibly could, giving her another couple of reminders to keep her going.

But it was not enough.

The danger had not been from those in front but from one behind.

The winner of the Champion Hurdle came past us with two strides to spare, winning the race by a head in a thrilling finish.

I was crushed. I had so believed we would win.

Had I, even then, gone too soon? Or not hard enough?

I pulled up, and Tom came out onto the course to meet us.

'I'm so sorry,' I said to him.

'Why?' he asked.

'Because we didn't win.'

'But you were second. That's much better than I thought she would be, especially being up against that lot.' He jerked his thumb towards the other runners, still mingling around on the track.

There were no TV interviews for those who didn't win, so Tom led Grapejuice straight through to the unsaddling enclosure, this time to the space reserved for the second.

The owner and Freddie were waiting there for us.

'Hard luck,' Freddie said to me as I dismounted. 'I hoped for a moment that you might actually do it.'

'So did I. I'm so sorry.'

'No need to be sorry. You gave her a great ride.'

'But you said to me before the race that she could win this.'

'*Could*,' he said. 'Of course I told you she *could* win, but I didn't really expect her to. Not up against the champion hurdler. But she damn well nearly did. And she trounced the other mare, the one that beat her at Cheltenham.'

He smiled at me, but I could still read the disappointment in his face, and I caught him looking enviously over at the trainer of the winner.

Grapejuice's owner, meanwhile, seemed delighted to have secured the sizable prize money for coming second, enough to cover the horse's training fees for the next year.

'Well done, young lady,' he said to me as I removed my saddle.

'Don't forget to weigh in,' Freddie said.

The jockeys who rode any horse that won prize money had to weigh in, down to tenth place in this race.

I carried my saddle up the steps to the weighing room, comfortable in the knowledge that I was in no rush this time, because the fourth race was the Foxhunters' Chase, a race for amateur riders over the Grand National course.

I weighed in before retreating into the female changing room for a rest. There were three other girls in there now, all of them excitedly getting ready for their first trip over the big Grand National fences.

'You'll do fine,' I said to them. 'Remember to keep kicking.'

It seemed strange to me that I was now the comparatively seasoned professional, giving these amateurs advice.

'I watched your win earlier on Multistorey,' one of the girls said. 'It was so exciting.'

'Thank you,' I replied.

'Jockeys out,' called an official through the internal speaker, set up next to the wall-mounted television.

'Good luck,' I said as the three girls nervously exited the changing room.

Maybe I wished I was going out with them.

Chapter 17

MY FOURTH RIDE OF THE day was in the two-mile Red Rum Handicap Steeplechase, named after the much acclaimed, and only, three-time winner of the Grand National.

It was the race in which I had been declared to ride, and that was because Freddie had two horses running. Hence, he'd had to engage another jockey to ride the one that Adrian should have been on.

My horse was called Sans Chichi, a six-year-old French-bred chestnut gelding that had started its jump-racing career in France, before being sold and brought over to England.

It didn't have great recent form, but two years ago, it had won a race at Auteuil, in Paris, on very heavy going. However, its official UK rating was still low, and it had been handicapped to carry only ten stone and two pounds in this race. And, as this was a handicap, I also received my three-pound allowance, which brought the weight down further to only nine stone, thirteen, while the top-rated horse would be carrying twenty-nine pounds more, at twelve stone.

This favourable handicapping of Sans Chichi had not escaped the notice of the betting public, and he was currently second favourite at five-to-one.

I sat in the changing room and watched the Foxhunters' Chase on the television, keen to see how my lady-jockey companions fared.

One of the girls was unseated after a blunder at the fifth fence, another pulled up her horse three fences from home when well behind, and the third finished a very creditable eighth to collect a small cash prize for the horse's owner.

I changed into Sans Chichi's red and grey silks and then went to find my valet to sort out the weight cloth, before weighing out and giving my saddle to Jason. I then went back into the changing room to wait to be called.

The three girls returned from their adventure in the Foxhunters', very chatty and happy to be back safe and uninjured, but full of stories of derring-do out on the track.

'I couldn't believe how big the Chair looked as we approached it,' one of them said. 'I was so scared I nearly peed my pants.'

She should meet Liam Carson.

I realised that it was the first time I had thought about him all day. With luck, he'd have broken his neck in a fall at Plumpton. Then I swiftly reprimanded myself for wishing such a thing on anyone and especially on a fellow steeplechase jockey. But I did wish he would leave me alone.

'Jockeys out,' came the call through the speaker.

For the fourth time today, I went down the steps from the weighing room to the parade ring to join Freddie on the grass.

'This one's simple,' he said to me. 'Don't let them hang around. We want a good gallop to make the most of the weight differential. It's only two miles, so go to the front if necessary, to maintain the pace. The start is just before the cross fence. One and a half times round the Mildmay course, and stick tight to the inside rail round the bends if you can. It will save you many lengths.'

'Got it,' I said.

He then gave similar instructions to the jockey riding his other runner, although it was carrying twelve pounds more than mine.

The mounting bell was sounded, and Jason came over with me, while Freddie went to the other jockey.

'Go for it, girl,' Jason said to me, giving me a leg-up. 'You're on fire.'

I gathered the reins and smiled down at him.

'Thanks.'

And go for it I did, taking the lead at the second fence after I felt we were going too slowly. I then stuck firmly to the inside rail all the way round the turns, taking the shortest route.

Only at the second last did I see another horse, when the highly rated top weight came briefly past me, but Sans Chichi thought nothing of that, and instantly stepped up a gear in pursuit.

And it was the extra twenty-nine pounds that made the difference.

As the leader laboured under his heavy burden, Sans Chichi ran as if he were on springs, leaping high and far over the last fence, taking back first place, and never letting it go again before the finish line.

Another winner. Three out of four. And second in the other one.

I was buzzing.

And so was Freddie when I joined him in the unsaddling enclosure. As I dismounted, he hugged me, tears in his eyes.

'Fabulous,' he said. 'Three winners in a day. Thank you so much. I've never managed that before here at Aintree. And it is all the more unexpected after Adrian called me this morning. It simply proves that I was right in hiring you.'

Now I was almost in tears as well, as I removed my saddle.

'Don't forget to weigh in,' Freddie said. 'Then I'll see you in the car when you're ready.'

On my way into the weighing room, I was approached by a young woman holding a clipboard and wearing a headset.

'Imogen,' she said, blocking my way in. 'I'm Sue Black, ITV Racing. Could you come and give a short interview to the team? For the day's round-up?'

'Sure,' I said. 'Just let me weigh in first.'

I went in and stood on the scale.

'Nine stone, thirteen,' said the Clerk. 'Sans Chichi. Weighed in.'

I quickly went into the female changing room and brushed my hair before going back outside. Sue Black was waiting for me.

'Follow me,' she said and set off at speed.

I followed her past the Dick Francis statue and round to where three ITV Racing presenters were standing behind their little podiums, on the terrace overlooking the parade ring. Sue gave them a 'thumbs-up' sign.

'And now we have the star of the day joining us live on air,' said the lead presenter. 'So welcome, Imogen Duffy.'

I was waved over to stand next to him and given a hand-held microphone with a green foam top that had *ITV Racing* printed on it in white letters.

'Thank you,' I said, holding the microphone up to my mouth.

'Three winners on your first ever day at Aintree,' said the presenter. 'Can you believe it?'

'Not really. When I arrived here this morning, I thought I was only riding in one race, so I've been very lucky.'

'When did you find out you would be riding in four?'

'At about twelve o'clock, after Adrian Shaw called Freddie Swinton to say he had flu and wouldn't be coming.'

'And you have certainly made the most of your chances. Riding Multistorey to victory must have been a thrill.'

'A great thrill,' I agreed. 'I schooled him at home after his fall in the Gold Cup, and he came back strongly today. Jumped beautifully. A great horse.'

'And you're already odds on with the bookies to win this year's Leading Jockey at the Meeting award. What do you think of that?'

'It's much too early to predict that. This is only the first day, there are still two more days to go.'

'But no one else has had more than one winner so far, and you have three. How many rides do you have tomorrow?'

'It depends on whether Adrian recovers overnight. Five if he doesn't, otherwise only two.'

'Freddie Swinton seems to have great faith in you. And I see that he's declared you to ride Hightown Harry in the Grand National.'

'Has he? That's news to me. But I suspect it will be subject to Adrian Shaw being still unavailable.'

'It would be a bit hard to jock you off after your performance today, don't you agree?'

I smiled at him and said nothing.

'Well, thank you for joining us, Imogen. Good luck tomorrow, and on Saturday in the National.' He turned from facing me to look directly into the camera. 'Ladies and gentlemen, that concludes our coverage of the first day of this year's Grand National meeting. Please join us again at two o'clock tomorrow on ITV Racing for day two, which includes the Topham Chase over the Grand National fences. Until then, it's goodbye from Aintree.'

He went on looking into the camera for a moment longer, then Sue Black shouted 'Off air', and everyone relaxed.

'Thank you, Imogen,' she said. 'We'll hope to see you again over the next couple of days.'

I went into the changing room, showered, and changed from my racing clothes into my going-home-wear of denim jeans and a sweater.

My choice of outfit was in stark contrast to most of those worn here today by the local Liverpool girls. They treated Aintree like their own backyard Royal Ascot, so they arrived dressed to the nines and wearing flashy hats. Many also had large areas of bare flesh on display – shoulders, backs, stomachs, and incredibly long legs under very short skirts – something that would have been more appropriate for going racing in the height of summer, rather than in the cold and wet of early April. But they didn't care. They came here to see and to be seen, and they had a fine time warding off the chilly conditions with a copious intake of alcohol.

I took my riding kit through to leave with my valet, who would wash and dry everything overnight, ready for racing tomorrow.

I'd never ridden in more than two races on any single day before, let alone four, so I was totally spent, and I hardly had the strength to walk to Freddie's car in the trainers' car park.

On the way out of the racecourse, I turned on my phone and it downloaded a mass of new text messages, almost all of them from my parents, expressing their joy at my three victories and then my TV interview that had been shown in Ireland, but there was also one too from Cormac Fitzgerald, the trainer from Thurles.

Brilliant, it read. *I told you that you were destined for greatness.*

It made me smile.

Freddie was at the car ahead of me, waiting patiently in the driver's seat.

'Sorry,' I said, climbing in next to him. 'I was caught by ITV Racing for an interview.'

'And well deserved,' he said.

'They told me that I've been declared to ride Hightown Harry in the Grand National. Is that right?'

'Absolutely right,' he said. 'I had to declare his jockey by one o'clock today, and I could hardly name Adrian Shaw when he'd told me he has the flu.'

'But, if he's better on Saturday, will *he* ride Hightown Harry?'

'Maybe,' Freddie said. 'Maybe not. I don't have to decide right now.'

He drove out of the trainers' car park onto Ormskirk Road. It was only five miles to the house in Knowsley, but I was fast asleep well before we arrived.

Freddie shook my knee.

'We're here,' he said.

I roused myself from my slumbers, and such was the depth of sleep into which I had quickly descended that I wasn't totally sure where I was.

'Where?' I asked, sleepily.

'The house in Knowsley.'

Oh, yes. The house in Knowsley. Where Adrian and Mandy Shaw had been due to stay tonight. But now they weren't coming, so here I was, alone with only Freddie, just as I had worried about.

He and I went in together through the front door – at least he didn't offer to carry me over the threshold.

'What do you want for supper?' he asked. 'Mandy was meant to be cooking a meal for us. She was bringing all the food with her. I'll see what's in the fridge.'

Predictably, the answer was not much. Only a pack of butter, some five-day-old milk, and a loaf of sliced white bread of the same vintage. And I was starving. All I'd had to eat since breakfast were three high-energy protein bars that I had grabbed from the jockeys' canteen between races.

'Do you want to go out and find somewhere to eat?' Freddie asked. 'Not that we'll get a table anywhere decent round here during Grand National week.'

'Isn't there a local takeaway? I could murder a curry.'

In the end we found that we could order by phone, pay by credit card, and have our food delivered from an Indian takeaway in Prescot, the next-door area to Knowsley.

When the food arrived, we sat opposite each other at the kitchen table.

'Glass of wine?' Freddie asked. 'To celebrate your three wins.'

'Our three wins,' I corrected. 'And that would be lovely.'

'What do you fancy? Red, white or champagne?'

Champagne sounded good but it always went straight to my head, and I needed to be fighting fit if I was going to ride the following day.

'A small glass of red would be good, thanks.'

He collected a bottle from his box, plus two glasses from a cupboard, and poured the wine.

'Cheers,' he said. 'To us, and to more successes tomorrow.'

We clinked our glasses and ate our curries.

'Have you heard at all from Adrian?' I asked, between mouthfuls.

'Yes, he sent me a video message earlier, congratulating you for winning on Multistorey.'

He removed his phone from his pocket and showed me the message.

'Well done, Imogen,' Adrian said from the screen. 'Brilliant ride on Multistorey. I'd better be careful, or you'll be taking my job.'

'That's nice of him,' I said.

But he hadn't looked well on the video, with sunken eyes and bluish lips, and he had coughed throughout.

'He won't be fit for tomorrow, that's for sure,' Freddie said. 'And probably not for Saturday either. Mandy called me and she's worried he'll try to get back for the National, even if he's not really well enough. No one will thank him for passing flu on to the other jockeys in the changing-room, and it's most unlikely he'd have enough energy to ride over four miles anyway, not after two full days in bed.'

'So I'll be riding five tomorrow?'

'Yes,' Freddie said. 'And three more on Saturday. I'm going to tell Adrian he won't be riding even if he turns up. You will definitely be riding Hightown Harry in the Grand National.'

My heart rate jumped at the thought.

'Has a conditional jockey ever won it?' I asked.

'Must have,' Freddie replied. 'Lots of amateurs have won it, so why not a conditional? David Mullins must have been one when he won on Rule The World in 2016. He was only nineteen. And Bruce Hobbs was even younger than that, at seventeen, when he won it in the 1930s, but I doubt they called them conditional jockeys back then.'

He topped up my glass.

'Go easy,' I said. 'I have five rides tomorrow!'

He laughed. 'And we will have to leave here early. All my runners for tomorrow are already in the Aintree Racecourse stables. They came up in the horsebox this afternoon. I want to go and see them have a short pipe-opener before racing, so I've arranged with Jason to meet me on the track at seven thirty.'

'OK,' I said. 'In that case I'm going up to bed. I'm pooped.'

I stood up, and he did too. He came round the kitchen table and took my shoulders in his hands.

'Really well done today,' he said. 'I'm so proud of you. Sleep well.'

He bent down and gave me a slight peck on the cheek, then he let me go.

I looked up at him.

'You sleep well too,' I said. Then I turned away from him and went upstairs to the room where I had put my suitcase earlier.

It was clearly a girl's bedroom – maybe a young teenager. On one wall were pinned several posters of heart-throb young male pop stars, plus one of Taylor Swift, while on a shelf opposite were a line of soft cuddly toys, as if she had not totally left her childhood behind. The duvet cover on the single bed was a girly patchwork of pink squares, with a matching pink pillowcase.

I lay down on top of the duvet and called my parents.

'Darling, you were brilliant,' my father said, and I could hear my mother repeating it in the background.

'Thank you. And I have some other news to tell you. I'm riding in five more races tomorrow, and I'll also be riding in the Grand National on Saturday. On a horse called Hightown Harry. And he's well fancied.'

'That's fabulous,' Dad said, but there was also a touch of wariness in his voice. 'But please be careful.'

'I will,' I promised, but jump jockeys being overly careful was not conducive to them winning races. They always have to balance risk against reward. If I'd been careful on City Flyer at the second-last fence of the Champion Chase, I wouldn't be here now.

Telephone call over, I undressed, put on my pyjamas, and went to bed.

And I was asleep almost before my head hit the pink pillow.

Chapter 18

I WAS WOKEN BY A GENTLE knock on my bedroom door.
'Imogen,' Freddie called from outside. 'It's gone six. We must leave in under an hour. I'm going downstairs. I'll make you some coffee.'

'OK. Thanks. I'll be down in a minute.'

I dragged myself out from under the warm covers, went to the bathroom, and then dressed. I'd slept well, but I still felt tired, and that was after only four races. What would I feel like later this afternoon, after five?

Apart from the coffee, Freddie had also made a mound of toast using the loaf from the fridge, and he'd found a jar of marmalade in one of the kitchen cupboards.

'Will the Fergusons mind?' I asked.

'Too bad if they do. They charge me enough. Much more than would be required to buy hundreds of jars of marmalade.' He laughed.

I drank my coffee and ate three slices of toast and marmalade.

'Right, are you ready to go?'

'Raring,' I said.

Freddie collected his car keys from the table in the hallway, then we went out of the front door and walked together, side by side, down the front path.

A photographer stepped out from behind a bush and started snapping away at us, the flash on his camera lighting up repeatedly in the early morning gloom.

'What the bloody hell?' Freddie shouted. 'Get the hell out of here.' He waved a dismissive hand at the man, but he took no notice, and went on shooting, his camera clicking away rapidly with multiple shots.

'Stop that, do you hear?' Freddie yelled, and he now advanced towards the photographer, bunching his fists as if he was about to use them.

'Freddie,' I shouted urgently. 'Leave him alone. That's what he wants you to do. Let's get in the car.'

Freddie suddenly stopped and turned towards me. Then he unlocked the car and we both got in. He started the engine, and reversed out onto the road, while the snapper went on snapping.

'Bloody paparazzi,' he said. 'I've had trouble with them before.' He drove off angrily. 'Why did he want pictures of us anyway? It must have been you he was after. You're the celebrity now, after yesterday.'

*   *   *

In the early morning mist, Jason, Freddie and I watched our Friday runners having a gentle canter along the all-weather strip inside the main course. There were six of them in total. I would be riding five, and Freddie had declared another jockey to ride the sixth, because he had two runners in the first race, the three-mile novice chase.

Satisfied, Freddie told Jason and the lads to take the horses back to the racecourse stables.

But we were not the only people out at this early hour.

As usual for the Grand National meeting, a strong contingent of Irish horses had crossed the water, and most were also stabled at the racecourse, some of them for three or four days prior to their races. Their trainers were out doing the same as us, watching their own strings at exercise.

In addition, there were the betting touts – a row of a dozen or so men, standing to one side or leaning on the white running rail, all with raised binoculars, checking how each horse was moving, looking for anything out of the ordinary in their action, something that might affect their performance in a race.

Even though there were no saddle-cloth numbers or convenient names to see, the touts would be able to instantly recognise every horse after many years of studying them. Some worked for the big bookmaking companies, passing useful titbits of information to their bosses to help guide their offered odds, while others would be independents, who would later try to sell tips to the incoming public.

There was also a TV camera crew, collecting atmospheric footage to use later in their broadcast, and several more photographers, but thankfully, these particular snappers were more interested in the horses than in the human beings.

'Right,' said Freddie to me as his horses departed, 'now that we're here, let's walk the National course.'

In recent years, the Grand National start has been moved further away from the packed and noisy grandstands, to reduce the stress on the horses. This shortened the race slightly, but at four miles and five hundred and fourteen yards, it is still the longest jump race on either the British or Irish calendar.

'Now, remember not to go off too fast,' Freddie said as we stood beside the starter's rostrum. 'Over the years, many horses have set off like a cavalry charge, only to come to grief by overjumping at the first. They've recently moved the fence closer to the start, to try and prevent that, but some still go too fast, perhaps seeking either death or glory.'

I didn't want death, although I wouldn't mind the glory.

We walked to the first fence.

'This is the first in the National,' Freddie said, 'but also the seventeenth, because you jump it twice.'

I looked at the bright green coloured obstacle. It was like no other fence I'd ever been close to before.

'It might look quite soft, with all this spruce lying on top, but the core is pretty stiff underneath, so it takes some jumping. And the landing side is slightly lower than the take-off, and that tends to pitch a horse forward. They've levelled it up a lot recently, so it's much easier than it was, but still be ready.'

I nodded.

We continued down the long straight that ran directly away from the grandstands, past the third, the first of the open ditches, and then on towards the sixth, Becher's Brook, perhaps the most famous fence in all of horse racing.

'It's named after Captain Becher,' Freddie said as we stood next to the mighty obstacle. 'His horse fell here during the first ever Grand National in 1839, and he ended up in the brook that then ran along the far side.'

I noticed that the fence was set slightly at an angle, and I remarked on it to Freddie.

'That's why some horses tend to swing out slightly to the right beforehand, so that they can then jump it at an angle to the left but watch out that they don't obscure your horse's view of the fence.'

We moved round to the landing side, from where the fence looked much taller than its official height of four feet and ten inches.

'There's a significant drop here,' Freddie said. 'Mind you, not as much as it used to be. But it's still there, and more on the inside than on the outer, so stay a little wider if you can. You won't lose much ground.'

I swallowed hard and nodded again.

That's if I get this far.

Then we walked on to the Foinavon Fence, named after the 1967 winner.

Foinavon was the only horse to avoid a massive pile-up on the second circuit, when two loose horses at the front of the field turned sideways, running along the take-off side of the fence rather than jumping it. The remaining runners piled into them, causing some of the jockeys to be thrown over the fence without their horses.

All of them were forced to stop, all except Foinavon, who was so far behind at the time that he was able to simply gallop round the outside of the mayhem, jump the fence unhindered, and continue on to win the race unchallenged.

Next up was the Canal Turn, where the racecourse made a ninety-degree turn to the left, close to the Leeds and Liverpool Canal that gives the fence its name.

'You need to jump this at an angle,' Freddie said. 'Otherwise, you'll lose too much ground. Swing to the right on the approach to the fence and then cut across it, but be careful not to get too close to the inside corner, or you might get badly squeezed by others cutting across you.'

'OK.'

Having made the turn, we were now on our way back towards the grandstands – just visible in the distance but still almost a mile away.

Next there was a line of four fences, the first called Valentine's Brook – named after a horse called Valentine that was reputed to have somehow jumped the fence with its hindlegs first during the Grand National of 1840.

The third of the four was another open ditch, and then the fourth had a ditch on its landing side.

'If you're still in contention after you've jumped this for the second time, then you're in with a great chance. Only two plain fences to go. But your horse will be tiring by now so don't ask him for any more mighty leaps, just a couple of steady jumps.

'And then you have to negotiate the long run-in. You still have more than a quarter of a mile to go after the last – and history shows us that anything can happen. In his first National, Red Rum was fifteen lengths behind at the last fence, but he still won it.'

We walked on, back across the Melling Road, where Fibresand is spread over the tarmac on race days to allow the horses to gallop over it, and on towards the other most famous of Aintree fences – the Chair.

As we approached, I could understand why one of the girls yesterday had nearly peed her pants with fear. The fence looked huge, its five-foot-two-inch height somehow amplified by its narrowness. With a five-foot-wide open ditch in front, it was a formidable challenge.

'You only jump this once,' Freddie said. 'Kick hard into it. Don't hesitate. Chuck your heart over and catch it on the other side.'

It wasn't only my heart that I was worried about.

It was the rest of me as well.

* * *

It was too much to expect that Friday would be as good for me as Thursday, and it wasn't, but it was still pretty good nevertheless, although it didn't start too well.

My mount in the first race, the three-mile chase, finished a poor seventh of the eight starters – and it would have been eighth if one of the others hadn't fallen at the last fence.

But on a slightly brighter note, Freddie's other runner in the race won in a close finish under another jockey, the horse having a much higher official rating than the one I'd ridden.

It's strange how your expectations can change so rapidly.

Only three days ago I'd been ecstatic at having a ride of any sort in this race – even if it had been on a donkey – but now part of me felt slightly aggrieved that, as the current acting stable number one, I hadn't been switched onto the higher-rated horse.

But I told myself that I really shouldn't complain. I had all of Adrian's other declared horses to ride.

There were nineteen runners in the second race, a Class 1 handicap hurdle over two and a half miles, and I was on the top weight, a highly rated animal that had won on its last outing at Kempton three weeks previously. Hence, this time the weight differential was not in my favour. While my horse was struggling under twelve stone, the eventual winner was carrying sixteen pounds less, and it beat me into second place by two lengths.

After another quick change, I was out again for the third race, this time a highly competitive two-mile novice hurdle.

A horse is defined as a *novice* if it hasn't won a race of the type – hurdle or steeplechase – before the start of the current jump season.

As the jump season now runs from the beginning of May until the end of April – and we were now only three weeks from that end – some horses that were still officially defined as 'novices' could in fact be very experienced. Indeed, the one I was riding today was running in its eighth novice hurdle race of the season, and he had won three of them.

However, he didn't notch up his fourth win, not on this occasion.

He made a bad mistake at the fifth hurdle, and I did well just to stay on him. But it caused him to drop to last of the eight runners, and he was always thereafter trying to catch up. He was disputing third place as we approached the last, but he weakened during the long run-in and finished fifth.

'Never mind,' Freddie said when he met us in the unsaddling area for those that didn't finish in the first four. 'That'll be his season over now. I had thought of running him in the Novices' Final at Sandown on the last day, but he clearly needs a rest. It's been a long, hard season for him, but he'll be back in the autumn after his summer holidays, won't you, my boy.' He patted the horse fondly on its neck. 'Now, Imogen, don't forget to weigh in – there's prize money for fifth in this race.'

Freddie didn't have a runner in the fourth race, so I sat alone in the changing room preparing myself mentally for the fifth, the Topham Handicap Steeple Chase, raced over two miles and five furlongs of the Grand National course. It would be my first experience of riding over the big fences, and it would have been wrong to say that I wasn't nervous.

There were twenty-four runners, and the twenty-four jockeys were crammed into the stewards' room for a briefing before the race.

'Have you all read the letter sent to jockeys about horse welfare, and the need to pull up if you're not in contention?' asked the briefing official.

We all nodded.

'Good. Remember to take your time, especially at the start. Don't go too fast too soon. In this race you jump two plain fences before the Chair, which is the third. The Chair is the narrowest fence on the racecourse, so make sure you spread out over the whole width to give your horse a good view. The one after the Chair is the water jump, which is right in front of the stands, so it gets the greatest scrutiny.

'Then you have a complete circuit ahead of you, but you don't jump the Chair or the water again. You bypass them to the finish. Finally, may I remind you to have respect for the rules concerning the use of the whip. It is a measure of your professionalism, and very important to the sport on its biggest public stage. Are there any questions?'

No one had any questions.

'Right, then,' said the official. 'Briefing over. Good luck, everyone, and come home safely.'

The briefing hadn't exactly filled me with confidence. I'm sure *Good luck, everyone, and come home safely* had been said to First World War soldiers just before they went over the top at the Battle of the Somme.

I joined Freddie and the owner in the crowded parade ring.

'I'm not expecting too much,' he said. 'Try and keep with them as long as possible, and enjoy yourself.'

Enjoy myself! Was he crazy?

But then I thought about it for a moment. I didn't have to do this job. I could have been home in Ireland, working in a factory, as a teacher, or on the buses. I was only here because I wanted to be – so I *would* go out and enjoy myself.

With this positive frame of mind, I took my horse out onto the track and cantered him down to the start.

The roll call was taken, girths tightened, and then we were off.

The Topham Steeple Chase commemorates the Topham family who ran the Grand National from the 1840s until 1973, and in particular Mrs Mirabel Topham, the charismatic former Gaiety Girl who, as racecourse chairman, initiated this race in 1949.

All twenty-six runners popped over the first two fences without mishap, and then it was the Chair.

What had Freddie said?

Kick hard into it. Don't hesitate. Chuck your heart over and catch it on the other side.

I kicked hard while some of those around me seemed to be hesitating, and I sailed over without any problems, catching my heart in the process.

I laughed out loud. What had I been worried about?

Next was the water jump, and then it was the run of six fences down to Becher's Brook.

Maybe Freddie hadn't been expecting much, but we were still well placed, and up with the leading group of eight as I steered my mount slightly wider at Becher's, to avoid the worst of the drop.

I also stayed wide at the Canal Turn to avoid getting squeezed on the inside, was running fourth at Valentine's, and had moved up to third as we crossed the Melling Road, with only two plain fences remaining.

I laughed again – I *was* enjoying myself, hugely – and I think my happiness transmitted itself to my horse. He seemed to be enjoying it too.

We were still in third as we jumped the last fence, but I could see that both of the pair in front were tiring, one of them not even keeping a straight course as it made its way towards 'the elbow', that point where the temporary rail directs you past the outside of the Chair.

But my horse was full of running, and he fairly ate up the ground, sweeping past both the others in the final hundred yards to win by two lengths.

I couldn't stop laughing.

Maybe it's the unexpected victories that we treasure the most.

Freddie was beside himself with joy, and he even came out onto the course to meet us.

'Wonderful, wonderful,' he said, grinning like the Cheshire Cat.

Another on-track TV interview followed, and then Freddie walked alongside as the stable lad led the horse into the unsaddling enclosure and to the space reserved for the winner.

Four wins for me, five for Freddie. And still another whole day to go.

We'd be the talk of the town.

And indeed, we were, but not for that reason.

Chapter 19

MY FIFTH AND LAST RIDE on Friday afternoon was in the final race of the day, a conditional jockeys' and amateur riders' handicap hurdle over two miles, in which I was riding the betting favourite, with high hopes of yet another victory.

For a change, I was one of the most experienced riders, with most of the others claiming seven or five pounds, as opposed to my three.

But, as things turned out, my experience didn't count for anything.

With nineteen runners in the race, we were all tightly bunched together as we jumped the third flight of hurdles, the one that would be the last on the next circuit. But the horse right in front of me clipped the top with its front legs and crumpled down to the turf. I did my best to avoid the bodies on the floor, but we had nowhere to go.

Being 'brought down' is the worst outcome for any horse and rider, not least because it is always so sudden and unexpected. Often, it's not good for the horse that falls first either, with half a ton of following horseflesh crashing into it. But, on this occasion, thankfully, both horses and both jockeys were uninjured – the animals jumping up and galloping away rider-less, while the humans were quickly attended to by the chasing medics.

'You OK?' asked a racecourse doctor, crouching down beside me.

'I'm fine,' I said, spitting out a clump of grass. 'Just fed up.'

'No pain anywhere? Any blurred vision?'

'Neither,' I said. I stood up.

'Report to the jockeys' medical room,' the doc said, and he returned to his vehicle, while I picked up my whip, ducked under the white running rail, and started the long trudge back to the weighing room.

It was not quite the end of the day I had been hoping for.

Freddie was waiting for me.

'You all right?' he asked.

'Perfectly. How's the horse?'

'A bit shaken up, but he'll be OK.'

'Good.'

'I gave your saddle to the valet. Ready to leave in ten minutes? I'll wait in the car.'

I went into the medical room and was cleared by the senior racecourse doctor, the same one I'd seen the previous morning. Then I quickly showered and changed, before going out to join Freddie in the car.

'That was a shame,' he said. 'But I have a feeling that tomorrow will be a day to remember.'

It certainly was that.

But it wasn't anything to do with the horses.

* * *

Friday afternoon rush-hour traffic, combined with those leaving the racecourse, meant that the journey back to Knowsley was slow and tedious.

As we turned off the motorway, Freddie's phone rang. He answered it on his hands-free system.

'Is that Freddie Swinton?' said a male voice through the car's speakers. 'My name is Gordon Woods. I'm a journalist with the *Daily News*.'

The *Daily News* was a red-top tabloid, well known for its celebrity culture.

'Yes, I'm Freddie. How can I help you?'

'We're running an article about the meteoric rise of Imogen Duffy in our Grand National special edition tomorrow, and we would love to include a quote or two from you, as her employer. She's had remarkable success over the first two days of the Aintree meeting. What do you put that down to?'

Freddie smiled across at me and put a finger to his lips.

'Good horses, strong teamwork and dedication,' he said. 'Imogen and I work well together, along with the rest of my staff at home in Lambourn. We're all striving for the same outcome – winning races.'

'I believe it was you who recently brought her over from Ireland, to ride for your stable. How would you describe your partnership?' he asked.

'Fruitful. These last two days have proved what a good decision it was of mine. I suspect there are other trainers who now wish they had been as quick off the mark in securing her services.'

'And would you describe your working relationship as close?'

'Yes, I would. Very close, and I hope it brings us even greater success in the Grand National tomorrow.'

'Thank you, Freddie. That will do nicely.'

Gordon Woods hung up.

'There you are,' Freddie said, turning to me. 'I told you that you're the celebrity now.'

*   *   *

Our pre-Grand-National dinner that night turned out to be a less impressive affair than I had been expecting.

Adrian and Mandy Shaw had already confirmed they weren't coming, and Susie Swinton and Freddie Junior had been held up for hours by a multi-car accident on the M1 north of London. Susie rang to say that they had decided to turn round and go back home. Perhaps they'd come up in the morning – or maybe they wouldn't bother.

Nevertheless, the cook arrived at seven o'clock, as requested, and produced a feast of caviar blini canapés followed by lobster thermidor, king crab squid ink ravioli, marinara sauce and a parmesan foam, with individual coconut crème brûlées for dessert. The fact that only Freddie and I were there to eat it didn't appear to dampen her enthusiasm.

Freddie opened a bottle of Chablis to help wash it all down, and we sat at the kitchen table eating like royalty, toasting another day of success on the track.

The cook washed the dishes before she left, and the leftover food went into the fridge. Then it was time for me to go up to bed.

'I'm leaving here again at seven,' Freddie said. 'To go and watch the horses have a canter. You can come with me if you want, or you can stay here in bed.'

'No, I'll come with you.'

'But we don't need to walk the course again, so we'll probably come back here for breakfast afterwards, and to change. Night, night, Imogen. Sleep well.'

'Thanks,' I said. I yawned. 'I think I will sleep well, although my nerves are jangling a bit for the National tomorrow.'

He laughed, but there was no goodnight peck on the cheek this time, for which I think I was grateful.

*   *   *

I was woken by a loud banging on my bedroom door, in stark contrast to the gentle knock of yesterday.

'You're not going to fucking believe this.'

Freddie was shouting loudly on the landing outside.

I opened the door a fraction.

'What is it?'

He shoved a newspaper through the gap; it was today's *Daily News*. The headline was in bold black, inch-high letters running right down the whole front page: IS TOP GRAND NATIONAL TRAINER SCREWING HIS JOCKEY, WHO IS HALF HIS AGE?

I stared at it. A cold chill ran down my spine, and I had a sick feeling in the pit of my stomach.

'But that's a lie.'

'Of course it's a bloody lie,' Freddie said. 'But look at this.'

He took back the paper and opened it. On pages two and three were spread a series of three large colour pictures. The first was the two of us walking together down the front path of the house – obviously taken by the paparazzi photographer yesterday morning – and, due to the angle from which it was shot, it looked like we were holding hands.

But it was the other two that were more worrying.

Someone had snapped the very moment when Freddie had hugged me in the unsaddling enclosure after Sans Chichi's win in the Red Rum handicap on Thursday afternoon. Out of context, it could very easily be taken as being a loving embrace.

And even more alarming was the third one.

It was a photograph of Freddie leaning down and giving me the goodnight kiss on the cheek on Thursday night. It had been taken through the kitchen window of this house by someone who must have been standing in the back garden, in the dark, spying on us.

'Bloody Gordon Woods,' Freddie said. 'I'll have his guts for garters. He's twisted my words. It says here that I was asked if our relationship was close and he quotes me as replying that it was very close, and that Imogen and I work well together as a couple. I'll damn well sue him.'

I remembered what the lawyer, Jim Wilson, had said about suing people for defamation – that you were unlikely to recover all your costs, even if you won, and how you had to think very carefully about the financial consequences if you lost.

I started to read the article printed round the pictures.

It was unpleasant reading, but like the front-page headline, it was all couched as questions. *Is Grand National trainer screwing his jockey? Are they having an affair? Are they a romantic item?*

Whereas the article gave the very strong impression that the answer to all the questions was 'yes', it didn't actually say so in black and white. And the newspaper's lawyers must have pored over it for hours, checking and rechecking, before it was printed, to ensure it didn't make them liable to legal action – none that they would go on to lose anyway.

I read on in trepidation, and it was the fourth paragraph that particularly caught my eye.

An unnamed fellow Irish jockey told me that he wasn't really surprised. 'Imogen Duffy has developed a bit of a reputation for her sexual exploits,' he said. 'It's not only the horses that she rides. There's a story going round the racecourse changing rooms that she slept with three male jockeys on the same night last month, at the Cheltenham Festival.'

Liam Carson.

It was all bloody Liam's fault.

And I'd bet a pound to a penny that he had been the one in the garden taking photos through the kitchen window.

In fact, I was sure he would have organised the whole damn thing before taking it to the *Daily News*. We had simply fallen into his trap like lambs to the slaughter. And now he'd be laughing his bloody head off.

'So, what do we do?' Freddie asked.

'Ignore it,' I replied. 'Be like the British royals – never complain, never explain.'

'But it's libellous,' Freddie said. 'If I don't sue, everyone will believe it.'

'Everyone will believe it anyway, whatever you do. The paper's fancy lawyers will have made sure it was classified as "fair comment" or "honest opinion" before it was published, so suing will simply be a waste of an awful lot of your money. And it would also mean that the story stays in everyone's consciousness for months, if not for years, whereas, if you do nothing, they will have all forgotten about it by this time next week.'

'You sound very calm about it all. Aren't you angry?'

'Very,' I said. 'I'm bloody furious. But I was given some very good advice by an Irish defamation lawyer, and I think he's right – ignore it, and move on.'

'But this could destroy my reputation.'

'I doubt it. It's not as if they've accused you of doing anything illegal.'

In fact, it might very well *enhance* his reputation. It had never done any harm to a man's prestige for people to believe he was having sex with a much younger woman. Quite the opposite. It had certainly never caused Al Pacino or George Clooney any problems, nor Rod Stewart or Paul McCartney.

But for the woman involved, it could be a different matter altogether. She was often cast as the villain of the piece – the entrapping filthy slut. Hence, in a male-dominated sport, my own reputation might be in tatters, and my job too, if Freddie reckoned that getting rid of me as his jockey was the best way to stop the tongues wagging.

'How did you get this paper?' I asked. 'Did you go out for it?'

'No. Someone rang the doorbell. When I opened it, no one was there, but this was lying on the doorstep.'

Liam, I thought again. It was just the sort of cruel thing he would do.

'What now?' Freddie asked.

'Let's go and see the horses.'

* * *

There was no photographer lurking in the bushes outside the house, but there were quite a few at the racecourse when we arrived, snapping away at the horses that would later be running in the Grand National, and there was also a journalist with them from the *Racing Post* newspaper. I recognised him.

As Freddie and I walked from the car park to the exercise area, the journalist came rushing over towards us, with one of the photographers in tow.

'Ignore them,' I said, and I took Freddie's arm.

'What on earth are you doing!' he hissed, snatching his arm away.

'If they think there's no story, they'll leave us alone.'

'But you'd be making the story.'

'No, I wouldn't,' I said. 'The story will only be if we deny it.'

'But I do deny it.'

'I know, but trust me,' I said, taking his arm again. 'Say nothing, and they'll soon go back to the horses.'

'Morning, Mr Swinton,' said the journalist, pen and wire-bound notebook at the ready. 'Have you any comment to make?'

The camera shutter was clicking constantly, but still I didn't let go of Freddie's arm.

'About what?' he said.

'The front page of the *Daily News*?'

I could feel the tension increase in Freddie.

'Say nothing about us,' I repeated quietly to him. 'Talk about your horses.'

'I'm only here to see my horses exercise,' he said strongly, 'not to comment on tittle-tattle.'

'And how about you, Imogen? What have you got to say?'

I didn't reply at all. I simply turned away.

'Is it true?' he asked. 'Are you a couple? Did you sleep together last night?'

Thankfully, Jason arrived at that point, and Freddie's three runners for the day also appeared from the racecourse stables, including Hightown Harry, who looked magnificent in the morning light. Freddie turned away from the journalist and spoke quietly to Jason, their heads bowed.

With no answers forthcoming to his questions, the hack soon lost interest and returned to studying the equine stars, taking his snapper with him.

'There,' I said, letting go of Freddie's arm. 'All over, and tomorrow's newspaper headlines will be about the winner of the Grand National, not about us.'

Not unless we are also the winners, I thought, *and I wouldn't mind that.*

But it wasn't quite that simple.

Chapter 20

S USIE SWINTON CALLED WHILE FREDDIE and I were in his car on the way back to the house for breakfast, after watching the horses exercise.

'There's a bloody reporter from the *Daily News* outside my front door,' she shouted down the line. 'He's asking me for my reaction to their front-page story.'

'It's not true,' Freddie said calmly.

'I don't believe you,' Susie went on shouting. 'Freddie Junior and I are definitely not coming today now. I have no intention of coming face to face with your latest damn floozy.'

She hung up without even saying goodbye.

I could tell that Freddie Senior was disappointed, and also that he was angry, very angry.

'I'll bloody get the bastard who did this.'

'It was Liam Carson.' I said it slowly. 'I'm so sorry. It's all my fault. He's trying to get at me, and you're the collateral damage.'

'How do you know it's him?'

'Because the article refers to a lie that he's been peddling about me sleeping with three male jockeys in one night at Cheltenham. That's not true either. He made it up to get me fired from my job with his father. I am quite certain that Liam was the unnamed

Irish jockey quoted. And the story is only going round the racecourse changing rooms because he keeps telling it.

'And I also believe it was him who took the photo of us through the kitchen window. He's been stalking and watching me all along. I reckon he set the whole thing up and then went to the paper, knowing they'd jump at it. Because his full-frontal attacks to physically harm me haven't worked, he's now trying to hurt me in other ways. The more success I have, the more determined he becomes to destroy me. He'll be hoping that you fire me as well.'

'But how could he take the photo? You told me he was riding at Plumpton.'

'He was, but only in the first race. That was at one thirty. He would have had plenty of time to get to Liverpool by the time that picture was taken. I bet he couldn't believe his luck when he saw you kiss me goodnight.'

We had a very subdued breakfast of coffee, with more marmaladed toast.

What was worrying me was that Freddie hadn't immediately said that he wouldn't fire me. But at least I'd be riding his horses today, as I was the declared jockey, and I wasn't ill or injured, but it was hardly an ideal preparation for the biggest race day of my life.

* * *

I couldn't say that arriving at Aintree on Grand National day was easy.

My own advice to Freddie, to simply ignore it and get on with things as if nothing had happened, was proving difficult to follow.

We agreed to arrive separately at the racecourse. Consequently, Freddie organised a taxi to collect me from the house.

Before that, I packed all my stuff into my suitcase, and left it in the hallway, ready to be collected after racing. But I had no real idea where I would be taking it. Would I be returning to Lambourn with Freddie in his car? Or taking the train south instead? Or even going west to Holyhead to catch the overnight ferry to Dublin?

The taxi dropped me at the designated drop-off point near the main racecourse entrance, and hence I had to bypass the large queue of racegoers waiting to go in through the turnstiles, in order to get to the designated jockeys' entrance.

After my TV interviews of the last couple of days, several people recognised me. Some of those wished me luck for today, while others told their friends, none too quietly, that I was the jockey who was mentioned on the front page of the *Daily News*.

One man even asked me outright if Freddie Swinton was any good in bed and, if he wasn't, then he was always available to take over. He thought he was being frightfully funny, and he laughed expansively, along with many of those around him.

I didn't join in.

Eventually, I reached the entrance and used my jockey ID card to go through.

The crowd was noticeably larger today than on the two previous days and I had to run the gauntlet through them as I made my way towards the weighing room, their comments clearly audible behind me.

'Oh, look, that's Imogen Duffy. She's the jockey who's sleeping with Freddie Swinton.'

'I know, and she's only half his age.'

'Do you think he only gave her those rides in exchange for sex?'

'It shouldn't be allowed.'

It was as much as I could do not to turn round and shout out to them that it wasn't true, but that would have made things worse.

Even the racecourse official outside the weighing-room door seemed to give me a strange look – or was that just my imagination?

'Hello, look out, here comes Lolita,' crowed one seasoned professional loudly as I walked in.

'Fuck off,' I said to him.

'Yes, and that's exactly what I hear you've been doing.'

He guffawed loudly.

I sought sanctuary in the female changing room, but I wasn't alone there either. There were three other girls in there, and I didn't get much solace from them.

When I complained to one of them quietly about the comments I had heard from the crowd, all she said was that I'd made my own bed, and now I had to lie in it.

'But it isn't true,' I said. 'It's a lie. It was made up by the newspaper to sell copies.'

She didn't believe me.

'It's been going on forever,' she said. 'Overly ambitious women sleeping with their male bosses to get an unfair advantage over the rest of us. You make me sick.'

I was taken aback by the intensity of her reply.

I knew that all jockeys are competitive, both male and female – I am too – but the rivalry is normally saved for when we are out racing on the track, rather than manifesting itself in the changing rooms.

I decided to say nothing more, for fear of provoking an even stronger response. But the episode had unsettled me, and I was still out of sorts when I went out to the parade ring for the first race, a three-mile handicap hurdle.

Freddie was already there along with the owner of the seven-year-old bay gelding that I was due to ride. I stood next to the owner, on the far side from Freddie, so that the parade-ring photographers couldn't get a snap of us standing together.

The gelding had won at the Cheltenham Festival on its last outing, ridden by Adrian, but after that win, the handicapper had raised his official rating by six points, so he was carrying more weight today against some of the same rivals in the twenty-one-runner race.

'The start is just before the last hurdle,' Freddie said, 'so after jumping that, you then have two complete circuits to go. He likes to be held up to make a late run, so settle him down towards the rear of the field for the first lap, and then make your way forward during the second. He stays on well. Got it?'

There was a distinct sharpness in his tone, which must be due to the stress that he would also be feeling.

'Yes,' I said.

The bell was rung, and Freddie gave me a leg-up onto the horse. I could almost feel the stares of those around watching as he touched me, all of them thinking not about a leg-up, more a leg-over.

The groom led the horse out onto the track, and I cantered him down to the start.

The starter called the roll call to ensure everyone had arrived.

'Duffy,' he called.

'Yes, sir,' I responded, holding up my hand.

211

'Duffy says yes to everyone,' one of the other jockeys called out, and most of the rest of them laughed at him. I blushed.

Thankfully, we were soon under way, and as instructed, I settled the gelding at the rear of the field as we negotiated the first bend in front of the grandstands. Here we remained for the next complete circuit.

Only as we were going down the back straight for the second time did I ask him to quicken. I pulled out slightly to give him, and me, a better view and only then did I see that two horses had gone on ahead rather more than I had realised.

I was now playing catch-up, big time.

I passed some of the other runners as we rounded the far turn. But I had no choice but to go outside of them, hence I was nowhere near the inside running rail, and I remembered what Freddie had said about how it cost you many lengths to go wide.

As I straightened up for the last three hurdles, plus the final run to the line, there were still four horses ahead of me, two of them quite a long way ahead.

As we jumped the second last, I was up into third, but I quickly realised that I wasn't going to overcome the leading two. I had given my horse too much to do and not enough time to do it. Try as he did, we were still two lengths adrift at the winning post, despite finishing much faster than both the first and the second.

For the first time ever, Freddie was cross with me – and he was really cross with me.

'Why on earth did you let them get away from you like that?' he demanded angrily as I dismounted. 'I told you to be towards the rear of the field, not right at the back of it, and you should have been watching more closely what was going on at the front. You were so late in reacting that you had to go very wide round the far turn. That alone probably cost you the race.'

And the owner was also far from happy, and his expression was one of annoyance rather than of disappointment. 'I told you, Freddie, that we should have had a proper jockey,' he said cuttingly. 'Not a damn claimer.'

I felt dreadful. They were right. We should have won the race, and it was because of my mistake that we hadn't.

If in doubt, blame the jockey, and they both clearly did.

'I'm sorry,' I mumbled, and then went up the steps to the weighing room to weigh in.

Could today get any worse for me?

The answer to that question was yes, it could get worse, much worse.

* * *

My next ride was in the third race, the Freebooter Handicap Steeplechase.

This time there were sixteen runners, and my horse was well handicapped with ten stone and eleven pounds on its back. And it was being quoted by the bookmakers as the third favourite, at odds of six-to-one.

I tried to put the memory of my previous ride out of my mind as I went down to the parade ring.

'Three miles and a furlong,' Freddie said. 'It starts down the far end of the home straight, and then you have two complete circuits to race. Nineteen fences in all. Tuck him in behind the leaders, so he doesn't run too freely early on. But keep your bloody eyes open this time, so that no one gets a jump on you.'

'Yes,' I said. 'I will.'

213

As I'd been told, I tucked him in behind the leaders at the start, running in fourth or fifth place as we jumped the three fences in the home straight and then swung left-handed away from the stands and down the back stretch.

We were still in the same position as we passed the crowd for the second time, and I was tight to the rail, taking the shortest route. But I misjudged the stride coming to the cross fence for the second time. I asked my mount for a big jump, but he decided to put in a short stride instead, by which time we were far too close.

He ploughed through the top of the birch and, although he miraculously didn't go down, he had lost much of his momentum, and at the very point when those around me were turning up the heat.

There was no way back.

I'm not convinced we would have won the race anyway, but my mistake had probably cost us a place. We trailed in sixth.

Freddie was not pleased with me again. I could tell from his demeanour, even though, this time, he said nothing. Nor did I. Nothing needed to be said. We both knew it had been my fault. I unsaddled the horse and walked miserably to the weighing room, weighed in, and went into the female changing room.

I looked up at the clock on the wall. It showed me it was a quarter to three. The Grand National was the fifth race on the card, due off at four o'clock. Just seventy-five minutes to go before the big one, and my heartbeat was already beginning to rise with excitement.

I decided to stay in here, away from the acid comments that were still being directed my way, either about the *Daily News* story or more recently about my riding ability.

But there was a knock on the door and an official was there, telling me that Freddie Swinton wanted to speak to me outside.

I went out.

I could tell immediately that Freddie was anxious, and he didn't really look at me, not in the eye anyway.

'Imogen,' he said. 'I'm sorry, but I've taken you off Hightown Harry.'

I stared up at him in disbelief.

'But how can you?' I asked. 'I was declared to ride him, and I'm not unwell or injured.'

'One of the other horses in the National has been judged to be lame by a vet, so he won't run. He was due to be ridden by Tom Grande, who's therefore now without a ride, and the rules of racing allow for a jockey to be switched onto another horse if his is a non-runner in the same race.'

'Oh.'

Tom Grande was second only to Adrian Shaw in the current champion jockeys' table.

'I wouldn't normally have done this to you, but the owner is insisting. He's been trying to win this race for years, and Hightown Harry is the best horse he's ever had. He watched your races earlier today, and he says that if you ride his horse instead of Tom Grande, and you don't win, he will send all his horses to another trainer. And there are ten of them in my stable.'

I felt like telling Freddie to get some bloody backbone and stand by me, and that he didn't need owners who dictated to him like that. But I could see that it would be pointless. Ten sets of training fees were a lot to lose, and I'd hardly covered myself in glory so far today, even if I had done on Thursday.

'Oh,' I said again.

'So can I please have back the Hightown Harry silks I gave you earlier.'

I went into the changing room, hardly feeling my feet on the ground. I took the yellow and blue checked silks off my peg and took them out to him.

'How do I get home?' I asked gloomily.

'What do you mean?'

'I mean, how do I get home tonight?'

'In my car, of course. What are you talking about?'

'I just feel ... abandoned.'

'Don't be so fucking stupid,' Freddie said. 'I'll see you after the race.'

He took the silks and walked away, while I went on standing there, looking out across the parade ring, not quite knowing how I really felt.

I hadn't been expecting to have a ride in the Grand National when I'd arrived here on Thursday morning, so why was I so bereft that it had now been snatched away from me? And did I still want Hightown Harry to win, for Freddie and the stable's sake, or did I want him to lose, to spite the owner?

The spite won.

I returned to the female changing room and hid myself away.

The change of jockey for Hightown Harry was announced over the racecourse public address system, and also on the television, so everyone now knew that I'd been jocked off, including my parents who would be watching at home. They had even asked some friends round to watch the race with them.

I was close to tears. I felt like I'd let them down.

* * *

The three other girl jockeys were all riding in the Grand National, and I found it hard watching them change into their silks and get ready for the race, so much so that I went and hid in the ladies loo.

None of them had said anything to me as they changed, but the one who had castigated me earlier had an 'it serves you right' smug smile on her face.

She was another one who I vehemently hoped didn't win the race.

Only after the 'Jockeys out' call had been made through the speakers, did I venture back into the changing room.

I changed out of my riding clothes into jeans and a sweater, then I sat on the bench watching the television.

I was frustrated. And I was also angry.

Yes, I was angry with the owner of Hightown Harry for demanding my removal from his horse, and with Freddie for not telling him where to go. But most of all, I was angry with Liam Carson.

I placed the fault for my poor performances in the first and third races squarely in his camp. Even though I'd tried very hard not to be, I *had* been distracted by the newspaper story, and its fallout.

The lewd comment at the start, about Duffy saying yes to everyone, had weighed heavily on me, and I had been thinking about it during the first race, rather than keeping my mind firmly on the matter in hand. Just a few moments of inattention had cost me the win, and for the same reason, I had been slow in spotting that my horse's stride wasn't right in the other race.

It was just my hard luck that Tom Grande's declared horse was now a non-runner, but even then I might have kept the ride on Hightown Harry if it hadn't been for those two earlier errors – and Liam was the direct cause of both.

'And they're off in the Grand National, the world's greatest steeplechase,' said the excited television race caller.

I didn't really want to watch it, but of course, I did, and my eyes were continually drawn towards the bright yellow and blue checked colours of Hightown Harry.

To increase horse welfare, the number of declared runners in the Grand National is now set at a maximum of thirty-four, and this year, with one non-starter, there were thirty-three making the cavalry charge towards the first of the thirty fences.

It was a far cry from way back in 1929, when twice that number went to post. Of the sixty-six starters that day, only ten completed the course, with eight of them refusing to jump the third fence, and five more doing the same at the Canal Turn. All in all, twenty-one horses refused to jump because of the congestion, one of them ridden by Keith Piggott, Lester's father.

None of the thirty-three runners today refused at the first fence, and none of them fell either.

Hightown Harry was up near the front, close to the inside rail, as the field jumped the line of fences down towards Becher's Brook for the first time.

Tom Grande is too far to the left, I thought.

That's where the drop at Becher's was at its greatest. But the horse cleared it with ease, while two others, further out, came to grief, depositing their jockeys on the turf before getting up and galloping away riderless. One of the jockeys, I noted with a smile, was the girl who had berated me.

I bet she wasn't feeling quite so smug now.

There were twenty-six runners still in the race, and closely bunched, as they jumped the Chair and the water, before setting out on their second circuit, with Hightown Harry still prominently placed in the leading half dozen.

Despite having raced for over two miles by this stage, the pace began to quicken and some of those in the rear were beginning to struggle. The old Grand National adage about 'hacking round the first circuit and racing round the second' was clearly more than an old wives' tale.

Becher's second time round claimed no victims, even though Hightown Harry still jumped it on the inside, again coping easily with the larger drop.

Horses at the rear of the field, those clearly out of contention, were now being pulled up by their jockeys, heeding the warnings they had been given in the pre-race briefing about horse welfare and the need not to flog a dead horse.

As the race came towards its climax, the excitement of the crowd began to boil, and I stood up and took a step closer to the television to get a better view of the screen.

Hightown Harry was the first horse past the winning post, but he wasn't the winner, because by this stage he was riderless.

Just as Freddie had told me not to, Tom Grande had ridden too close to the inside corner of the Canal Turn the second time, and he had been squeezed badly against the wing of the fence by another horse cutting right across him, which resulted in Tom being unseated.

Being unseated is simply a more polite way of saying that the jockey fell off, very different to the situation when the horse itself falls and the jockey goes down with it.

I could imagine Hightown Harry's owner being absolutely furious, especially if Freddie told him that I wouldn't have done that.

I was now the one with the 'it serves you right' smug smile on her face.

Chapter 21

THE JOURNEY HOME WAS A sombre affair, mostly conducted in silence but with much unsaid.

Freddie and I left the racecourse before the last race to avoid the worst of the traffic, stopping briefly at the house in Knowsley to collect our stuff, including the unopened case of Bollinger.

It had been a terrible day for both of us, despite me being crowned leading rider of the meeting with four wins plus two seconds, while Freddie picked up the award for leading trainer with five wins.

They were scant consolation for the dashing of both our high hopes for success in the main event, although for differing reasons.

As we neared home, Freddie finally talked to me, but he didn't mention anything about our day at Aintree.

'I decided not to declare My Wife's Mink to run at Stratford tomorrow because we've had no rain, so you can have the day off,' he said. 'But you're declared to ride at Windsor on Monday. I won't be going. Shall I tell Jason you'll go in the horsebox?'

'No,' I said. 'I'll take the car. It's time I became more independent.'

'OK.'

He drove on a few more miles.

'Then you have your court case in Thurles on Thursday?'

'Yes.'

'And then your three-day suspension the following week?'

'Yes.'

'Why don't you go home to Ireland for a while? Stay out of the limelight for a bit. Give this bloody *Daily News* thing a chance to blow over. I'll tell James not to declare you to ride anything after Monday, and I'll tell the stable staff that you won't be riding out at all this week.'

Was he also telling me that my job was over? That I'd been fired?

'But I will be coming back again?' I asked, somewhat forlornly.

'Of course,' he said, but to my ears, he didn't sound too convincing. 'Ask the judge to issue a restraining order against Carson, to keep him away, so he can't keep pestering you.'

It was not pestering that I was afraid of. More like dying.

'I don't suppose the judge will order anything,' I said. 'It's not a very serious charge. And would an Irish restraining order have any effect in England anyway?'

'You can but try.'

'OK. I'll go home on Monday evening, after racing. There's a nine o'clock flight from Heathrow. I feel I need to get away from here for a while anyway.'

Hence, we agreed that I would ride as declared at Windsor on Monday afternoon, then go home to Ireland that night, ready for the court case in Thurles on Thursday. I would then remain in Ireland until after my suspension was served the following week.

And for the next two nights, I would stay in my cottage, with the new security chain firmly attached, rather than in Freddie's house.

*   *   *

Sunday wasn't a much better day than Saturday.

I spent most of the day inside, hiding from the world, but I did venture out for an hour or two in the morning, mostly to reacquaint myself with the car, in preparation for Monday.

I drove to Hungerford, the local town about ten miles away, to have a coffee and also to buy some milk and a microwavable Thai curry from Tesco for tonight's supper.

I parked in the supermarket car park and walked through to the high street to find a café.

There were about a dozen people already sitting in there, most of them in a large group of middle-aged women, and the Grand National was very much their main topic of conversation. The winner was trained locally, and there was even talk that he might be paraded through the town that very afternoon.

I paid for and collected my coffee from the counter, and then sat at a table in the far corner from them, keeping my head down, hoping that no one would recognise me.

'I had a fiver each way on him,' said one of the group. 'And at twenty-eight-to-one. Made me a hundred and seventy quid.'

'You're buying all the coffees then?' quipped another.

'No bloody chance. It's all gone on my electric.'

The chatter between them went on for a bit about how disgraceful it was that energy bills had gone up so much. But it soon returned to the racing.

'Don't you think it's a rum do about Freddie Swinton sleeping with that young girl jockey,' one of the women said. 'And it says in the paper today that he removed her from his horse in the National yesterday because their secret affair became public. They reckon he'll now dump her, both from his bed and from his stable, to try and kill the story. Talk about getting caught with his pants down and his willy hanging out.'

The rest of them laughed. I didn't.

I quickly finished my coffee and left.

But there was no respite for me in the supermarket.

I collected the milk and the Thai curry from the shelves and took them to the self-service checkout. Alongside the tills were racks of newspapers. The *News on Sunday*, sister paper to the *Daily News*, had a bold headline: SWINTON TAKES REVENGE.

I didn't want to read the story beneath, but of course, I did.

A reliable source has disclosed to the News on Sunday *that the racehorse trainer Freddie Swinton replaced Imogen Duffy as jockey on Hightown Harry in the Grand National in revenge for her revealing their affair to the media. The source, who wishes to remain anonymous, claims to have overheard a heated exchange between the two outside the weighing room at Aintree shortly before it was announced that Tom Grande was to ride the horse in Duffy's place.*

I dropped the milk and curry onto the supermarket floor and rushed outside in tears.

A reliable anonymous source!

It had to be bloody Liam Carson again.

224

I sat in the car sobbing, but also shaking with fear, and with anger.

After a while, I recovered enough to go back inside the shop to buy the milk and meal, then I set off towards Lambourn in the car.

After crossing under the motorway, I missed the first turning to Lambourn and soon found myself in the village of Great Shefford. Here I took the turning to the left, signposted LAMBOURN 4 MILES.

I thought that I recognised the road and realised it was the way Freddie had driven me home from Newbury Police Station, and sure enough, I soon passed a sign saying: EASTBURY – PLEASE DRIVE CAREFULLY.

I did drive carefully, in fact I went very slowly, because I was looking for something – Boxtree Stables.

They were on the left-hand side about halfway through the village, behind a tall flint and red-brick wall. I pulled into the gravel driveway and stopped next to the sign that read: BOXTREE STABLES – SOPHIE BURNETT, RACEHORSE TRAINER.

I didn't continue in the car up the driveway. I had no real desire to do so, and I certainly didn't want to see Liam. But I stepped out of the car and took half a dozen strides towards the gates in the wall, which were wide open. Through them, I could see a block of brick-built stables, and a line of dormer windows in the tile roof above them – probably the flat where Liam lived.

Somehow it helped me to have a physical location at which to direct my bile.

Another car came along the road towards me and indicated to turn right, into the driveway, just where I was blocking the way. The driver hooted at me.

I hurried to my car, waved a hand of apology towards the female driver, quickly climbed in, backed out onto the road, and drove away.

The rest of the day didn't improve much either.

I checked the declarations for my one race at Windsor, a three-mile handicap chase. It was designated as a Class 4 contest, which meant that it was limited to horses that had an official rating under a certain value. Hence, all the runners would have substantially lower ratings than those I had ridden against at Aintree in the Class 1s, and the much smaller purse on offer reflected that difference in class. Not that it meant that the race itself would be any the less competitive.

Thankfully, Liam Carson was not scheduled to ride in the same race, but I was dismayed to see that he had been declared in two of the others, the first and the fourth on the seven-race card, which meant he would be at the racecourse most of the afternoon.

I decided that I would arrive during the first race, and depart during the fourth, so that he wouldn't see me come or go. The rest of the time I would stay hidden away in the female changing room, only appearing from there to ride in the third race.

Next I tried to book my flight home for Monday evening, but there was a big Republic of Ireland versus England football match taking place in Dublin on Tuesday night, and all flights from Heathrow were already full. The earliest I could get one was Wednesday morning, and so I booked myself a seat with Aer Lingus, optimistically buying myself a return ticket for the following week.

I just hoped that Liam wouldn't be on the same aeroplane.

Finally, I did some washing, ate my curry, and went to bed early, having first checked that all the doors and windows were firmly locked.

* * *

On Monday morning, I woke early, as my body clock always dictated, but I had nowhere to go. I wasn't expected to ride out, and Freddie Swinton had made it quite clear I should stay away from his yard, something that suited me just fine under the present circumstances.

But somehow I felt trapped in this cottage, almost imprisoned, and I longed to be outside. So I went for a run, going east this time so that I wouldn't be seen by the other lads riding up the all-weather gallop, or even by Freddie standing at the top of the hill with his high-power binoculars.

It felt good to be out in the spring air, pounding across the grass or alongside fields of fast-growing wheat and barley shooting up from the earth in the annual miracle of plant growth.

I was out for well over an hour, before returning home for a hot shower and a welcome breakfast of fresh scrambled eggs on buttered toast.

* * *

I drove myself to Windsor races, but my luck didn't change.

As planned, I waited in the jockeys' car park until the first race started before quickly making my way to the weighing room and the relative safety of the female dressing room.

There were two other lady-jockeys riding at the meeting so I felt it was unlikely that Liam would burst in, as he had done at Newton Abbot. Neither of the two were the same ones who had been riding at Aintree, but nevertheless, I kept myself to myself.

There were ten runners in the third race, the three-mile chase, and my mount was carrying ten stone and twelve pounds. I weighed out in good time, gave my saddle to Jason, and returned swiftly to the changing room to wait.

'Jockeys out,' came the call, and I stood up, collected my skullcap and whip, and went out.

Liam was standing by the weighing-room door, blocking my way to the parade ring.

'I told you you'd regret it,' he said menacingly.

'Get out of my bloody way,' I said.

'And there's more to come.' He laughed, a nasty brutal cackle.

He finally stepped aside and let me through, but the encounter had hardly left me in the right state of mind to ride three miles over nineteen fences.

'You OK?' Jason asked when I joined him.

'Fine,' I said automatically.

'Did Freddie give you any instructions?' he asked.

'No.'

'Right. Well, in that case, just do your best. He jumps well but he's a bit one-paced, least he has been in his previous races.'

And one-paced he turned out to be again today, and a pretty slow one pace at that.

We finished a bad fourth of the eight finishers. Not great, but not a total disgrace, and at least the horse had jumped well enough, and I hadn't fallen off.

'Not too bad,' Jason said in the unsaddling enclosure. 'Don't forget to weigh in.'

'Jason,' I said. 'Will you please come in with me, while I weigh in?'

He looked at me as if it were a strange request, which it was. But I felt I might be in need of some protection.

And there's more to come.

What had Liam meant by that? More newspaper lies, or more physical attacks?

'OK,' Jason said, 'but quickly. I have to look after the horse.'

He told the stable lad to take the horse out, and to wait for him by the testing barn, in case it was selected for dope testing. In major races the first four home are routinely tested, but for a Class 4 race, it is usually only the winner, sometimes together with the second, occasionally the third, or any other horse selected at random by the stewards.

Jason came with me into the weighing room, but there was no sign of Liam, and I felt rather foolish. I weighed in, and thanked Jason, who then rushed off, shaking his head in bewilderment.

I quickly changed out of my racing clothes and then drove home without incident, parking the car alongside the cottage.

I knew that Liam couldn't be watching me as I went in, because I had left Windsor as the runners for fourth race were going down to the start, so he had to be a good way behind me, even if he'd left immediately after the race and driven back faster than I did.

But I felt far from safe.

What if he tried to prevent me from getting to the District Court at Thurles on Thursday? So that I couldn't give evidence against him. And I was now more determined than ever to do that.

Against my better judgement, I decided that I would stay in my cottage tonight, but tomorrow, I would pack a small hand-luggage bag and spend Tuesday night in a budget hotel near Heathrow, ready for my early flight to Dublin on Wednesday.

I did fleetingly think about asking Stacey if she could arrange my travel to the airport – perhaps asking Spencer to drive me – but the thought of going into the stable office filled me with unease.

I could just imagine what she and the others would be thinking, and then saying about me after I'd gone. I decided I would organise my own taxi to Hungerford railway station, and then I'd catch a train from there to Heathrow.

I had a bowl of corn flakes for my supper, then I tried to watch some television before turning in for another early night, once again propping a chair under my bedroom door handle.

But I couldn't get to sleep. I had too many things swirling around in my head, not least the gripping fear that I may have ridden my last horse for Freddie Swinton. It felt a bit like my life was over.

* * *

I checked myself into a hotel on the northern perimeter of Heathrow airport, and so paranoid had I become that I used a different name to my real one, and paid in advance with cash, which I had withdrawn from an ATM at Hungerford Station. The male receptionist didn't question it or ask me for any identification.

I went down to the hotel bar, sat in a quiet corner, and ordered fish and chips, with a large glass of red wine to help it down, all paid for again with cash.

My father had agreed to collect me from Thurles, and I was really looking forward to seeing my parents again. Amazingly, I had only been away for three and a half weeks, but it felt like so much longer.

After dinner, I lay on my hotel bed watching television, but I purposefully avoided any news programmes. I didn't want to know what else was happening in the world.

I woke early, caught the hotel courtesy bus to the airport terminal, and used one of the automated check-in machines to print my boarding card, before going through security to the departure lounge.

I bought myself a coffee and a croissant.

I was looking forward to some of my mother's home cooking.

The flight was called, and I made my way to the gate, presenting my passport and boarding card to the woman at the desk.

She turned and gave my passport to one of two men standing beside her.

'Are you Imogen Duffy?' the man asked.

'I am,' I replied.

'My name is Detective Constable Madan of Thames Valley Police.' He took a step towards me and placed his hand on my arm. 'I arrest you on suspicion of the murder of Liam Carson.'

PART 2

SID HALLEY

Eight months later

Chapter 22

'SID, CAN YOU *PLEASE* COME and help me with this bloody Christmas tree?'

It was mid-morning and my gorgeous wife, Marina, was struggling through the front door, dragging an enormous Norway spruce that wouldn't have looked out of place in Trafalgar Square.

'Why on earth did you buy one so big?' I asked.

'Because you told me we needed a big tree, or it would be totally lost in this hallway. The man at the Christmas-tree farm said this one would be perfect. He's just delivered it.'

I bet he thought it would be perfect, and the price would have been perfect too, at least for him.

I helped her carry it into the centre of the room, where a red-painted metal stand was waiting, its circular hole ready to take the trunk. And, to my eyes, the hole didn't look anywhere near big enough for this monstrosity.

'I didn't mean you to get one quite as big as this,' I said.

'Well, you should have come with me, then,' she said sardonically, 'instead of playing bloody games on your computer.'

That was a bit harsh, I thought. I'd been completing some share transactions online, selling various stocks and buying others, looking for a profit, trying to earn us a living, and enough to pay Saskia's horrendous school fees, which were also attracting extra taxation.

Saskia was our daughter, now aged sixteen. She was our only child, and consequently hugely spoilt. We had tried for more children, vigorously and often, but nature in that respect had not been kind to us. Hence, we made the most of what we had, and she brought us great joy as we observed her quickly changing from an adolescent girl into a fully-fledged young woman.

Together, and with difficulty, Marina and I managed to lift the arboreal giant into a vertical position and, much to my surprise, the trunk fitted neatly into the hole in the stand, with hardly a millimetre to spare.

'There,' Marina said. 'Perfect fit. That was the one thing I did measure.'

Why had I ever doubted her?

No one could ever accuse my wife of being stupid. With a PhD in biological chemistry, a background of cancer research, plus a sizable canon of scientific papers published in the most esteemed global medical journals, she was now much sought after as a guest lecturer by many of the world's top universities, including Oxford and Cambridge in the UK, and Harvard, Yale and Princeton in the US.

I, meanwhile, was an ex-steeplechase jockey, an ex-private investigator, an ex-security consultant, and an ex-transplant guinea pig. In fact, I was pretty good at being an ex. I had even once been an ex-husband, but that felt like it was a long time ago, in a previous life, long before I met and fell hopelessly in love with Marina, to whom I was certainly not an ex.

Not yet anyway, although we'd had a few ups and downs.

We were currently on an up and had been now for the last few years, and I think we both hoped that this up would last our lifetimes.

But being an ex-husband meant that I had an ex-father-in-law, and we were now living in his house. At least, I always thought of it as *his* house, but it was now his ex-house, as it actually belonged to Saskia. Hence, Marina and I now paid rent to our daughter to live in it, along with her.

My ex-father-in-law, Rear Admiral Charles Roland, was in his nineties and his formerly ramrod-straight back, legacy of an early life spent in the Senior Service, was finally beginning to curve. But his brain remained sharp and as bloody-minded as ever.

He had two daughters – Jill and her younger sister Jenny, who had once been my wife.

Both had eventually married into pots of money, but neither had produced any offspring, so, one day, Charles had announced that he was giving his beloved home at Aynsford to the only granddaughter he knew, Saskia, even though she was not actually related to him by blood, more by adoption by him as an honorary granddaughter.

'All I have to do is live another seven years,' he had said, 'and she'll have it free of bloody inheritance tax.'

'What about Jill and Jenny?' I had asked at the time. 'Won't they expect to inherit it?'

'Probably,' Charles had said to me with a sly smile, 'but they don't need the money. And they don't even like the place – neither of them ever comes here to see me, and I can't remember when we last had a family Aynsford Christmas together. All they would do is sell it, and that would break my heart, even if I was dead. And, anyway, there's plenty of my other capital that they'll eventually get their hands on. My investments have done extremely well over the years, not least due to your advice, Sid.'

That had been six years ago now, and I think that it was only Charles's determination to live those seven years that was keeping him alive.

He had twice had extensive treatment for cancer, once for his prostate and another for a type of leukaemia that had left him feeling very unwell. It had finally been seen off with the help of an experimental gene-therapy trial that Marina had managed to sign him up to, even though he was well over the prescribed age.

But both had taken their toll on his overall health, and last year, Charles had decided that he needed greater care than could be provided by his long-term live-in housekeeper, Mrs Cross, who was by then well into her seventies and in need of some care herself.

So he had checked himself and Mrs Cross into separate rooms at the Godswell House retirement home in a nearby village. It was now where they both lived very happily.

Mrs Cross somehow still looked after him and called him Admiral, as she had always done, while he played chess during the day against the other residents, and then regaled them nightly at dinner with stories of his exciting adventures on the high seas, all from a time when the Royal Navy still did almost rule the waves.

The previous July, Marina and I had sold our house two miles away over the hill and had moved into Aynsford with

Saskia, the owner. This would be our first Christmas here, and we wanted to make it special, not least because Charles and Mrs Cross were coming to stay with us for the festivities.

'What do you think?' Marina asked, standing back and admiring the tree.

'Great,' I replied, 'but do we have enough lights and baubles for it?'

'I bought some more of both, and a new angel for the top. The skirt on our old one has become so torn and threadbare that she looks more like a prostitute than an angel.'

'How are you going to get her up there?' I asked, looking up to the very top of the tree.

'I'm not. That's your job. Go and get the stepladder.'

At this point, the front doorbell rang. I answered it.

'Mr Halley?' asked the man standing there. 'Mr Sid Halley?'

'Yes,' I said. 'How can I help you?'

'It's not me that needs your help,' he said in a slightly lilting Irish accent. 'It's my daughter, and you are her last hope.'

'What sort of help does she need?' I asked warily.

'She needs you to investigate a murder.'

'I'm sorry,' I said. 'I don't investigate anything these days. Get the police to do it.'

'They have. But they've come up with the wrong answer.'

'I'm sorry,' I repeated. 'As I said, I don't investigate anything any more, so you've wasted your time coming here. You need to leave now. Goodbye.'

I started to close the door, but he put his foot in it, preventing it from closing.

'Mr Halley,' he said. 'How's your wife?'

'Look,' I said angrily, opening the door wide again, 'if you think that by threatening my wife, I will change my mind, you can bugger off. Or else I'll call the police.'

I started to close the door again.

'I promise you that I'm not threatening your wife,' he said defensively. 'I was just asking how she was. In particular, how is her left leg? I once saved that leg and quite likely her life. I'd like to know it's still doing OK.'

I opened the door wide once more.

'Who did you say you were?' I asked.

'I didn't, but my name is Patrick Duffy. I'm a doctor. A surgeon. And I specialise in emergency medicine. Many years ago, I was one of the team of surgeons that treated your then girlfriend, Marina van der Meer, at St Thomas' Hospital in London, when she'd been shot.'

I could still recall that day so well, despite the passing of seventeen years. Even now, I went hot and cold remembering the terror I had felt that I would lose her.

I stared at the man in front of me, with his horn-rimmed spectacles and neat, greying hair, dressed in a blue blazer with a white shirt and smart striped tie.

He didn't look like a threat.

'Well, Dr Patrick Duffy,' I said. 'In that case, you'd better come in.'

* * *

I took Patrick Duffy through into the kitchen where he sat on one side of the table, while Marina and I sat opposite, and he told us about that day at St Thomas' Hospital, from so long ago.

'The bullet had torn right through the popliteal artery behind your knee,' he said to Marina. 'Destroyed it completely. If it hadn't been for the prompt application of a tourniquet by the attending ambulance team, you would have bled out and died on the street within only a few minutes. As it was, you had lost so much blood by the time you arrived at the hospital that your blood pressure was hardly readable.'

I gripped Marina's hand tightly under the table.

'Of course, we transfused many pints of blood into you, but every time we eased the tourniquet, it would simply pour straight out again onto the floor. None of it was going down into your lower leg. And we were running out of time because your calf and foot were beginning to die due to lack of a blood supply. The senior consultant believed instant amputation of the leg above the knee was the only course of action that might save your life, and even that was far from certain.'

Marina was staring at him, hanging on his every word.

'I was only a lowly registrar then, but I'd been researching a new technique using nylon catheters, and I suggested that we try it on you. I have to say that the consultant wasn't at all keen, but I stuck to my guns and convinced him that the major surgery required to amputate most of your leg, when your blood pressure was already so low, would likely prove fatal anyway, so what did he have to lose.'

'What did you do with these catheters?' I asked.

'I used two of them as bypasses. Obvious really, and it's now a regular treatment, but back then it was very new and experimental. I opened your inner thigh some way above the wound, inserted the catheters into your femoral artery, and we used them to divert oxygenated blood outside of your body, bypassing

241

the tourniquet, round the knee, and then back into your leg again. They are similar to the tubes we use in a heart-lung machine, but of a much smaller diameter. There was just enough blood flow to keep your lower limb alive, giving us the time to repair the artery itself, which we did by transplanting some veins from your other leg. There is no question the procedure saved your leg. It may have even saved your life.'

Marina was now in tears, and she stood up and went round the table to hug this man, who had so suddenly and unexpectedly come into our home.

'How can we possibly thank you?' Marina asked, wiping her eyes.

'By helping my daughter.'

* * *

Dr Patrick Duffy stayed well on into the afternoon.

Over lunch, he told us a bit about his life, and how he was still working in emergency medicine, now as the head of department at Tipperary University Hospital, where his wife also worked as a midwife. He then told us about his daughter, Imogen, and her abusive boyfriend.

'Hold on a minute,' I said interrupting him. 'Imogen Duffy. I've heard of her. She's a jockey. Didn't she win the Grand National?'

He shook his head. 'She won the Topham Trophy at the Grand National meeting, and she was also leading jockey there. And she won the Champion Chase before that, at the Cheltenham Festival, in March.'

'I remember. She caused a huge sensation. But then she suddenly disappeared, almost as fast as she'd arrived.'

'That's because she's been in Bronzefield Prison for the past eight months.'

'Prison?' Marina said with concern. 'Why?'

'She's on remand, awaiting trial for murder. The abusive boyfriend was found dead in his flat, with a carving knife driven through his heart.'

Marina winced.

'And the police are convinced that Imogen did it.'

'Why?' I asked.

'Because her fingerprints were found on the knife.'

'Ah.'

'But she didn't do it,' Patrick said urgently. 'She knows nothing about it. She was horrified when she was arrested at Heathrow. She didn't even know Liam Carson was dead.'

'What was she doing at Heathrow?' I asked.

'She was boarding a flight home to Dublin. That's where she was stopped by police.'

I wondered if she'd been trying to flee the country. The police would have certainly thought so. But at least she hadn't been trying to board a flight to somewhere that didn't have an extradition treaty with the United Kingdom, such as North Korea or Iran, not that she could take a direct flight to those places from Heathrow anyway.

Patrick went on to tell us about how Imogen had been questioned for three days, before being charged with murder and then denied bail for the past eight months because she was deemed to be a flight risk.

'But the police must have had some other evidence, rather than just her fingerprints on the knife?' I said.

'That was the most compelling. But there is also a witness who saw her close to the murder scene. And she'd been previously warned by the police for threatening Carson with a knife. And there was a witness to that, too.'

It didn't sound very good.

'Is there any DNA evidence against her?' Marina asked.

'I haven't seen any, but who knows what the prosecution are hiding, ready to spring on us at the trial.'

'But the law demands that all the evidence they have must be disclosed to the defence,' I said. 'When is the trial?'

'It's been set for January. Starts on the twelfth. At Reading Crown Court.'

Just five weeks away and with Christmas in between.

'Does Imogen have a lawyer?' I asked.

'Yes, but I don't think he's much good. I've tried to get her to change, but she seems to like the one she's got. But he keeps telling her that she should plead guilty to manslaughter on the grounds of diminished responsibility, as a result of Carson's continued abuse of her. He clearly thinks she did it.'

Maybe he was right.

'He says she could get only ten years, maybe even less. She could be out in four or five. But she refuses to even countenance it. She is adamant that she didn't kill Carson, so why should she plead guilty to doing so?'

'And what do you think?' I asked.

'I'm terrified she'll be convicted of murder and get a life sentence, perhaps spend the next twenty-five or thirty years in prison for something she didn't do.' He was almost in tears. 'I'm not sure her mother could take that. These last eight months have exacted a huge toll on her, and on me. She's our only child.'

His tears were now flowing freely, and I could see he hated it, turning his face away from us so we wouldn't see him cry.

But we had, and I could understand them. How would I feel if Saskia was facing a conviction for murder, when I was convinced she hadn't done it?

'What do you want Sid to investigate?' Marina asked, close to tears again.

I looked at her in total surprise. For years, she had forbidden me from investigating anything, ever since a Northern Irish ex-terrorist had almost killed us both, along with Charles and Saskia too, to say nothing of our much-loved dog, who had died at his hands.

'I want Sid Halley to find out who really killed Liam Carson,' Patrick said slowly. He looked straight at me. 'I think you're our only hope.'

* * *

Before he went, Patrick Duffy helped me put the new angel up on the top of our enormous Christmas tree. He steadied the stepladder, while I went up to its top, holding the angel in my good right hand, not that my left hand was bad. In fact, it was a miracle.

A combination of a serious racing fall and a sadistic villain had resulted in my losing my left hand completely. For many years I had used a plastic and steel myoelectric replacement, but good as it was at picking things up, it had no feeling and was never really part of me.

But ten years previously, I had been offered a new flesh and bone hand – a transplant.

At first, it had been difficult for me to adjust psychologically to the change, but as time went on, the new hand had gradually become mine rather than someone else's, and now it was an integral part of my being, and I was back to thinking of myself as two-handed rather than one. But I still had to take a cocktail of pills every morning to prevent the rest of me physically rejecting the newcomer.

I agreed with Patrick that I would go and see Imogen's lawyer and to delve a little into the evidence.

'I'll do it quietly,' I told him. 'Under the radar. I work best that way. So please don't tell anyone.'

'But you will go and see Imogen as well?' he asked adamantly.

'Let me hear what the lawyer has to say first, and then I'll decide.'

I could see that he was disappointed.

'I promise I'll go and see her, if it will do any good.'

'But you need to hear what she has to say,' he persisted.

'Sid, you must go and see her,' Marina said resolutely.

'OK, I will. But let me speak to the lawyer first so I know what to ask her. I'll do that this week, and I'll visit her at Bronzefield during the week after.'

And that was how we left it. Patrick gave me the lawyer's details, while I gave him mine to pass on to Imogen, as she would have to book me into the prison system in order to have a visit.

Marina hugged Patrick again at the front door, as he was leaving. 'I am sure Sid will do his best for your daughter,' she said to him.

But would my best prove her innocence or her guilt?

Chapter 23

THE BRASS PLAQUE OUTSIDE THE front door read: *Ashe, Brook and Pollard, Solicitors at Law*.

I pushed the button on the intercom box.

'Hello,' came a voice from the tiny speaker. 'Can I help you?'

'My name is Sid Halley,' I said. 'I have an eleven o'clock meeting with Mr Archie Brook.'

A buzzing sound emanated from the door, and I pushed it open.

After Patrick Duffy had left, Marina had insisted that I get on with my investigation straight away. 'He saved my life,' she'd implored. 'We owe it to him to at least try.' So, I had called the law firm and made the appointment.

Their offices were in Reading, about an hour's drive from Aynsford, and I had been given a slot to see Mr Brook the following morning.

So here I was.

But Archie Brook was not quite what I was expecting. For a start he was very young, and he wasn't wearing a suit. He also had no tie, just an open-necked shirt above khaki chinos and white-soled running shoes.

He stood up from behind his desk when I went in and held out his hand. I shook it, but he also saw me look him up and down.

'Dress-down Friday,' he said. 'I wear a suit and tie on other days, and on Fridays too, if I have to go to court.'

'Sorry,' I said. 'I was expecting someone much older.'

'I'm twenty-seven,' he said, although he didn't look it. 'I've been a qualified solicitor now for more than four years. You can check me out on the Law Society website.'

'I already have. It says you were admitted to the Society as a solicitor in 1976. But that would have been more than twenty years before you were born.'

'Ah,' he said with a smile. 'That would be my grandfather. He's also called Archie Brook. He's the Brook that's in the firm's name. He's seventy-three now, but he's still registered here, and he even does some work occasionally. But I am on the Law Society register too, just a bit further down.' He smiled again. 'Please take a seat.' I did as he asked, and he sat down again as well. 'Now, how can I help you, Mr ...' he looked down at the papers in front of him, '... Halley.'

'I'm here about Imogen Duffy.'

'Ah, yes, a very sad situation. Nice girl. And the victim was a nasty piece of work, by all accounts. Probably deserved what he got, but the law doesn't work like that. Where would we be if all those that deserved to die could be murdered without any payback?'

He laughed, although it wasn't a laughing matter.

'You seem convinced that she's guilty,' I said.

'Pretty open-and-shut case, I'm afraid. The murder weapon came from her kitchen, and it has her fingerprints on it. A witness places her at the murder scene, and she admits to previously threatening the victim with a knife. Not much hope really.'

'Surely admitting to having previously threatened the victim with a knife is hardly evidence that she used it against him on a totally separate occasion?'

'Maybe not on its own. But it does tend to imply intent, which is one of the stumbling blocks I've encountered with the prosecution service, regarding my attempts to lessen the charge. I've been trying to get it reduced to manslaughter, on the grounds of diminished responsibility, caused by the victim's abusive behaviour towards her, but ... no luck so far. And she's not exactly playing ball. It's well known in legal circles that the only difference between *killing for revenge* and *diminished responsibility* is a good psychiatrist, but she refuses point-blank even to see one.'

'Perhaps that's because she didn't do it,' I said.

He gave me a look that seemed to imply that he thought it was me who should see the psychiatrist.

'Are you sure you're a suitable solicitor for this client?' I asked. 'You are meant to be working on her behalf, not for the prosecution.'

'I am working on her behalf,' he replied sharply, more than somewhat piqued. 'I am trying very hard to get her the best possible outcome, and to save her from being sent to prison for the rest of her life.'

'Can I please see the case files?'

'Not without the express permission of my client,' he replied rather condescendingly. 'I've said too much to you already.'

'Have you not had her permission? Her father was going to arrange for Imogen to call you this morning.'

'I'm afraid prisons are not always as helpful as they might be in allowing the inmates to use the telephone, even though the rules clearly state that those on remand should be able to consult their legal representatives at any time.'

As if on cue, the phone on his desk emitted a long beep. He didn't pick up the handset, rather he pushed a button next to it.

'Mr Brook,' said a female voice through the speaker, 'I'm so sorry to interrupt you but I have Imogen Duffy on the line, and she is insistent that she speaks to you right away.'

'Thank you, Miss Williams,' Mr Brook replied. 'Please put her through.'

There was a click and then a sweet Irish voice came on the line.

'Archie,' it said breathlessly. 'Someone called Sid Halley is coming to see you.'

'He's already here,' Archie replied. 'Sitting right in front of me.'

'Oh. Good. Please give him all the help he needs, including access to all the documents. I want him included in my defence team.'

'OK. I will. Are you all right?'

'I suppose so. The other girls and I put up a few Christmas decorations yesterday. We made them from loo roll and some coloured pens.'

'Well, don't you worry. I'm doing everything I can at this end, and I'll give Mr Halley what he needs.'

'Thanks,' Imogen said. 'I must go. There's a long queue behind me for the phone.'

She hung up and Archie switched off the speaker.

'Doing everything I can at this end?' I said sarcastically. 'Have you interviewed the witness who claims to have seen her at the murder scene?'

'Well, no,' he replied. 'But I have seen her police statement.'

'Her?'

'Yes, she's a racehorse trainer. She owns the stables where Liam Carson's body was found.'

'What's her name?'

'Sophie Burnett.'

I didn't recognise it, but many years had passed since I'd had day-to-day dealing with racehorse trainers. I knew a Brian Burnett. He'd been a trainer twenty years ago. I'd even ridden for him. Perhaps he had been a relation, maybe her father.

Archie Brook pushed a button on his phone.

'Miss Williams,' he said. 'Could you please bring in the Imogen Duffy case files?'

'Certainly, Mr Brook.'

After a few moments, an attractive young woman came in carrying a brown cardboard document storage box, which she placed on Archie's desk.

'Thank you, Miss Williams,' he said, smiling at her in a certain way.

It made me wonder if they referred to each other as Miss Williams and Mr Brook when there wasn't anyone else to hear them. Somehow, I doubted it.

Archie removed the lid from the box and lifted out the contents. There weren't that many papers – perhaps only three- or four-inches depth of them in total.

I didn't think that boded particularly well for Imogen.

I'd been involved in some legal cases where the documents filled so many of these brown cardboard boxes that a sack truck was needed to transport them all to court.

'How did Imogen come to appoint you as her solicitor?' I asked.

'I was a duty solicitor with the DSCC when she was brought into custody after her arrest.'

'DSCC?'

'Defence Solicitor Call Centre. It's where the police call if an arrested person requests legal representation. I was one of the duty solicitors, so I was assigned to Imogen's case, and so I went to Loddon Valley Police Station.'

'Where's Loddon Valley?'

'In south-east Reading. Near the M4. I was assigned to Imogen for her first police interview, and I've just sort of carried on with her ever since. She didn't know any other solicitors.'

'How often are you a duty solicitor with DSCC?' I asked.

'About once a month. The firm encourages all associates to be on the rota, as a civic duty. Imogen was just lucky to get me.'

Or unlucky, I thought.

'Have you instructed a barrister for her case?' I asked.

'Of course,' he said. 'The trial is only five weeks away now. I instructed counsel way back in June, for the Plea and Trial Preparation Hearing. That's when the trial date was set. And, soon after the hearing, we submitted our defence statement and our list of witnesses.'

'What did the defence statement say?' I asked.

'Basically, that Imogen Duffy wasn't there, and she didn't kill the victim.'

'Anything else?'

'It took issue with some of the prosecution disclosure, in particular their claim that Imogen was seen by a witness at the stables during the time when the murder could have happened.

At the same time, I also made an application for legal aid. Imogen now has no job, no home, and no assets. Any money she did have was used up pretty quickly by her initial legal fees.'

Legal aid is a government scheme to ensure that members of the public are not barred from receiving legal assistance and advice just because they can't afford it. Legal representation is a right, not simply a privilege for those who are able to pay for it.

But it didn't always mean you would get the best represent-ation available.

Legal aid doesn't pay as much as privately funded clients, and therefore many top lawyers don't sign up for it.

'Which barrister did you instruct?' I asked.

Archie looked down at the papers.

'Donna Lewis. She's from London. Burton Chambers. Inner Temple.'

'And how often do you speak with her?' I asked.

Not often, I thought, if he'd had to look up her name.

'Every couple of weeks or so. She calls me to find out if there's been any progress with reducing the charge. Or if our client has considered changing her plea.'

'So, she also thinks Imogen is guilty?'

He didn't reply.

'Have you discussed with Donna Lewis your strategy for the trial?'

Again, there was no reply, so the answer was obviously 'no'.

'How many murder cases have you dealt with?' I asked.

'This is my first.'

Young Archie Brook was clearly out of his depth.

* * *

I spent over four hours at the offices of Ashe, Brook and Pollard, Solicitors at Law.

I sat and read through all the documents in a vacant conference room, while Archie had numerous appointments with other clients.

There was the usual stuff – copies of the charge sheet, the police interview transcripts, scene of crime and forensic reports, results of a search at the home of the accused, her bank and credit card statements, post-mortem report on the victim – together with copies of several witness statements.

I started with the first interview transcript.

Archie had obviously told Imogen to reply 'No comment' to all the police questions. A lot of solicitors did. They would say that it was better to find out first what evidence the police have collected, rather than giving them any useful information to use against you. I could understand their reasoning, but I felt that it tended to simply make the accused look guilty.

'How did you arrive at the airport?'

'No comment.'

'Where did you sleep last night?'

'No comment.'

'Did you murder Liam Carson?'

'No comment.'

'Is your solicitor an idiot?'

'No comment.'

OK, so the final question and answer weren't actually in the transcript, but the others were.

By the subsequent interviews, the legal advice had clearly changed, and Imogen was then answering the police questions.

'Have you ever seen this knife before?'

'Not that I'm aware of.'

'Is it not the carving knife from the block in your kitchen?'

'Maybe. It does look like that one.'

'Did you take this knife to Boxtree Stables and use it to murder Liam Carson?'

'No.'

'How do you account for it being found embedded in his body?'

'I can't.'

'Have you previously threatened Liam Carson with this knife?'

'If it is the one from the block in my kitchen, then yes, I have.'

'So, are you glad that Liam Carson is dead?'

'I wouldn't say that I am glad, but I'm not sorry either.'

'Why is that?'

'Because he has attacked me twice, and he's been telling awful lies about me to the newspapers.'

'Is that the reason why you killed him?'

'I didn't kill him, but I think he deserved to die after all the harm he's caused.'

'Harm to whom?'

'Me, and to Freddie Swinton. He said dreadful things to the press about us, none of which were true.'

'Why did you use a false name to check in at an airport hotel?'

'Because I was afraid of being recognised.'

'Why did you pay the hotel in cash rather than using your bank card?'

'Because I didn't want them to know my real name.'

I sighed. The answers she had given were just as incriminating as the 'No comments' had been, maybe more so, and she'd also provided them with the motive they would have been searching for.

No wonder they had charged her.

And the four witness statements weren't any more beneficial to her case either.

The first was from the airport hotel receptionist, stating that he recognised the photo he'd been shown by police as that of the young woman who had checked in to the hotel using the name Alison Brown, paying in advance for her room with cash.

The second was from a man called Simon Potter, maintenance man at the stables where Imogen Duffy had worked in Lambourn. It stated that, on the Wednesday prior to the murder, he had collected the key to Imogen Duffy's cottage from the key cupboard in the stable office, before walking round to the cottage to fix a security chain on her front door. When he arrived at the cottage, the front door had been wide open. He rang the doorbell and Miss Duffy shouted at him to come in. He walked through to the kitchen only to discover that Liam Carson was already in there, and Miss Duffy was brandishing a carving knife in a threatening manner. Mr Carson then left and he, Simon, removed the knife from Miss Duffy's possession before calling the stable office for assistance.

The third witness statement was from a policeman, PC Tate, who had interviewed Imogen on the Wednesday before the murder, when she had attended Newbury Police Station to complain of Mr Liam Carson's behaviour towards her, in particular his stalking and harassment of her, his threats to kill her, and his theft of some underwear from her home.

The statement contained a detailed account of the interview, which had been conducted in the presence of Mr Freddie Swinton, who had accompanied Miss Duffy to the police station. A note, purportedly delivered to Miss Duffy's address by Mr Carson, was examined and retained for a fingerprint check. Miss Duffy admitted having touched the note, so her fingerprints were taken so they could be eliminated. The PC had indicated to Miss Duffy that there was not much for the police to go on, not without corroboration from a third party. It would simply be her word against his, but he, PC Tate, had nevertheless agreed to speak to Mr Carson, which he then did by telephone.

PC Tate went on to record that, on that call, Mr Carson had laughed at the accusations, denied any form of harassment or stalking, and insisted that he'd never threatened Miss Duffy in any way nor had he ever been inside her cottage.

PC Tate then detailed how he had received a call from Imogen Duffy later in the afternoon of the same day, alleging that, since their meeting that morning, Liam Carson had forced his way into her home and threatened her, and that she had repelled him by brandishing her carving knife.

PC Tate had subsequently interviewed Liam Carson at Boxtree Stables. Mr Carson agreed that he had been to Miss Duffy's cottage, and he had taken with him a bouquet of red roses, as an apology for any distress he might have inadvertently caused. However, he had been met with nothing but hostility from Miss Duffy, including being threatened with a knife. After discussion with a senior officer, it was decided not to take any action against Miss Duffy, but she was issued with an official warning for threatening another person with a knife.

It didn't read particularly well for Imogen, and the fourth witness statement was no better.

The racehorse trainer, Sophie Burnett, stated that she had attempted to turn into her driveway at Boxtree Stables late on Monday afternoon, only to find another car blocking her path. A young woman, whom she picked out in an identity parade, and she now knew to be Imogen Duffy, had been hurrying down the driveway away from the stables. The young woman had waved a hand in apology, before quickly climbing into the car and driving it away at speed.

The statement went on to say that she, Sophie Burnett, had discovered Liam Carson's dead body on the bed in his flat above her stables when he failed to turn up for work the following morning, after she had gone to look for him. And very distressing it had been for her too.

Next, I read the post-mortem report.

I attended the scene of the death at about 10 a.m. to discover a 27-year-old male with a single knife wound to the chest. The deceased was a slightly built but well-nourished and muscular individual. A knife, with a 20cm blade, was still in situ in the chest, slightly to the left of the middle of the anterior chest wall, some 11cm below the sternal notch. Most of the blade was inside the body, with the remaining 4cm outside, together with the knife handle.

Rigor mortis was well established, as was livor mortis, which had become mostly permanent. An attempt was made to measure the core temperature of the body, and it was estimated to be approximately 25 degrees Celsius. The ambient room temperature was quite high at 21 degrees. The corneas of the eyes were fully clouded, and the intraocular pressure was well reduced. Considering all these factors, I made an estimate of time of death as being between eight and eighteen hours prior to my arrival at the scene, so between 4 p.m. on Monday and 2 a.m. on Tuesday.

Quite a large window, I thought, but I knew that determining the time of a death was always tricky. Only in Hollywood films did a pathologist confidently state, having briefly examined the remains, that the victim died at 2.15 a.m. precisely, as if it were an exact science.

I read on.

The body was then removed to the mortuary at the Royal Berkshire Hospital in Reading, where I continued my examination.

The knife had entered the chest between the fourth and fifth ribs, fractionally to the left of the sternum, and appeared to be stuck in place due to having sliced through part of the bone of rib 4, which had subsequently 'gripped' the blade, making it impossible to remove without surgically excising the rib.

On careful removal of the knife, the wound was found to be vertically placed, wedge-shaped and approximately 16cm deep. The knife had been directed downwards on the supine body with great force, piercing the skin, the subcutaneous tissue, the intercostal muscle between rib 4 and 5, and also the bone of rib 4, before puncturing the pericardium and the anterior wall of the left ventricle, at a level some 8cm above the apex. The blade had then travelled on through the posterior wall of the ventricle. These two punctures had caused immediate and catastrophic haemorrhaging, and the pericardial cavity was found to contain in excess of 600ml of blood, while all the other organs were pale. There were no other injuries present, and the stomach was empty.

I consider that the cause of death was pericardial tamponade – compression of the cardiac muscle by an accumulation of fluid in the pericardial sac – and shock, both due to the knife wound. Cardiac arrest would have been almost instantaneous, unconsciousness would have followed within a few seconds, and brain death within a few minutes.

Or, in layman's terms, Liam Carson had died due to being violently stabbed right through the heart with a carving knife while he'd been lying on his back, and the knife had become stuck in him.

The scene of crime report was rather less revealing.

The deceased was found lying face up on his bed with a knife still embedded in his chest. There had been minimal external bleeding although a few blood spots were present on the bedclothes, together with signs of some blood spray, presumably from the wound during impact. This blood was swabbed for further analysis. There was no sign of forced entry, and no indication of a struggle between the victim and the assailant. All surfaces were dusted for finger- and handprints, including the visible parts of the murder weapon, and a number of swabs were also taken for DNA examination. There were no obvious footprints visible, even in ultraviolet light, and no CCTV recordings were available to be viewed.

Accompanying the written report were some graphic photos, mostly of Liam Carson taken from every possible angle. He had been naked when he died, the bedclothes only covering the lower part of his body, and the carving knife appeared incongruous, standing upright in the middle of his chest, like the handle of an upturned bricklayer's mortar board.

The search of Imogen's cottage had thrown up nothing of interest other than the fact that the knife block in the kitchen had one vacant space, where a carving knife should have been. Some of Imogen's clothes had also been retrieved from the laundry basket and sent for forensic analysis, along with several pairs of shoes from her wardrobe.

But it was the forensic report that was the most revealing of them all, or not, depending on how you viewed it.

Yes, Imogen's fingerprints were indeed found on the knife, but not on its handle. Her right forefinger- and thumbprints had been discovered on either side of the blade, close to where it met the handle. But I reckoned there was no way anyone could have driven that knife through a man's heart by only holding it by the blade, and certainly not with just one finger and a thumb. I believed that the assailant must have either worn gloves or had wiped the handle clean, possibly both.

The report stated that all the blood found at the scene had belonged to the victim, and no DNA from anyone else had been detected from any of the many swabs taken. Similarly, all finger- and handprints lifted from inside the flat had been those of the deceased, apart from those two found on the blade.

In addition, no blood had been found on any of the clothes or shoes taken from Imogen's cottage. The only down point was that several small stones found stuck in the tread of two of Imogen's car tyres matched the size and style of the gravel on the Boxtree Stables driveway, but that was hardly conclusive proof that she'd been there at all, let alone at the time of the murder.

A forensic analysis of the GPS records on Imogen's mobile phone had shown that she'd been to Eastbury village on three occasions, but not at the supposed time of the murder. But the police would almost certainly have assumed that she had been 'casing the joint' on those prior visits, and she had simply left the phone at home on the day she went there to kill.

The analysis noted that there was no record of any calls from Liam Carson, and not a single message from him had been found on the phone. But it did show that she had twice searched 'using a knife in self-defence' on the internet, but thankfully there were no searches for 'how to murder with a knife'.

Overall, to my mind, it was all unconvincing and circum-stantial.

If the prosecution were relying on Imogen's fingerprints being found on the knife as conclusive evidence that she had murdered Liam Carson, I felt they were on very shaky ground. All it really proved was that the knife blade had once been held by her, and it might well be the one missing from the knife block in her kitchen.

But that didn't prove that she had used it to kill him.

Chapter 24

I LEFT THE OFFICES OF ASHE, Brook and Pollard with a sheaf of notes I had made from the papers I thought were most relevant.

Marina was in the hallway when I arrived home at Aynsford.

She added one final bauble to the Christmas tree, before standing back and admiring it.

'What do you think?' she asked.

'It's wonderful,' I said. And it was wonderful too, with lots of shiny globes, stars and other ornaments, together with a multitude of little white lights. 'Well done.'

She collected the empty decoration boxes.

'Did you have any luck with the lawyer?'

'The prosecution seem to be relying very heavily on the fact that it was the carving knife from Imogen's kitchen that was left behind at the murder scene, firmly stuck in Liam Carson's chest.'

'Well, they would, wouldn't they, especially if they found her fingerprints on it.'

'They were only found on the blade.'

'But that *is* the sharp bit.'

Our conversation was interrupted by my mobile phone ringing.

'Hello,' I said, answering.

'Sid, it's Nigel Falkirk, from *The Times*. We've been sent a press release via the Press Association that says you are investigating the Liam Carson killing. Is that correct?'

'Who's it from?' I asked with a heavy heart.

'Chap called Patrick Duffy. He claims you will exonerate his daughter, Imogen, who's currently on remand for the murder.'

So much for me asking him not to tell anyone. He'd only gone and told all the newspapers plus the broadcast media.

'Are you going to run the story?' I asked.

'Depends if it's true. Is it?'

'I'm just having a quiet look at the evidence,' I said. 'Nothing more.'

He laughed. 'The Sid Halley I know never had a quiet look at anything. So, you are investigating it. Can I quote you?'

It didn't make any difference if I said *yes* or *no*. He'd quote me anyway.

'So do you think the girl jockey is innocent?' he asked.

'I haven't studied the evidence yet, and I wouldn't tell you what I thought anyway. We'd both get done for contempt of court if you publish a quote like that at this stage. It would be seen as prejudicial to a fair trial.'

'Our lawyers will sort that out.'

'Well, I'm still not giving you anything. Be it on your own heads.'

He laughed again. 'I'm always here if you have anything to say.'

'OK, Nigel. But I won't have anything to tell you. If I find anything, I'll be saving it for the trial.'

I disconnected, his laughter still resonating in my ears.

So now what?

My nice quiet look at the evidence, under the radar, had been blown wide open. I was quite sure some of the papers would run the story even if Nigel didn't. I sighed. In my experience, if people knew I was investigating something, they tended to clam up and refuse to speak to me. Not that such a response had ever stopped me trying.

'Who called?' Marina asked.

'A reporter from *The Times*. It seems that Patrick Duffy has told the world that I'm investigating Liam Carson's death, and that I will exonerate his daughter.'

'You'd better get on with it, then.'

* * *

HMP Bronzefield is a Category A, top-security prison, situated just a couple of miles south of Heathrow airport, and is the largest all-female prison in Europe.

I was meeting Archie Brook there. He had booked a legal consultation with his client, and I'd been cleared by the prison authorities to join them for the hour-long visit.

I arrived in good time, but Archie was ahead of me, waiting in the visitor reception area.

'We have to leave everything in one of these lockers,' he told me, pointing. 'Keys, phone, money, wallets and so on. And cigarettes and lighters. We can only take in legal papers plus one pen. We get searched. And we have to show the pen when we come out to make sure it's not left behind to be used as a weapon.'

It was my first time in a prison proper, although I had once spent an uncomfortable night in a police cell.

Having had our photo IDs checked against their lists, passed through a metal detector and submitted to a rub-down search, we were taken from the reception area through gates in two five-metre-high perimeter fences, and then into the main prison building. There, we were shown into the 'Visits Hall', a large airy space with windows across one end. But even these windows had steel bars across them.

There were lots of chairs, red ones for the prisoners and blue for the visitors, set out in groups of five, one red and four blue, with the red and blues on opposite sides of low round tables. In one corner were stored some toys, no doubt for children visiting their mothers.

'Social and family visits are in the afternoons,' Archie said. 'Only legal visits in the mornings, so we shouldn't be interrupted.'

And, indeed, we were the only ones there.

Archie and I sat down on two of the blue chairs and waited.

The round clock high up on one wall loudly ticked off the seconds – tick, tick, tick . . . It made me realise that everything relating to prison life was about time.

Tick, tick, tick . . .

The seconds seemed to pass so slowly here, and I was only visiting. For the inmates, time and a strict daily routine controlled their lives utterly.

Doing time.

It said it all.

A metal door slammed at one end of the hall, and I turned to see a young woman being escorted in by a male prison officer. She was smaller than I had been expecting, her lack of stature emphasised by the oversized baggy grey prison-issue clothing she was wearing.

She was led over to us, and she sat down on the red chair opposite.

'If you need me just shout,' said the officer. 'I'll be over by the door.'

He moved away, well out of earshot for normal conversation.

'Hello, Imogen,' Archie said. 'This is Sid Halley. He'd like to ask you some questions.'

I smiled at her, but she didn't smile back.

'If you've come to try to get me to change my plea, you're wasting your time.'

'I haven't,' I said. 'I promise. I watched you win the Champion Chase at Cheltenham last March. Great ride.'

She suddenly perked up, even smiling.

'It was one of my better days.'

'I won it too.'

'When?'

I laughed. 'Before you were born. But I still remember it as if it were yesterday. Great feeling, isn't it?'

'The best. But it seems like it was in a different lifetime to now.'

She resumed her rather miserable persona.

'How are things in here?' I asked.

'The boredom is the worst part,' she replied. 'And the food. It's awful – so tasteless and stodgy. I try not to eat it. That's why I've lost loads of weight.'

'Do you get on all right with the other women?'

'They're OK, I suppose. A lot of them find God in here, constantly praying for forgiveness, but I've spent most of my life trying to avoid anything to do with religion. But there's not much chance to get to know them anyway. We're locked in our cells for long periods, sometimes eighteen hours a day when they're short-staffed, which is most of the time. And there's no internet access. That's the worst bit. You have no idea what's going on outside.'

'Don't you get access to a television?'

'Occasionally, but it's heavily restricted, and they never show any of the bloody racing.'

I laughed loudly, and she joined in, laughing along with me, suddenly without inhibition.

I had finally made contact with her inner self, peeling away the defensive layers she had obviously created to cope with prison life.

'I thought you'd be in your own clothes,' I said. 'As you're on remand.'

'We can all wear our own clothes if we want, even the convicted girls. But it seems easier to wear this.' She waved at the grey.

And more anonymous, I thought.

'So, what do you want to ask me?' she said.

Where did I start?

'Have you ever been to Boxtree Stables in Eastbury village?'

'Not right into the stables, no, but I did pull into their driveway.'

'Why was that?'

'I wanted to see where Liam Carson lived.'

'So you went into his flat?'

'No. I just pulled the car into the start of the driveway. I climbed out and walked up to look through the gates. But I didn't go in.'

'But your car did block the driveway?'

'Yes, and typically, another car came along from Lambourn and wanted to turn in. The driver hooted at me, so I ran down the drive to move mine.'

'Did you see the driver?'

'Only through the windscreen. It was a woman.'

'And when was that?'

She thought. 'The day after the Grand National. Around lunchtime.'

'On the Sunday?'

'Yes.'

'Are you quite sure about that?'

She thought again. 'Yes. I'd been to Hungerford for a coffee. But it was a terrible idea. That bloody newspaper had another story about Freddie and me on the front page. I saw it in Tesco's. But it's all untrue.'

'Can you remember which newspaper ran the story?'

'The *Daily News*. More like the *Daily Bloody Fake News*.'

'And you're sure it wasn't on the Monday of that week?'

'Quite certain,' Imogen said. 'It was on Sunday. I rode in a race at Windsor on that Monday afternoon. It was the last ride I had.'

She sounded woeful.

'There may be a chance again,' I said, trying to be encouraging.

'I doubt it. Not after this.'

But Lester Piggott returned to race riding aged fifty-five, after having been in prison for over a year, and he won the Breeders' Cup Mile just ten days later, and went on to win his thirtieth British Classic. But Lester had been exceptional in so many different ways, and the annual UK jockey awards were now even called 'The Lesters'.

'There's a female witness who claims to have seen you in the Boxtree Stables driveway on Monday afternoon.'

'Then she's mistaken, or she's lying. I was there on Sunday.'

'Not on Monday as well?'

'No. I definitely only went there once.'

Now it was time for the big question – the elephant-in-the-room question – the one we had been avoiding up to now.

'Who killed Liam Carson?' I asked her.

'I don't know. It wasn't me. Perhaps Freddie Swinton did it.'

'Why would he?'

'Because he was bloody angry with Liam. He was the one telling the lies to the newspapers. He told everyone that Freddie was sleeping with me, someone half his age, but it wasn't true. Liam made it all up to get at me, but both Freddie and I had a really rough time at Aintree because of it.'

'But why would Freddie use the knife from your kitchen?'

'I don't know. But he did have a key to my cottage, and he thought I was going to Dublin on Monday night, when in fact I had booked a seat for Wednesday.'

'Why didn't you go on Monday night?' I asked.

'Because there were no seats left on any flights. Ireland was playing football against England in Dublin the following evening. Hence, the first flight I could get was early on Wednesday morning.'

'And you were arrested trying to board it?'

'Yes.'

'Was the carving knife still in the block in your kitchen on that Monday evening?'

'I don't know. I don't remember seeing it. And I wouldn't have needed to use any knife, because I only had a bowl of corn flakes for supper that night.'

'So it could have gone missing earlier in the day, while you were at Windsor races?'

'I suppose so.'

'Who else had a key to your cottage?'

'I know there was one hanging in a cupboard in the stable office. Anyone could have taken that. And Louisa, the cleaner. She also had one.'

We might be thought of as clutching at straws, if we tried to claim that her cleaner was the murderer.

'Tell me about threatening Carson with the knife. How did that happen?'

'He forced his way into my cottage. I grabbed the carving knife from the block and shouted at him that I'd stab him if he came any closer.'

'And did he come any closer?'

'No. Because at that point the stable maintenance man had turned up, and Liam went away.'

'And would you have actually stabbed him?'

'Probably. I was that frightened of him. No one has any real idea what he was like. Not even my dad.'

'Then tell me,' I said.

She spent the next half hour describing how Carson had controlled everything about her life, how he had been jealous of her success, and how he had taken every opportunity to belittle her. And when she had finally plucked up the courage to walk out on him, she described his violent reaction and how he had told her categorically that he would rather kill her than let her leave him.

'But the analysis of your phone made special note of the fact that there were no calls or text messages from him.'

'That's because I changed my number when I came to England, and he never got to know the new one. There were plenty of messages before that, on my Irish SIM. Horrible they were too – how he was going to hurt me and why I'd always regret leaving him.'

She went on to recount how he had attacked her at her parents' home and also how he had tried to put her through the wing of a fence at Newton Abbot. She finished by telling me that on the occasion he had forced his way in, and after she had threatened him with the carving knife, Liam had told her that, the next time, he would bring his own knife.

'It was all very frightening,' she said.

'It must have been,' I said sympathetically.

'Funny, though,' she said with a wan smile. 'At least I feel safe in here, knowing that he can't get to me.'

'But he's dead,' I pointed out.

'Yeah,' she said. 'That helps too.'

Chapter 25

'How did it go?' Marina asked when I arrived home.

'Pretty well. She seems like a nice girl.'

'Does that mean you don't think she's a murderer?'

'I didn't say that. Everyone thought that Harold Shipman was a nice doctor until he turned out to be the most prolific serial killer of modern times.'

'But did you find out anything that helps Imogen's case?'

'Not much. I now have a better idea of how frightened she was of Liam Carson, but that doesn't really help. Possibly the reverse. But she did say that the eyewitness is totally wrong to claim that she was anywhere near the scene at the time of the murder.'

'What are you going to do next?'

'I've arranged with Imogen's solicitor that we should have a meeting with the barrister as soon as possible. To work out our strategy for the trial. The trouble is that everything shuts down soon for two weeks over the Christmas and New Year holidays. I'd also like to go and talk to one of the witnesses, but that's not as simple as it sounds.'

'Why?'

'Because the prosecution doesn't like the defence talking to their witnesses. Not before the trial. I am meant to apply in writing to the prosecutor, and then wait patiently for the reply, which would probably be that the witness doesn't want to speak to me anyway.'

My wife smiled at me. 'But you're going to go and see them anyway, without asking first.'

'Exactly,' I said, smiling back at her. 'She's a racehorse trainer and she has a runner declared at the Cheltenham December meeting tomorrow. I thought I might just turn up and, by accident, find myself standing next to her.'

She laughed. 'Can I come and watch?'

Marina hadn't come to the races with me for so long that I couldn't remember when was the last time. But it had certainly been several years ago.

'I would absolutely love you to come and watch, but who will be here for Saskia when she gets back from school? It's the last day of term, so she'll be home earlier than usual.'

'I think Sassy's quite old enough now to look after herself for a few hours. I'll ask Fiona to give her a lift home.'

Fiona was a neighbour from the next village, whose daughter went to the same school, and we often shared runs.

'OK,' I said, somewhat surprised. 'That would be great.'

Ever since Saskia, then aged six, had been kidnapped from her primary school on the orders of a Northern Irish ex-terrorist, Marina had been extremely protective of our daughter, perhaps excessively so. Never before had she entertained the idea of Saskia being left alone for a couple of hours, even in our own home.

'We've received some more Christmas cards,' Marina said. 'And there are also a couple of letters for you, they're all on the side table.' She pointed.

I looked through the cards, checking there wasn't one from someone to whom we hadn't already sent one – there wasn't.

The two letters were underneath the cards, one in a brown envelope, one in a white.

The brown one contained a reminder from the DVLA that my car tax was due by the end of the month, but the white one's contents were all the more sinister.

If you know what's good for your health, Mr Halley, you'll stop investigating the Liam Carson murder. You have been warned!

I read and reread the message. It was printed on a sheet of nondescript plain white paper and, understandably, it was unsigned.

'What is it?' Marina asked.

I screwed up the paper. 'Nothing, just a marketing flyer for a retirement home offering me a free gift if I visited.'

I picked up the white envelope. The address was also printed rather than handwritten, and the postmark showed that the first-class stamp in the top right-hand corner had been franked at the Royal Mail Swindon Mail Centre at 18.12 the previous evening.

The Swindon mail centre was just a few miles west of Lambourn, and it was where mail collected from the post boxes in the village would be franked.

I also screwed up the envelope, and I put both in the recycling bin in the kitchen.

Nigel Falkirk had written a piece in the previous day's *Times* Diary.

I hear that former champion jump jockey turned private invest-
igator, Sid Halley, is back on the trail, this time searching for a

murderer, and he's determined to prove a fellow jockey innocent. 'I'm just having a quiet look at the evidence,' Halley said, but in my experience, Halley has never had a 'quiet' look at anything.

The whole thing was couched in very general terms without mentioning any names, something that the newspaper's lawyers must have insisted on. But anyone with any intelligence would have been able to work out which murder I was investigating. And several other papers had run with the story too, in much the same manner. So now everyone would know.

And it had clearly caused a stir somewhere, with someone.

But did they really believe that threatening me would stop me investigating? If so, they didn't know me very well.

Hence, I suddenly became more determined than ever to discover the truth.

* * *

On Friday morning, Marina and I went to Cheltenham races.

Their two-day mid-December meeting is not on the same scale as the Festival, with only about ten thousand here on this day, compared with seven times as many for the Gold Cup in March, but there was still quite a queue to get in at the north entrance.

As with all professional sports, horseracing has had its share of problems with the mental health of its retired participants, especially the jockeys. In recent years, the Racecourse Association and the Professional Jockeys Association had come together to introduce an excellent scheme in which all retired jockeys, who have successfully ridden out their claim, are able to apply for a Jockey Recognition Badge that provides them with ongoing complimentary car parking, plus free entry to all racecourses.

The programme aims to provide jockeys with a sense of community following their retirement, to assist them with their change in circumstances, and to support their mental health.

As I qualified, I had applied to the scheme and, because I had also been a professional jockey for more than fifteen years, I was entitled to have a companion badge as well. Hence, I no longer needed to rely on my very old and battered metal 'Jockey' badge to try and blag my way in.

Marina and I used our new passes, and we sailed through the turnstiles without problem.

'Let's go and find some lunch,' I said.

'It's only half past eleven.'

'But the first race is at ten past twelve.'

As always, in December, racing started early due to the sun going down before four o'clock, there only being one more week now until the shortest day. As a jockey, I had always hated this cold and dark month, yearning for the return of spring, with its longer days and the great jumping festivals at Cheltenham and Aintree to look forward to.

We settled on a coffee and a sandwich in the Vestey Bar.

'It's much nicer here than I remember,' Marina said. 'I have the memory of it being a huge scrum to get anywhere, and all the bars were ankle-deep in spilt beer.'

'It can still be a bit like that at the Festival,' I said. But all racecourses had worked hard to improve their facilities for racegoers, and Cheltenham was no exception.

'So, in which race is the lady trainer's horse running?' Marina asked.

'The second.'

'And where and when are you going to ambush her?'

The same two questions had been milling around in my own head for some time. Ideally, it had to be in a place, and at a time, when she couldn't just walk away, but also when she was not too busily engaged with her horses.

During the Festival meeting, many of the trainers for each race remain in the parade ring to watch it on the huge television screen set up at one end. It saved having to push through the large crowd to get to that part of the grandstand reserved for owners and trainers, from where the view wasn't that good anyway.

Some trainers stayed in the parade ring at the other meetings too.

If Sophie Burnett remained in the parade ring to watch the second race on the big screen, that would be the ideal time for me to go and stand next to her, and to engage her in 'innocent' conversation.

We watched the first race from the grandstand steps near the betting ring.

Marina insisted on placing a bet, choosing a horse by its name, rather than by its form. Hence, she wagered ten pounds on the nose of Sassy But Sweet.

'Our daughter's called Sassy,' she said, holding out the bank-note to the bookmaker. He smiled at her, took the money, and gave her a white printed ticket in return. Marina looked at it.

'I get eighty pounds back if it wins,' she said excitedly.

But, despite Marina shouting encouragement, Sassy But Sweet didn't win, although the horse gave her a good run for her money, finishing a close second in the eight-horse contest.

The loss of her ten pounds – or rather my ten pounds – didn't seem to dampen Marina's spirits. 'Let's bet on the next race as well,' she said, hanging onto the sleeve of my coat.

'Maybe on the third,' I said. 'It's time to go and find Sophie Burnett.'

'Who?'

'The lady trainer we've come here to see.'

'Oh, yes. Right.'

We walked, arm in arm, through the grandstand and on towards the parade ring. I used my Jockey Recognition Badge to gain access, and we went across and stood on the terrace in front of the weighing room.

'Sid Halley!' called a voice behind me.

I turned round to find Bernard Parkin sitting on one of the benches beside the weighing-room wall, a walking stick by his side and his trademark checked flat cap on his head.

'Hello, Bernard,' I said, smiling at him. 'I thought you'd be dead by now.'

'Not quite,' he said with a laugh. 'But nearly. I'm ninety-five. But I've still got all my marbles.'

Bernard had been the official Cheltenham Racecourse photographer for more than fifty years, and he had attended almost every Gold Cup here since Golden Miller had won it a record five times in a row in the 1930s. He had certainly photographed me many times during my riding career, both as a victor and as a faller.

'I hear you're back investigating the wicked,' Bernard said. 'I knew you couldn't leave it alone for very long. How's it going? Caught anyone yet with blood on their hands?'

'If only,' I said.

'Come on, Sid,' Bernard said, imploring me to give him something juicy. 'I love a bit of gossip. It's all the fun I have these days.'

'Sorry, Bernard. I have nothing to report. I must be losing my touch.'

He laughed again, but I could tell he didn't believe me.

'Pose for a snap?' he asked. 'With your lovely wife?'

'Of course.'

Bernard produced a camera that was almost as old as him, and he stood up and took a picture of us both. 'I'll send you a copy,' he said.

'Thanks, Bernard,' I replied. 'It's very good to see you again.'

'I remember when you won the Champion Chase here,' he said wistfully. 'What a ride that was. You always were the best, that's until . . .'

He tailed off and glanced down at my left hand.

'Almost as good as new, now,' I said, holding it up and flexing the fingers. 'I had a transplant.'

'I could do with a whole-body transplant,' he said. 'There's far too much wrong with this one.'

We laughed together this time.

I spotted Sophie Burnett walking into the parade ring.

'Sorry, Bernard,' I said. 'I have to go now. Stay well.'

'What you mean is "stay alive".' And we laughed again.

Marina had been listening to our conversation.

'I wish I'd seen you ride as a jockey,' she said as we moved away. 'Everyone says you were the best.'

I smiled at her. 'Don't believe everything you hear.'

But I had been pretty good, and I'd been champion jockey on three occasions. And almost every night, I still dreamt that I was riding winners.

*　　*　　*

Sophie Burnett was petite, brunette, and appeared fully in control.

Her runner in the second was obviously owned by a syndicate, and she was surrounded in the parade ring by a group of six large men all wearing identical scarves, each knitted in the same red and blue colours as the racing silks worn by the jockey who soon joined them on the grass.

Marina and I stood to one side of them, listening to their good-natured banter.

'Is he going to win?' one of the men asked.

'Depends on whether Sophie's given him the go-faster juice,' said another.

'Or doped the rest with sleeping pills,' added a third.

They all laughed, clearly enjoying their day out at the home of jump racing.

A bell was rung, and Sophie and the jockey went over to the horse. She gave him a leg-up onto the horse's back, and then she returned to join the men sporting the red and blue scarves. None of them showed any signs of going to the grandstand.

I could have done without the owner sextet being with her, but this was as good an opportunity as I was likely to get.

I held Marina's hand and pulled her a little closer.

As I was glancing across at Sophie, she turned and stared straight at me.

'Aren't you Sid Halley?' she asked, taking a couple of steps towards me. 'You used to ride for my father-in-law, Brian Burnett. I'm Sophie Burnett.'

She held out her hand and I shook it.

This was going to be easier than I had feared.

'That was a long time ago,' I said. 'How is he doing?'

'Sadly, he's no longer with us. I took over the yard from him. I've had it now about ten years.'

'Sophie Burnett,' I mused. 'Didn't you employ that jockey who was murdered?'

She nodded. 'Liam Carson. Nasty business.'

'When was that?' I asked.

'Back in April. I discovered his body.'

I pulled a face, in sympathy. 'Did they get the person responsible?'

She nodded again. 'The trial's next month. I'm a witness.'

'So you saw something?'

More nods. 'I saw the murderer as she was leaving.'

'She?'

'It was his girlfriend.'

'And you're sure she did it?'

'Her fingerprints were on the knife that killed him.' She said it in a manner that expressed no doubt whatsoever that Imogen was guilty.

Sophie looked up at the big screen. The horses were still circling down at the far end of the home straight, at the two-mile-one-furlong start.

'So how come you saw this girl?' I asked her.

'Her car was blocking my drive when I tried to use it. I hooted at her to move it. She ran down the drive, climbed in and drove away very quickly.'

'Lucky you saw her,' I said. 'Had you seen her at your stables before with Liam Carson?'

'No. I saw her there just the once.'

'Were you going in or out of the stables?'

'In,' Sophie said. 'Her car was in my way.'

282

'And you're sure it was that particular day?'

'Positive,' she said. 'I was coming home from the races. I was in a hurry to be back to feed the dogs and for evening stables.'

'From Windsor races?'

'Yes.' But then she looked at me quizzically. 'How did you know that? What are all these questions about?'

'They're off,' called the race commentator over the public address, as the race started.

Sophie's attention instantly switched from me to the big screen.

'Come on,' I whispered to Marina. 'Time for us to go.'

* * *

Maybe Sophie Burnett had indeed given the horse some go-faster juice, or the others might have been half asleep, but the red and blue silks won the race easily, by five lengths.

Marina and I watched from the viewing steps as there was much backslapping and high-fiving going on in the unsaddling enclosure.

That was good, I thought. Perhaps Sophie Burnett would be sufficiently distracted by her win not to remember my questions, or at least not enough to warrant reporting the encounter to the police.

But she had seemed pretty determined that she'd seen Imogen at Boxtree Stables on the Monday, rather than on the Sunday as Imogen had claimed.

Was one of them mistaken?

Or was the other purposefully lying?

Chapter 26

MARINA LOST ANOTHER TEN POUNDS of my money on the third race, and the novelty of gambling was beginning to wear off.

'You need to take more notice of their form,' I said. 'Rather than choosing only by their name or their colours.'

We watched from the windswept grandstand steps as her choice in the fourth race, the one with the jockey wearing a fetching cerise and scarlet outfit, finished second to last. Another tenner down the drain.

We popped into the Cottage Rake bar to warm up.

'If you're so damn clever,' Marina said, sipping a cup of coffee, 'you can choose the one to bet on in the next.'

I looked in the racecard at the list of runners for the fifth race. It was a two-and-a-half-mile handicap chase for 'veteran' horses, that is those over ten years of age, so they'd been around for a while, not that it helped me pick which of the ten runners might be the winner.

But I did notice that one of them was trained by Freddie Swinton.

'Come on,' I said, taking Marina by the hand. 'Quick. Leave your coffee. I'll choose one later. There's someone else I want to talk to.'

'You'll use any bloody excuse.'

I ignored her, and we rushed to the parade ring.

I knew what Freddie Swinton looked like – who in racing didn't? And I'd even ridden against him, towards the tail end of my career, when he'd been a still-wet-behind-the-ears young conditional.

The horses were coming into the ring from the saddling boxes, together with their connections, and I spotted Freddie Swinton, standing on the grass at the far end, with a man I assumed was his horse's owner.

Marina and I went over to stand next to him.

'Imogen Duffy sends her love,' I said.

Freddie stared at me.

'I read that you were back snooping, but what the hell is Sid Halley doing going anywhere near Imogen Duffy?' he asked. 'I tell you, that girl is nothing but trouble. I made a big mistake bringing her over from Ireland.'

'But she's a good jockey.'

'It's not her riding skills that are the problem, more her social ones. Then she goes and kills someone.' He shook his head.

'She didn't do it.'

He laughed. 'Convinced you of that, did she? Has an answer for everything, that one. I'm well shot of her.'

'Did you sleep with her?' I asked. 'Like the papers said you did?'

'I bloody did not,' he retorted, getting quite angry. 'Is that what she told you?'

'No,' I said. 'She did not. In fact, she vehemently denies it.'

He calmed down a little.

'But several pictures show Imogen holding your arm.'

'That was her idea, and a bloody stupid one it was too. She said it would help the story go away, but it didn't. It made things worse. Caused me all sorts of problems with my ex-wife. And my son. He still won't speak to me.'

'But you weren't very enamoured with Liam Carson.'

'No, I bloody wasn't. He was a right little shit.'

'Is that why you killed him?'

Freddie stared at me again.

'I did not kill him,' he said calmly. 'The police investigated me and cleared me. I have an alibi.'

'Where were you?'

'In London, not that it's any of your business.'

'I think that it is my business. Anything connected with this case is my business. So, where were you?'

'I don't have to answer your questions,' he said defensively.

'As you like,' I said. 'But you may be forced to answer them in court.'

'I was at the dentist.'

'All night?'

'I had a four o'clock appointment in Wimpole Street. After that, I had dinner with a friend, and I stayed the night in a hotel.'

'Who was the friend?'

'Just a friend.'

I wondered if it had been a lady, perhaps a married lady – married to somebody else.

'Where was your dinner?'

'In a restaurant.'

'Which restaurant?'

'I forget.'

I didn't believe him.

'Which hotel did you stay in?' I asked, not really expecting him to answer. But surprisingly, he did.

'The Granby. In Great Portland Street. Near the BBC.'

'Were you alone at the hotel that night?'

'That is not relevant.'

'But you missed the following morning's exercise at your stables?'

'Yes.'

'And how often does that happen?'

'Almost never, unless I'm away racing up north or in Ireland. Or I'm on holiday.'

'How convenient for you that you were away on that particular night,' I said sarcastically.

'Very,' he said. 'Now excuse me. I have a race to see to.'

He turned away from me and spoke to Adrian Shaw, his jockey, who had just arrived.

'Do you really think Freddie Swinton did it?' Marina asked.

'I don't know. The police must have checked out his alibi. But maybe he had engineered his alibi because he knew something would happen.'

'You mean he hired a hit man?' Marina's eyes were as big as saucers. 'How exciting.'

We stood and watched as the jockeys were tossed up onto the horses' backs, and then went out onto the course.

Freddie Swinton walked over to me.

'And you can tell Imogen Duffy that she needs to arrange for someone to fetch the rest of her belongings. I currently have them stored, but if they're not collected soon, I'll dispose of them.'

'OK,' I said. 'I'll tell her.'

But I thought that her belongings were the least of her worries.

* * *

Marina and I walked towards the grandstand, but I stopped on the way at a bookmaker's pitch and wagered twenty pounds on Freddie Swinton's horse.

He may or may not be a murderer, but he was a damned good racehorse trainer. That, at least, was beyond a reasonable doubt. And Adrian Shaw wasn't the champion jockey for nothing either.

We watched the race from the grandstand steps again, and both of us cheered madly as Adrian Shaw managed to force his horse to the front with only a few yards to go before the finish line.

'Fabulous,' Marina said, hugging me. 'How much did we win?'

I looked at the ticket.

'Eighty pounds,' I said. 'But that includes the stake. So we've made sixty pounds profit.'

'Brilliant! Let's do it again. Then I can buy a new handbag.'

She seemed to have conveniently forgotten about the thirty pounds she had previously lost.

'I think it's time for us to go home,' I said. 'I've spoken to everyone I came here to see.'

'Spoilsport.'

'I also want to avoid the traffic, otherwise we'll be late getting back, and Saskia will wonder where we are.'

That swung the decision, so we made our way towards the exit.

There were two large men in dark coats waiting outside, and as Marina and I passed them, they fell into step behind us.

Oh, God, I thought.

I remembered the note I'd been sent.

If you know what's good for your health, Mr Halley, you'll stop investigating the Liam Carson murder. You have been warned!

I'd been beaten up in a racecourse car park once before, and I had no wish to be so again.

I gripped Marina by the arm and hurried along towards our car, but I could still hear the footsteps behind us on the gravel, and they seemed to be getting closer.

Well, I wasn't going to simply wait to be attacked from behind.

I pushed Marina forward and quickly turned round, bunching my fists, ready for the fight.

The two men didn't break stride, they simply walked straight on.

'Afternoon,' one of them said as he passed me.

I turned to watch them walk off, past Marina, and then onward, no doubt innocently towards their own car.

'What was all that about?' Marina asked with concern.

'I thought we were being followed,' I replied, feeling some-what foolish. 'But we weren't. Not maliciously anyway.'

'Are you all right?' she asked.

'Yes, I'm fine. Sorry. I must be getting paranoid in my old age.'

And, of course, we reached our car safely and made it home to Aynsford with no mishaps, and Saskia was delighted to see us.

'Three whole weeks off school,' she said excitedly.

'But you must have some mock exam revision to do,' I said.

'Don't be such a killjoy,' she moaned. 'I'll do it after Christmas. When does Grandpa arrive?'

'Not for another twelve days,' Marina said.

'It must be odd for him, coming here for Christmas,' Saskia said. 'After he lived here for so long.'

'I'm sure he'll have a great time,' I said.

But I did find it odd, me living here rather than Charles.

Aynsford had always been the sanctuary to which I had escaped when in trouble. Ever since, many years ago, Charles and I had become friends over a game of chess.

I think it is safe to say that, back then, Admiral Roland had not approved of his younger daughter marrying a jockey. He had despised horseracing, believing that anyone connected with it was either a rogue or a moron. I, meanwhile, considered him to be a relic of the past – a dinosaur – and the worst example of a pompous, class-ridden bigot.

He had initially dismissed me as a stupid little man, who had left school aged fifteen with no qualifications. On top of that, I was illegitimate, and at a time when those things mattered, at least to him.

That my twenty-year-old window-cleaner father had fallen to his death from his ladder only three days before his wedding to my then nineteen-year-old mother, and I'd been born eight months later, had not appeased him. Nor had the fact that my still-unmarried mother, knowing she was dying of a kidney ailment, had removed me from my grammar school and, because I was small, had apprenticed me to a racehorse trainer in Newmarket, so that I would have somewhere to live after she was gone.

I think you could have safely said that Charles and I didn't get on.

But a game of chess had changed all that.

On one of our rare, painful Sunday visits to Aynsford, and while Jenny was upstairs sorting things in her childhood bedroom, he had asked me in frustration if I played chess.

'I know the moves.'

So, we had played a game, and I had beaten him easily.

He had made the critical error of underestimating his opponent, and he stared long and hard at the board, fingering the bishop with which I had caught him in a classic discovered check and hence captured his queen.

Jenny and I had gone to Aynsford more often after that, and Charles and I always played chess, winning and losing in about equal measure. It was the start of a period of mutual respect between us, which slowly developed into a firm and close friendship that had even survived the acrimonious breakdown of my marriage to his daughter. Over time, Charles's interest in horseracing grew, and to such an extent that he was eventually invited to act as a steward at his local racecourse.

For more than twenty-five years, Charles had been my muse, my best friend, and my mentor, such that whenever I'd had a difficult decision to make, or any other sort of dilemma, I would come here to Aynsford and drink whisky with him, and seek his measured and perceptive advice.

So, indeed, it did feel odd that it was now me who sat nightly in his favourite armchair in front of the roaring fire in the drawing room, and that it would be *me* welcoming *him* to Aynsford for Christmas.

Chapter 27

THE IMOGEN DUFFY TRIAL STRATEGY meeting took place on the following Tuesday morning, at Burton Chambers, in the Inner Temple, on the north side of the Thames in the City of London.

Archie Brook and I were welcomed by Donna Lewis, the instructed barrister. I took her to be in her forties, and she seemed competent and reasonably self-assured. She showed us into a conference room overlooking the Inner Temple gardens.

The name Temple derives from Temple Church, built here by the Knights Templar in the twelfth century, when they occupied the precinct, the Templars themselves having originally taken their name from the Temple of Solomon in Jerusalem.

After the suppression of the Knights Templars by Pope Clement V in 1307, the Temple area of London became a hub for the English legal profession, an appropriate change considering the negotiations between King John and the English barons had taken place at Temple, prior to the sealing of the Magna Carta at Runnymede in June 1215, a document that became the foundation of all British law.

Middle Temple and Inner Temple remain two of the four great Inns of Court, the others being Lincoln's Inn and Grey's

Inn, slightly further north in London, and every practising barrister in England and Wales has to be a member of one of the four.

'So where do we start?' Donna Lewis said.

'We should start from the premise that Imogen Duffy is innocent until proven guilty,' I said. 'Let's have no more talk of changing pleas or of diminished responsibility. Imogen has made it quite clear that she didn't kill Liam Carson, and it is our job to stop the prosecution from proving that she did.'

I could see from the expressions of the other two that they didn't really believe it.

'What is the evidence against her?' I asked rhetorically. 'As I see it there are just two things. One, the knife had her finger-prints on it, and was most likely from the knife block in her kitchen, and second, the eyewitness account by Sophie Burnett.'

'How about the prior threatening of Carson with a knife?' Donna asked.

'That's hardly physical evidence of murder,' I said. 'In fact, there is no physical evidence at all in this case, other than those two fingerprints. No blood splatter was found on any of Imogen's clothes or shoes, and no DNA of hers found at the scene. There is no forensic evidence whatsoever to show she was ever in Liam Carson's flat.'

'But there is nothing to show she wasn't,' Archie said.

'That's the problem,' I agreed. 'And she wouldn't be the first person to be convicted of murder not because there was over-whelming evidence she did do it, but because there is nothing to show that she didn't.

'Take Timothy Evans. He was convicted and hanged for murdering his daughter even though there was nothing that really suggested he killed her. But there was also nothing to show he hadn't done it, and his assertion that John Christie must have been responsible wasn't believed. Christie even gave evidence against Evans at his trial. But three years later, Christie finally confessed to the killing, just before he too met the hangman on separate murder charges. By then, of course, it was far too late for Evans. His body was already rotting away within the grounds of Pentonville prison.'

'What about Imogen's fingerprints on the knife?' Archie said.

'But they were found on the blade, not on the handle. Have you read the pathologist's report? The knife was driven into the chest with such force that it sliced right through one of Liam Carson's ribs. There is no way that could have been done by only holding the knife by the blade. Those fingerprints simply show that Imogen had once held the blade of the knife, not that she had used it to kill.'

'But that still leaves the witness,' Donna said.

'Yes, the witness,' I said. 'How reliable is she?'

'What do you mean?' Archie said.

'Sophie Burnett claims she saw Imogen in the driveway of Boxtree Stables on Monday at six o'clock. Imogen says she was there on Sunday lunchtime, not on Monday. And Liam Carson was certainly alive on Monday afternoon because he rode in two races at Windsor Racecourse.'

'Well, Imogen would say that, wouldn't she?' Donna said. 'Especially if she was guilty.'

'But some other things also don't add up,' I said. 'Firstly, Liam Carson was naked when he died. I've seen the photographs of the scene. What was he doing lying naked on his bed at six o'clock on a Monday, when he'd been riding at Windsor Racecourse earlier in the afternoon? I suppose it's possible, but highly unlikely. And if so, was he asleep? There were no defensive wounds on his hands, so he probably didn't see the person with the knife before he was stabbed.

'Secondly, Imogen told Archie and me that the car that arrived while she was blocking the driveway came from the Lambourn direction. If Sophie Burnett was on her way home from Windsor races, as she claims, she would have arrived from the other direction, especially if she was in a hurry.'

'How do you know she was in a hurry?' Donna asked. 'Perhaps she'd been to the shops in Lambourn on her way home.'

This was where I was on somewhat shaky ground.

'Because she told me that she was hurrying to get back for her dogs and for evening stables. That's why she says she hooted at Imogen to get out of the way.'

There was a long silence.

'Please don't tell me that you went to see her,' Donna said finally.

'No, I did not,' I replied. 'I was at Cheltenham races last Friday and she was there. And it was she who came over and engaged me in conversation, not the other way round. So I took the opportunity to ask her a couple of questions.'

I could tell that neither of them believed me. I probably wouldn't have believed me either, except that I knew what I was saying was the truth.

But Donna wasn't finished. 'It is improper practice for someone engaged by the defence to contact a prosecution witness without prior permission. Doing so might be considered as witness intimidation, or even perverting the course of justice. And they're both criminal offences.'

'I did not intimidate her, and I'm not engaged by the defence,' I retorted. 'I'm an independent investigator looking at the case on behalf of Imogen's father, and he's not paying me, so I'm not actually *engaged* by anyone.'

'Stop splitting hairs,' she said, dismissively.

'But that is exactly what we have to do. We need to split every damn hair available, if it helps to create a reasonable doubt in the minds of the jury. If we just drift along, never questioning anything, and not stretching the rules, then Imogen Duffy will spend the next twenty years in jail.'

Maybe they both thought she deserved to.

'This is what we're going to do,' I said. 'And if you two won't do it, then I'll find another barrister and another solicitor who will.'

I outlined my plan for how Donna should cross-examine the prosecution witnesses.

She and Archie sat quietly listening, occasionally nodding, and once or twice pursing their lips or shaking their heads.

'Are we all agreed?' I asked.

They both nodded.

'How about witnesses for the defence?' Archie asked. 'We provided a list of possible witnesses at the Plea and Trial Preparation Hearing.'

'Who's on that list?' I asked.

'There was Imogen herself, of course, and two others to act as character witnesses.'

'Who?'

'Her father, and Freddie Swinton.'

'I certainly wouldn't call Freddie Swinton as a character witness. The only things he'd say about Imogen's character at the moment would be detrimental to our case.'

'How do you know?' Donna asked.

'Because I also spoke to him, at Cheltenham on Friday. He told me that Imogen had caused him nothing but trouble, and that he was well shot of her.'

'He didn't say that when I spoke to him in May,' Archie said. 'He seemed quite supportive of her. That's why we put him on our list.'

'Well,' I said. 'He's not supportive any more.'

'So do we just call her father?' Archie asked.

'No,' I said intensely. 'We don't call anyone. Not even Imogen.'

'But how will the jury learn about Carson's awful behaviour towards her?'

'They won't,' I said. 'Not from us anyway. And that's definitely for the best.'

'Wouldn't it make the jury feel sorry for her?' Archie asked.

'I doubt it. It would simply plant a strong motive in their minds. We need to do everything we can to keep any details of his behaviour towards her away from the jury.'

'Sid's right,' Donna said. 'But won't the prosecution bring it up anyway, as a motive?'

'I expect they'll try. But all they have is the Newbury copper, and one single comment made by Imogen in her police interview, when they asked her if she was glad Carson was dead. They're probably relying on filling in the details during cross-examination, but if we choose not to put her in the witness box, they can't ask her anything. The prosecution can't call the defendant as a witness. Only the defence can do that, and we're not going to.'

'But will Imogen agree?' Donna asked. 'Ultimately it's her decision whether or not to give evidence.'

'Then we will have to convince her,' I said.

It's always a risk for the defendant not to give evidence. Not only does it take away the opportunity for them to stand up in the witness box and categorically tell the court that they didn't do it, but the jury can draw an adverse inference over their failure to speak in their defence.

However, it does prevent the prosecution from cross-examining them, and bringing up things that we would much rather the jury didn't hear.

It is said that defendants who don't give evidence, and are subsequently convicted, spend the whole of their sentence wishing that they had given evidence, while those who do and are also convicted, spend their whole sentence wishing they hadn't.

'So, we don't present a defence case at all?' Archie asked.

'That's right. In British courts, there is a presumption that the accused is innocent until proven guilty. It is for the prosecution to prove Imogen's guilt, not for us to prove her innocence. All we will do is to try and undermine their witnesses, to question their reliability, so that the jury can't be sure beyond a reasonable doubt. Not certain enough anyway to convict.'

'I hope you're right,' Donna said.

So did I.

*   *   *

Christmas at Aynsford was everything I could have hoped for.

Charles and Mrs Cross arrived with full fanfare at about eleven o'clock in the morning on Christmas Eve. I had offered to collect them, but Charles had already organised a taxi.

He stood in the hallway admiring the enormous Christmas tree.

'I used to have a big tree like that, just there, when my girls were small, and their mother was still alive. Such happy memories.'

Charles wasn't one for showing his emotions, more a stiff-upper-lip sort of chap, but there was clearly a tear in his eye.

Marina and I had discussed whether we should allow him to sleep in the master bedroom, with us moving out, but we had fully redecorated that room since our arrival, changing the very male, dark furnishings for lighter, pastel colours. And we had already moved his magnificent nineteenth-century teak and steel-banded Royal Navy officer's chest into the large guest room.

He had wanted to take the chest with him to the care home, but there hadn't been the space.

'You're in the guest room,' I said to him.

'Of course,' he replied, and I helped him up the stairs with his suitcase and his various other assorted carrier bags.

'Come down when you're ready,' I said to him as he stood stroking the polished wood of his much-loved naval chest. 'Marina has prepared some smoked salmon for lunch.'

Mrs Cross, meanwhile, asked if she could sleep in her old room up in the eaves, on the second floor.

'It's all ready for you,' Marina said. 'But if you'd prefer, you could stay in our other spare room on the first floor. It might make it easier for you with the stairs.'

'I'll be fine up top,' she replied with a smile. 'Just like old times.'

Saskia had always loved Christmas, and she was beside herself with excitement, behaving more like the little girl she had been, rather than the young woman she had become.

'Please can we play a game this evening?' she asked.

'Maybe,' I said.

'That's what you always say, then you just sit in the drawing room with Grandpa and drink whisky.'

I looked at her.

'All right,' I said decisively. 'Tonight, we will play a game. What do you have in mind?'

'Charades,' she replied firmly. 'We play it at school in our drama class. It's great fun.'

'OK,' I said. 'We will play charades after dinner.'

And we did, still sitting round the dining room table, although Charles and Mrs Cross both had trouble with the film titles *Star Wars: The Force Awakens* and *Mamma Mia: Here We Go Again*, while Saskia struggled to act out Charles's choice of *Coastal Defences of the British Empire in the Revolutionary and Napoleonic Eras* in the book category.

After we'd all had two turns each at acting out a title, and the game had ended in a draw, Charles and I retired to the drawing room and drank whisky.

'What's new?' Charles asked me, settling into his favourite armchair.

I sat in the armchair next to him and sipped my single malt.

'I've been investigating a murder.'

'Have you, indeed. Whose?'

'Someone called Liam Carson. He was an Irish jump jockey.'

He nodded. 'I think I remember reading about it. Stabbed, wasn't he?'

'Through the heart with a carving knife.'

'That would do it. But I thought they'd caught the killer.'

'That's who I'm working for.'

'The killer?'

'The supposed killer.'

'Are you trying for an appeal?'

I shook my head. 'Her trial's not until next month.'

'Her?'

'Imogen Duffy. She's another Irish jockey.'

Charles nodded again. 'Won the Champion Chase.'

'That's the one.'

'And you think she's innocent?'

'I think that the evidence against her is very thin.'

'That's not the same thing.'

'The problem is that if she didn't kill Carson, who did? And the knife certainly came from her kitchen.'

'No other suspects?'

'Only one, and he seems to have an alibi.'

'Seems to?'

'He claims he had dinner with a friend, but he won't say where, or with whom, and then he spent the night in a London hotel, maybe alone, maybe not.'

'Have you checked it out?'

'The police will have done that.'

'But the police are simply looking to prove their case, which is the complete opposite of what you are trying to do. They might have only found what they wanted to find, and then stopped looking any further.'

Marina came into the room. 'Come on, you two. Drink up. It's time for bed. There's only ten minutes now until midnight, and Father Christmas will be here soon.'

Charles and I stood up and drained our glasses.

'Now I must remember to go to bed in the guest bedroom tonight, not in the master,' Charles said, laughing. 'Otherwise, Father Christmas will never find me.'

I wondered how much Christmas cheer there would be in Bronzefield prison. Not much, I suspected. Staff levels would be so low on Christmas Day that the inmates would be spending most, if not all, of the day itself locked in their cells.

And I doubted that there would be a stocking hanging on Imogen Duffy's prison bedpost tonight, waiting for Father Christmas to fill it with presents, even if she had been a good girl this year.

Chapter 28

CHRISTMAS DAY DAWNED BRIGHT AND sunny.
Marina had done Christmas stockings for us all –
and I'd done one for her – and the five of us opened
the presents from them wearing our dressing gowns, drinking
coffee and eating toast around the kitchen table.

After that, Charles asked if he could go to the Christmas
morning service at the local church, so we dressed, and I went
with him.

He had such fun, meeting up with many former neighbours
and belting out 'Hark! The Herald Angels Sing' and 'O Come,
All Ye Faithful' at the top of his considerable voice.

Back at the house, I opened a bottle of champagne, and we
unwrapped more gifts. Then it was almost time for lunch.

Marina complained to me that she couldn't stop Mrs Cross
from being in the kitchen all the time, and from continually
washing up the pots and pans as she was cooking.

'She clearly thinks it's still her domain.'

I laughed. 'I suppose it's what she's used to.'

'I know she's trying to be helpful, but it's driving me mad.
She even poured away the water from the French beans that
I was saving to use in the gravy.'

When we had finally convinced Mrs Cross to sit with us at the dining room table for Christmas lunch, rather than remaining in the kitchen, Saskia asked her what her first name was, as we'd all been calling her Mrs Cross.

I looked at Charles, and he simply shrugged his shoulders.

'Elsie,' she said quietly. 'But I'm not very fond of it.'

So we continued calling her Mrs Cross, and everyone seemed happy with the arrangement.

I assumed there must have once been a Mr Cross, but I decided not to ask. Mrs Cross had been Charles's live-in housekeeper for longer than I had known him, and there had been no sign of a Mr Cross during that time.

We started our festive feast with a shrimp cocktail, then enjoyed roast turkey with all the trimmings, followed by stewed pears and hangop, a traditional Dutch dairy dessert, made from buttermilk and yogurt, which Marina had always eaten as a child at Christmas in Fryslân, her native province in the Netherlands.

With our stomachs full almost to bursting, we adjourned to watch the King's Christmas message on the television, before Charles and I settled down in front of the fire in the drawing room for another Halley/Roland tradition, the post-Christmas-lunch snooze.

Mrs Cross, meanwhile, insisted on washing up the dishes.

* * *

The following day, I took Charles to Kempton Park races for the King George VI Chase, while Marina and Saskia went to the opening of the sales in Oxford.

304

They asked Mrs Cross to go with them, but she declined, deciding to remain alone at Aynsford, where she seemed to be at her happiest.

As always, Kempton on Boxing Day was absolutely packed for one of the great steeplechase races of the year, and it didn't disappoint with the favourite, Multistorey, trained by Freddie Swinton, winning the big race by two lengths under Jimmy Tucker, himself recently returned from a serious shoulder injury.

After the presentations, I left Charles by the parade-ring rail, and made my way over to Freddie Swinton, as he was still answering questions from a group of racing journalists. He saw me coming and pursed his lips in displeasure and irritation.

I stood patiently as he answered the last of the questions, then he turned to me.

'What the bloody hell do you want?'

He said it quietly so the journalists wouldn't hear.

'I wondered if you have remembered the name of the restaurant where you dined with your anonymous friend on the night Liam Carson died.'

'No, I haven't. Now bugger off and leave me alone.'

He turned angrily away and marched off. I was clearly getting under his skin.

I went back to join Charles, who was leaning heavily on the rail.

'Are you OK?' I asked.

'Just tired. I'm not as sprightly as I used to be. I must be getting old.' He smiled.

'Would you like to go home now?'

He didn't say anything, but I could clearly see that he did.

'No problem,' I said.

We made our way to the exit, and Charles sat down on a chair while I fetched the car.

He slept most of the way to Aynsford, and we were both grateful to Mrs Cross, who somehow had a tray of tea and buttered toast magically ready for us when we arrived.

The girls appeared soon after, laden down with branded carrier bags.

'You have no idea how much we've saved,' Marina said.

I was more worried about how much they'd spent.

* * *

'I am sorry, sir, but there is no record of someone of your name having stayed at our hotel on that particular night.'

It was the morning after Boxing Day, and I was sitting at my desk in my study.

I had called the Granby Hotel in Great Portland Street, saying that I was Freddie Swinton, and had asked for a duplicate of my hotel invoice to be emailed to me, as I had lost the original and my tax accountant needed it.

'Are you sure about the date?'

'Positive,' I replied. 'But could you check the following day as well?'

I could hear a computer keyboard being tapped.

'Nothing on the following day either, sir. Sorry.'

'It's not your fault,' I said. 'I must be mistaken or have the wrong hotel.'

We disconnected.

How come, if the police had checked out Freddie Swinton's alibi, there was no record of him having stayed that fateful Monday night at the Granby Hotel?

I could think of several different reasons.

He might have given the wrong hotel name to me on purpose, just to be bloody-minded. Or, like Imogen at the airport hotel, he could have used a false name so no one would recognise him, after the newspaper stories. Or, if he was indeed with a lady friend, then the booking might have been in her name.

Or maybe the police hadn't checked his alibi at all, and he'd been lying when he told me they had. Or perhaps he had no alibi in the first place.

There was no mention of Freddie Swinton in any of the documents provided by the prosecution to the defence. But there wouldn't be, not if the police hadn't found anything about him that helped their case against Imogen, and he wasn't on their list of prosecution witnesses.

Maybe I should reassess my decision not to call him as a defence witness, perhaps hoping for a 'Perry Mason moment' when the witness breaks down under questioning, and suddenly confesses to the crime.

However, if Freddie didn't admit to murder, which he certainly wouldn't, he could do Imogen far more harm than good. Under cross-examination, he would likely bring up all the details of Liam Carson's campaign of hate towards her, and hence reinforce, in the minds of the jury, her motive for killing him.

Thankfully, we didn't need to make that decision right now.

Freddie Swinton remained on the defence list of potential witnesses, so we still had the chance to call him during the trial if we wanted to – that's if things were not going well, and the prosecution had managed to introduce all the stuff we were trying to keep out.

Not that Freddie's angry reaction to my questions at Cheltenham and Kempton would indicate that he'd be any use to us as a character witness for Imogen, whatever he might have said in the way of supportive comments to Archie back in May.

But if we did call him and he turned out to be hostile, we might then be at liberty to treat him so, perhaps even allowing us to sow a few seeds of doubt in the minds of the jury by providing them with a possible murder suspect who was different to the young woman sitting in the dock, someone who had every reason to hate Liam Carson as much as she did.

However, we would have to do it very subtly. Directly impeaching the credibility of your own witness was strictly against the rules – even if he was hostile to our cause.

* * *

Charles and Mrs Cross went back to their retirement home on New Year's Eve.

'Are you sure you won't stay to see in the New Year here?' Marina asked.

'Thank you, my dear,' Charles said, laying his hand on hers. 'But we've been here quite long enough, and we have a bit of a party at Godswell House tonight, and we'd hate to miss that. I'm meant to be speaking to the other residents about spending New Year's Eve away in a warship.'

'Which ship?' I asked.

'Which do you think?'

'*Amethyst.*'

'Of course. We spent New Year 1949 in Hong Kong harbour, before going up the Yangtze. I was just a young lad then, mind, but I remember it well.' He smiled broadly. 'One of the ratings had been ashore, and he'd somehow acquired a whole bag of Chinese firecrackers. We lit them all over the decks at midnight. They made a tremendous noise, but the captain was furious. He thought we were under fire.' He laughed, but then he suddenly became very serious. 'But for twenty-two of my ship-mates on that night, including the captain, that was their last ever New Year celebration. Within four months, they would all be dead.'

There were tears in his eyes and I tried to hug him, but he pushed me away in embarrassment. But he did hug Marina and Saskia, thanking them both effusively for a wonderful Christmas.

'Come for Christmas again next year,' Marina said, tears also welling up in her eyes.

'I will,' Charles replied. 'That's if I'm still alive.'

He made me think of Bernard Parkin, the Cheltenham Racecourse photographer, both of them making the most of their lives, while they still had them.

* * *

Our New Year celebrations at Aynsford were a lot quieter than Charles's had been in Hong Kong aboard HMS *Amethyst* in 1949.

Marina, Saskia and I just about managed to stay awake until midnight, to watch the fireworks from London on the television, before wishing each other a Happy New Year, and then immediately heading off to our beds.

'It somehow seemed so right to have had Charles here for Christmas,' Marina said to me as we snuggled together beneath the bedclothes. 'In truth, I'd been really worried about him coming – him feeling awkward about us living in his house without him, and us apologising to him all the time for making some changes – but it was fine. He should come and stay with us more often.'

'Why don't we ask him to come here for Easter?' I said.

'That's a great idea.'

*   *   *

On the morning of 2nd January, another note dropped through the letterbox in the Aynsford front door, again printed in bold black letters on a plain sheet of white paper.

I told you to stop investigating Liam Carson's murder. I won't warn you again.

I looked at the ubiquitous white envelope in which it had arrived.

Once more, the postage stamp had been franked at the Royal Mail Swindon Mail Centre, this time at 18.16 on 28th December.

Why did someone want me to stop investigating?

And was it a coincidence that it had been posted just two days after I'd spoken with Freddie Swinton at Kempton Park races?

Everyone knows that the only thing that's better than getting away with murder is to have another person convicted of it. That way, the police close the case and stop looking for anyone else.

John Christie must have been laughing all the way home to 10 Rillington Place, after his testimony helped convict Timothy Evans for a murder that he himself had committed.

Did the person who sent this note want Imogen Duffy to be found guilty for the same reason?

Back in the day, when I'd been a full-time investigator, I'd earned a bit of a reputation amongst the British criminal underworld.

'It's no good beating up Sid Halley, he'll just come after you harder.'

So they had resorted to beating up my then girlfriend, now my wife, and also kidnapping my daughter. And I suppose their tactics had worked, because I had left that life behind me – or almost.

But if someone thought that a couple of menacing notes were going to stop me now, they were very much mistaken.

Chapter 29

THE CROWN COURT BUILDING IN Reading has a very grand façade, built in the Baroque revival style, with multiple Ionic columns flanking large round-headed sash windows.

Above the main entrance is a balcony, fronted by an ornate stone balustrade, upon which sits a panel with a frieze of the Royal Coat of Arms of the United Kingdom, a reminder that all criminal trials prosecuted within its walls are done so in the name of the reigning monarch.

I queued to pass through the security check to get in. Having emptied my pockets into the tray, I walked through the metal detector.

It remained silent.

One of the peripheral advantages of having had a hand transplant, and hence no longer wearing a steel and plastic prosthesis, was that I no longer caused such machines to sound multiple alarms, and to flash large red warning lights. It had made passing through airports so much easier and considerably less embarrassing.

Once inside, I collected my stuff from the tray and then admired the grand lobby that reached up through the full height of the building, such that there were four square skylights in the ceiling, some forty to fifty feet above the geometrically patterned tiled floor.

But all this nineteenth-century grandeur belied the fact that the six courts in Reading were fairly modern, built in red brick onto the rear of the old part.

Imogen's case was to be heard in Court Number 2, on the first floor.

* * *

Much of the first morning of any murder trial is always taken up with legal presentations, introductions, and the swearing in of the jury.

Unlike in the United States, where potential jurors first have to complete a detailed questionnaire and are then regularly interrogated by both prosecutors and defence to determine their suitability, members of an English jury are simply selected at random from the local electoral register and are not required to answer any questions except to give their names and addresses, and to indicate if they are related to, or are a friend of the defendant or the witnesses.

'I swear by Almighty God that I will faithfully try the defendant and give a true verdict according to the evidence.'

I watched as the five men and seven women each took the oath in turn, trying to assess how they might react to the story that would shortly be unfolding in front of them.

I wondered if it was an advantage to have a majority of women on the jury or a disadvantage. Women could be very critical of their own sex, while men might be more forgiving of a vulnerable girl who had been so badly treated. Not that we wanted to tell them anything about that anyway.

All the while, Imogen Duffy sat immobile in the glass-fronted dock.

She had been brought to the court in a prison van, and Donna, Archie and I had been to see her in the court cells prior to the start of proceedings.

'Sit still all the time, unless you are told to stand up by either Donna or the judge,' I told her. 'Whatever happens, make no sound or movement, even if you disagree with what is being said, and you desperately want to shout out. Don't. Just sit quietly. Show no emotion. And try to look as small as possible.'

She would have no problem complying with the last part.

At only five foot, five inches tall, she had been one of the shortest steeplechase jockeys. And the long period of inactivity in Bronzefield prison had caused her muscle mass to waste, so that she now looked far more like an anorexic schoolgirl than the wiry, tough and highly toned athlete she had been nine months ago, when she'd easily been able to control half a ton of Thoroughbred racehorse jumping over fences at thirty miles per hour.

I reckoned that, in her current state, she'd likely have trouble controlling a Shetland pony.

We went through our strategy with Imogen and explained that we didn't want her to give evidence in her defence.

'Won't that make me look guilty?'

Donna explained to her that, even though an adverse inference might be drawn by the jury over her failure to give evidence, it wouldn't be anywhere near as bad as them hearing about her tumultuous relationship with Liam Carson during what would undoubtedly be a very aggressive cross-examination by the prosecution.

314

'OK,' Imogen said. 'I'll agree with what you think is best.'

The dock at Reading was at the rear of the courtroom, alongside the public gallery, although members of the public couldn't see the defendant, nor vice versa, because the glass between them was opaque.

Sitting in the gallery were several members of the public, and I noticed that one of them was Patrick Duffy, alongside a small woman who I took to be his wife, Imogen's mother. I waved a hand in his direction, and he nodded back at me. His face was very sombre, and there was some puffiness around his wife's eyes, as if she had been crying.

Facing the dock, behind his raised light oak-panelled bench, sat the judge. He was clothed in a violet-trimmed black gown, complete with bright scarlet sash, a judge's wig perched precariously on his head.

To the judge's right was the witness box and to his left were the jury, now sitting behind twelve desks, in two rows of six, their rather casual dress in stark contrast to the very formal attire of everyone else.

In front of the judge's bench, at a lower level, in the well of the court, sat the clerk and the usher, and in front of them, facing the judge, were the prosecution and defence teams, with, as tradition dictated, the defence being closest to the jury.

I took my seat at a table immediately behind Donna Lewis, next to Archie Brook.

'Who are those people?' I asked Archie quietly, indicating towards the five members of the prosecution team.

'The older man in front is Geoffrey Blandford,' Archie whispered. 'He's the main prosecuting counsel. The one next to him, also in the gown and wig, is the main man's junior barrister, the other three behind may be solicitors, the CPS, or even police. They're there to help and advise the prosecution.'

As Archie and I were for the defence.

My heart was beating fast with nerves.

With everyone settled into their proper places, the judge invited the prosecution counsel to outline the Crown's case.

Geoffrey Blandford stood up and turned towards the twelve good men and true – even though seven of them were, in fact, good women and true.

'Ladies and gentlemen of the jury,' he began, 'this case is one of violent murder within the competitive world of Thoroughbred horseracing.

'Liam Carson, a twenty-seven-year-old jockey, was found dead, lying on his own bed, in his own home, with a carving knife embedded in his chest, it having sliced right through his heart.

'We will show that the defendant, also a jockey, had the opportunity and the motive for the killing. In addition, the murder weapon was found to have the defendant's fingerprints on it, and you will hear from an eyewitness who puts her at the scene of the crime at a time consistent with the pathologist's estimated hour of death.

'We will demonstrate that the defendant is a liar and has used a false identity in order not to be identified. Furthermore, we will also lay before you evidence of a previous threat to the life of the victim by the accused, and with the very same knife that was ultimately used, by her, to commit the murder.'

As a final flourish he half turned and indicated towards Imogen sitting in the dock.

'In this way we will prove to you, members of the jury, so that you are sure that the defendant, Imogen Duffy, is guilty of the charge of murder, beyond any reasonable doubt.'

He stood there dramatically for several more seconds, still pointing at Imogen in the dock, before finally retaking his seat.

I noticed that Geoffrey Blandford's black gown was made of silk. That indicated that he was a KC, a King's Counsel, the most senior and experienced of barristers. I had considered whether Imogen should have also had a KC to defend her, but she was relying on legal aid and the judge had decided that the defence case didn't warrant the cost to the nation of a KC.

Not that I was particularly bothered by that. I didn't want her to appear to be 'over lawyered'.

People on minor motoring charges who turn up at the magistrates' court with a King's Counsel to represent them are almost certainly guilty but are doing their best to get off – the cost of the barrister far outweighing any likely fine they would receive if the charge were proved.

I suppose it was a risk for Imogen not to have a KC, but at no point did I want the jury to think that she was guilty simply because she had instructed a fancy lawyer. And, most importantly, a fancy KC might have also believed they knew best, and hence not done what I wanted them to do.

Donna Lewis would be fine.

The judge looked over at her. 'Miss Lewis, does the defence wish to make an opening statement?'

Donna rose. 'No, Your Honour.' She sat down again.

The judge looked down at the prosecution counsel.

'Mr Blandford?'

'Your Honour, before calling our first witness, we have three witness statements to read out to the jury, which have been agreed with my learned friend for the defence, who have no objection concerning their content.'

Section 9 of the Criminal Justice Act, 1967, allows witness statements, properly executed and signed, and over which there is no contention, to be read out in court and admitted as evidence, thereby saving the witnesses from having to attend court in person.

The prosecution junior barrister stood up and read aloud the three statements in turn, each of which I had previously read at Archie Brook's offices.

First was the statement from the airport hotel receptionist, describing how Imogen Duffy had used a false name – Alison Brown – and how she had paid in advance with cash, when checking in on the day before she was arrested.

Next was the statement from Simon Potter, the Swinton stables' maintenance man, describing how he had found Imogen in her kitchen threatening Liam Carson with a carving knife.

And third was the one from PC Tate reporting how Imogen had been to see him at Newbury Police Station on the Wednesday prior to the murder, to complain about Liam Carson's behaviour towards her, and how she had ended up being issued with an official police warning for threatening someone with a knife.

The junior barrister sat down, and the KC stood up again.

'The prosecution calls Detective Chief Inspector Miller.'

The usher went out of the court and returned with a man wearing a suit and tie, carrying a sheaf of papers. He confidently stepped into the witness box, and the usher stood in front of him.

'Please hold the Bible up in your right hand and read from the card.'

The witness put down his papers, and took the Bible, holding it up.

'I swear by Almighty God that the evidence I shall give shall be the truth, the whole truth, and nothing but the truth.'

The usher took back the Bible and returned to his place.

The KC rose and turned to the witness.

'Please tell the jury your name, rank and role.'

'I am Detective Chief Inspector Keith Miller. I lead the Thames Valley Police Major Crime Team within the Force Crime Operational Command Unit, based in Kidlington, north of Oxford.'

'And are you the senior investigating officer in this case?'

'I am.'

'And did you attend the crime scene, soon after the body of Mr Carson was discovered?'

'I did.' He referred to his notebook. 'My detective sergeant and I arrived together at Boxtree Stables, Eastbury, at eight twenty-five on that Tuesday morning.'

'DCI Miller, could you please tell the jury what you found at the scene?'

The Chief Inspector began to give a full description of what he had observed in the flat above the stables.

The KC interrupted him at one point.

'Your Honour, photographs of the scene are included in the prosecution bundle and are also available to the jury in their files. But I should warn the jury that the photos are rather graphic, as they show the deceased as he was found.'

As one, the twelve members of the jury reached forward for the white ring folders that were lying on each of their desks.

I watched as they opened the files and looked at the photos, the same ones I had seen at the offices of Ashe, Brook and Pollard, the ones with the carving knife still protruding from Liam Carson's bare chest.

Several members of the jury went a little pale, and quite a few looked across at Imogen in the dock, some of them with revulsion clear on their faces.

The DCI continued, describing how he had arranged for the scene to be isolated, for a forensic team to be summoned, as well as sending for a Home Office registered forensic pathologist to attend.

'And did you remain at the murder scene for an extended period?' asked the KC.

'Yes. I did. I remained there to supervise while the forensic team carried out their examination, and also until the pathologist arranged for the deceased to be removed to the mortuary at the Royal Berkshire Hospital. Then my sergeant and I secured the crime scene with padlocks and "Police line do not cross" tape.'

'What time would that have been?'

The DCI looked at his notebook again. 'Fifteen ten hours. Ten past three in the afternoon.'

'And what did you do next?'

'I telephoned my office. I was informed by a member of my team that a Thames Valley police constable, PC Tate, based at Newbury Police Station, who had become aware of the murder via the force's internal messaging system, had been in touch. He reported that only six days previously, he'd had need to issue an official police warning to an individual who had threatened Mr Carson with a knife.'

'Yes,' said the KC. 'PC Tate's witness statement has already been read to the court and admitted as evidence. Remind us of the name of the individual to whom the official warning was issued.'

'Miss Imogen Duffy,' said the DCI. 'The defendant.'

'And did you act on this information?'

'I did. I immediately called the officer at Newbury. He appraised me with the full details of his interview with Miss Duffy, including the fact that he had interviewed her in the presence of her employer, the racehorse trainer Mr Freddie Swinton. He also gave me Miss Duffy's home address. As Miss Duffy's residence was only a few miles down the road from Eastbury, I decided that my sergeant and I would pay her a visit right away, with a view to interviewing her, and perhaps making an arrest.'

'And what did you find?'

'No one answered my knocks on her door. So I went to the adjacent cottage, where the neighbour said that she might be at Mr Swinton's stables. Hence, I went to the stables and was told by staff in the office that she may have flown to Ireland, even though they were uncertain of her precise whereabouts. The staff then contacted Mr Swinton, who agreed to meet me at Miss Duffy's address, with his key to the front door.'

'And did you enter the premises?'

'Using the authority accorded to me by Section 17, subsection 2 of the Police and Criminal Evidence Act, 1984, and with the permission of Mr Swinton, the owner of the property, my sergeant and I entered the premises and carried out a preliminary search, as we had reasonable grounds for believing that Miss Duffy might be present.'

'And was she present?'

'She was not. But it was during this search that I observed a wooden knife block in the kitchen with an empty slot, indicating that a knife was missing. Further examination of the block, and of the murder weapon at a later time, indicated that the knife that was missing was identical to the one used to murder Liam Carson.'

'So it was that knife?'

'I would say so, yes.'

Donna Lewis rose from her chair.

'If it might please Your Honour, I feel that my learned friend is leading the witness to give an opinion, rather than sticking to the facts of the case.'

The KC turned and gave her a piercing stare.

'I agree, Miss Lewis,' said the judge. He turned to the detective. 'Please refrain from giving your opinions on subjects of which you are not an expert witness, Chief Inspector.'

But the KC wasn't yet finished with the knife.

'Once the murder weapon, the knife, had been recovered from the body of the victim during the post-mortem examination at the mortuary, was it sent for forensic analysis?'

'Yes. It was,' replied the DCI.

'Are you aware of the findings by the forensic laboratory?'

'Yes, I am. I have read the forensic final report. It is included in the prosecution bundle.'

He reached forward and lifted a copy of the report from his papers.

'Could you tell the court what was found on the knife?'

'The defendant's right thumbprint and her right index finger-print were discovered, one on either side of the blade.'

'Was this discovery made before or after her arrest?'

'Before. Miss Duffy had previously volunteered her finger-prints at Newbury Police Station. The prints found on the knife were compared to those, and an exact match was found.'

'So did you attempt to locate her?'

'Yes. Having been given the information that she may have already flown to Ireland, a check was made of airline passenger manifests to determine whether and when she had left. It was during that check that we ascertained that she had not yet departed from the UK, and was, in fact, booked on an Aer Lingus flight from Heathrow to Dublin on the Wednesday morning. I dispatched two of my team to the airport and they arrested her as she was attempting to board the aircraft.'

'Did you try to locate her prior to that time?'

'Yes. On Tuesday evening, I arranged for some officers to call several Heathrow airport hotels, but none of them reported having any guest with the name Duffy.'

'And do you know why that was?'

'We subsequently found out, when questioning the defendant, that she had indeed stayed overnight in one of the hotels we had called, but she had used a false name when checking in. And had paid for her room in advance with cash.'

'Yes,' said the KC. 'The court has already heard the witness statement from the hotel receptionist. In her interview, did the defendant say why she had checked in with a false name?'

'She claimed that she didn't want to be recognised or for anyone to know her real name.' His tone of voice left no doubt in anyone's mind that he believed such actions to be highly suspicious.

'Did she say anything else during her police interview?'

'She said that she wasn't sorry that Liam Carson was dead. When asked why that was, she replied that he'd been telling awful lies about her to the newspapers, and therefore he deserved to die.'

'The defendant said that Mr Carson deserved to die,' the KC repeated slowly. 'Thank you, Chief Inspector. No more questions from me, but my learned friend will probably want to ask you some.'

He said it with gritted teeth. Donna Lewis was clearly no 'learned friend' of his, not after her previous audacious intervention.

Donna stood up.

'Miss Lewis,' said the judge before she could speak, 'is your cross-examination of the witness likely to last long?'

'Yes, Your Honour. I do have quite a number of questions to ask of this witness.'

'In that case, I think we will adjourn for lunch at this point,' he said. He turned towards the jury. 'Ladies and gentlemen, we will begin again at two o'clock when the defence counsel will begin her cross-examination of Chief Inspector Miller.'

'All rise,' called the usher.

We all stood and bowed at the judge, who bowed back, before departing through a door to his chambers, no doubt for a fulsome lunch. I even wondered if he might wash it down with a small glass of wine.

I, meanwhile, could have done with a couple of stiff whiskies after that evidence.

Chapter 30

WE RESUMED AT TWO O'CLOCK, with the jury filing into their allotted places.

I had spent the lunch recess with Donna and Archie, both of whom now seemed even more convinced of Imogen's guilt.

'Come on,' I said to them urgently. 'We can undermine this witness's evidence. We just need to be clever.'

I went through the questions that Donna should ask and the way she should ask them. And I had also looked up DCI Miller's social media accounts.

The Detective Chief Inspector was shown back to the witness box.

'Please stand,' the judge said to him. He did so. 'I remind you that you are still under oath from this morning.'

'Yes, Your Honour.' He sat down again.

Donna now stood up.

'Chief Inspector,' she said. 'Could you give the jury some indication of your education and of your experience of criminal matters?'

The KC rose. 'Is that matter relevant, Your Honour? The fact that the witness has risen to the rank of Detective Chief

Inspector in the police service would seem to imply that he has sufficient knowledge and experience of criminal matters.'

'Miss Lewis,' said the judge. 'Is there a purpose to your line of questioning?'

'Yes, Your Honour, which will quickly become apparent.'

'Then please proceed. But be warned, I will not allow you to continue if I feel your questions are not relevant to this case.'

The KC sat down again and Donna turned back to the witness.

'Is it not true, Chief Inspector, that you started your working life as a civilian forensic scientist, before joining the police service?'

'Yes. I graduated from London University with a degree in forensic science, and I worked in a forensic laboratory in Oxford for three years, before joining the Thames Valley Police.'

'Did the laboratory you worked in deal with criminal cases?'

'All the time. It is how I became interested in police work, in particular in becoming a detective.'

'And during your time at the laboratory, did you write, or help to write, forensic reports for criminal cases such as this one?'

'Yes. Several of them.'

'Would that have been one of the reasons why you remained at Boxtree Stables supervising the forensic examination of the murder scene? That and to keep up to date with current forensic techniques?'

'You could say so, yes.'

'So would you agree with me that you are something of an expert in forensic matters?'

'Yes. I would.'

'After Miss Duffy was arrested, was a further search made of her home?'

'Yes. A forensic team and I carried out a full search of the property.'

'And were any items taken away for analysis?'

'Yes, there were. The knife block, several pairs of shoes, and various pieces of clothing were taken.'

'When you made your oath this morning, you swore by Almighty God that the evidence you would give would be the truth, the whole truth, and nothing but the truth. Is that correct?'

'Yes.'

'I am not implying in any way that the evidence you have given so far today has not been the truth, but it hasn't been the whole truth, has it, Chief Inspector?'

Donna paused.

'You told the court earlier that the forensic report stated that the defendant's right thumbprint and her right index fingerprint were found on the blade of the knife, but you didn't say what wasn't found.' She paused again. 'Was a forensic analysis of the defendant's phone carried out?'

'Yes.'

'And did you have any difficulty in unlocking the phone?'

'No.'

'Was that because my client freely gave the police the unlocking code?'

'Yes.'

'And did the phone have its Location Services enabled, allowing its position at any time to be recorded using GPS and Bluetooth?'

'Yes.'

'And did those records show that the defendant's phone had been in Eastbury village at the time of the murder?'

'No. But that doesn't mean the owner of the phone hadn't been there, just that she hadn't taken her phone with her.'

'That is mere conjecture, Chief Inspector. Let us stick to the facts.'

Donna paused again.

'Did they show that the phone had been near Boxtree Stables at any other time?'

'Yes. On three prior occasions. Two the previous week, and once more on the day before the murder.'

'On the Sunday?'

'Yes. At one o'clock in the afternoon.'

'On the Sunday?' Donna repeated. 'At one o'clock in the afternoon?'

'Yes.'

Another pause.

'During the forensic analysis of the defendant's phone, did you find her Aer Lingus ticket to Dublin for the flight she was attempting to board when she was arrested?'

'Yes, we did.'

'And was it a single ticket or a return?'

'A return.'

'A return ticket,' Donna said slowly. 'For the following week?'

'Yes, for the Wednesday.'

'And did she explain in her police interviews why she was attempting to board a flight to Ireland?'

'She said she was going home to see her parents.'

Donna paused once more.

'Was any CCTV footage available from Boxtree Stables on the day of the murder?' Donna asked.

'None that showed the access to Mr Carson's flat.'

'Did the police attempt to obtain any CCTV footage from anywhere else, footage that might have shown the assailant either going to or coming away from the murder scene?'

'Yes. Footage was obtained from some of the shops and businesses in Lambourn, and from several doorbell video systems in Eastbury village, for the period around when the murder could have occurred.'

'And did any of that footage show the defendant at any time?'

'No.'

'Let us now turn to the other matters in the forensic report,' Donna said, lifting it high in the air. 'How many swabs does this report say were taken at the scene, to determine the presence of any DNA?'

The detective leaned forward and picked up his copy, opening it at the relevant section.

'Fifty-five.'

'And how many of those fifty-five swabs returned a positive match with the DNA of the defendant?'

'None of them.'

'None of them,' Donna repeated. 'And how many other fingerprints of the defendant were found at the murder scene?'

'None.'

'And was there any other forensic evidence to show that the defendant had ever been inside Liam Carson's flat?'

'No.'

'Let's turn now to the items removed from Miss Duffy's cottage, in particular, her shoes and her clothes. Were these items subjected to a forensic search, perhaps looking for blood?'

'Yes.'

'And was any blood found?'

'No.'

'And was any DNA other than the defendant's found on these items?'

'No.'

'And yet the report indicates that there would have been a substantial degree of blood spray and splatter from the wound in Mr Carson's chest. Is that correct?'

'Yes.'

'So it might be expected that there would be some blood on the clothes, and maybe on the shoes, of the murderer?'

'It is a possibility.'

'And all the blood samples at the scene were found to belong to the victim, not to any other individual. Is that correct?'

'Yes.'

'And was the victim's blood found on any of the items worn by the defendant on arrest, or on any of the defendant's property subsequently seized from her home?'

'No. Only her fingerprints on the knife.'

'Yes. Let us consider that knife. The defence does not dispute the fact that the defendant's thumb- and fingerprints were found on the blade, but were any of her prints found on the handle?'

'No.'

'Indeed, were any fingerprints from any individuals found on the handle?'

'No.'

'Was any DNA residue found on the handle?'

'No.'

'Everyone knows what fingerprints look like. Any parent of a small child has had to clean them repeatedly off their windows.

But am I right in thinking that fingerprints are primarily formed by sweat, the aqueous-based secretions of the eccrine glands in the fingers, with additional greasy material from sebaceous glands, primarily from the head and forehead, due to contamination caused by the common human behaviour of touching the face and the hair?'

'That is correct.'

'And are these secretions left on an object in a pattern that matches those of the arches, whorls and loops found on the fingers themselves, patterns that are unique to any individual?'

'Yes.'

'And is there very often cell material also present in a fingerprint due to the continuous shedding of cells from the human skin?'

'Yes.'

'And do modern forensic techniques allow a DNA profile to be determined from such cell material found in a fingerprint?'

'I believe so.'

'Does the forensic report in this case indicate that such a technique was employed in an attempt to extract a DNA profile from the fingerprints found on the knife?'

'Yes, it does.'

'And was a DNA profile extracted?'

'No.'

'As an expert in forensic science, can you give the jury a possible reason for this failure?'

'No, I can't.'

'Might it be because the prints were not fresh, that they had been on the knife for some considerable time, maybe many days, before it was used to kill Liam Carson, and hence the cell material had degraded to such an extent that it was unable to provide a DNA profile?'

'It is a possibility,' the DCI said again.

'You have already told the jury that you entered Miss Duffy's home before she was arrested, using a key provided by her then employer, Mr Freddie Swinton. Is that correct?'

'Yes.'

'Were you aware that other keys to the property were also available? The cleaner had one, and there was another stored in an unlocked cupboard in the stable office. So, in fact, is it not possible that someone else could have entered Miss Duffy's home and removed the knife from the block while she was out of her house, maybe while she was riding at Windsor races on that Monday afternoon?'

'I suppose it's remotely possible.'

'Finally, let us turn to the question of the airport hotel, where the defendant used a false name when checking in, and where she paid in cash. The tone of your voice when answering questions from my learned friend seemed to imply that you believed her actions at the hotel to be suspicious. Would that be correct?'

'Yes.'

'But they were not suspicious at all, were they, Chief Inspector? Miss Duffy had been the subject of two very hostile front-page stories in the *Daily News* and the *News on Sunday* in the few days preceding the murder. Might it not have been that she was simply concerned that, had she used her real name, or had used a bank card with her real name on it, a member of the hotel staff might have contacted those publications to report her presence at their hotel, and hence subjected her to more unwelcome press attention?'

'I suppose that could have been the case.' But his tone clearly indicated that he still firmly believed Imogen had been acting suspiciously.

'I have just one more question. There is no phone evidence that my client was in Eastbury village at the time of the murder. No CCTV footage shows her making any movement. And it would seem to be the case that the fingerprints found on the knife's blade had been there for an appreciable period before the murder took place. So, is there any forensic evidence whatsoever that places the defendant at the scene of the crime, or any forensic evidence that indicates that she had been present when Mr Carson was killed?'

'No.'

'No,' Donna repeated slowly. 'Thank you, Detective Chief Inspector Miller. No more questions.'

Donna sat down, and I patted her back in congratulation.

'Any re-examination, Mr Blandford?' asked the judge.

The KC rose to his feet.

'Chief Inspector,' he said slowly, 'in your long and distinguished career in the Thames Valley Police Force, and before that in the forensic science service, have you ever encountered a situation where the person whose fingerprints are found on the murder weapon has not subsequently been found to be responsible for the killing?'

'Never,' replied the DCI.

'Thank you. No more questions, Your Honour.'

The KC sat down again.

'Thank you, Chief Inspector,' said the judge. 'You are discharged. I am sure that I don't have to remind you that you should not discuss your evidence with anyone – not with friends or family members, nor with any of your police colleagues, not until after this case is concluded.'

The detective stepped down from the witness box, and to my eyes, he appeared somewhat shell-shocked. I reckoned that he hadn't been expecting such a grilling from the defence when he had confidently arrived at court earlier that morning.

The judge looked at his watch.

'Mr Blandford, is your next witness here and ready?' he asked.

The KC half rose. 'Yes, Your Honour.'

'I think we'll have a short comfort break before you call him. Court will sit again in ten minutes, at three fifteen.'

The judge stood up.

'All rise,' called the usher.

The judge went out of the back of the court, while the jury returned to their holding area.

Donna turned round to me.

'You were brilliant,' I told her. 'Completely shot down his previous evidence.'

'Mostly due to your questions,' she said.

'So, who's next?' I asked.

'The pathologist,' Donna said. 'The prosecution are quite cross that we have insisted on him being here in person, rather than just having his report read out in court.'

'But you do know why?' I said.

'Absolutely. Don't worry, I'm ready for him.'

'We need to try and get him to revise his estimate of the time of death until after six o'clock on Monday afternoon. That's when Sophie Burnett says she saw Imogen at Boxtree Stables.'

'I'll have a go,' Donna said.

I stood up and stretched.

'Sid.' I heard the call.

I turned and Patrick Duffy beckoned me over to him.

'Hi, Patrick,' I said. I looked at the woman next to him.

'This is my wife, Kathleen,' Patrick said. 'We are very frustrated that we can't see Imogen. We don't even know that she's aware we're here.'

'I'll tell her,' I said. 'But I'm afraid I can't do anything else.'

'We are very grateful for what you are doing.'

He had a deeply worried expression on his face, as if he couldn't bear to imagine what might happen next to his daughter.

I smiled at him. 'Try and keep positive.'

I started to go back towards my place.

I looked to my right and there was Imogen, still in the dock, sitting next to a uniformed security officer who was at least twice her size. I waved at her.

'Both your parents are here,' I said. 'In the public gallery.'

She nodded. 'Thank you,' she mouthed.

Comfort break over, the judge returned to his raised position behind his bench, and he surveyed the court to check that everyone was in their proper place.

'Please bring in the jury,' he said to the usher.

The seven women and five men were shown into the court. When they were settled into their places, the KC rose to his feet.

'May it please Your Honour, the prosecution calls Dr Jonathan Andrews.'

The usher went out and soon returned with the witness, who entered the witness box and took the oath.

The KC was still standing.

'Please give your name and qualifications to the jury.'

'My name is Dr Jonathan Andrews. I am a Home Office registered pathologist and associate professor of forensic pathology at the University of Reading. I am a fellow of the Royal Society of Pathologists.'

He was quite a small man, with a receding hairline. But what hair he did have was long, white, and somewhat unkempt. He appeared to me to be like a cross between Albert Einstein and Doc Emmett Brown, the crazy scientist from the *Back to the Future* films. Half-moon spectacles, perched on the end of his nose, further enhanced the visual image of a mad professor.

'Thank you, Dr Andrews,' said the KC. 'And were you the Home Office pathologist who attended Boxtree Stables in Eastbury on the morning when Liam Carson was found deceased?'

'Yes.'

'And did you carry out an initial examination of the body at the scene?'

'Yes. I did.'

'And did you then have Mr Carson's remains removed to the mortuary at the Royal Berkshire Hospital for you to carry out a full post-mortem investigation?'

'Yes.'

'Dr Andrews, you will find your post-mortem report in the bundle in front of you. Please could you turn to it now.'

The witness reached forward and found the relevant sheets of paper.

'Could you please now read out your report to the jury.'

The doctor read out his full post-mortem report, which was the one I had seen at Archie Brook's office. He finished reading and placed the papers down again on the edge of the witness box.

'So,' said the KC, 'is there any doubt in your mind that the cause of Mr Carson's death was the knife wound to the heart?'

'No doubt whatsoever.'

'And could such a wound have been self-inflicted?'

'No.'

'Thank you, Doctor. No further questions from me.'

The KC sat down, and Donna stood up.

'Dr Andrews,' she said. 'In your report, you estimated the time of death as between eight and eighteen hours before the time you arrived at the murder scene. Can you explain why this is such a long period, and why you have not been able to be more specific?'

'Determining the time that someone died is not an easy task. Bodies of different individuals do not always behave in the same way after death, and there are numerous factors that affect how quickly tissues begin to decompose.

'There are three main methods of determining how long ago a person died, known as the classical triad – rigor mortis, livor mortis, and algor mortis.

'Rigor mortis is the stiffening of the corpse. It occurs after oxygen ceases to be delivered to the body's cells, resulting in the formation of actin-myosin filaments, which cause a short-ening of the muscle fibres. It begins almost immediately after death and is usually fully established some six to eight hours later. The body will then remain rigid for about twenty-four hours until the actin-myosin starts to disintegrate due to the breakdown of its proteins. In this instance, rigor mortis appeared fully established, indicating that death had occurred at least six to eight hours prior to my examination, but less than twenty-four.

'Livor mortis is the discolouration of the skin due to the pooling of blood and other fluids in the body, as a result of gravity. In Mr Carson it was well established, and had become mostly fixed, meaning that when pressure was applied to the skin, the discolouration did not disappear. This fixation normally occurs between eight to twelve hours after death.

'Algor mortis is the cooling down of a corpse after death from the normal live-body temperature of thirty-seven degrees Celsius, or ninety-eight point six degrees Fahrenheit in old money. But, contrary to popular belief, this is not an exact science. The rate of cooling is not linear and is governed not only by the ambient temperature of the surroundings but also by the deceased's mass to surface area ratio, body fat percentage, and their clothing, or the lack of it. And in this case, determining the core body temperature was not straightforward due to the pronounced rigor preventing the usual method of inserting a rectal thermometer.

'Overall, having taken each of these factors into full account, I am confident that death occurred at least eight hours prior to my examination, and maybe as many as eighteen hours prior.'

I could tell that we weren't going to be able to shake him on that score, but Donna tried once again nevertheless.

'Thank you, Doctor, for your very detailed reasons for your estimate of the time of death. But how confident are you that, in fact, death occurred less than *sixteen* hours before your initial examination, rather than eighteen?'

The doctor looked at her with a touch of disdain.

'Not particularly confident,' he said. 'And I'm also not particularly confident that it occurred longer ago than that. But I am very confident that it occurred somewhere between eight and eighteen hours beforehand.'

Even Donna now stopped trying.

'May I now turn to the injuries on the deceased,' she said. 'Were there any defensive wounds on the hands or arms?'

'No. As I wrote in my report there were no other injuries other than the single knife wound to the chest.'

'So, it might appear that the victim was unaware that he was about to be stabbed. Is there any medical way of determining if the victim had been asleep at the time he was attacked?'

'No. There isn't.'

'But do you consider it likely?'

The KC rose quickly. 'If it may please Your Honour, I believe that question is outside the expert scope of this witness.'

'I agree,' said the judge. 'Doctor, you should not answer that question.'

'Let me rephrase it,' Donna said. 'In your experience over many years of examining stab victims, have you ever come across a situation where a fully conscious individual, knowing they were about to be stabbed from the front, has not tried to defend themselves with their hands or arms?'

'No. I have not.'

'And would you say that substantial force was required to stab someone in the manner you have described, where the knife has passed so deeply into the chest cavity?'

'Yes. A very large amount of force would have been required.'

'In your expert opinion, and using your detailed knowledge of human anatomy, could such a deep and ferocious injury have been caused by someone holding the knife only by its blade, and with just their thumb and forefinger?'

'Absolutely not.'

'Indeed, might you expect the perpetrator of this act to be someone quite muscular, someone having the necessary strength to drive the knife through the chest wall, right through the bone of a rib, and then onward through the heart?'

'Yes. I would.'

Donna turned and signalled for Imogen to stand up. Conveniently, the large security officer also stood up next to her, making her look even smaller than she actually was. And every member of the jury turned their eyes towards them.

'Dr Andrews,' Donna said. 'Please look at the defendant in the dock. Do you consider that she would have sufficient strength to have committed this murder?'

The KC was now on his feet, but the judge was well ahead of him.

'Doctor, you should not answer that question. Miss Lewis …'

'No further questions, Your Honour.'

Chapter 31

'HOW DID IT GO TODAY?' Marina asked when I arrived back at Aynsford.

'Pretty well, I think. Donna Lewis did a really good job. Much better than I had been expecting. She did exactly what I'd asked her to do. Even more. But we still have Mrs Sophie Burnett to contend with. She's the eyewitness.'

'Is that a big problem?'

'It might be. It's the only real card the prosecution has left after today, but it's a biggie – it could be their ace of trumps. If the jury believes her, then it puts Imogen at the scene during the period in which the pathologist says the murder happened.'

'What are you going to do?'

'Try to make sure that the jury don't believe her, or at least create some doubt in their minds. I have a meeting arranged with Donna before court sits in the morning to go through our approach to her testimony. Ideally, we need to make Mrs Burnett admit she is wrong, or as a minimum, get her to question her memory of when she saw Imogen at Boxtree Stables.'

'What time do you have to leave in the morning?'

'I have to be at Reading by half past eight.'

'So it looks like I'll be doing the school run again tomorrow.' She raised her eyes to the heavens. It was usually my job to do the morning run.

'Thanks,' I said. 'But I'll collect her tonight.'

Saskia attended an all-girls predominantly boarding school just outside Banbury, although she was one of the day pupils.

She was meant to finish each day at half past six, but on Mondays she had orchestra rehearsal from seven until eight, on Tuesdays it was swimming training, Wednesdays and Thursday were play rehearsal nights and on Friday she stayed late for house supper, so she never actually left the school premises each evening until a quarter past eight.

And she had to be back there just twelve hours later, including on Saturdays. No wonder she spent most of Sunday sleeping. But she seemed very happy and was doing particularly well in her studies.

Thinking of Saskia, and my huge pride in having her as my daughter, made me wonder about Patrick and Kathleen Duffy, and how they were bearing up with their only child having been incarcerated in a foreign prison for nine long months. It can't have been easy for them to visit her, not when they both held down full-time jobs in the HSE, the Irish national health service.

Marina and I had breaded plaice fillets, minted new potatoes, and garden peas for our supper. One of the advantages of Saskia staying late for a school-based activity was that she was provided with an evening meal, eating it with the boarders.

'I stopped at Godswell House to have coffee with Charles this morning,' Marina said as she finished her fish. 'On the way home from dropping Sassy.'

'How was he?' I asked.

'In great form, and still full of thanks for Christmas. He asked about your case, and I told him the trial had started. He was quite interested. You should give him a call.'

I remembered what Charles had said about checking Freddie Swinton's alibi. I'd had no luck calling the hotel that he claimed he had stayed in, and I'd done nothing else since. Perhaps I should have done something more.

But what?

It was now January and Freddie claimed to have stayed at the Granby Hotel in Great Portland Street on a Monday night in early April. No normal person could remember everything they did on a particular day nine months ago – not unless it was the day they had committed murder.

Freddie Swinton was still on our witness list, so we retained the option of calling him to give evidence, although goodness knew what the judge would say if Donna asked one of her defence witnesses to prove his alibi for not having committed the crime.

No comment.

*　*　*

Saskia came running out to the car, putting her violin case on the back seat before climbing into the front next to me.

'Hi, Dad.'

Much to my disappointment, Saskia had long ago stopped calling me Daddy.

'Had a good day?' I asked.

'Excellent. Did you know that a female praying mantis eats her male mate after they have sex? You wonder why he does it.'

The urge to reproduce is obviously extremely strong.

'A few of the girls want to form a feminist club called Mantis.'

'Do you?' I asked.

'Not really. I'm more into boys than they are.'

'Any particular boy?' I asked casually.

'Harry Styles, mostly. Although I do still love Taylor Swift.'

We laughed together – happy and relaxed.

What joy Saskia brought to my life and to Marina's.

And I imagined that Imogen brought the same joy to Patrick and Kathleen Duffy – at least, she would if she were free.

* * *

'Please state your name?' asked the KC.

'Sophie Burnett.'

'And are you the owner of Boxtree Stables?'

'I own the stables jointly with my husband, Bobby Burnett. But I, alone, hold the trainer's licence.'

'The racehorse trainer's licence?'

'Yes.'

'And how long have you been the racehorse trainer at Boxtree Stables?'

'For ten years. I took over the licence from my father-in-law, when he retired.'

Mrs Burnett was standing up in the witness box, rather than sitting down, and she was wearing a royal blue jacket over a white open-necked blouse.

'Did you employ the jockey Liam Carson?'

'Not exactly employ,' she said. 'Professional jockeys are self-employed. But we had an arrangement.'

'What sort of arrangement?'

'He would act as my stable jockey, and in return he would have the use of the flat above the horses, rent free. It's not so much a flat, more of a bedsit, with a kitchenette at one end. There's an outside wooden stairway up to the door, at the end of the stable block.'

'And how long had this arrangement been in place by the time Mr Carson died?'

'Only ten days. Since he had arrived from his home in Ireland.'

'And how did this arrangement come about? Did he answer an advertisement?'

'No. It was by word of mouth. My previous stable jockey was moving on to a bigger stable, and he told me he had a friend who was looking for a job near Lambourn. The friend was Liam Carson. Hence, I spoke to Liam on the phone and invited him to come over from Ireland to ride for me, for a three-month trial period.'

'Did Mr Carson say why he particularly wanted to come to the Lambourn area?'

'Yes, he did. He said his girlfriend had recently been appointed to ride for Freddie Swinton, and he wanted to be near her.'

'Did he tell you his girlfriend's name?'

'Yes he did. Imogen Duffy.'

'The defendant?'

'Yes.'

'So did you see Miss Duffy at Boxtree Stables often during those ten days, while Mr Carson was living there?'

'No. I saw her just the once.'

'But you knew it was her?'

'No. Not when I saw her. I learned that later.'

'Mrs Burnett,' said the KC, 'could you please tell the court how it was you saw the defendant at your stables.'

She described how she had come to turn into her driveway only to find it blocked by another car. She had hooted, and the driver, a young woman, had run down the driveway, jumped into the car, and driven it away at speed.

'And this occurred on the evening before you found the body of Liam Carson?' asked the KC.

'Yes.'

'At what time?'

'It would have been when I was returning from Windsor races. Around six o'clock.'

'But you didn't recognise the driver?'

'No. In fact I thought nothing of it at the time, but I later mentioned it to the police.'

'When did you mention it to the police?'

'I'm not sure. It would have been either on Wednesday or Thursday. After Liam was found dead.'

'Yes, let us go back to the Tuesday morning, and the discovery of the victim's body,' said the KC. 'Who was the first person to find Mr Carson dead?'

'I was.'

'At what time was that?'

'Seven thirty. Liam had been due to ride out one of my horses and he hadn't turned up at seven o'clock as we had arranged, so I went to find him, in case he had overslept.' She paused. 'It was a great shock to find him.' She visibly shivered at the memory. 'I have been trying ever since to forget what I saw, but the mental image keeps reappearing in my mind – all day, every day.'

'I am sorry to distress you, Mrs Burnett, but I have to ask you to tell the jury what you found.'

She gripped the sides of the witness box, as if needing the support.

'Liam was lying on his bed, on his back, with a knife stuck into his chest. It was horrible.' She shivered again.

The KC paused for several seconds before going on.

'Mrs Burnett, when you went up the stairs to the door of the flat, was it open or closed?'

'It was closed but was not locked. I first knocked on the door, but as there was no answer, I tried the handle and went slowly in.'

'How far in did you go?'

'I'd only taken a couple of steps inside when I saw him. I immediately turned round and ran outside again. I may have screamed, I'm not sure. I know I felt sick. Then I telephoned the police.'

'Did you go back into the flat?'

'No, I did not,' she said adamantly.

'So, you were sure Mr Carson was already dead?'

'Quite sure. There was a deep purple colour to parts of his body, and there was also the repugnant smell of death. I've encountered that smell before when I've had horses die in my stables.'

Some members of the jury wrinkled their noses in disgust.

'How long did it take for the police to arrive?'

'The first car was there in about fifteen minutes, and many more followed over the next hour or so. All hell broke out.'

The KC paused and looked down at his papers.

'When did you discover the identity of the woman that you had seen in your driveway?' asked the KC.

'After I had attended an identity parade at a police station in Reading.'

'When was that identity parade?'

'I think it was on the Friday afternoon after the murder.'

'And at that identification parade, did you positively identify the person that you saw in your driveway on the evening before you discovered Liam Carson's body.'

'Yes, I did. It was Imogen Duffy.'

'Imogen Duffy,' the KC repeated slowly, no doubt for the benefit of the jury. 'The defendant in the dock. Thank you, Mrs Burnett. No further questions from me.'

The KC sat down.

Donna stood up.

'Mrs Burnett, I represent the accused. I am sorry that you have had to relive what must have been a dreadful experience for you, and that you have the recurring mental image of finding Mr Carson dead in his flat that morning. However, I would like to ask you to bring forward in your mind another mental image, that showing the moment when you first saw the defendant in your driveway. Please now close your eyes and think hard.'

Donna paused for a second or two.

'In this new image, is the defendant on your left or on your right?'

'On my right.'

'You are preparing to turn right into your driveway?'

'Yes. But it is blocked by her car.'

'Yes, but what exactly is the defendant doing when you first see her?'

Sophie Burnett thought for a moment.

'She's standing by the gate.'

'Is she facing in towards the stables, or facing out towards the road?'

'In. Towards the stables.'

'So, she is clearly visible?'

'Yes.'

'Not out of sight behind the gates or the wall of your property?'

'No.'

'And what do you do?'

'I hooted at her to move her car.'

'You are impatient for her to get out of your way?'

'Yes.'

'What does she do when you hooted at her?'

'She hurries down the drive, gets into her car, and drives away.'

'So, her car is pointing outwards?'

'No. Inwards. She has to reverse out onto the road first.'

'Thank you, Mrs Burnett. Now I will ask you about your movements on the Sunday before the murder. Can you recall how you spent the day?'

'Yes, I can. That was my husband's and my wedding anniversary, and we had all our adult children home for Sunday lunch.'

'And did you cook the lunch?'

The KC half rose. 'Is it relevant who cooked the lunch, Your Honour?'

'Miss Lewis?' asked the judge.

'I hope that the relevance may become apparent, Your Honour.'

'Then continue.' The judge turned to the witness. 'Mrs Burnett, please answer the question.'

'Yes, I cooked the lunch.'

'And at what time did you sit down to eat?' Donna asked.

'I believe it was around one thirty.'

'And what did you eat?'

The KC was getting very restless in his chair, but he didn't rise.

'We had roast beef.'

'With roast potatoes? Yorkshire puddings? Plenty of vegetables?'

'Yes. All of those.'

'You were in your kitchen the whole morning preparing the meal?'

'Yes.'

'Did you go out at all on that Sunday? Perhaps to buy a Sunday newspaper, or a bottle of wine, or to get a missing ingredient for the lunch? Please think carefully.'

Mrs Burnett was silent for a few long seconds, as she thought.

'I may have had to nip to the local shop for some plain flour, to thicken the gravy.'

'May have?'

'I know I had to do it once, but I can't remember if it was on that specific occasion.'

'Now let us turn to the following day, the Monday. You told us earlier in your testimony that you spent the afternoon at Windsor races, is that right?'

'Yes. I had two runners.'

'Both ridden by Liam Carson?'

'Yes.'

'And you arrived home at six o'clock?'

'Yes, about then. I was held up after the second of my races because the horse was selected for testing.'

'Testing?'

'Dope testing. Any horse in a race can be selected by the stewards to go to a special barn where it remains until it urinates. The urine is then sent away to be tested. On that day, my stable lad wasn't feeling well, so I stayed with the horse. And I had to wait quite a long time for it to pee.' She smiled.

'Hence, you left the racecourse later than you had planned?'

'Yes.'

'And you were therefore in a hurry to get home?'

'Yes. I had the dogs to feed, and I also wanted to be back before evening stables finished. That's why I was so impatient when I found my driveway blocked.'

'And you drove yourself home from Windsor?'

'Yes.'

'Along the M4 motorway to junction 14, the Hungerford turn-off?'

'Yes.'

'And then through Great Shefford?'

'Yes. It's by far the quickest route.'

'Mrs Burnett, you have already told us that in your mental image of the defendant in your driveway, she was on your right, and you were preparing to turn right into your driveway. But if you were arriving home from the Great Shefford direction, and Miss Duffy was in your driveway at that point, she would have been on your left, and you would have been turning left into your driveway. Can you explain this inconsistency in your testimony?'

Sophie Burnett remained silent for quite a long while, a look of puzzlement on her face, plus an increasing degree of embarrassment.

'No, I'm sorry, I can't,' she said eventually.

'I put it to you,' Donna said, 'that you did not see the defendant in your driveway on the Monday afternoon at all, but at one o'clock on Sunday, when you were returning home from the other direction, after having nipped quickly to a local shop in Lambourn to buy some plain flour to thicken your Sunday-lunch gravy – and at a time when you would also have been impatient to get into your driveway because your lunch was almost ready to serve. Isn't that the case, Mrs Burnett?'

The witness looked around her, as if searching for some help. None was forthcoming.

'Mrs Burnett,' said the judge. 'Please answer the question.'

'It must have been on the Sunday. I'm not very good with my days.'

Her answer was barely audible, but we did all hear it.

'No more questions, Your Honour.'

Donna sat down.

'Mr Blandford, do you wish to re-examine?' asked the judge, looking towards the prosecution bench.

Geoffrey Blandford just sat in his chair shaking his head from side to side.

I didn't know whether it was just to indicate that there would be no re-examination of the witness, or because he now realised that that part of the prosecution case was in tatters.

'Mrs Burnett,' said the judge. 'You are now free to go. Do not discuss your evidence with anyone until after the trial is concluded.'

She stepped down from the witness box and made her way out of the court, all the while staring resolutely down at the blue-carpeted floor.

I wondered if she was in tears.

I actually felt quite sorry for her. All she'd done was make an honest mistake, but one that could have been crucial, had it not been properly challenged.

The judge looked at his watch. 'I think we will adjourn for lunch at this point. Court will sit again at two o'clock.'

'All rise,' called the usher.

Chapter 32

'THEY'VE GOT NOTHING LEFT,' ARCHIE said excitedly. 'They have no forensic evidence, and their eyewitness has turned out to be worse than useless.'

Donna, Archie and I were in a small conference room adjacent to the court.

'Let us not get overconfident,' I said. 'The prosecution still have motive and opportunity, and don't forget that the murder weapon clearly came from Imogen's kitchen. It had her fingerprints on it. We can't get away from that.'

'What happens next?' Archie asked.

'The prosecution still have some witnesses they could call,' Donna said. 'The policeman from Newbury is on their list, and the airport hotel receptionist, but we have already accepted their witness statements without objection to the content, so what would be the point?'

'They may still want to question the Newbury policeman in court,' I said. 'Even though we've already heard his witness statement, they can still call him. They could have him repeat, live to the jury, how he gave Imogen an official police warning over threatening Liam Carson with the very same carving knife that was ultimately used to kill him. And he could also tell them in person what Imogen said about Carson's behaviour towards her, to try and strengthen the motive. They must realise by now that we won't be calling the defendant as a witness, so they won't be able to ask her about it directly.'

'Can't we claim that there's no case to answer?' Archie said.

'We will definitely be doing that,' Donna agreed. 'But that will be after the prosecution have closed their case. For now, we just have to wait and see what they do next.'

'They must have really believed they had introduced enough evidence to convict,' Archie said.

I remembered what he had said to me in December, when I first went to see him at his offices in Reading.

Pretty open-and-shut case, I'm afraid. The murder weapon came from her kitchen, and it has her fingerprints on it. A witness places her at the murder scene, and she admits to previously threatening the victim with a knife. Not much hope really.

Perhaps the prosecution had thought the same, and complacency had set in, and they were now trying to back-pedal ferociously.

'I can't believe they haven't yet mentioned anything in court about those newspaper articles,' I said. 'Being able to show that Liam Carson was the anonymous source for those stories would have surely bolstered Imogen's motive for killing him.'

I had acquired copies of the relevant *Daily News* and *News on Sunday* from a newspaper archive company, and their front-page stories on those two days certainly made for explosive reading. And they would have also provided Freddie Swinton with a pretty strong motive for murder.

'There's no one on their witness list from any newspapers,' Donna said.

'Can they add witnesses at this late stage?' I asked her.

'Yes, they can, but they would need to get permission from the judge. And they would have to go through the correct protocol of first obtaining witness statements, and then allowing the defence time and access. Permission is usually only granted if compelling new information has come to light since the trial started, or something has cropped up from previous testimony. I can't see how newspaper articles published nine months ago could be considered as something new.'

'Could they call Freddie Swinton?' I asked. 'Even though he's on the defence list?'

'They could,' Donna replied. 'There is no property in a witness. Anyone can be called by either side, even if they're on the other side's list. The only exception is that the prosecution cannot call the defendant. Only we can do that.'

I just hoped that the prosecution hadn't discovered another unexpected rabbit to be pulled out of a hat, with which they could still ambush us. Not that ambushing the defence in court was meant to be allowed.

* * *

At two o'clock sharp, Donna, Archie and I were in the courtroom, as instructed, ready to resume.

Imogen was also back in the dock, her parents and a few others were sitting patiently in the public gallery, and the usher was waiting to be instructed to bring in the jury. But there was no sign of the KC or the rest of the prosecution team, nor of the court clerk, nor the judge.

'What are they up to?' Archie asked.

'Maybe the prosecution is throwing in the towel,' Donna said.

356

I doubted that.

After five minutes, the clerk returned to the court, and shortly afterwards, the prosecution team arrived, but no one said anything to Donna, to Archie, or to me.

'All rise,' called the usher.

We all stood up as the judge took his place.

He did not instruct the usher to bring in the jury, something that usually indicated that there was about to be some other matter to deal with, rather than the introduction of more evidence – the jury was always excluded from legal argument between the judge and counsel.

The judge cleared his throat.

'I am informed by the court clerk that the prosecution wish to make an application.'

The KC stood up.

'Yes, thank you, Your Honour. The prosecution applies to be permitted to call an additional witness in this case, one who was not previously on our list.'

Just as I had feared.

'We wish to call Mr Gordon Woods. He is a journalist.'

I recognised the name. He had written both the explosive newspaper articles in the *Daily News* and the *News on Sunday*.

The judge turned towards the defence bench. 'Miss Lewis, do you have any objection?'

'Would Mr Woods's testimony relate to any matters that have come to light since the beginning of this trial?' Donna asked.

The judge turned back towards the prosecution.

'It would not,' said the KC. 'It would relate to articles he wrote in early April.'

'Before the murder?' Donna said.

'Yes.'

'Then the defence objects strongly to this request, Your Honour, on the grounds that there is no just cause for the prosecution to enter a new witness at this late stage, not when they must have been aware of any potential significance the witness might have had prior to the submission of their witness list. The defence has the absolute right to be forewarned of the prosecution case and to have the time to prepare counter argument. Calling a new witness at this late stage would hinder that right, and in our view may be detrimental to a fair trial for the accused.'

The judge looked again at the KC. 'Mr Blandford?'

'If it may please Your Honour,' the KC said in his most ingratiating tone. 'The Criminal Procedure Rules state that the overriding objective is that criminal proceedings should be conducted justly, and further defines *justly* as convicting the guilty, as well as acquitting the innocent.' He emphasised the word *guilty*, while he almost mumbled *innocent*. 'The prosecution considers that, in order to provide the jury with the necessary evidence to make their decision in this case, this new witness is essential.'

The judge looked at him. 'Mr Blandford, those very same procedure rules also state that, to manage a criminal case justly, the court should treat the prosecution and defence fairly, recognise the rights of the defendant, and progress the case efficiently and expeditiously. I happen to agree with the defence that the prosecution had every chance to determine the importance of this witness at an earlier stage, and no compelling new evidence has come to light since the start of these proceedings that has changed that importance. For those reasons, I refuse the prosecution's application.'

Both the KC and Donna sat down again, but their body language couldn't have been more contrasting. The KC looked totally crestfallen, while Donna appeared positively upbeat.

'Well done,' I whispered quietly to her.

'Mr Blandford,' said the judge, 'are you ready to continue?'

The KC half rose. 'Yes, Your Honour.'

The judge instructed the usher to bring in the jury.

'Ladies and gentlemen of the jury,' the judge said to them, when they were all seated in their allocated places, 'I apologise that you have been kept waiting, but we are now ready to continue.' He then turned to the prosecution. 'Mr Blandford?'

The KC stood up.

'That is the case for the prosecution, Your Honour.'

He sat down again.

Not so much pulling a rabbit from a hat. More like tossing out a damp squib.

But what else could they do? The Newbury policeman probably wasn't even here – not after his witness statement had been accepted by the defence.

The judge turned towards Donna.

'Miss Lewis?'

She rose to her feet.

'Thank you, Your Honour. The defence wish to discuss some legal issues.'

The judge nodded. No doubt he could guess what the legal issues would be.

He turned towards the jury.

'Ladies and gentlemen of the jury. Counsel and I will discuss legal matters now, and then we will adjourn for the day. You will not remain in the court for our discussions, so you will have an early finish this afternoon. The court usher will see you out, and you are free to go for today. Please be here, ready to resume, at ten o'clock tomorrow morning. In the meantime, I remind you not to discuss the case between yourselves, or with anyone else, including with your partners, friends or families. And remember what I said to you at the beginning of the trial. You must not do your own research, and you must certainly not look up events surrounding this case on the internet. If you do, it is a very serious matter, one that could result in me sending you to prison.'

And with that stark warning still ringing in their ears, the twelve members of the jury stood up and were ushered out of the courtroom. We waited in silence until the door was firmly closed behind them.

'Miss Lewis?' invited the judge.

'Your Honour, the defence wishes to make a submission that there is no case for the defendant to answer. There is absolutely no evidence, forensic or otherwise, that places my client at the scene of the crime during the period within which the pathologist confidently stated that the murder was committed, nor any evidence that would indicate that she was present when Mr Carson died. The only supposed eyewitness has now admitted under oath that she was mistaken in placing the defendant at the scene on the appropriate day. For these reasons, we feel that it would be unsafe to put the question to the jury, and hence respectfully request that you should dismiss the case due to a lack of evidence.'

Donna sat down.

'Mr Blandford?' said the judge.

The KC stood up.

'Your Honour, the prosecution maintains that the defendant has a very strong case to answer. She had opportunity and motive. She is known to have visited the scene, the murder weapon came from her home and had her fingerprints on it, and she had previously threatened Mr Carson with the very same knife that was used to kill him. In addition, she said in a police interview that Mr Carson deserved to die. Subsequent to the murder, she used a false name when checking into a hotel to prevent detection, and she was attempting to flee the country when arrested. Whereas, if each of these points was considered in isolation, it might raise unease, taken together they create a compelling narrative that the defendant committed the murder. The prosecution urges you to reject this submission, to continue with the trial, and to put the question to the jury.'

The KC sat down again.

The judge was silent for quite a few long minutes before speaking.

'Thank you, Miss Lewis and Mr Blandford. I will consider this submission and give my ruling in the morning. Court is now adjourned. We will sit again at ten o'clock tomorrow.'

'All rise,' called the usher.

After the judge had departed, Donna turned round to me. 'That didn't sound too hopeful, but at least he didn't instantly dismiss our submission. He's probably leaving the decision until tomorrow so he can consult with another judge first.'

'Is he allowed to do that?' I asked.

361

'Yes. But the final decision is his. But if he does rule there is no case to answer, the prosecution can immediately state that it intends to appeal the ruling, and then it goes to the Court of Appeal for them to make the decision.'

'Is that likely?'

'Not likely, but it is possible. And, at the same time, the prosecution could also appeal the previous ruling that they couldn't bring in a new witness. The judge will want to make sure he's absolutely bulletproof before making a no-case-to-answer ruling. It wouldn't look good for him if it was overturned on appeal.'

'So, you think it's more likely that we will go on?'

'I would say so, yes.'

Donna glanced around her to make sure no one was eavesdropping on our conversation.

'But,' she said quietly, 'as we've decided that we won't call any defence witnesses, the whole case might be over by tomorrow anyway.'

It was suddenly crunch time.

Chapter 33

I DROVE MYSELF HOME TO AYNSFORD, but if anyone had asked me about the journey afterwards, I wouldn't have been able to recall any of it, because my mind had been busy with other matters.

After the judge departed, Donna and I had spent a couple of hours in the empty courtroom discussing the content of her closing speech.

When I arrived home, I found to my delight that Marina had asked Charles to join us for supper, and she had already collected him from Godswell House.

'How's it going?' Charles asked, when I gave him a tumbler of whisky in the drawing room.

'Difficult to say. I felt we were doing all right, but every time I think we're getting on top, the prosecution comes back at us with a vengeance.'

'Just like at Edgehill.'

'What?'

'The Battle of Edgehill.'

'Were you there?' I asked.

He laughed. 'Even I'm not that old. It took place in 1642. But it should have been a resounding victory for King Charles

363

the First and the royalists. It could well have decided the English Civil War at the very first battle. But the royalist cavalry went AWOL from the battlefield, chasing the parliamentary mounted troops for miles. After that, whenever the royalist foot soldiers got on top, the parliamentarians kept coming back at them. So, in the end, it was inconclusive.'

'There won't be anything inconclusive about this trial,' I said. 'I can't see it being a hung jury. We'll get an answer one way or the other, and maybe as soon as tomorrow.'

I took sip of my own single malt.

'You're really invested in this trial, aren't you?' Charles said.

'I suppose I am.'

'You always were determined to win. That's why you became champion jockey rather than just an also-ran.'

It was true. Even as a young child, I'd been highly competitive in the primary school playground. As the smallest boy in the class, I'd had to be, simply to survive. I didn't really believe that the derogatory social stereotype *small man syndrome* particularly applied to me, but maybe it did. I didn't consider myself as being overly aggressive or domineering, regardless of how others might see me.

Inside I was a pussycat.

'So, what's left?' Charles asked.

'We've decided not to call any defence witnesses, not even Imogen.'

'Is that wise?'

'I believe so. We really don't want her cross-examined about her volatile relationship with Liam Carson. It would give her a strong motive to kill him. So, we'll now move directly to the final speeches by the prosecution and defence counsels.

Then the judge will sum up, before sending the jury out to deliberate.'

'And what are her chances?'

'Middling,' I replied. 'It all depends on how much significance the jury place on the fact that it was her knife that was found stuck in the victim's body. That's our major stumbling block.'

'And quite a big one too, I imagine.'

'Huge.'

I took Charles home to Godswell House on my way to collect Saskia from school.

'Good luck,' he said, as I dropped him outside the front door.

'Thanks,' I said. 'I think we will need it.'

* * *

'My ruling is that there is a case to answer,' said the judge. 'I will provide my reasons in writing later. We will now continue with the trial. Bring in the jury.'

The jury filed in – twelve ordinary people with an extraordinary duty to perform.

When they were all settled into their allocated places, the judge turned to Donna. 'Miss Lewis?'

She stood up.

'The defence calls no witnesses, Your Honour.'

The judge raised his eyebrows in surprise, so much so that they almost disappeared under his wig.

'Miss Lewis, have you made your client aware that she has a right to give evidence in person, and a failure to do so may result in the jury drawing such inferences as seem proper?'

'Yes, Your Honour,' Donna said. 'I have, and she is aware.'

'Members of the jury,' the judge said to them. 'The defence have decided to call no witnesses in this case, not even the defendant. That is their right. They do not need to prove the innocence of the defendant. It is for the prosecution to prove her guilt, and to prove it so that you are satisfied so as to be sure of her guilt. I am the judge of the law, while you are the judges of the facts, and it will be your decision alone as to whether the defendant is guilty or not guilty. We will now hear the closing speeches of both the prosecution and the defence counsel, after which I will sum up the case and give you directions on the law.'

He turned towards the prosecution.

'Mr Blandford?'

The KC stood up.

'Thank you, Your Honour.'

He took a sip of water, and then turned to the jury.

'Ladies and gentlemen of the jury, let us look at the undisputed facts of this case.

'Liam Carson was found dead, with an eight-inch carving knife blade still embedded in his chest, a blade that had pierced his heart in two places, which resulted in his death. We heard from the Home Office pathologist that, in his expert opinion, such a wound could not have been self-inflicted, hence we are looking at a case of murder. The murder weapon belonged to the defendant, and her fingerprints were found on it. And just six days before Mr Carson's lifeless body was discovered, we have heard that the defendant threatened him with that very same knife.

'In her police interview, the defendant stated that she was not sorry Mr Carson was dead, and also that she believed he deserved to die. We know she had a motive to rid herself of Mr Carson, because she claimed in that police interview that Mr Carson had told lies about her to the newspapers. And she also attended Newbury Police Station to complain that he was stalking her, harassing her, and stealing from her. But we have heard no evidence of that behaviour, other than the word of the defendant in her police interview, and we know, don't we, that she is a liar. She lied when checking into a Heathrow airport hotel, giving a false name, so that she wouldn't be recognised, prior to her attempting to board an aeroplane to a foreign country.

'And finally, when given every opportunity to do so, the defendant has chosen not to give evidence in this trial, something that may be her right, but one from which you are entitled to draw an adverse inference. When taking all this indisputable evidence together, there is only one clear verdict you can deliver, and that verdict is guilty of the offence of murder.'

The KC sat down again, looking rather smug, as indeed he might.

Donna stood up.

'Ladies and gentlemen, the prosecution has tried to paint a convincing argument that the defendant is guilty, but there are many, many gaps in what they have told you. They claim that my client had the opportunity to kill Mr Carson, but so did I, and so, I expect, did most of you. They make the claim that she had opportunity simply because she has no verifiable alibi for the time of death. Alibi is a Latin word meaning elsewhere. But Imogen Duffy was indeed elsewhere. She was at home when this heinous crime was committed, home alone, and therefore without witness to that fact.

'Let us look at what else the prosecution has failed to mention. Fifty-five separate swabs were taken at the crime scene. Fifty-five. And not a single one of them contained the DNA of the defendant. The whole of Mr Carson's flat was dusted for finger-prints, and none were found belonging to the defendant, other than those two on the blade of the knife, prints that we have heard were old rather than fresh, so old in fact that a DNA profile was unable to be obtained from them, not even when using the most modern of techniques.

'We were also told by the pathologist that there was no way the fatal injury could have been administered by someone holding the knife only by its blade, but no fingerprints nor any DNA belonging to the defendant were found on the knife handle. And the pathologist further stated that a substantial amount of force, likely from a strong muscular individual, would have been required to drive the blade through the chest wall, passing right through the bone of a rib, and onwards through the heart.'

Donna turned round briefly and looked at Imogen in the dock, and I saw most members of the jury also look that way.

'The defence does not dispute the fact that the murder weapon is the knife that was found missing from the knife block in the kitchen of the cottage in which my client was living at the time. But we have already heard from Chief Inspector Miller that Mr Freddie Swinton had a key to the cottage, and also Mr Potter, the maintenance man, stated in his witness statement that he had collected a second key from the key cupboard in the office at Mr Swinton's stable yard. So, in fact, anyone might have been able to access her home to remove the knife. Maybe someone came into the cottage while the defendant was out, maybe while she was riding at Windsor races on the Monday afternoon, to take the knife, to throw suspicion onto my client and away from them.

'Following her arrest, a thorough extensive forensic search was made of the defendant's home and no evidence whatsoever was obtained that might have indicated that she was present when Mr Carson died. Both the pathologist in his report, and DCI Miller in his testimony, stated that there would have been a substantial degree of blood spray and splatter from the wound, but despite this comprehensive hunt, no blood of the victim was found on any of the clothes, or on the shoes, belonging to the defendant. And there was no evidence found on her mobile phone that showed she had been present at Boxtree Stables at the time of the killing.

'The prosecution called a witness, Mrs Sophie Burnett, who they claimed could place the defendant at the scene of the crime during the period within which the murder was carried out. However, as you heard, Mrs Burnett was mistaken and actually identified Miss Duffy at Boxtree Stables at about one o'clock on the Sunday, not on the Monday, as she had originally claimed. And there is no question that Mr Carson was alive after one o'clock on that Sunday, because he rode as a jockey in two races at Windsor Racecourse on the following afternoon.

'And as for checking into a hotel using a false name, that is not evidence of murder. She was just a young woman trying to avoid press intrusion, after salacious articles about her had appeared the previous weekend. It wasn't as if she was attempting to travel on false documents. The prosecution would have you believe that she acted like a guilty person, fleeing the country to foreign soil, but this is so far from the truth. She was going home to Ireland, not to South America, or some other far-away destination without an extradition treaty with the United Kingdom. She simply planned to spend a few days with her parents, before returning. She even had the return air ticket on her mobile phone. Does that sound to you like a guilty person who was running away?

'There is absolutely no direct evidence that proves that my client was present at Boxtree Stables when Mr Carson was murdered, or that she had anything to do with this crime. The judge will soon direct you that, in order to convict, you have to be sure that the defendant is the person responsible for this murder, and I put it to you that, based on the evidence you have heard, there is no possible way you can be sure she is the killer, so you must return a verdict of not guilty.'

Donna sat down again.

That was the last thing she could do to persuade the jury.

Now it was all up to the judge, and of course, to the jury itself.

The judge cleared his throat.

'Ladies and gentlemen of the jury, I will now give you some directions as to the law, and also sum up the case.

'As I said to you before, I determine the application of the law, while you determine the facts of the case, and you alone consider those facts to come to your verdict.

'The prosecution brings the case, and the prosecution must prove it. This is the burden of proof. The defendant does not have to prove her innocence. The prosecution can succeed in proving the defendant is guilty of the offence by making you, the members of the jury, satisfied so that you are sure of guilt. Nothing less will do. This is the standard of proof required.

'If, after considering all the evidence, you are sure of guilt, the verdict must be guilty, but if you are not sure of guilt, the verdict must be not guilty. You may have heard the term *beyond a reasonable doubt*, but being satisfied that *you are sure of guilt* has the same meaning.

'The element of the offence is simple. The defendant is charged with murder. In English law, a crime of murder occurs when a person of sound mind unlawfully kills another living human being, using actions that were intended to kill, or at least to cause grievous bodily harm. You may consider that stabbing someone through the heart with a carving knife would constitute such an action.

'In this case, there is no direct evidence that the defendant committed the crime. There is no CCTV footage showing her killing Mr Carson, and no forensic evidence that places her at the crime scene at the time of death, or which later demonstrates that she was present when Mr Carson died. Instead, the prosecution is relying on what is known as circumstantial evidence. This means pieces of evidence relating to different circumstances, none of which on their own directly proves the defendant is guilty, but which, say the prosecution, when taken together, prove that she is. The fact that the murder weapon was from her home could be an example of such circumstantial evidence, but that is a matter for you to decide.

'The defendant chose not to give evidence in this courtroom, and no further defence witnesses were called. However, you have heard Miss Lewis suggest that the evidence on which the prosecution relies does not prove the defendant's guilt at all, and that there are too many gaps and too many unanswered questions, such as who could have had access to the defendant's home. The fact that the defendant did not give oral evidence means you are entitled to draw such inferences as you seem proper, but it is not evidence of her guilt.

'You have heard all the evidence to be presented in this case, and no more shall be presented to you, even if you feel that there are still questions to be answered. You must decide which, if any, of the pieces of evidence you have heard are reliable, and which, if any, are not. You must then decide what conclusions you can reasonably and fairly draw from those pieces of evidence you do accept, taking them all together. You must not, however, engage in guesswork or speculation about matters that have not been proved in evidence. Finally, you must weigh up all the evidence and decide whether the prosecution have made you sure that the defendant is guilty.

'As you may know, English law permits me, in certain circumstances, to accept a verdict which is not the verdict of you all. Those circumstances have not yet arisen, so that I must ask you to reach a verdict upon which all of you are agreed. Should, however, the time come when it is possible for me to accept a majority decision, I will give you a further direction.

'You will now retire to consider your verdict. First, you will need to select a foreman or forewoman from amongst your number, to assist with your deliberations and to announce your final verdict in the court.'

I watched as the five men and seven women left the court, trying unsuccessfully to read their body language. One or two of them looked at Imogen in the dock, but I didn't know whether that was a good sign or a bad one.

When the door was closed behind them, the judge looked down at counsel.

'Experience has shown that I am the worst predictor of how long a jury will take to come to a verdict,' he said. 'I will certainly allow them the whole afternoon, and tomorrow morning too, if they need it, before even considering giving any direction concerning a majority verdict. We will now adjourn for lunch. If you intend leaving the court building, please ensure the clerk has your contact details, so that you can be informed if there is a verdict or if the jury wish to ask a question.'

The judge stood up.

'All rise.'

We rose and bowed, and the judge bowed back before departing.

'What now?' I asked.

'We wait,' Donna said.

'How long for?'

'Maybe an hour, perhaps two, or even up to a week. Who knows?'

'Is a short wait a good sign, or is a long one better for us?'

'Impossible to tell. The murder trial of OJ Simpson lasted a whopping ten months, but he was acquitted after only a few short hours of deliberation, even though everyone was convinced he was guilty – everyone, that is, except the twelve members of the jury. But John Haigh, the acid-bath murderer, was found guilty after just fifteen minutes of deliberation.'

'So, what are our chances?' I asked.

'You tell me,' Donna replied. 'Would you convict her?'

'The ownership of the knife is the big problem.'

'No kidding. It's really the only thing the prosecution have against her, but it might be enough. It all depends on whether the jury can see past that.'

'Let's go and have some lunch,' Archie said.

But there were too many nervous knots in my stomach to allow me to eat.

It reminded me of how I used to feel as a jockey before a really big race such as the Grand National or the Cheltenham Gold Cup. I could even remember one year not being able to eat any Christmas dinner because I was so nervous about riding the short-priced favourite in the King George VI Chase on Boxing Day.

I had always felt that a good dose of nerves helped me concentrate, but there was nothing to concentrate on here. There was not a single thing more I could do.

We just had to wait.

And to hope.

Chapter 34

Two HOURS LATER, MY NERVOUS state hadn't improved one iota, in fact it had become worse.

All sorts of scenarios were constantly playing out in my mind.

Were they trying to convince a few reluctants to return a guilty verdict?

Or a not guilty one?

I tried to reply to some of the emails I had received on my phone, but I couldn't focus on anything else other than what my mind was imagining was going on in the jury room.

I found it impossible to sit still, so I paced up and down in the area just outside the courtroom, counting my steps back and forth, wearing a track into the carpet. Eventually, I needed some fresh air.

'I'll be outside the building,' I said to Archie.

I went down the stairs to the impressive lobby. Patrick and Kathleen Duffy were sitting together on a bench to one side. Patrick saw me and came over. He looked pale and haggard.

'What's taking them so long?' he asked, clearly agitated. 'Surely they must see that she's innocent.'

'Keep calm,' I said, trying to be reassuring. 'Juries work in mysterious ways.'

'And why on earth didn't Imogen give evidence, to tell the jury she didn't do it?'

'Because we felt it was best not to allow the prosecution to bring up in cross-examination all the animosity that had existed between Imogen and Liam Carson. It would have fuelled the idea of a motive in the minds of the jury.'

'But if they had known all that, they might have realised how nasty he was towards her.'

'Indeed, they might, and that might also have made them think that Imogen killed him because of it.'

He stared at me, but then he nodded, as if he realised why.

'We just have to wait,' I said. 'I know it's hard.'

'It certainly is,' he agreed. 'And it's not been helped by having Michael Carson sitting behind us all the time in the public gallery.'

'Michael Carson?'

'Liam's father. Imogen worked for him once, that's until he fired her for breaking up with his son. He's been chuntering on all the time under his breath to us about how evil Imogen is, that she's a murderer, and how he hopes that she dies in jail. Kathleen and I moved seats to get away from him, but he then moved too, to be behind us again. I think he's as unpleasant as Liam was.'

'I'm sorry,' I said.

I left the Duffys in the lobby and went outside, going down the steps and across the road into Forbury Gardens Park, breathing the fresh air in deeply. It was a cold crisp January day, but the sun was still shining brightly in the clear blue sky, a combination I had always enjoyed, especially when riding out early on the gallops.

I wandered aimlessly around the park, past the open bandstand and the huge bronze lion set high on a grand stone plinth. I read the plaque attached to one end of the plinth.

This monument records the names and commemorates the valour and devotion of 11 officers and 318 non-commissioned officers and men of the 66th Berkshire Regiment who gave their lives for their country at Girishk Maiwand and Kandahar and during the Afghan Campaign 1879–1880.

It made me realise that, however much the world changes, some things remain just the same.

I wondered how all those officers and men from Berkshire, whose names are inscribed on twelve bronze panels, six on either side of the plinth, had made the four-and-a-half-thousand-mile journey all the way from Reading to Afghanistan in the 1870s with no planes, no motor vehicles, and precious few trains.

They had probably walked much of it, only then to die there.

Did their parents, wives and children, left behind to grieve their sons, husbands and fathers, think that their sacrifice had been worth it, just to ensure some far-away spot was shaded British Empire pink on the world map?

'Sid, Sid!' I heard someone shouting my name, snapping my brain from hundred-and-fifty-year-old mental images of distant lands back to the here and now.

I quickly turned to see Archie running towards me.

'Sid, we have a verdict.'

He turned and ran back towards the Crown Court building, and I followed, my heart pumping fast, and not just because I was also running.

* * *

By the time I arrived at Court 2, nearly everyone else was there already.

Patrick and Kathleen were in the public gallery. I waved at them, then looked past them at the man sitting behind. Michael Carson had a broad weatherbeaten face under a mop of untidy greying hair.

As I walked to my seat, I smiled at Imogen in the dock, but she didn't smile back. In fact, she was shaking with fear.

I sat down next to Archie.

'What do we think?' I asked him, but all he did was shrug.

The usher brought in the jury, and I tried to see if any of them would look at Imogen. I thought it might be a good sign if they did, but they all kept their eyes down as they took their seats. Was that a bad sign?

'All rise,' called the usher.

We all stood up and the judge came in, bowing to us all before taking his seat. We sat down again.

The court clerk stood up and faced the jury.

'Would the foreperson please stand.'

The woman at the far end of the front row stood up, and the clerk turned to face her directly.

'Have you reached a verdict upon which you are all agreed? Please answer "yes" or "no".'

'Yes,' said the woman.

'On the charge of murder, do you find the defendant guilty or not guilty?'

I held my breath.

'Not guilty.'

There was a disturbance in the public gallery.

Patrick Duffy shouted 'Yes', and he punched the air, while Michael Carson, behind him, stood up, rage clear in his broad face.

'What the bloody hell is going on?' he shouted. 'Imogen Duffy murdered my son.'

He started shouting abuse at the jury, accusing them of being racist against the Irish, which was strange because Imogen was Irish too.

The judge intervened.

'Mr Carson,' he said loudly, leaning right down to his microphone so that his voice boomed through the courtroom speakers. 'You will sit down quietly, or I will instruct the bailiff to remove you from the court.'

Michael Carson didn't wait for the bailiff. He stormed out of the court of his own accord, still shouting abuse at everyone, especially the jury, and also threatening revenge on Imogen and her family.

When the door to the public gallery was finally closed, and we could only faintly hear Michael Carson still ranting away outside, the judge faced forward, towards the dock.

'Miss Duffy, you have been found not guilty of murder by this jury. You are now free to go. However, you will need to go down to the cells to deal with the release paperwork and to collect your belongings.' He turned to the jury. 'Thank you, ladies and gentlemen of the jury, you are now discharged.'

Donna made no application for defence costs as Imogen was on legal aid anyway.

'All rise,' called the usher.

The judge bowed to us, and us to him, before he departed back to his chambers.

It was suddenly all over. Just like that.

Not guilty. Finished. Go home.

Donna turned round to me, all smiles.

'Well done,' I said to her.

'Well done you, for all your help,' she replied.

Mr Blandford, the prosecution counsel, came over to our side.

'Congratulations, Miss Lewis,' he said, not quite meaning it. 'We should never have called the lady racehorse trainer. That's what did it for us.'

I didn't really agree with him. Without her, and without any forensic evidence, the case would probably have never come to trial in the first place. But it had, and a not guilty verdict had been delivered.

Mr Blandford drifted away, no doubt to lick his wounds.

'We'd better go and see Imogen,' Donna said. 'She might need some help with the release papers and her stuff.'

The three of us went down to the cells level, below the courts, where we had seen her before the trial started.

She was back in one of the cells, but this time the door had been left wide open, because she was a free woman.

There were lots of hugs and tears.

'What can the police do now?' Imogen asked.

'Nothing to you,' Archie said. 'They've had their chance. They can't try you more than once for the same crime.'

That wasn't entirely true. Since 2005, the *double jeopardy* rules have changed in England and Wales, such that people previously acquitted of the most serious of crimes, including murder, could be retried if *new and compelling* evidence was found against them.

The change was primarily a response to the fact that, in some cases, modern DNA profiling technology had proved beyond any doubt whatsoever that some individuals, acquitted prior to DNA testing being available had in fact done the deed. The DNA evidence was considered sufficiently compelling to warrant a new trial.

However, in the United States, protection against double jeopardy remains enshrined in the Fifth Amendment to the US Constitution, the same amendment that allows you not to have to answer questions that might incriminate you.

'The police will likely look again at Freddie Swinton,' I said. 'He had motive. I tried to check his alibi but without success. There's definitely something dodgy about it.'

'Freddie didn't do it,' Imogen said.

'How do you know?' I asked.

'I just do.'

I stared at her, and there was a moment of huge realisation in my brain.

Oh my God!

Michael Carson had been absolutely right.

Imogen Duffy had indeed murdered his son.

*　*　*

I felt immense unease.

Sid Halley had always righted wrongs, protected the innocent, and brought the guilty to book. But now I had been instrumental in doing the complete opposite.

I quickly made my excuses and left, passing Patrick and Kathleen Duffy as they waited expectantly for their daughter outside the custody area.

Patrick started to move towards me, but I didn't stop to speak to him. I didn't want to. Instead, I walked fast through to the grand lobby, and then out into the fresh air.

I felt sick.

If anyone knew a daughter, it was her father.

So, had Patrick Duffy known all along that Imogen was guilty?

Had he been deceiving me ever since he first came to my house in early December, simply playing on my feelings of gratitude towards him for what he had done, all those years ago, to save Marina's leg?

Or had he been fooling himself as well as me?

I was confused and also somewhat angry.

I drove myself home to Aynsford, but the journey did little to lessen my anxiety.

'How did it go today?' Marina asked, as I walked through the front door.

'She was found not guilty,' I said.

'But that's marvellous.' Marina clapped her hands together in excitement. 'Why didn't you call me to tell me the good news?'

What did I say? That I now wished the verdict had been guilty?

'I'm going to see Charles,' I said instead. 'I'll collect Saskia afterwards.'

'Is everything all right?' Marina asked with concern.

'Everything's fine,' I said. 'I just need to talk to him.'

But I could tell that Marina wasn't convinced. She knew, as I did, that I only *needed* to talk to Charles when something was troubling me, and I was severely troubled by what had happened.

* * *

'Are you sure she did it?'

Charles and I were sitting in his room at Godswell House.

I had brought with me the remains of the bottle of Glenmorangie ten-year-old single malt, which I'd purchased for his stay over Christmas, although I was only having a very small one, as I had to drive.

'Pretty sure.'

'But you're not certain?'

'If you mean have I got unequivocal proof, then no, I haven't.'

'So, what's the problem?'

He made it sound so simple.

'The problem is that if I hadn't got involved, she would almost certainly have been convicted. But I did get involved, and it was through me that enough doubt was planted in the minds of the jury, such that they acquitted her. But now I don't have that same doubt in my own mind.'

Charles took another sip of his whisky.

'As I see it, you have two options,' he said. 'First, you can forget about it and get on with your life, or second, you can continue to fret over it and drive yourself to distraction. Either way, there's nothing you can do that will change the outcome of the trial.'

I didn't feel he was being very helpful, although he was probably right.

'I just feel uncomfortable, as if I've been used.'

He laughed.

'Just like all those other people *you* have used in the past to get what you wanted.'

It was true. I'd previously employed a bit of deception and subterfuge here and there, but that was somehow different.

Or was it?

I left him to finish the final few mouthfuls of whisky from the bottle and went to collect Saskia from school.

'Hi, Dad,' she said, climbing into the car.

'Had a good day?' I asked

'Great, thanks. I got my maths mock exam result back. I got a 9, that's equivalent to an A star.'

'Well done, darling. That's brilliant.'

I suddenly realised that I would also do anything I could to get my own daughter off a murder charge, including a bit of deception and subterfuge, even if I believed she was guilty.

* * *

At eleven o'clock the following morning, I was enjoying being at home and not having to rush again to Reading.

The front doorbell rang.

'Are you expecting a delivery?' I asked Marina.

'Not that I can think of.'

I went to the door, expecting more ME + EM dresses for Marina, to be tried on, rejected, and then sent back. It was like a ritual in this house.

But there was no courier with a familiar black box. Instead, there were three people standing outside on the driveway: Patrick, Kathleen and Imogen Duffy.

'We couldn't go home to Ireland without coming here first to thank you,' Patrick said.

'You'd better come in,' I replied.

I took them through to the kitchen where Marina was delighted to see Patrick again and to meet Kathleen and Imogen.

It seemed too early for celebratory champagne, and in my mind, it was not appropriate, so Marina made us all coffee, and we sat around the kitchen table drinking it.

'Sid was brilliant,' Patrick said. 'He talked Imogen's counsel through it all and he exposed the gaps in the prosecution case. We owe him everything.'

I felt strange, basking in such praise, after the many thoughts I'd had during a restless night.

'So, what are you going to do now?' I asked Imogen.

'Go home to Ireland and try and regain my fitness. Cormac Fitzgerald, the first trainer I rode for, has promised to find me some rides.' She smiled. 'Who knows, I might be back at Cheltenham one day.'

'Come with me,' I said, standing up. 'I have something to show you.'

I took her through into my study, picked up a small silver salver from a bookcase and handed it to her.

She read the inscription engraved around the edge.

Presented to Sid Halley, winning jockey of the Champion Chase, Cheltenham Racecourse.

'Wow!' she said. 'I really thought you'd been kidding me.'

'Why did you leave the knife behind?' I asked.

385

She stared at me.

'What do you mean?'

'Why did you leave your kitchen carving knife stuck in Liam?'

She looked from side to side, her eyes widening in panic. She said nothing, but her face reddened in a blush.

'Couldn't you get it out?'

She still said nothing.

'It's all right,' I said. 'I'm not recording anything.'

Still nothing.

'Imogen,' I said. 'I know it was you who killed Liam. You had both the motive and the opportunity. And it was your knife. You were extremely clever not to leave any forensic trace or to be caught on any CCTV. So why did you leave the knife behind?'

She went on staring at me, perhaps deciding what to say.

'The bloody thing wouldn't budge,' she said eventually, slowly and quietly. 'I pulled and pulled at it, but it was stuck fast. In the end, I had to leave it.'

'But you failed to wipe the blade?'

She nodded. 'I wiped the handle, but I didn't realise that my prints were already on the blade.'

'How did you know Liam's flat wouldn't be locked?'

'He never locked his door. We argued about it when I lived with him in Leighlinbridge. He said he had nothing worth stealing, so what was the point.'

'What did you do with your clothes?' I asked.

There was a long pause, and I waited patiently.

'Tuesday is dustbin day in Lambourn, and the bin lorry comes early, before seven most weeks.'

'That was a big risk.'

'Not really. I obviously didn't use my own bin. I put everything I was wearing in there, right down to my socks and knickers, including my shoes, riding gloves and the surgical face mask I'd worn. According to the West Berkshire Council website, eighty-five per cent of the rubbish from Lambourn goes straight to a local incinerator to provide power from waste.'

'How did the CCTV in Lambourn village not spot you?'

'Because I went over the fields. I checked out the route when I went for a run on Monday morning, and there was easily enough moonlight to find my way to Eastbury at one a.m. on Tuesday.'

'Was he asleep?'

'He was, but he woke up as I stabbed him. He stared up at me. But then his eyes glazed over as he died. The moon was shining through the window so I could see his face clearly. It was horrible. But by then what was done was done. I couldn't undo it.'

She was now crying.

'I'm so sorry,' she said, sobbing. 'But he would have killed me for sure if I hadn't done something. There is absolutely no doubt about that in my mind.'

She stared at me through watery eyes.

'What are you going to do?' she asked quietly. 'Will you call the police?'

'Right now, I'm going to return to the kitchen to finish my coffee.'

I gave her a few moments to compose herself, and then we went to join the others.

'Sid showed me the trophy he was presented with for riding the winner in the Champion Chase,' Imogen said. 'It's fabulous.'

'So you two have a special connection,' Patrick said.

Indeed we had.

Patrick looked at his watch. 'We must go. We have a flight to Dublin to catch.'

I saw them through the hall to the front door.

Imogen and Kathleen went out towards their waiting taxi, while Patrick turned back to me and held out his hand.

'Thank you, Sid,' he said. 'I'm so grateful.'

I shook his hand, but I didn't let it go.

'Why did you send me those threatening notes?' I asked him.

He looked at me and began to shake his head.

'Don't deny it,' I said. 'I know it was you.'

He started to pull away, but I went on holding his hand, gripping it tightly with my good right.

He looked me in the eye.

'I'd heard that threatening Sid Halley would make him look even harder, to keep him at the job.'

'And you posted them in Lambourn to convince me that someone else, other than Imogen, was responsible for the murder? But that isn't true, Patrick, is it?'

He shook his head fractionally again. And his face was full of pain at the sudden realisation that someone else knew the whole truth.

I thought back to the overwhelming fear I had felt at Cheltenham Racecourse, when I'd believed that Marina and I were about to be attacked in the car park.

'I think I have fully repaid my debt to you, Patrick Duffy,' I said. 'Don't ever come here again. Do you understand?'

He nodded again, and I let go of his hand.

I watched as he walked across the gravel to the taxi, climbed in, and was driven out of my life.

I went back into the kitchen and sat down next to Marina.

'That was nice.'

'She did it,' I said.

'Did what?'

'Imogen Duffy murdered Liam Carson.'

Marina turned and looked at me.

'She admitted it,' I said. 'When I took her into my study. She told me everything.'

I recounted to Marina all that Imogen had said. 'And Patrick Duffy knew all along.'

'So, what are you going to do about it?'

'Perhaps I should contact the police. If Imogen's clothes didn't get burnt in the incinerator but went to landfill, they might be able to find them and test them for Liam Carson's blood. That would be the *new and compelling* evidence needed for a new trial.'

'Now, why on earth would you do that?' Marina said with irritation. 'You heard how Carson threatened to kill her. She was surely only acting in self-defence.'

'The law of self-defence states that you can use *reasonable* and *proportionate* force to defend yourself. It does not include driving a carving knife through the heart of a sleeping man.'

'Perhaps she thought it was her only choice. Look at the size of her. She clearly wouldn't have been able to defend herself against him when he was awake.'

'But I feel as if I've been used.'

'So what?' Marina said. 'I use you all the time.'

'How?'

'I use you to satisfy my enormous sexual appetite.'

I reached across and stroked her back.

'Are you hungry now?'

'Always. For you.'

Despite it being nearly lunchtime, we went upstairs to bed.

Nothing else really mattered.